WHITEWASH

ALEX KAVA

WHITEWASH

MIRA

All the characters in this book have no existence outside the imagination of the author, and have no relation whatsoever to anyone bearing the same name or names. They are not even distantly inspired by any individual known or unknown to the author, and all the incidents are pure invention.

MIRA is a registered trademark of Harlequin Enterprises Limited, used under licence.

Published in Great Britain 2007
MIRA Books, Eton House, 18-24 Paradise Road,
Richmond, Surrey, TW9 1SR

PB ISBN: 978 0 7783 0207 0

58-1107

Printed in Great Britain
by Clays Ltd, St Ives plc

This book is dedicated to two amazing women:
Patricia Kava, my mom, whose silent support comes with
lots of love by way of lighted candles,
delicious popcorn balls, a nod and a smile.

and

Emilie Groh Carlin (1922–2005)
My first book without you only makes me miss
our discussions, your stories and your
words of encouragement more than ever.

AUTHOR'S NOTE

Thermal Conversion Process (TCP) is not a figment of my imagination. It is a very real and amazing process that converts refuse and other waste material into oil. It's an exciting and viable energy alternative. EcoEnergy, its CEO, facility and employees, however, are all figments of my imagination. Please forgive any mistakes or inaccuracies about the process, as well as any twists of the facts, I may have made to fit my storyline.

1

Thursday, June 8
EchoEnergy Industrial Park
Tallahassee, Florida

Dr. Dwight Lansik refused to look down. He hated the smell wafting up from the steel grates beneath his feet, reminding him of an odd concoction—fried liver, raw sewage and spoiled meat. He knew that no matter how many times he'd shower or how hard he would scrub—leaving his skin red and bruised—he'd still be able to smell it. That's why he usually avoided the catwalks overlooking the tops of the silver-gray tanks and the maze of pipes that connected them. He especially avoided walking over this particular holding tank, its massive lid left open like a huge, smiling mouth while the last trucks of the day emptied into it. But this was exactly where Ernie Walker had asked to meet.

That was Ernie, always wanting to emphasize whatever his moronic point might be by going to the extreme. Just last week the man had insisted Dwight meet him directly under the flash-off water pipe so Dwight could feel the excessive heat for himself. "Ernie, you could have just told me the damn thing's too hot," he scolded the plant manager, who had simply shrugged and said, "Better you feel it for yourself."

As much as he hated to admit it, Ernie was right. Had he not dragged Dwight to the Depress Zone he would have never discovered the real problem, a much more serious problem than an overheated flash-off water pipe. And how would he? His job kept him down in the lab, exactly where he was supposed to be, *where he preferred to be,* analyzing and calculating cooking times and coking temperatures. He dealt in recipes and formulas.

His wife, Adele, used to tease him and the memory brought a sting. She'd been gone almost a year and he still missed her terribly. Yes, she used to tease him—or was it goading—that he could break down any carbon-based object, including himself, just by looking at it. To which he confessed he already had. At a lanky hundred and fifty pounds he knew he amounted to exactly thirty-one pounds of oil, six pounds of gas, six pounds of minerals and a hundred and seven pounds of sterilized water. But that was the sort of thing he was supposed to know. He certainly couldn't be expected to know whether or not every depressurization valve was fully functional or that all distillation columns remained unclogged. *That* was Ernie's job.

However, it wasn't Ernie's job to mess with the computer program that regulated and controlled the process—the directions and temperatures, which stage, how long and how fast the feedstock moved through the pipes, what was depressed and separated and released. No, that wasn't Ernie's job. It was supposed to be Dwight's and only his. As the creator of the software program he was the only one with the authority and the access to change it and make adjustments. But those greedy bastards found a way to override it, to override him. And now Dwight hoped Ernie hadn't discovered yet another telltale sign before Dwight had a chance to do something about it.

Suddenly Dwight grabbed the railing to steady himself. Had the steel grate beneath him started to vibrate?

He twisted around to look toward the ladder at the end of the catwalk. Would he even be able to hear Ernie climb up the wobbly metal slats? The safety earplugs muffled all the mechanical churning, the hissing and clanking of the pipes and coils that zigzagged from tank to tank, the hiss of hydraulics and the whine of rotors and pulleys, even that sloshing of the liquid below. Despite the momentary sway, there was no one where the railing ended.

He waited, expecting to see Ernie's hands reach up over the top of the ladder that poked up toward the sky. Another tanker truck rumbled below, grinding gears and sending up a cloud of diesel fumes. And the catwalk started to vibrate again. There were no hands on the railing, no sign of anyone coming up. Perhaps it had only been the truck's vibration. That or Dwight's imagination.

He adjusted his safety goggles and checked his watch. End of the day. Where the hell was Ernie? Dwight had hoped to leave a bit early, but now he'd be stuck in traffic. The men at the airport Marriott would end up waiting for him. Did he care? Why should he? They couldn't start without him. They had nothing without him. After several brief phone calls he knew they wanted any information he had. Hell, they were lucky he had decided to do the right thing.

It was his grandmother who had insisted he be named after the great general Dwight D. Eisenhower, but never once in his life had Dwight Lansik acted like a general. Instead, ever the meek, obedient soldier or servant churning out the brilliant, heroic work and letting everyone else take all the credit. It was about time he took charge.

And so what if he was a little late getting to the hotel? It wouldn't matter. These guys were chomping at the bit for the information he had, anxious vultures, ready to rip and shred and destroy everything he had worked so hard to create. They'd wait.

He forced himself to look down. The soupy glop they called feed-stock sputtered and swirled beneath him in the 2,500-gallon tank, waiting to get sucked down and into the massive, sharp blades that would chop and dice and mince it all into pea-sized sludge. Putrid gases erupted from the mixture quite naturally without any elec-tronic interference or prodding. No, this stink was not man-made, but simply the natural and inevitable results of dumping together rotting slaughterhouse waste: slimy intestines, rust-colored blood and bright-orange spongy lungs floating and bobbing alongside rotting chicken heads with the eyes still intact and staring. Surely chickens had eyelids?

Christ! That smell. His eyes burned despite the goggles. Stop looking down, he told himself, willing his gag reflex to hold out.

He glanced at his watch again, giving it a twist on his bony wrist. The Rolex was worth more than his car, a frivolous gift from the CEO when they inaugurated this plant. He wore it to remind his sub-ordinates how vital he was to the company, when in fact, he thought it a gaudy waste of money.

Where the hell was Ernie Walker? How dare he make him wait up here in the scorching sunlight and the disgusting fumes.

Dwight leaned against the railing, hoping the sway of the catwalk would stop. He was getting nauseated. His undershirt stuck to his back like a second skin. He pushed at the carefully rolled sleeves of his crisp oxford, unbuttoning the collar and loosening his tie all in two quick motions. Nothing helped. The muffled noises blended together in a roar that began pounding inside his head. He yanked off the yellow hard hat and swiped at his forehead. He felt off balance, a bit dizzy, so he didn't even notice the man come up behind him.

The first blow slammed him into the railing, knocking the air out of his lungs. He doubled over, his stomach wrapped around the metal. Before he got a chance to catch his breath he felt his legs being lifted out from under him.

"My God!" he yelled as he grabbed the railing.

His fingers clutched tight, hanging on even as he felt his body swing over. His feet kicked and slipped against the inside concrete. There was nothing: no ledge, no cracks. His legs thrashed and his rubber soles fought to make contact. His arms ached and his fingers gripped the metal already slick with his own sweat.

He tried to look up, tried to plead but his voice sounded small and far away, it, too, muffled by the earplugs, and he knew it was lost in the vibration, the screech and clanking. Still he begged between gasps to the shadow above him, a hulking figure with the sun behind adding a halo effect. His goggles had fogged up. His hard hat had plunged into the soup. And the earplugs continued to make his screams sound like they were only in his head.

When the pipe came smashing down on Dwight's fingers he was sure the bones had snapped. Despite the pain, he gripped and clawed at the metal, but his fingers were quickly becoming useless. He felt his body giving out from under him just as the pipe cracked over his head.

He plunged into the sludge. Consciousness slipped away. He could hear the vibration of the soup slosh around him, more like ocean waves crashing into him. Through a swirling blur of rust-colored water and blue sky he saw the wide-eyed chicken heads bobbing alongside him.

Dwight Lansik knew all too well that it would take only minutes before the liquid sucked him down, swallowing him whole, and that he would simply become a part of the very formula he had created. So he was grateful when everything finally went black.

Colin Jernigan marched through the crowded lobby of the Marriott Hotel, trying to find someplace quiet while his cell phone continued to vibrate. He shouldered his way past two lethargic businessmen, almost tripping on the oversized cases they dragged behind them.

"Yeah," he finally barked into the phone. Nothing. He pushed his way out the revolving door, trading chatter for car engines and still straining to hear. "Go ahead."

"Meeting just got canceled," he finally heard a male voice say.

Though he didn't recognize the caller it didn't matter. If the man had this phone number he had been approved to make this call. Colin didn't answer. He didn't need to because immediately there was a click then the buzz of a dial tone.

He slipped the phone into the pocket of his jacket. He was neither surprised nor disappointed, both worthless emotions he had long ago discarded. Still, his fingers found the gold tie bar and he rubbed his thumb over it as if for good luck while he straightened his tie using the reflection of the empty valet booth's glass.

He rubbed his eyes and took a good look at his reflection. He looked like hell. Soon all his hair would be prematurely gray. The broad shoulders were slumped enough to remind him to straighten them. An ache in the back of his neck announced that maybe the gray wasn't all that premature.

It had been a wasted trip. A whole day blown. He wasn't looking forward to telling his boss. She'd be pissed; that, he already knew for certain. Briefly he wondered what it was that made Dr. Lansik back out at the last minute.

Colin Jernigan shrugged and checked his watch. Then he started looking for the airport shuttle. He'd catch some sleep on the trip back. Maybe he'd even make it to Washington before the eleven o'clock news.

2

The phone had wakened Sabrina Galloway almost an hour before her alarm clock was set to go off. Now she snapped it off and replaced it on her nightstand. Even as she sank back into the pillows she found herself waiting for her heart to stop galloping and her breathing to return to normal.

What did she expect? This was exactly why she had uprooted her quiet, predictable life in Chicago and moved to Tallahassee. And she *had* given the hospital permission to call at any time of day. Still, it startled her each time the phone rang before sunrise.

"Did I wake you?"

The tone was always the same—abrupt, authoritarian and unapologetic. Even though it was a different nurse every time, each one said similar things. In the beginning Sabrina had tried to remember their names. Now that the calls became more frequent she had gotten lax in her manners, which would have made her father angry or at least it would have in another time. Not so much anymore.

"I know it's early," the nurse had continued, "but I'm getting ready to end my shift." This, too, was a frequent reason, whether the call came past midnight or before 6:00 a.m.

"Of course I understand," Sabrina said and bit down on her lower lip. Truth was, she didn't understand why someone on the next shift couldn't call her at a more reasonable time, at a time that wouldn't automatically jump-start her heart and put her into emergency mode, that is, if there wasn't an emergency. At this rate would she be able to tell when the real emergency came?

"He tried to leave the premises again," the woman said without alarm or urgency. More than anything, she sounded annoyed, like she was talking about an errant teenager breaking curfew. And almost as an afterthought she added, "He's demanding to see you. Dr. Fullerton seems to think it might settle him down a bit if he does see you."

Sabrina promised to be there as soon as possible, only to have the nurse tell her that sometime in the afternoon would be just fine. It wasn't that they didn't have the situation under control. So why did they need to wake her during that time frame reserved for alarm and emergency, triggering a panic that stuck with her for the rest of the morning? She knew better than to ask. She already had, once, only to be lectured that they were following her instructions, honoring her request that she be notified each time it was required to use restraints and sedate him.

"We aren't required to contact you," the charge nurse reminded Sabrina at the end of that lecture. It was strictly a "courtesy call."

Sabrina sat up on the edge of the bed, waiting for the tightness in her chest to ease. Each time she expected the worst or at least something similar to that phone call two years ago. The one that started all this. She rubbed her hands over her face. Was it only two years ago? The tightness in her chest gave way to an ache, not much better but familiar. She still missed her mom.

She reached for her running shoes exactly where she had left them next to the nightstand, ready for her so she wouldn't have to fumble around in the faint blur of morning. Despite the phone call Sabrina always woke up before sunrise. Her daily routine had been her saving grace, giving order to the sudden chaos that had taken over her structured, predictable life. She slept in her sports bra and jogging shorts instead of pajamas, so she couldn't talk herself out of her morning run. It was a habit she had developed when she moved to Florida. In those first weeks it took all her effort to push out from under the covers. She kept telling herself she needed to be strong for her dad. She couldn't afford to lose him, too.

She began making the bed as soon as she was out of it, pulling the corners taut. Before she finished she found herself sitting on the edge. She hated that they had to restrain him again. The first time she visited him with the leather straps binding his arms to the bed rails like some criminal she demanded they let him go home with her, never even considering that she wouldn't be able to take care of him and work at the same time. The charge nurse—the same one who reminded her it was a courtesy for them to even call—quickly squelched Sabrina's heroic gesture, explaining that since her father signed the commitment papers himself only he and Dr. Fullerton could release him. And of course, Dr. Fullerton would not.

She snatched the folded gray T-shirt waiting on the corner chair and wrestled into it. Her mind raced through her work schedule, already adjusting and reorganizing her day to accommodate the un-expected road trip. She would ask her boss if she could leave early.

It was Friday. Shouldn't be a problem. With any luck she could be driving back home just as it started to get dark. It was silly and she felt as though she were ten whenever she admitted it—because the rumors and stories certainly sounded like old superstitions told over a campfire—but she hated the idea of being stuck in Chattahoochee after dark.

In the kitchen she heard the first timer click on and within a minute the room began to fill with the aroma of freshly brewed coffee. Seconds later the refrigerator's ice machine clattered into its dispenser the requisite amount of ice needed for her breakfast smoothie.

While she waited for the coffee, Sabrina retrieved the rolled-up newspaper from her doorstep and set right the flowerpot the carrier continuously aimed for. A glance at the local headlines made her long for the *Chicago Tribune*. Who'd ever guess she'd miss tales of murder and embezzlement in exchange for county-festival schedules and new city zoning rules. It was almost a year since her move and Tallahassee, Florida, still didn't feel like home. She couldn't imagine that it ever would. But it wasn't Florida's fault.

She had lived in Chicago all her life. In thirty-five years her biggest move was from downtown to the suburbs. She never felt alone in the city of 2.8 million, not even when the winters dragged on and on. Of course, restlessness would set in. How could it not with the mountains of black, smudged snow and ice piled up along the streets? In the bleak midwinter, bundled strangers passed each other with no eye contact, all of them focused on one single thing—warmth and getting back into it. But that was just a part of winter living in the Midwest.

Her schedule and routine kept her busy. Her students kept her entertained. And until two years ago she had a family who was her lifeline: a slightly neurotic but loving mother, a brilliant, doting father and a reckless but charming brother who had also been her best friend. She never imagined they'd all be swept away in less than a day.

No, Florida wasn't the problem. It didn't take a Ph.D. for Sabrina to figure out what she was feeling came from deep inside her, not around her. If nothing else, warm and sunny Florida could and should be a catalyst. At least the residents of Tallahassee made eye contact when they met you on the street. Though Sabrina suspected it was to look her over and quickly determine—although they didn't say it, their eyes did—"you're not from around here, are you?"

She wondered how they could tell. What exactly was it that gave her away?

She glanced through the newspaper, taking time to read only the headlines as she poured a quarter cup of skim milk into a mug and filled the rest of it with coffee. Below the fold on page three a headline caught her attention: Jackson Springs Bottled Water Recall.

She drove by the family-owned bottling company every day on her way to EchoEnergy. She shook her head, not really surprised. As a scientist she believed the federal government did a poor job of regulating municipal water supplies, allowing much too high levels of arsenic and other dangerous contaminants in regular tap water. That they thought they could regulate bottled water any better was a joke. She sipped the lukewarm coffee and worried more about the caffeine in it than the water. She hadn't gotten a decent night's sleep since she moved to Tallahassee and yet she knew caffeine was probably the least of her worries. She only wished it could be that easy.

Her friend Olivia liked to remind her that within less than a year Sabrina had picked up and moved to a part of the country she had never even visited before. Throw in a new job in an industry she had never been a part of and add to it the role of caregiver. "Of course it's the caffeine that's stressing you out and keeping you awake at night," Olivia would conclude, her tongue firmly planted in her cheek.

Sabrina gulped down the coffee and set aside the mug. Her fingertips absently rubbed where the diamond ring used to be on her ring finger. She'd never had it resized and it was loose. She constantly worried about losing it as she pulled on and off latex gloves on a regular basis. The ring sat safely in its box in her dresser drawer, tucked away so she wouldn't lose it down a drain.

Who was she fooling? She had really taken it off because all of its meaning and promises had already gone down the drain. This move had cost her much more than she'd ever anticipated.

Actually, the new job was a lifesaver. She was a scientist, after all. She thrived on new puzzles, concocting solutions to unsolvable problems, finding alternatives to old, worn-out remedies. It came naturally, instinctive, an insatiable curiosity. It was about time she was out in the real world confronting the challenges instead of sitting back, debating and theorizing them. For ten years she had focused so much of her attention on making tenure that maybe she had forgotten the thrill of discovery.

When she was a kid this job at EchoEnergy would have been exactly the kind of stuff she had dreamed about doing. Growing up, her older brother, Eric, played football and put together model cars while Sabrina begged for her father's hand-me-down microscopes so she could get a better look at what particles made up a regular clump of dirt. She'd spend hours figuring out how to separate those particles and several more hours experimenting what happened when you added water to each. While Eric discovered girls, Sabrina was

breaking down the elements in sulfuric acid and chromium phosphates. The summer of her fifteenth birthday her mother was ecstatic to hear that Sabrina had been spending every afternoon with Billy Snyder, until she learned the two of them had been creating a flashlight that glowed in the dark without the use of batteries.

Her mother's harshest recrimination was, "You're turning out to be just like your father."

Her mother had never been able to say it without a smile, and Sabrina knew it was more a compliment than an accusation. That was her mother, melodrama and sarcasm as much creative tools as her paintbrushes and clay. Sabrina knew it was obvious her parents loved each other, though they gently teased and goaded one another. Her mother called Arthur Galloway's inventions "worthless contraptions" even as she clapped and fought back tears of joy during his demonstrations. However, her father's contraptions were usually the root of all family arguments and, according to her mother, the cause of all their hardships and heartache. But her father never seemed to mind, only grinning at her mother's outbursts and placating her with a kiss on the cheek while telling her he "was indeed crazy, crazy in love" with her.

Sabrina had to admit that she didn't remember any hardships. She couldn't remember the family ever—not once—going without. Her father's teaching job at the university always provided more than enough. It wasn't until after her mother was gone that Sabrina realized all those arguments, all those hurled accusations were simply her mother's way of saying that she knew Arthur Galloway could have been a famous inventor if only he hadn't been saddled with a family and monthly responsibilities. That she understood he had sacrificed something larger than the sum of all of them, and she wanted to make sure he knew, over and over again, that she hadn't asked for any of it. Almost as if she was also giving him a reason, or perhaps a second chance, to change his mind, the ravings of a woman who could never believe she was worthy of her good fortune. The fact was that Meredith and Arthur Galloway were crazy in love with each other. In the end it wasn't her mother's petulance that drove Arthur Galloway crazy or drove a wedge between her children. Instead, it was the absence of that petulance, the absence of her mother that had ripped them all to shreds.

Something slid and crashed outside, startling Sabrina. She jumped even as she recognized the sound, then winced at a second crash. She raced across her living room to the sliding glass door.

"Hey, cut it out," she yelled, shoving open the door.

Too late. The huge white cat batted a paw, sending a third terra-cotta flowerpot off the deck railing.

"Come on, Lizzie, give me a break."

Sabrina grabbed the broom that had become a common fixture in the corner of her small patio. She waved it in front of the cat before Lizzie could swipe at the next pot in the row. It took Sabrina weeks of yelling to realize the feline terror was stone deaf, so even raising the broom did no good unless it was in the cat's line of vision.

On a morning like this the last thing Sabrina needed was to have to deal with Lizzie Borden.

3

Tallahassee, Florida

Jason Brill left the concierge's desk shaking his head. It was ridiculous what this hotel considered a king-sized suite. The so-called manager didn't even know enough to be embarrassed by it, his bush-garden eyebrows raised in surprise at every one of Jason's questions like he couldn't quite imagine why a noisy and empty minifridge wasn't quite the same as a well-stocked minibar. Jason straightened his tie and gave his shirt cuffs a tug as if the altercation had included more than a tongue-lashing. He wanted to hit the guy. In the past he would have. He knew his boss would be okay with the room, but Jason wasn't okay with it.

He balled up his fist around the key card to the pathetic suite and jammed it into his back trouser pocket. His job was to ensure that the senator got only the best and that he would be well taken care of. A particularly difficult task this morning since none of the goddamn hotel staff—not a single one with English as a first language—even knew who Senator John Quincy Allen was. Okay, so it was one more good reason to support his boss's stand on immigration, which pretty much supported sending the whole goddamn lot back and building a wall.

Earlier Jason had considered pulling up stakes and going to a different hotel, but it probably wouldn't make much difference. There wasn't a decent four-star hotel in the entire city. Now he wished the senator hadn't been hell-bent on staying overnight. Maybe he could convince him to take a flight back after the tour. If nothing else, he could at least save the senator from the head chef's runny omelet. Jason could still taste the damn thing. The grits had been runny, too, not that Jason understood why every breakfast in the South had to include that stuff, anyway. Again, the omelet wouldn't matter to the senator. The grits would, though the man wouldn't complain. There'd be only that drop of the eyes and a slight nod as if to say, "So this is the best you could do."

God, he hated that look of disappointment, a look that said, "So this is how you repay me." Sometimes he'd rather the man chew him out instead. Jason's uncle Louie used to say, "It ain't healthy for a man not to say what's on his mind. You keep it all bottled up, eventually you blow up." Uncle Louie wasn't much of a scholar, but he knew a thing or two about common sense, which was certainly one thing Jason discovered to be lacking in D.C. big-time.

But Jason also knew the difference between people who inherited good manners and discipline and those who had to learn it from scratch, the difference between Senator John Quincy Allen and Uncle Louie. It was the difference between Jason walking away from that stupid-ass manager instead of slamming the bastard's smug face into the wall.

He rolled his shoulders and stretched his neck, but knew the tight ball of tension was there for the day. He flipped open his cell phone as he reached the bank of elevators and punched the Up arrow. While he waited he scrolled down his phone's call list. The elevator doors opened to two chattering maids and Jason held the door open, standing back. When they noticed him their conversation stopped immediately in midsentence—pretty obvious even if he didn't understand the language. The older one bowed her head as she passed by while the younger woman smiled at him, a wonderfully coy smile as though she had no clue she had a nice ass. But then she glanced back over her shoulder as if to make sure he noticed the tight ass. It only reminded him that this discipline thing pretty much sucked and it certainly couldn't be healthy for a twenty-six-year-old male.

It wasn't like there was some chief of staff how-to-behave manual or that anyone had ever come right out and told him what was and wasn't acceptable behavior for a senator's chief of staff. No, that much he'd figured out for himself. It didn't take long for Jason to realize that politics were constantly one major innuendo after another whether you were making deals or breaking balls. They even gave the insinuations fancy names and phrases like "the politics of personal destruction." But where Jason came from it didn't matter what you called it or how polite you did it, breaking balls was still breaking balls.

His cell phone started ringing as soon as he stepped into the elevator.

"Jason Brill," he said.

"Brill, it's Natalie Richards."

He couldn't help smiling, speaking of ball breakers. "Hello, Natalie Richards."

"What's this about changing the venue for the presummit reception?"

"Well, I'm fine. Thanks for asking. And how are you?"

"Cut the crap, Brill. I don't have time for that cute-ass sense of humor of yours. And I don't appreciate it when people start playing musical chairs and not bothering to let our office know."

"Come on, Ms. Richards. Your team's in charge of the entire energy summit. This is just a reception, a personal reception that Senator Allen is throwing for a few of his friends and acquaintances who happen to be coming to the summit." Though he was pretty sure Richards knew it wasn't just a reception but a celebration. If all went well, Senator Allen's hard work would be rewarded with EchoEnergy being the first American oil-producing company supplying all the vehicles of U.S. troops. It was worthy of a celebration even if it was a bit premature.

"Friends and acquaintances," Richards said, "who just happen to be all the heavy hitters."

"Not to worry. Your boss is going to be invited." *Despite trying to trip up this deal every step of the way.* He wisely kept the last part to himself.

"That's not the goddamn point, Brill, and you know it."

"All I know is you're making much ado about nothing."

"You can't continue to—"

Jason began tapping the cell phone against the elevator wall, then brought it back to his ear only to interrupt her again. "I think I'm losing you, Ms. Richards. I'm in Tallahassee. In an elevator and I—"

He clicked the phone off and slipped it into his jacket pocket. He'd probably be sorry later on, but he had more important things to do right now than to suck up to the White House. More important things like stock a fucking minifridge.

4

EchoEnergy

Almost noon and Sabrina still hadn't been able to track down her boss. She was certain she could leave an hour or two early without his permission, but she'd at least like to clear it with him, especially if he had anything he wanted her to finish up over the weekend. Dr. Lansik was on the schedule but no one had seen him all morning. The man kept to himself and hardly ever left the lab or his small office at the far end of the lab. No one probably would have even noticed he was missing if Sabrina hadn't started asking for him.

"Maybe something happened at his home...a sick child perhaps," Pasha Kosloff suggested in his Russian-accented English. He said this without looking up from the vials he was filling with a murky-brown liquid.

Sabrina didn't say anything despite knowing their boss didn't have any children. Instead, she watched Pasha's long, delicate fingers place each vial carefully into the centrifuge. His tall, lanky frame slouched at the shoulders and bent at the waist, hunched over the metal contraption. He moved in slow motion as if he were creating a masterpiece, every gesture deliberate, almost painstakingly so.

Sabrina's own work sat in the distiller that took up the far corner of the lab, an old monstrosity that would need to hum and vibrate for another half hour before she could check on it. She glanced at her watch and stuffed her hands into the worn and sagging pockets of her lab coat.

"Maybe he's having an affair," Anna Copello suggested. "You know, sneaking out from work during the day so his wife won't get suspicious."

Sabrina knew this explanation wasn't possible, either, at least not the wife part. Though she wasn't surprised at Anna's suggestion. The young woman seemed to have a talent for seeing the very worst in everyone. Sabrina glanced at Michael O'Hearn, the oldest of the group, a fit, compact little man with wild black hair and a goatee that was almost completely silver. He would know their boss the best. Despite his thick protective goggles she could see him rolling his eyes at Anna.

"I don't think so," O'Hearn said. "I believe his wife died last year."

Sabrina knew this wasn't true, either, and she stared at O'Hearn. How could O'Hearn not know the truth?

"Oh, that's awful," Anna gasped and even Pasha looked up from his vials. "Why didn't he tell us?"

"He's a private man," O'Hearn insisted. "If you paid any attention you'd have heard him mention that his wife's gone."

Sabrina escaped to the corner, pretending to check the gauges on the distiller. She couldn't believe how little every one of them knew about their boss. Especially O'Hearn. She understood that the two men had been colleagues long before they came to spearhead EchoEnergy's Product Laboratory. Sabrina had worked with Dwight

Lansik for a shorter period than any of them, and yet she seemed to be the only one who knew he had no children and his wife was not dead, though she was, indeed, gone.

In fact, it was quite by accident that Sabrina had learned the truth. Shortly after she started, she came in early on a Sunday, not unusual for either her or Lansik, but this particular Sunday she caught him sleeping on the old blue sofa in his office. Not just sleeping but with his robe, toothbrush and slippers in place as if it had been his routine for some time. He grudgingly confided that his house had not been the same since his wife was gone.

At first Sabrina thought he meant that his wife had passed away. He had made it sound like a painful process, more that of a brokenhearted widower than an abandoned husband. But among the scattered paraphernalia was also a crumpled set of staple-bound papers, official-looking documents with the first page stamped Divorce Decree.

It wasn't any of Sabrina's business. Lansik was her boss, not a friend or a member of her family. What happened in his personal life was…well, personal.

The phone started ringing in the adjoining office and all of them stopped and stared. Finally Sabrina pushed open the door, hesitating as she looked around, checking the blue sofa before she reached for the phone on her boss's desk.

"EchoLab," she answered.

"Ms. Galloway?" a woman's voice asked, startling Sabrina so much she stepped back. Why would anyone presume she would answer her boss's phone?

"Yes?" she said so quietly she wondered if the woman had heard her.

"This is Anita Fraiser from Mr. Sidel's office. He asked me to contact you. He needs you to meet him outside Reactor Area #1 at one o'clock. You'll be giving the VIP tour."

"Wait a minute. I had no idea there was a tour today. I'm sure there must be some mistake." William Sidel was the CEO of EchoEnergy and Sabrina was quite certain she'd remember an appointment with him, let alone a tour.

"No, no mistake. You were on the list."

"The list?"

"Let's see here," the woman said and Sabrina could hear pages being flipped and shuffled. She glanced outside the office, into the lab, and everyone was now staring, not bothering to disguise the fact that they were straining to listen in. "Yes, it's right here. Your boss has you listed as the lead if for some reason he's gone."

"Has he called in sick?" Sabrina couldn't believe he would purposely do this to her.

"All I know is that Dr. Lansik will not be in at all today. So again, that's one o'clock, Reactor Area #1."

5

Jason Brill was pleased. It was just as he had anticipated. Put the senator in the middle of some hot-topic environmental issue and they will come. They, of course, being the media. Now Jason was glad he'd talked the senator into the navy-blue suit, crisp white shirt and red tie though the senator fought him on the shirt, insisting white was for ultraconservative pricks and definitely not moderate Democrats.

Jason made it sound like it wasn't a big deal. He told the senator he could wear whatever he wanted, but for some reason the navy suit with a white shirt made him look taller. And on a photo op where they would be on their feet the entire time, Jason knew he didn't have to say anything more. Without another word Senator Allen was peeling off his blue oxford and replacing it with the freshly pressed white shirt Jason had waiting for him on a hanger in the hotel closet.

The drive from Tallahassee was not one of Florida's most scenic.

The senator had shot Jason one of those subtle, furrowed-brow looks of disapproval that Jason knew so well.

It did look like the middle of nowhere. On the edge of the Apalachicola National Forest there were more pine trees than Jason ever expected to see in Florida. The limousine spent little time on the interstate, almost immediately taking a narrow two-lane blacktop with dirt shoulders that the car veered onto when meeting several large tanker trucks too wide for their own lane. The trucks barreled down the highway, obviously used to the locals giving them the space they needed.

Twice the limousine driver, who introduced himself as Marek Zelenski, ended what appeared to be a game of chicken by skidding off the concrete and into the dirt. The second time the car slammed to a full stop was followed by a diatribe from Marek, a slew of profanities in what Jason could only guess was Polish. He glanced in the rearview mirror with a quick apology in broken English and pulled the car back onto the road.

"Looks like they're in dire need of a new road bill down here." Jason tried to make light of the situation, but the senator shook his head.

"Other than those tankers we've seen very little traffic," the senator pointed out. "No sense wasting the taxpayers' time and money."

Jason started nodding in agreement instead of simply saying he was sort of joking when he'd stated the obvious. But then he caught a glint in the senator's blue eyes.

"Also, no traffic means no voters," the senator added with a smile. "Which means a waste of *my* time and money."

That was when Jason wondered if he would regret this whole fiasco. It had been his idea, after all. A surefire way for the senator to promote his position at the upcoming energy summit and at the same time tap into all the positive press EchoEnergy was getting. And why shouldn't he? The senator had helped EchoEnergy from the very beginning, lobbying to get the federal grants to build the facility and later garnering the tax incentives that allowed the plant to hire and operate. In the last several years EchoEnergy earned an incredible reputation with environmental groups and was now the darling of the news media, like some shining beacon in the energy war. Why shouldn't the senator capitalize on some of that? After all he had done he deserved some accolades and recognition as being a pioneer in this new breakthrough technology.

But for some reason Senator Allen wasn't crazy about Jason's idea, once even suggesting that he didn't want to risk upstaging the media focus for the energy summit. Jason's whole point was not to upstage the summit as much as it was to highlight the senator's role. Once the summit began so would the competition for media attention. Usually the senator took advantage of opportunities like this. Jason didn't get it.

They passed through the industrial park's electronic gate, stopping only briefly at the security hut where Jason was surprised to see the uniformed guard, alert and at attention, reminding Jason more of a marine barracks than a commercial processing plant. And the limousine didn't get an easy pass. Credentials were checked, the young man taking his time to examine details and match photos to faces.

It wasn't until they drove to the end of the road—a much wider, smoother path than the state highway they had left—that the plant could be seen through the thick forest that lined three sides of what Jason knew to be a hundred-acre property. It looked like a strange small town. On one side, what Jason figured must be the office complex, were five to six modern steel-and-glass buildings—two and three stories high—surrounded by a landscaped park. A slice of the river behind the park disappeared into the forest.

On the other side of the industrial park were about a dozen giant silver tanks like high-rises glinting in the sun. Steel-grated catwalks instead of glass skywalks connected them. A maze of pipes, some a foot in diameter, and huge electric coils snaked along the tanks and overhead—all a shining white as if the plant had only finished construction. All of the pipes eventually attached each of the tanks to the top of one building that took up the back side of the park, a massive corrugated steel structure with no windows and very few doors.

Jason had to admit he expected something else, something dingy and dark, considering the long line of tanker trucks—that he now realized were companions to the ones that almost ran them off the highway—were carrying either chicken guts or fuel oil. Yes, he was impressed and he looked to Senator Allen, hoping to see the same reaction only to find the senator sitting back against the soft leather car seat with…absolutely no reaction.

They approached the office complex, turning the final corner to the entrance. And that's when Jason saw them. They were parked on sidewalks and filling the circle driveway, all jockeying for the best spot. Jason counted nine news vans. He didn't bother to count the crowd surrounding the entry to the building. But when he glanced at the senator, he noticed the man was now sitting forward at the edge of the seat, rubbing his hands together like he was getting ready for a feast.

He gave Jason a rare but genuine pat on the back as he said, "Good job, son."

6

EchoEnergy

Sabrina kept thinking there had to be some mistake. She was the last person on their team whom Dwight Lansik would choose to lead in his absence. Not for lack of ability or experience, but simply because she had been the last hire. She knew the man had a rather strong opinion about seniority, with disloyalty being the only thing that could uproot it. Taking that into consideration, O'Hearn would be the next in line, and then Anna. When Sabrina told the others about being assigned as tour guide, she could see the question in their eyes, too. Though she couldn't imagine any of them would really want the assignment. If it was up to her, she'd gladly pass.

Anna was the only one who dared to ask out loud, "Mr. Sidel requested *you* to give the tour?" She raised one of her perfectly shaped eyebrows to emphasize that she was not pleased. She was always doing that, using facial expressions to say what she really thought.

Pasha had commented once that he saw a physical resemblance between Sabrina and Anna, but Sabrina failed—or perhaps refused—to see anything the two might have in common. Sabrina knew the woman was several years her junior and yet Anna Copello had a way of making her feel like she was one of Anna's problem students. Sabrina, according to Anna, was constantly using glass vials that Anna had set aside for herself, or documenting results using a substandard method. For some reason Sabrina had rubbed Anna the wrong way from the second she arrived at EchoEnergy. O'Hearn had once joked that with Sabrina's arrival, Anna was no longer the only beauty in their group of mad scientists. And Sabrina couldn't help wondering if that was true. Anna certainly treated Sabrina as if she was the spoilsport.

"His secretary said my name was on the list," Sabrina offered, trying to defend herself when it looked like Anna was waiting for an explanation.

"The list?" At this, Anna turned to O'Hearn, crossing her arms over her chest. "There's a list?"

O'Hearn simply shrugged and swung his chair back to face the computer screen like it didn't matter to him one way or another. Pasha had already wandered off to complete his work. Anna looked around at both men, then threw her hands in the air as if the situation was hopeless. Without even a glance at Sabrina, she stomped off.

Sabrina slipped back into Lansik's office. While on the phone she had seen a file folder labeled Tour Briefing. It was right there on his desk when she replaced the phone, straddling his in-box pile, tempting her, daring her. It wasn't like Sabrina to touch anyone else's belongings, let alone take them, but she found herself thinking that if Lansik had gotten her into his mess, he certainly couldn't complain about her taking a peek and utilizing the same information he had planned on using.

She slid the bulging file folder that included a spiral six-by-nine-inch notebook inside her briefcase. She'd return it later, after the tour. Then she escaped her colleagues to find refuge at a small bistro table in the EchoCafé, the same table in the corner by the window where she sat every day for lunch.

Same table, same time, same lunch. Her brother used to call her a slave to her routine, claiming it was too rigid for her to ever really enjoy life. This from a guy who couldn't hold a job or maintain a relationship for more than six months. She might be boring, she argued, but she had a career she loved, money in the bank and a roof over her head. More than Eric could say for himself. Though how would she know? She hadn't seen him in over two years.

Over her usual egg salad on wheat she glimpsed one or two of Lansik's notes, his chicken-scratch handwriting almost impossible to decipher. She hadn't taken more than two bites of the sandwich. She knew she was eating only to settle her nerves, and she wasn't sure why she was nervous.

She had done formal presentations all the time when she worked at the university, some of them—not many—impromptu. And she knew the thermal-conversion process backward and forward. It had fascinated her enough that she insisted on knowing every aspect. She could do this tour. So what was bothering her? How unexpected and sudden it was or the fact that Lansik had chosen her above the others?

Sabrina had met the CEO of EchoEnergy, William Sidel, only once. Well, she hadn't actually met him. O'Hearn had pointed him out to her at one of their employee-appreciation events. Sidel had been patting a lot of backs and making everyone laugh, but he never seemed to make his way over to the group of scientists. O'Hearn claimed it wasn't personal, but simply that he avoided them so he didn't have to pretend to know what they were talking about. According to O'Hearn, William Sidel was an incredible entrepreneur when it came to getting investors and lobbying the government, but the man had no idea of, or interest in, the day-to-day process.

Sabrina stopped at the lab to stow her briefcase, almost making her late. Now, as she hurried to Reactor #1 to meet the man who had recently made the covers of *Forbes, Time* and *Discover* magazines, Sabrina wondered if she should have also stopped at a restroom. At least to check for food in her teeth, wash her hands, maybe give her hair a swipe. Instead, she pushed a strand behind her ear.

She was nonchalant about her appearance—too nonchalant her mother had always complained. She glanced down at herself: the lab coat was bright white and pressed, even if the pockets sagged a little from her constantly putting her hands in them. Her black trousers were part of her standard wardrobe. There were six other pairs, exactly the same, back in her bedroom closet. Years ago Sabrina resigned herself to the fact that she had no fashion sense. Her artistic and sometimes flamboyant mother had confirmed it, going a step further and declaring Sabrina "fashion retarded." To which Sabrina usually responded, in her own defense, that if Albert Einstein could wear the same outfit every single day, then so could she.

Even her jewelry she kept to a minimum—classic but simple: an eighteen-karat gold rope chain that had belonged to her mother and a Movado watch her father had given her when she made tenure. As she approached Reactor #1 Sabrina decided that had she known about the tour this morning she still wouldn't have changed a single thing about her appearance or herself.

She'd do just fine and she stuffed her hands, sweaty palms and all, into her lab-coat pockets.

7

Washington, D.C.

Natalie Richards shook her head while she watched the small TV in her office.

"Do you believe this guy?" She pointed at the TV screen, only glancing at the man sitting in her guest chair. Ordinarily she'd be equally frustrated with his sitting back, all relaxed with his legs crossed as though he really were a guest. She kept her eyes on the TV. Her hands rested on her ample hips when she really wanted to strangle something...or someone.

She had already flipped through the channels. Senator John Quincy Allen was live on every blasted cable channel. And unless a terrorist attack or natural disaster happened in the next few hours he would, undoubtedly, lead all three of the evening broadcast-news channels.

She kept the sound turned down, not out of courtesy to the man who occupied her guest chair, but because she was expecting the phone to ring. Her boss would be furious and it wouldn't take long. News traveled fast in this town. At least Natalie wouldn't need to be the messenger of this bad news.

"So what's he up to?" Now she came around behind her small, ornate desk and looked Colin Jernigan in the eyes—tired eyes. He probably hadn't gotten any sleep the last few days. She swore every time she saw him these days those brilliant blue eyes seemed to get dimmer and dimmer and his close-cropped hair more and more peppered with gray. If she remembered correctly he wasn't even forty yet. Poor bastard, not that it hurt his looks any. He was still fit, trim and handsome, and most annoying to her was that he was as calm as ever. Nothing seemed to faze him. No doubt just one of the reasons he was the best in the business. Or at least he used to be. Forget about the physical wear and tear. That meant nothing. Natalie Richards prided herself on being able to look someone in the eye and see what was bullshit and what was passion. But in this case what she didn't like was what she didn't see at all, what she hadn't seen in quite some time—a missing spark behind his eyes.

"Anything?" she asked when he still didn't respond. "I've got to have some line of bullshit, some credible bullshit or my ass is gonna get one helluva kickin'."

"I have no idea why Senator Allen does the things he does." Then he gave her a rare smile. "I'm surprised you don't know. I thought you were the most powerful woman in this town."

"I will have you know I *am* the most powerful *black* woman in this town," she said, besting his attempt at humor. "And that's about as good as saying I'm the most beautiful woman in the dugout. Not like there're dozens of us coming up to bat."

She leaned against the desk and crossed her arms, getting serious again. "Listen, if the senior senator from the great state of Florida screws up the energy summit I will personally kick your ass."

"My ass? Not his?"

"I can't control his. I can control yours."

She didn't expect him to flinch even if she hoped he would. She reminded herself that she wouldn't trust him if he did flinch easily. What a wicked circle politics had become.

A knock at the door interrupted them.

"Come on in!" Natalie yelled.

Her assistant opened the door. "Excuse me, Ms. Richards." Then she stood back to let in a young man dressed in black jeans, leather boots and leather jacket, a laminated ID badge swinging from a cord around his neck. His tangle of hair was matted down from the helmet he now carried tucked under one arm. Had it not been for the leather messenger pouch he handed across the desk, Natalie would never have allowed him in her office dressed this way. As soon as she took it, he turned and was gone without a word. Her assistant smiled, nodded and closed the door gently behind her.

"You're back to using messengers?"

"We never stopped. Let all those other idiots use e-mail and then be shocked when someone accesses all their precious messages they thought they deleted. This—" she opened the pouch and pulled out the single envelope fastened with a wax seal "—can't be traced. And even if someone hijacked it and opened it, they'd never know what it meant."

"Seems a bit archaic in this vast technological world, doesn't it?"

She raised an eyebrow at him. "Not like your methods aren't a bit archaic?" She grabbed the TV remote from the corner of her desk and shot it at the TV screen, clicking it off. "So tell me, what went wrong?"

"I don't know."

"Not acceptable," she said, shaking her head slowly. She had learned long ago that her gestures garnered more authority than her words ever would.

"Forgive the pun, but maybe Dr. Lansik simply chickened out."

She stared at him, raising her eyebrow and giving him a frown that indicated she wasn't in the mood for puns or sarcasm or any more of his usual dry humor.

"You'd have me believe this is all some coincidence? The senator's tour not even twenty-four hours after a botched meeting? A coincidence," she repeated, enunciating the word syllable by syllable.

"I don't believe in coincidences." He said it with no apology, but he shifted in his chair slightly, just enough for her to recognize she had him on the edge. She had him exactly where she wanted him.

"It's getting too late to wait around for another opportunity like this. You hear what I'm saying?" But she didn't expect him to respond. "You know we have to have this all taken care of before the energy summit?"

"Dr. Lansik decides not to talk, then disappears. I can't get blood from a turnip," he said, but at least he wasn't smiling.

"What about one of the other scientists?"

"It doesn't look hopeful. This close to the summit? I wouldn't count on it."

Natalie Richards tapped the envelope she had pulled out of the leather pouch and without opening it, she handed it to him.

"Then we need to move on to plan B." She hoped he had come up with something—anything else. She didn't like plan B. "Your next assignment," she told him, folding her arms across her chest. "William Sidel can get oil from chicken guts. I'd rather you bring me back blood from that turnip."

8

EchoEnergy

Sabrina was beginning to wonder why William Sidel had insisted she lead this tour. So far he interrupted her every step of the way. It surprised her. Sidel had the reputation of being a charmer. Of course, everything she knew about the man came from articles and news clips instead of firsthand. A *Time* magazine article called him a "wizard," a modern-day Rumpelstiltskin who had found a way to magically spin garbage into oil. His magic would most likely continue if EchoEnergy was awarded a $140-million government contract to supply the entire U.S. military. That feat alone, the article had contended, would be a major coup considering the contract had never gone to a domestic company, but rather the same Middle Eastern oil company. Sabrina knew that obtaining that single contract could mean the difference between EchoEnergy becoming a serious supplier of alternative oil or simply remaining an interesting novelty.

Meeting him in person today, for all his supposed charm and wizardry, Sabrina didn't think him charming or magical. Instead, William Sidel resembled the ex-linebacker that he had been in college. Still a large man, Sabrina noticed his middle overlapped his belt just enough to betray his lack of an exercise regimen. However, he did still possess a boyish face along with the mannerisms to match. In fact, he reminded Sabrina of a middle-aged frat boy who didn't trust that his deep voice and physical presence would demand enough attention, so he compensated with outbursts, offhand observations or awkward jokes. At first it had been extraneous information he interjected between Sabrina's pauses as if he was uncomfortable with only the hum and rattle of the pipes overhead. She wondered if perhaps he was simply as nervous as she was.

Sabrina started to explain to the group of fifteen, several potential investors and one senator that, "Thermal conversion speeds up the same process of pressurization and extreme heat that the earth has been doing naturally to turn carbon-based objects into oil. We take that same—"

"You know, that reminds me of my third-grade teacher," Sidel suddenly interrupted. "I could never get that earth science crap." He laughed. He was the only one who did. Sabrina and the others stared at him and yet he continued. "You know what she'd do if we forgot our homework? She'd make us stand facing the blackboard with our noses pressed into a chalked circle. And let me tell you, this schnoz took up quite a bit of the blackboard."

This time several in the group laughed. And that's when Sabrina saw Sidel relax; his hands came out of his trouser pockets and he shifted his weight, no longer looking like he was ready for the next tackle. Sidel was that guy who demanded constant attention but did so in such a manner that no one really minded, or rather, no one really

minded for the first few times as long as the humor was self-depre-
cating and not aimed at anyone else. Sabrina was used to dealing with
men like Sidel, but in the past they were usually her students, not
her boss. One thing she knew for certain was that guys like Sidel
quickly became more annoying than entertaining.

"But it must take a tremendous amount of fuel to run this place,"
Glenn Owens, an investor, said.

"In our case, it takes plenty of guts," Sidel joked.

Owens didn't laugh. "Seriously, is the output worth the input?" he
asked, this time directing his question to Sabrina and purposely
turning away from Sidel.

Owens had been introduced as a billionaire from Omaha who had
made a good deal of his fortune investing decades ago alongside billionaire Warren Buffet. The tall, silver-haired gentleman had dressed
casually—a blue Ralph Lauren polo and khakis—as if the tour had
been a last-minute side stop on his way to play golf. However, there
was nothing casual about his manner and when it looked as if Sidel
would answer the question again, Owens put up a hand to silence
him.

"We're 85 percent energy sufficient," Sabrina answered after an
uncomfortable pause. "That means for every 100 BTUs in feedstock,
we use only 15 BTUs to run the process. The oil can be used immediately to fuel electrical-powered generators. Most of it goes a step
further and we distill it into vehicle-grade diesel and gasoline."

"And what about waste removal?" Owens wasn't satisfied.

"Nothing hazardous comes from feedstock, which is the only
carbon-based garbage we process. Also with feedstock everything is
used in some capacity," Sabrina explained. The efficiency of EchoEnergy was one of the selling points that had lured her to the position.
"What's not separated off as oil is shunted and sold to be used in high-

concentrate fertilizer. The depolymerization takes apart materials at the molecular level..." Sabrina stopped. She was losing them with her jargon. She smiled and tried again, "Anything dangerous is destroyed by the high temperatures so the runoff is flushed then brought back to room temperature. It's clean enough by EPA standards to be used again in the next cycle or released into the river."

"If I might just add to what Dr. Galloway said." Sidel stepped forward, serious now. "Our runoff is so clean the plant isn't even required to register as a waste-management industry by the EPA."

"Sounds too good to be true," Owens insisted.

"That's why I wanted you to take a look for yourself, Glenn," Senator Allen said as he patted Owens on the back. "It's the wave of the future." The senator addressed the group of men on the tour. "This plant, and hopefully others like it, will be our freedom from foreign oil companies. Think about it—" and now he had managed to move into the center of the group "—oil from refuse, from slaughterhouse garbage. Never again will we be held captive by Middle Eastern oil sheikhs. No more guises of war over oil. It truly is quite remarkable."

Sabrina watched from the sidelines, waiting patiently for some sign that the political speech was finished. She realized now this was probably why Jason Brill, Senator Allen's chief of staff, had argued earlier when Sidel announced at the beginning of their tour that no media would be included. Still, Sabrina couldn't help thinking Mr. Brill was probably relieved. Despite the senator's eloquent voice and refined posture the yellow hard hat and plastic goggles didn't quite flatter his slight frame, making him look a bit like a caricature, a bulbous yellow bobble-head with alienlike goggle eyes.

Senator Allen gestured toward Sidel, reaching up to put a congratulatory hand on the big man's shoulder and bringing him back into the fold. "And this man is the genius behind it all."

That's when Sabrina noticed it as she was standing back and waiting.

The sounds from above weren't the familiar hum and swish of wet feedstock, sloshing and being flushed. Instead, there was a high-pitched ping and rattle like pebbles traveling within the pipes. She stepped away from the men and listened, trying not to look up and stare. A glance told her the valve to Reactor #5 was open.

Impossible. And yet, the sound confirmed it.

There was solid matter, unrefined bits and pieces traveling into the reactor, a reactor that wasn't used for anything other than releasing clear, liquid runoff.

She looked over at William Sidel, who was now smiling and joking again. She could hear him inviting the group to take a detour and "get a good look at the magic feedstock." He reminded Sabrina of a chef eager to share his secret ingredient. He turned her way and for a second she thought he had noticed her looking up at the valve. Should she give him a wave, distract him and pull him aside?

The men were all laughing again. No, it was definitely not the time to mention what might be a dangerous mistake. Besides, how did she know for certain? Perhaps Lansik had made the change recently. There was probably a logical explanation. She'd need to check it out before she went off sounding like Chicken Little, and the odd but seemingly appropriate analogy made her grimace as she followed Sidel with the rest of the group.

9

Jason Brill couldn't believe how bad it smelled. And he wasn't even thinking about the rotting chicken guts. It was the stink inside the limousine that challenged his gag reflex and brought him close to up-chucking his own lunch.

Jesus! The entire limousine smelled like vomit despite having all the windows rolled down. Yet he tried not to look away from the senator, tried not to look repulsed.

Marek handed Senator Allen another wet towel. "I not get stench out for weeks," the limo driver said, shaking his head and not bother-ing to hide his disgust. Then he climbed into the front seat totally unaware of the senator looking up and staring at the back of the driver's head like that was exactly where he'd like to shoot a poisoned dart.

Jason refrained from helping, other than offering to hold a dis-carded towel or two. Unlike Marek, he knew when to sit back and shut up. He knew that the navy suit was probably toast. Instead of focusing on the smell, he concentrated on what had happened. Jason couldn't help thinking that asshole Sidel knew exactly what he was doing when he took them all up the catwalk that overlooked the holding tank with his "magic feedstock."

Whatever his intention, it didn't matter. What Jason would never forget was that Sidel had laughed like some fucking frat boy when Senator Allen started puking over the railing, yelling not to worry, they could break that down, too, with the rest of the "magic" garbage. Jason used to teach guys bigger than Sidel a lesson with an elbow to the kidneys and a fist to the throat. It seemed cleaner and more fair than the way the senator insisted things be done. And all Jason could think at the time was, "Thank God there weren't any media around."

Sidel had gone too far. After everything the senator had done for him the man should be licking the vomit off Senator Allen's Italian-leather shoes, not pointing and laughing. Jason had never understood the connection between the two men. He knew they had both attended Florida State University at the same time, but he couldn't imagine them being friends even as young men. They seemed too different. Sidel had been a linebacker for the Seminoles while Senator Allen headed the debate club. And yet there appeared to be a strong allegiance, at least on the senator's part.

Allegiance, unrelenting loyalty, Jason certainly understood. The whole concept was one he had had to learn the hard way. He came from people who trusted no one, who knew how to steal and cheat and lie so well they didn't realize there were boundaries. Jason supposed it wasn't much different than politicians. No wonder he had been attracted to D.C. when he was old enough to buy a motorcy-cle—a sleek, powerful Yamaha—and drive as far away as possible. He got a job as a courier and muscled his cycle around the capital, squeezing in and out of traffic, pushing the limits, breaking a few rules. But then he banged up himself and his bike when he darted in front of a black SUV.

Jason still delivered the bloodstained package despite three broken ribs and a badly bruised knee. The SUV owner, some hotshot foreign diplomat, threatened to have Jason's license pulled. Didn't matter, the bike was busted up worse than Jason. He figured he was out of business.

Three days later he got a message from the courier service that the recipient of his last delivery wanted to meet him. Immediately Jason thought he was fucked, another asshole upset about the blood, or maybe there had been something important inside that got crushed. He never imagined that the recipient had heard the rumors about Jason's heroic delivery and actually wanted to offer him a job. Senator John Quincy Allen told Jason he reminded the senator of himself when he was a young man. Evidently it was something good because less than two years later Jason Brill became the youngest chief of staff to a U.S. senator on the Hill. No one had ever shown such trust in Jason before.

Now Jason couldn't help wondering what William Sidel had done to garner such trust. Everything he had read about the man painted him as a simpleminded, down-home good ole boy who happened to be a bit of an entrepreneurial whiz. Sidel had no particular talent. Instead, he possessed something much better—the gift of bullshit, the ability to ignite and excite others about his schemes using only words and promises, getting them to follow, to believe, to create, to rally and even to invest. Only, thermal conversion wasn't a scheme at all. It was brilliant, but it also wasn't Sidel's idea. He had bought the patent, hired one of the founding scientists, then added to and improvised the process enough to claim it as his own.

Sidel's witty repartee made him the life of the party and his annoying banter made him everyone's buddy only by default because no one wanted to end up as the butt of his one-sided jokes. The man could pull a zinger even on the best of the best. Jason remembered when a cocky reporter from *E: the Environmental Magazine* tried to attack Sidel by calling him a snake-oil salesman, Sidel quipped, "It's not snake oil, it's real oil. You'd know that if you were smart enough to read your own magazine."

And the thing is, Sidel was right. It was the real deal. It was an ingenious process. Jason was proud the senator was a part of it. But he didn't trust Sidel and he wasn't sure why Senator Allen did.

"How do you put up with that guy?" Jason couldn't help it. He had to ask.

"Who? Sidel?"

"Of course, Sidel."

Senator Allen finished wiping his silk tie, balled up the last towel and tossed it on the floor across from them. "He gets things done, my boy. He gets things done." And then he turned to watch the miles of pine trees pass by outside the limousine window as if that was all the explanation that was needed.

10

Sabrina rushed back to the lab to hang up her lab coat and retrieve her briefcase. She'd be late, but hopefully she could get to Chattahoochee before dinner was served. It pained her to think of her father needing to be spoon-fed because they refused to take off the restraints. Despite the circumstances she was relieved that the tour had to be cut short.

She wasn't surprised to see O'Hearn and Pasha still working. Pasha's family had all remained in Moscow. O'Hearn had claimed he was a dedicated bachelor though he had mentioned a son once. Earlier, when they had all drawn blanks trying to figure out where Dwight Lansik might be, Sabrina thought it remarkable how little they knew about their boss. And with the exception of Anna Copello, whom Sabrina knew nothing about nor did she wish to know, none of them had anyone to go home to.

She was on her way out again, car keys dangling, when Pasha asked, "The tour good? No?" He stopped on his way to the back storage area, waiting for an answer. Usually Pasha didn't even bother to look up from his work. That he had bothered to ask made her realize that the three of them had probably continued to discuss the subject while she was gone.

"It was good," Sabrina said, despite remembering the malfunctioning valve to Reactor #5. "Until Mr. Sidel had everyone take a look into the holding tank."

"Ow, that couldn't be good." O'Hearn crinkled his nose, the mention enough to revive the memory of the stink.

"Senator Allen puked right over the railing," she told them.

O'Hearn let out a rare laugh, but Pasha turned his head.

"Puk-ed?" Pasha didn't understand the word.

"He tossed his cookies," O'Hearn said, smiling and enjoying the Russian's confusion. "He upchucked his lunch."

Sabrina hated that O'Hearn poked so much fun at Pasha, once even claiming it was his superficial revenge for the cold war.

"He vomited," she said before O'Hearn could continue.

"Oh, right. That no good." Pasha finally nodded and continued to the storage room.

Sabrina started to leave again. She glanced at O'Hearn, who now sat in front of one of the computers. Not much got past O'Hearn. If changes had been made to the system, he would probably know. She checked to make sure Pasha was out of earshot then stopped beside the bank of computers. She waited for O'Hearn to look up at her.

"Do you know if Dr. Lansik reprogrammed the process to include Reactor #5?"

"Five's only for Grade 2 garbage—plastics and metals."

"Yes, I know."

"We're not set up to process plastics and metals. Too many toxins are given off. We'd have to find a way to dispose of the toxins." O'Hearn was matter-of-fact. "We have a long way to go before we use Reactor #5. That's probably another forty million dollars away."

"Yes, I know all that." Sabrina tried to keep her patience intact. She didn't need a lecture. She knew this process inside and out, and she also knew what she had heard and seen. The valve to the reactor looked like it had been opened. She was almost certain. "But is there any reason Dr. Lansik may be using Reactor #5? Maybe to increase production?" Only Lansik controlled the computer software that ultimately cranked the gears and lifted levers or, in this case, opened valves.

"There's no reason for Reactor #5 to be open except to process Grade 2 garbage," he repeated. But this time he scratched his head, his fingertips disappearing into the wild mass of hair. He cocked his head as he looked up at her, his dark eyes becoming slits as though he was trying to see what she was getting at. "Why do you ask?"

"Nothing, really," she said and immediately regretted it. Of course he knew it was something at this point. How much did she want to tell him? If it turned out she was wrong and she hadn't heard what she thought she heard, and if the valve wasn't opened at all, she would look like a fool. On the other hand, if there was a malfunction… "It's just that on the tour today I thought it looked like the valve to Reactor #5 was opened. That's all. But I'm sure I must have been mistaken."

She didn't tell him that it also sounded like gravel running through the pipes, exactly what it would sound like if ground-up, pea-sized plastic and metal were, in fact, running through those pipes instead of soupy, soft chicken guts. Even the bones would not make the type of sound she'd heard.

O'Hearn was still staring up at her, not convinced.

"Everything always looks a little backward to me when I'm down there, anyway," she added with a smile, playing his male chauvinism to her benefit for a change. It was the sort of thing Anna Copello would say and none of them would question. "For all I know I was probably looking at the valve to Reactor #3 the whole time."

"That's probably it." He nodded, satisfied, and he turned his attention to the computer screen.

Sabrina tightened her grip on her briefcase, hesitant and standing there as if she were waiting to be excused, probably the result of too many years in academia. She had never been a very good team player, too much of a loner to depend on others. She had been at EchoEnergy almost a year and still knew little about her colleagues. But that was obviously the atmosphere Lansik promoted. Look how little any of them knew about Lansik. If there was a problem he might not share it with the rest of them unless he needed their help to fix it. She decided to wait and talk to Lansik about it.

O'Hearn looked up at her again. "Was there something else?"

"No, nothing else. I guess I'll see you on Monday," she said. "Or tomorrow?"

"Not tomorrow. I have plans this weekend," he said, shifting his weight and tapping the keyboard, abruptly cutting off any further discussion. He sounded a bit defensive this time.

Sabrina didn't care and she didn't wait to find out. She was simply relieved to escape.

11

William Sidel waved a hand at Glenn Owens, motioning for him to make himself comfortable in one of the two black leather chairs reserved for guests. Sidel's corner office was a triangle, two of the three walls floor-to-ceiling glass, triple-paned to block out the sounds of trucks below and positioned to look out over the Apalachicola River. However, guests faced only one of the walls of glass and instead had the best view of what Sidel liked to privately call his wall of honor. There, framed photos and magazine covers defined his life and reinforced to visitors just how important he was.

Sidel knew Glenn Owens wouldn't be impressed by the political photos. Okay, cancel out the ones with both Presidents Bush and Clinton along with the current president. Although he caught Owens's eyes lingering on the one of Sidel with Reagan. Likewise, he was pretty sure Owens wouldn't care much about any of the framed magazine covers with Sidel's face next to headlines like The Environmental Wizard.

No, he knew exactly what would move Owens to respect him, to open up his checkbook. And Sidel refrained from grinning when he saw Owens's eyes slide down and stop at the photo of Sidel with General Schwarzkopf and another next to it with him in the middle of a group of National Guardsmen. Never mind that the latter was shot outside a training camp in Florida. Sidel had purposely had the photo cropped tight so the background remained indecipherable in the hopes it would be perceived as some mess-hall barracks in Iraq.

"Senator Allen seems to think this process of yours is our ticket away from OPEC and all those Middle Eastern bloodsuckers." Owens didn't waste time or words.

Sidel was pleased. Rather than answer immediately, he went to the mahogany cabinet behind his desk and slid open the top, revealing an assortment of bottles and glasses. Without asking, he broke the seal on a bottle of Johnnie Walker Blue, poured two fingers and handed it over the desk to his guest.

Owens didn't bother to hide his surprise. It was just one of the unpublicized facts Sidel had been able to dig up on the man who thrived on privacy. Well, Sidel hadn't actually dug it up himself. That's what he had staff for.

"You saw for yourself. The poor guy can't stomach to be around this stuff and yet that's how much he believes in it." Sidel poured himself some of the Scotch to be polite though he didn't much like it. He'd rather have a couple of beers. He held up his glass in a salute and watched Owens take a long sip. He wanted to tell the silver-haired tightwad that he'd end up filthy rich without Owens's measly ten-million-dollar investment. But then it wasn't necessarily the money that mattered to Sidel. He could already buy whatever he wanted, whomever he wanted.

The phone interrupted. Sidel looked at Owens and he raised his eyebrows and shrugged. "This must be terribly important for my staff to interrupt us."

He grabbed the phone and instead of a greeting said, "What is it?"

"We have a problem."

Sidel caught himself from jerking forward and blinked in surprise, glancing down to see, indeed, that the call had come in on his direct line.

"That's why I pay you the big bucks," Sidel said, shooting Owens a smile. "If there's a problem, take care of it." And he hung up the phone.

12

Washington, D.C.

Abda Hassar pulled his taxicab to the curb and waited. Delivery trucks and vans were required to go around to the back. Two Capitol police officers patrolled the front, one with a whistle constantly in his mouth, the other waving through limos and scolding vans attempting to double-park. But at this time of day Abda was allowed to park without reprimand or notice.

He opened a new bag of sunflower seeds and popped several into his mouth. This was his second bag. He hadn't had anything to eat all day. His tongue shoved the seeds into his cheek, and he began sucking the salt from the roasted shells. He pushed his Ray-Ban sunglasses up to rub the exhaustion from his eyes. Three hours of sleep a night used to be enough. Not anymore. By day he drove his cab. It allowed him a communications system without drawing suspicion. By night he handed out assignments and strategized their plan.

He pulled down the bill of his Red Sox baseball cap and sat back, his head leaning against the headrest. He wanted to close his eyes just for fifteen minutes, even ten. But of course he couldn't risk it. He avoided looking at those who passed the cab trying to determine whether it was available. Sometimes he got an idiot or two who tapped the window and slapped the hood to get his attention. *Couldn't they read the Off Duty sign lit up on top?* Americans were simpleminded and rude.

Abda glanced at his laminated license on the sun visor. The silly smile bothered him, a flagrant disguise that he worried more than anything else would trip him up. The photo, taken only a year ago, looked like a boy, clean-shaven, close-cropped hair and that smile. His friend and associate, Khaled, had suggested he smile, not just for the photo but often.

"Americans expect us Arabs to scowl and look sullen," Khaled explained. "Be friendly and polite. Greet them. Wish them a good day and always, always smile. They will not know what you are up to."

Abda had been in America almost ten years now. After 9/11 he practiced his English until his Middle Eastern accent was all but gone. He wanted no association with the mongrels who flew planes into buildings with innocent people. There were much better ways to accomplish a goal, to make a powerful statement. And if anyone needed to pay with a life it should be a company or a country's leaders, not its people. This was what Abda Hassar believed. This was what brought him to this mission.

When fares asked him where he was from—and they always did despite his near-flawless English—he told them his mother was French and his father an Arab, leaving out that his father was also one of the richest oil sultans in the United Arab Emirates. Why then was he driving a lowly cab would no doubt be the next question and, of course, suspicions would be raised. But Abda had discovered early on that Americans would much rather talk about themselves.

"Are you visiting our magnificent capital for business or pleasure?" was all Abda needed to ask. He had decided that taxicab drivers were like bartenders, cheap therapists. And so he heard tales of despairing divorces and cocky career successes.

Abda saw him coming down the front steps and he snapped to attention, sitting up in the seat. Then he caught a glimpse of himself in the rearview mirror, his eyes reprimanding him.

"Settle down," he told himself. He was a lowly errand boy, who was already being used as a simple messenger. He would never be taken seriously. And yet here Abda was waiting for him almost like a slave, anxious and attentive for the scraps his messenger would leave behind.

Abda tried not to allow his power to be siphoned away. He could not be crippled by a dependence on those who would much rather be his enemies than his comrades. Yes, a common goal brought them together, but ideologies kept them adversaries. Was it wrong to let your enemies use you if you were using them back?

"Fifteen and Constitution," the young man said as he opened the door and slid in without glancing at him, pretending he had never gotten into Abda's cab many times before.

Abda smiled, playing the game as he greeted him, "Good afternoon on this beautiful day."

The young man ignored Abda, wasting no time and pulling out files, riffling through them with one hand while he punched away a text message on the small handheld machine. It was machines like this one that Abda had decided would be the ultimate downfall of human communication. No terrorist act, no massive-scale war, but a simple machine that had civilized men and women tapping out messages to each other rather than sitting down face-to-face.

Abda stole a glance in the rearview mirror, pretending to check traffic as he pulled the taxi away from the curb and eased his way onto the street. The man was not much younger than Abda and yet already their lives were so very different. He wondered where this young man would be ten years from now, or twenty years. It wouldn't take long before his constant frown would leave wrinkles around his mouth and an indent in his brow. The blond hair would show bits of gray. The tanned skin would leather. The expensive gold bracelet that dangled from his wrist would no longer hold the significance he believed it projected. And the eyes he hid behind fake eyeglasses—designer glasses that he hoped made him look older and more serious—those eyes would fade and lose their spark and see even less than they pretended not to see now. But more than anything else Abda wondered if in ten to twenty years the young man's soul would be content. At least Abda knew that his own would be content whether today or twenty years in the future.

Within minutes they reached his passenger's destination. Before Abda pulled the taxi to a full stop the man was handing him a ten for the fare and opening the door.

Abda knew he wouldn't want a receipt or change, but he asked anyway and then thanked him when the man shook his head.

He pulled the taxi back into traffic before he could attract attention or be waved down by another fare. Only now did he realize his palms were sweaty and his head throbbed to the beat of his heart. He was almost afraid to check the rearview mirror, the dread and the anticipation just as strong as that first day the tall, blond man had climbed into his taxi.

Finally he willed his eyes to look and immediately relief washed over him when he saw the small envelope with the familiar wax seal, left in the middle of the backseat, waiting for him.

13

Florida State Hospital
Chattahoochee, Florida

Sabrina hardly recognized the man fidgeting in the recliner, his hands constantly moving, his fingers drumming every surface, sometimes poking only at the air. His eyes darted everywhere except to hers. His body rocked gently back and forth though the recliner was not a rocking chair. Even his tongue flicked in and out, moistening his lips, rolling around and pushing out his cheeks as if it was no longer comfortable inside his mouth.

It had taken Sabrina over an hour in traffic, getting to Chatta-hoochee later than she had hoped. Thankfully they had taken off the wrist restraints before she arrived. But at what cost to him? She wasn't sure she wanted to know. The drugs they used only seemed to demolish what was left of his brilliant mind, either zoning him out or making him a jittery mass of nerve endings. It was bad enough that he tuned in and out of reality, blending memories, hallucinations and pipe dreams all together for a surreal world that no one else shared.

"I had peas for dinner," he told Sabrina like a four-year-old who said anything that came to mind.

"How about next time I visit I sneak in a cheeseburger for you?" she asked and waited for some glimpse, a flicker of the man she knew. But he didn't even look at her. His eyes darted back and forth, watching an imaginary ping-pong game behind her.

"Eric was here yesterday," he said as casually as he had announced the peas.

At first she thought she had misunderstood him. Sabrina tried to catch his eyes, tried to determine what level of reality he was in this time.

"He looked good. He's over on Pensacola Beach."

"Dad, Eric's somewhere in New York or Connecticut. He's not here in Florida." She wasn't sure why he would get this mixed up.

"No, no, he has a new job." Then he leaned forward, but still without meeting her eyes he whispered, "He's on a secret mission. I'm not supposed to tell anyone he was here."

She hesitated then said, "Eric wasn't here, Dad."

She could sit through hearing about his other hallucinations, but not this one. She couldn't. She wouldn't. Her brother hadn't been in touch with anyone for over two years. His choice. He didn't even know about Chattahoochee.

"I think you might have imagined seeing him, Dad."

She reached for his hand, hoping to stop or at least slow the rocking motion. He let her hold it for only a few seconds and then he jerked it away, poking uncontrollably at the ceiling.

"He lives above a boathouse and watches the dolphins in the bay." There was no anger, no impatience that she didn't believe. He said it as a matter of fact.

She gave up. If there was some comfort he could draw from imagining his only son had come all the way from New York to visit, then why should she deprive him of that?

"He works for a guy named Howard Johnson."

She smiled and nodded, biting her lower lip and thinking, *God, I miss you, Dad.*

Then suddenly his eyes met hers and held them as if he had heard her thoughts. And without any other change in appearance he said, "You won't forget pickles and onions on that cheeseburger."

Sabrina sat forward, holding her breath and searching his eyes. "Dad?"

"Maybe some fries, too?"

There was a pause as she sat completely still, not sure whether to hope.

"You got it." She finally smiled, but kept on the edge of her seat, wanting to take his hand again, wanting a bit more reassurance, but he was already drumming the arms of the recliner.

Before she could breathe a sigh of relief, his eyes were darting away. She needed to take comfort in having him there with her if only for a few seconds. She couldn't be greedy. They had told her it might be only a little at a time, a spark here and there. All of her research told her it was possible for him to come back as suddenly as he had left. It also told her he might never come back.

He was tapping his feet when he said to her, "I'm having lunch with your mom tomorrow."

And suddenly Sabrina's heart sank to her stomach. He wasn't coming back. At least not anytime soon.

14

Jason Brill wanted to hit Delete as he scrolled the missed calls on his cell phone's queue. He'd listened to only three messages, but could guess the others were similar. Someone had leaked it to the media about the senator's mishap. Jason wouldn't be surprised if it had been William Sidel. Though he couldn't figure out what the hell Sidel had to gain. Embarrassing the senator in front of a small group was one thing, but even an overgrown prankster like Sidel would recognize it was a mistake to royally piss off his direct link to government subsidies, tax incentives and possibly a $140-million-dollar contract.

Senator Allen refused to do anything about the media inquiries. He said he wouldn't dignify the reports with a response.

"The entire matter is ridiculous. I've been feeling a bit under the weather. Possibly the flu," he said as if he really believed it might be true.

But then he insisted Jason cancel all their weekend plans in the area, even surveying the site for the energy summit reception. He wanted to head back to Washington first thing in the morning.

Jason had nodded, biting his tongue when he knew it was a terrible mistake. He could already see the headlines, Senator Upchucks and Runs. And all the wonderful sound bites about freedom from foreign oil and saving the environment, everything from before the tour would be shelved, forgotten. Thank God there wasn't any video or photos of the senator hanging over the railing and spewing his lunch into the tank of chicken guts.

Jason wiped a hand over his jaw and watched Senator Allen sipping Chivas. A glance at the shelf above the minifridge and a quick count of the empty miniature bottles in a neat row told him perhaps it was a good thing he had canceled the weekend schedule. Jason would rather manage the media than the senator's "day-after misspeaks" that included anything from mixed metaphors to border-line racial slurs.

Jason knew Senator Allen had a big heart. The man cared about things like welfare moms finding good jobs that would help get them back on their feet. He pushed for higher minimum wages and sup-ported tax cuts for the middle class. It was because he championed the American worker and was so passionate about it that sometimes he got carried away and called illegal immigrants "parasites."

"He was trying to make a goddamn point," the senator said suddenly after a long silence of sipping and staring out the window at the night lights of Tallahassee.

"And what point would that be?" Jason asked, knowing they were both still thinking and talking about William Sidel.

"I told him last week that the contract might not pass through the Appropriations Committee."

"I thought it was a sure thing," Jason said, keeping himself from adding, *Why the hell didn't you tell* me *last week?*

The timing of the contract was supposed to be perfect for announcing at the energy summit. Jason had arranged this tour as a precursor, an early reminder that Senator Allen had been the driving force. The media had already begun to call the contract "a smart, brave assurance" that EchoEnergy's thermal conversion was, indeed, "a liberation from foreign oil." And Jason had orchestrated it so that all of the attention and credit would be directly connected to Senator John Quincy Allen.

The man tipped his glass at Jason as if it was no big deal and simply said, "My boy, rarely is there a sure thing." But then he sat forward, raising his index finger and tapping it against his lips, a familiar gesture signaling Jason that he had an idea, that he was ready to fight back. "There is one thing I want you to do."

Finally, Jason thought, anxious and ready to take on William Sidel. "Sure, anything," Jason said.

"I want that fucking Polack deported."

"Excuse me?"

"That limo driver. I want him gone."

Jason stared at his boss. He was serious.

He watched Senator Allen sit back, satisfied and sipping his Chivas, a grin now replacing the scowl.

15

Sabrina had taken a wrong turn on her way home from Chatta-hoochee, her mind a million miles away. Her condo was dark except for a lamp in the far corner of the living room, set by a timer so that Sabrina never had to enter a pitch-black house. Her first impulse was to check for voice messages. No blinking red light on the cordless phone's base. She couldn't help thinking, out of sight, out of mind. Her friends back in Chicago were more colleagues than friends, even Olivia, whose e-mails had become less frequent and now included a forwarded joke or inspirational message instead of any personal message. They had their own families to worry about. Sabrina could certainly understand that.

What she couldn't understand was how quickly, how easily Daniel had given up. Before she left Chicago, she had tried to give him back his ring. It wasn't fair, she had told him, since she didn't know how long she'd be gone. At the time he'd laughed and said she needed to stop analyzing their relationship as if it were a scientific equation.

"This is a matter of the heart," he told her, ironically treating her a bit like one of his own students, going into a poetic explanation. "And the heart is not a thinking organ."

They were so different from each other she wasn't sure why she thought the relationship would work. Maybe she simply hoped to replicate her parents' love affair, only to realize in her failure how truly extraordinary theirs was.

Sabrina dropped her car keys and wallet into the middle desk drawer and left her briefcase alongside the carved ball-and-claw foot of the cherry-wood writing desk. The desk and her mother's upright piano were the only two pieces of furniture that made the trip with her from Chicago, not that she had much to begin with. It was easy to sell her secondhand bargains that she used to decorate her studio apartment and simply buy new things for the Florida condo.

Her new salary at EchoEnergy made her professor's salary look like a pittance. Another reason Daniel's phone calls had become less frequent. Last week, or was it two weeks ago, he had all but accused her of wanting to stay in Florida because of the money. "Maybe your father would get better quicker if EchoEnergy didn't pay those huge bonuses," he had joked, then apologized. But Sabrina still felt the sting.

Now she ran her hand over the smooth rosewood of the upright piano, circa 1905. More than a hundred years old and still a beauty, one of the few left that had been made by Bush and Lane of Chicago. Just the sight of it brought back memories that calmed and nourished her. Her mother's musical and artistic talents were as volatile as her emotions. She played the piano rarely and impulsively, often waiting to be coaxed and usually giving in only at their famous neighborhood parties when Sabrina's father joined her and when she had a large enough audience gathered around who pledged and promised to sing along. "To drown out my mistakes," her mother would say with a laugh, though everyone knew there wouldn't be a single mistake.

It was the happiest Sabrina had ever seen her mother and father when they were sitting at the piano with a crowd of friends. They'd play all the old big-band tunes, fun stuff to sing like "All of Me," "Boogie Woogie Bugle Boy," and "Chattanooga Choo-Choo." But always, without fail her mother would end the evening with "When You Wish Upon a Star," and all the giggles and previous belting out of gibberish would quiet, giving in to the soft melody and the light but sobering message.

Sabrina could barely tap out "Chopsticks." Eric had been the one who had inherited their mother's musical talent, but not the interest. Sabrina closed her eyes and brushed her fingers over the keys, wishing that she could hear it for a second or two, just the way it was back then, mixed with the laughter and Uncle Teddy's baritone adding harmony. She wouldn't even mind adding the smells—her mom's best friend, Verda May's, cigarette smoke, the scent of candle wax and even the burnt cinnamon from her mother's failed attempt at baking apple pie. Always at the last minute she'd send Sabrina's father out to Della's Bakery around the corner to pick up a replacement dessert. The parties, the laughter, the music, everything ended when her mother ended.

Sabrina plucked at a few keys, the beginning of "Chopsticks." Someday she'd take lessons, if only to be able to play "When You Wish Upon a Star."

She heard a scraping sound out on the patio. That damn cat. Sabrina slid open the glass door, ready to grab the broom. She stopped herself when she caught a whiff of lavender. She could feel a presence even before she could make out the old woman's shape, sitting next door in the wicker chair. The scraping sound must have been the chair's feet scooting against the cement floor, and now Sabrina could hear the chink of ice cubes in a glass. In the still of the night she could even hear the purring of a content Lizzie somewhere close by.

"Miss Sadie?" Sabrina said gently, not wanting to startle the old woman who had keen hearing, unlike her cat.

Out of the dark came the familiar smooth, deep voice. "Come join me, dear."

Sabrina heard the clinking of more ice as she felt her way around the hedge of crepe myrtle that separated their patios. Her eyes adjusted to the dark and she could see the outline of Miss Sadie, her crinkled hair pulled into a neat bun at the back of her head. Her wire-rimmed eyeglasses were still in place despite the dark and on the small table beside her sat the tall glass of what Sabrina knew was whiskey and water on ice. Also on the table was an ice bucket, tongs and another glass and she remembered it was Friday night. Though unspoken and unplanned, they had spent every Friday night since March right here in the dark, sipping whiskey and water on ice, usually just sitting quietly, listening to the night birds and watching the stars.

They shared bits and pieces, glimpses of their pasts, never whole stories. It wasn't necessary. It was difficult to explain. They were like two old friends who already knew enough about each other to know they liked what they knew.

Sabrina took her place in the rickety wicker chair beside the old woman. She added several cubes of ice to the empty glass, poured the whiskey a third of the way and splashed it with water. She took a long sip, tonight grateful that the bite of liquor was stronger than usual.

"I just got back from Chattahoochee," she said and she saw Miss Sadie nod. She could feel Lizzie rub up against her leg and begin a rumble of purrs. Oh sure, on this side of the crepe myrtle Lizzie befriended her. On the other side she swatted down potted plants like they were pesky mice.

"Chatt-a-hoo-chee." Miss Sadie drew out the word and tasted it with a sip of whiskey. "My momma used to scare the living daylights out of us with threats she'd send us off to Chattahoochee if we misbehaved."

"Did it work?"

"My little brother, Arliss, ended up there for a spell in '55. He was long past being a child by then, but I suppose you could say it was misbehaving that put him there. Times were much different. It was either there or the state prison. Nothing like now."

Sabrina leaned her head back and looked up at the stars. There was something about Miss Sadie's voice that made everything she said sound like a melody. Maybe it was the southern accent mixed with the deep richness of each word, slow and smooth as molasses. It soothed Sabrina more than the whiskey, more than anything else in her life right now. The old woman had become a staple in Sabrina's life, someone she didn't need to explain herself to, someone who didn't want anything from her.

"How is your daddy?" Miss Sadie asked, inviting as little or as much as Sabrina wished to share.

"I don't know," Sabrina confided. "I honestly don't know."

Miss Sadie nodded again, satisfied. That was all Sabrina had to say, as if the old woman knew exactly the confusion and uncertainty Sabrina felt without her having to put it into words. She got the feeling there wasn't much in life that surprised Miss Sadie anymore. The old woman liked to say that at eighty-one she had "seen it all, up one side and down another."

They settled into a comfortable silence, sipping their whiskeys, and Sabrina tried to erase the day's events. After a long while she finally asked, "Whatever happened to Arliss?"

In that same melodic voice Miss Sadie said, "Five days after he got to Chattahoochee he stripped the sheet off his bed, rolled it up into a knot and hanged himself."

16

Abda decided to park his cab several blocks from his destination. No use drawing attention to it. He spit out the last of the sunflower shells into the palm of his hand, opened the window and tossed them out. He gathered everything he needed, pulled on his baseball cap and headed to the restaurant on foot.

It was crowded as usual, but they were already waiting for him in their corner booth. Abda slid in beside Khaled and said nothing. Qasim looked ridiculous in what Abda recognized as a designer T-shirt. He wanted to point at the embroidered emblem and reprimand his friend for wearing such a thing. But he knew this was what Qasim needed to do to fit in.

The waitress named Rita brought him coffee and remembered the extra cream without him asking for it. She had served them many times. She believed they were students and had even helped Qasim with his make-believe American literature class. He still carried the thick book. It sat on top of a notebook in its usual place beside his coffee cup. Pieces of paper stuck out from the pages as if marking passages.

Qasim played his role a bit too seriously, and sometimes Abda worried there would come a time when it was no longer a role. Was it possible Qasim would forget? Abda had always believed he needed to worry more about Khaled, the quiet intellect, whose eyes—never his voice—often challenged Abda's dedication to doing everything and anything that was necessary. Abda knew Khaled thought himself better able to lead and more committed to their cause. But there could be only one man in charge and they could not afford the luxuries of jealousy, resentment or distrust. Khaled knew this and he would never put his own personal beliefs above or before the mission. This idea that an individual could come before his nation was a frivolous, selfish, Western concept. Abda hoped that Qasim also remembered this as he enjoyed wearing bright-colored clothes with ridiculous brand-name logos and even more ridiculous price tags.

They ordered sandwiches and as soon as the waitress left them Abda brought out a calculus textbook from his backpack. From between the pages he slid the envelope with the now-broken wax seal. He carefully withdrew a single sheet of paper and unfolded it in the middle of the table. The three of them huddled around it as if it were some sacred text. Qasim took out a pen and opened his notebook, pretending to take notes, continuing to play out his charade as a student.

The diagram had been sketched on plain white paper that looked unremarkable at first glance. In truth, when Abda first opened the envelope left on the backseat of his cab and found only this diagram with its odd penciled-in codes, he felt the air leave his lungs. He thought for certain he had been duped. That suddenly the transfer of information had stopped and in its place was some penciled hoax.

Now as he watched his friends stare at the sketches on the paper he realized their confusion.

He pointed to a rectangle drawn at the top. "The head table." His finger slid down to several circles, tapping one at a time as he whispered, "The delegates from Europe, the representatives from American oil companies, members of Congress."

Abda saw their eyes go from confusion to realization to excitement as they, too, started to see the meaning of the codes.

"The banquet?" Khaled said softly and Abda could see him restraining a smile.

Abda took Qasim's pen and circled several of the penciled-in codes of two to three letters, sometimes with a number.

"It is not only every table arrangement, but every seat assignment," he told them. "We now know exactly where our target will be seated."

17

"A tall latte with steamed milk instead of cream, and a shot of espresso. Anything else?"

"No, that's it," Sabrina said, taking the coffee in one hand while handing the woman her Visa card with the other. The credit card provided her a detailed account of her monthly spending, so she used it constantly to appease her obsession with order and organization. Along with electronic BillPay she no longer found the need to ever carry cash.

Sabrina had made this exchange every Saturday morning for almost a year with the small Asian woman who ran EchoEnergy's Coffee Shack, and yet every Saturday the woman pretended both the order and Sabrina were new to her. Neither woman called the other by name despite their employee badges prominently displaying their names in bold letters alongside their mug shots. One woman clipped hers to the strap of her coffee-stained apron, the other to the lapel of her white lab coat, and that alone determined the difference, the boundaries between them. It hadn't taken Sabrina long to understand the social hierarchy within the corporation.

Quite honestly, the lack of familiarity didn't bother Sabrina. She liked her privacy, even liked maintaining a level of anonymity, something she had gotten used to and had taken for granted living in Chicago. It wasn't much different than being a professor and keeping a social distance from her students. Or at least that's how Sabrina looked at it, despite thinking it a bit contradictory to EchoEnergy's fundamental philosophy. The industrial park sprawled over 100 acres in the middle of nowhere and prided itself on the small-town atmosphere it had created, providing fitness, recreation and dining areas that made it look more like a miniresort than a manufacturing park. There was even a dry cleaner, bank branch and convenience shop that sold anything from a gallon of milk to Seminole T-shirts.

CEO William Sidel often bragged that his 267 employees were one big happy family. Lansik had used his own version of that spiel during Sabrina's job interview. Working in a small, communitylike setting had been the last thing Sabrina was interested in. She already had family members who had become strangers to her. She didn't need more strangers pretending to be family.

On Saturday mornings it should have been particularly difficult for Sabrina not to get to know the few who walked the halls of the West Park, which included the laboratories, offices and café. Even the plant ran with what they called a skeleton crew of only about two dozen over the weekend. But that's when the class separation, the hierarchy, revealed itself. Anyone with a white lab coat stood out, almost detached from the rest of the company and unapproachable, getting a respected nod and courtesy "hello" but nothing more, as if everyone believed the scientists had much more important things to do. After all, it was the scientists' mystery process that kept them employed. So all Sabrina had to do was slip on her white lab coat and suddenly she gained the privacy and anonymity she craved.

Most of the time she loved Saturday mornings. She took refuge in the silence, the closed doors, the absence of phones ringing and computers humming. This morning she turned on all the lights in the lab and her office. The misty fog of sunrise had been pushed out by heavy bruise-colored clouds, swollen and bloated and threatening to burst at any moment. They rumbled overhead, sealing in the hot, steamy air.

She noticed Dwight Lansik's office door was still open, left ajar just as it had been the entire day before. She knocked before entering. They were usually the only two at work on Saturdays, he, of course, already here since he had been spending the nights. Out of curiosity Sabrina opened his closet door. There in the middle of the floor was his ratty duffel bag.

This didn't seem right.

Okay, maybe he and his wife had suddenly reunited. He wouldn't need to stay here anymore. But would he leave his personal items? She glanced over her shoulder and hesitated, then knelt beside the bag. She pulled back the main zipper. Everything looked to be in perfect order, folded and tucked. She opened one of the smaller side zippers to find a wallet and car keys. Now, *that* was strange.

Sabrina left the duffel bag and moved to the one window in Dwight Lansik's office. She stretched and twisted, but still couldn't see the corner of the back parking lot, close to the river, the spot where all the plant crew migrated. She had walked out one evening with Lansik and when he headed in the opposite direction he had joked that his Crown Victoria looked much more impressive among the Chevys and Fords than in the West Park lot with all the Mercedeses, BMWs and Lexuses.

She went back to the closet and grabbed the keys out of the duffel bag. Something definitely wasn't right.

18

When Natalie Richards was a little girl she dreamed of being a black Emma Peel. She watched the popular TV show *The Avengers* faithfully and according to her momma she had even been able to mimic a pretty darn good British accent. It didn't take long for the little girl, or by then a young woman, to realize there wasn't any room in government intelligence or the Justice Department for a woman, let alone a black woman. Once in a while she wished her momma was still alive to see how far her little girl had come. Today was not one of those days. With the energy summit less than a week away there was still too much at risk.

She stood in her office, looking out of the window. Thankfully, the building was quiet on Saturday, though not the outside. A crew with a jackhammer started ripping up a portion of the sidewalk down the street. But at least the phone remained silent and she'd take that jackhammer noise any day over the phone calls she'd dealt with all week.

She glanced back at her desk, the notes and maps and diagrams spread alongside file folders and to-do lists all dealing with the energy summit. On the edge of her desk were folded copies of the *Washington Post* and the *Times*. She hadn't bothered to read more than the headlines. She didn't have the patience to wade through small-minded rantings about the energy summit's expectations and obligations.

The media had pushed this president to focus on foreign oil and the U.S. dependency. What they didn't realize, what they didn't care to understand was that foreign oil wasn't just about oil. It was about continued relationships. It was about diplomacy and maintaining a level of friendship and influence in a region that spawned and harbored terrorists. How could anyone not understand that? It seemed so simple to Natalie Richards, but then she had grown up in a neighborhood where she had to deal with bullies every day of her teenage life.

The last president understood and he even drew a line in the sand: "You're either with us or against us." Despite the jokes about "cowboy diplomacy" it had been absolutely necessary at the time. It had worked. In fact, it had worked so well that this current president thought he had the luxury of backing away, of relaxing and pretending things had changed. But things don't change overnight. People don't change.

Natalie and her boss were a part of a group that believed the attitude of this current president threatened to demolish all that goodwill built up among those who had backed the United States. And he was doing it recklessly by taking away contracts and going back on age-old agreements. It wasn't right and it would cost the country more lives in the long run. Thank God, Natalie's boss recognized that and had the balls to do something about it. The difficult part, the unfair part, was not letting anyone know, especially when adversaries like Senator John Quincy Allen so blatantly and so vocally lobbied and promoted his pet project, EchoEnergy.

Natalie had to put aside the file on EchoEnergy and now she flipped open her classified dossier on Allen. She hadn't been able to find anything...yet. He hid it well, but if Natalie couldn't find anything on William Sidel and EchoEnergy she was determined to find Allen's Achilles' heel. Every politician had one. Some were just more difficult to find than others. Allen came off as the protector of the common man's rights and environmentalists' advocate, yet it was rumored that he owned a resortlike mansion on South Beach where he intended to retire. He preached about the United States's need to decrease its dependency on foreign oil, but then he voted against drilling in Alaska's ANWR. He was called a maverick when he sided with Republicans, proposing an amendment to define marriage, yet Natalie had never once met the senator's wife. Only in Washington, D.C., was it possible to get away with such contradictions.

Natalie shook her head. Suddenly, she seemed to have the weight of the nation's future piled somewhere on her desk. It could have been—no, it should have been—a very simple business deal, if only Dr. Dwight Lansik hadn't changed his mind. Instead, she had to resort to plan B and damn it, she had enough to worry about without some sort of covert operation becoming part of her job.

She smiled at that term *covert operation*. Perhaps in a way she had become a sort of twenty-first century black Emma Peel.

19

EchoEnergy

Sabrina stood back and stared at the dirty white Crown Victoria. Thunder growled overhead, the clouds bloated and slow moving. The parking-lot lights blinked on as the sky continued to darken. There was no breeze, nothing to break up the thick, humid air. On the weekends there was no rumble of trucks, no hiss of hydraulics, only the distant hum that joined with the croaking of frogs from the river's bank. She'd never noticed before how close this parking lot was to the river.

She held up the electronic keypad attached to the keys. She knew it was Dwight Lansik's car. Yet when she pushed Unlock she jumped at the sound of the doors unlocking.

There could still be a logical reason for his disappearance. There could have been an emergency and someone could have picked him up. If he had left in a hurry that would certainly explain the car and the duffel bag. Whatever had happened wasn't really any of her business.

She checked inside the car, opening the driver's door and glancing behind seats, not sure what she was looking for. Then she popped the trunk, walking slowly, almost hesitant to look inside. Did she really expect to see the body of her boss tied up and tossed back there? Thankfully, it was empty and she released a long sigh, not realizing that she had been holding her breath. Too many movies, she decided, blaming the storm clouds above for inducing her slasher-movie mentality. So her boss had played hooky. Maybe that's all it was.

Finally she locked the car and headed back to the lab. The rain might start any second and Sabrina had learned the hard way that thunderstorms in Florida weren't anything like in the Midwest. Until she moved to Florida she had never seen rain come down so hard and for so long, drenching sheets of it, that would begin full force and so suddenly as if a huge water spigot had been opened.

Sabrina glanced back at the car and this time caught a glimpse of the rolling river between the trees. William Sidel had chosen this property specifically so he could be on the Apalachicola River. The forest surrounded the park on three sides and the river created a natural border on the fourth side. A swatch had been cleared in the middle of nowhere so that the park was protected by a fortress of trees and water. Some had suggested Sidel simply wanted his company to be a part of the natural environment he loved and hoped to save. Others called him paranoid and accused him of isolating his manufacturing plant from scrutiny.

A closer rumble of thunder made Sabrina quicken her pace. But in midstride she stopped. Whether it was only the weather or a hunch, something wasn't right. She turned and headed to the plant instead of the lab.

She found the door to Reactor #5 locked. Of course it was locked.

Every door to every building was locked. The reactor wasn't being used, and yet, standing on this side of the door, she could feel the vibration.

Sabrina pulled out her security pass key card. Few employees had clearance for all the working areas of the plant. All the scientists and most of the engineers had full clearance. She slipped the card into the slot, but the electronic eye continued to blink red. She looked over her shoulder. Was it possible they had already restricted access? She tried again, this time slowly. The light flashed green for several seconds then finally the lock clicked. She yanked the door open before it flashed back to red.

Sabrina had never been inside Reactor #5. It had been exactly what O'Hearn had said yesterday afternoon. It was offline for future use, for a process they weren't prepared for, that they couldn't afford. Sabrina entered slowly, taking careful steps. A huge transparent water tank, two stories tall, stood in the middle of the room. Steel ladders climbed up its sides and grated catwalks crossed over the open top. She recognized it as a flushing tank. There was a similar one in Reactor #3 that the flash-off from the depressurized feedstock spilled into, almost like the final rinse cycle of a washing machine. All of the nutrients and cooked oil were separated and pumped to other tanks, but the leftover water was forced into the flushing tank where it was cleaned up one last time before being released into the river.

Sabrina could hear the pinging sound inside the reactor more clearly. There was no doubt that feedstock of some sort ran through the overhead pipes. She had been right when she thought the valve was open. The whirl of machinery vibrated all the way to the floor. Huge fans spun and buzzed, but the room radiated heat. And with all the activity, the flushing tank, the most important part of the process, the part that cleaned up the final mess, sat idle without a gurgle.

20

EchoEnergy

Leon hated that the guy thought he could just add on another hit like some two-for-one deal.

"But you're already in Tallahassee. It's not like you need to make another trip," the guy said in a smug voice that grated on Leon's nerves.

He'd worked for mob bosses less presumptuous than this asshole. How'd he think this worked—*Oh, by the way, while you're still in town you mind killing one more person?*

It was bad enough that Leon had given in to the demand of no guns or knives. Christ! He should have charged extra for that alone. Didn't these assholes realize it took some creativity to figure out how to off someone and make it look like an accident? He wasn't a goddamn magician.

If all that wasn't bad enough, here he was again at this stinking guts factory. The place gave him the creeps. It wasn't natural what they were doing. He didn't care what anyone said. 'Course, someone else must think it's not natural or Leon wouldn't be back.

Whatever was going on wasn't up to Leon to figure out. He didn't get paid to form opinions or make judgment calls. The reason why this two-bit chicken factory seemed to be cleaning house of their white-lab-coat staff wasn't any of his business. That they chose to use his services rather than hand out pink slips with their last paychecks was actually good for Leon's business. It'd be silly to question it. He just didn't like the asshole's attitude.

This fucking weather put him on edge. Christ! These clouds looked like something alive, gunmetal gray, ghostly globs crawling overhead with bellies ready to burst open. Angry demons with enough electricity to light up the sky for miles. This kind of stuff wasn't a good sign, not that he was superstitious. There was just too much about this he didn't like.

For starters, he didn't like that the target was a woman. Not that he hadn't taken out women before, but all the times before—*okay, it was only twice*—but both times the women were slutty con artists who should've known better than to steal or cheat on their mob-boss boyfriends. This woman wasn't like that. As far as Leon could tell, she wasn't like any of his previous hits. It wasn't that big a deal. The price was right. Hell, like the asshole said, he was already here. Even had the credentials and security key card.

He had watched her checking out the Crown Victoria, realizing even before she popped the trunk that it wasn't her car. That's when it occurred to him that it might be the goddamn other guy's car. It was probably the reason she needed to disappear, too. A shame, really. She was a good-looking broad.

21

EchoEnergy

Back in the lab Sabrina pounded the computer keys. The lightning flashed now in sets of three and four, not finishing before the thunder came in slaps and crashes. She probably shouldn't be on the computer. She tapped in her password for the third time and for the third time she was denied access. The computer continued to ask for it, insisting on a special code. Yesterday morning her password alone had worked fine. All she wanted to do was check the processing line for Reactor #5.

Lansik was the only one with the code to change the process, but any one of the scientists, including her, had access to view it. Which she had done just yesterday, logging on to check and post operational stats. A glimpse of the real-time program would show the flow, the temperatures and output and help her figure out the problem. Now all of a sudden the computer required a code just to view the system.

She sat back and ran her fingers through her wet hair, wanting to yank instead. She was soaking wet, creating a puddle around her. It wasn't like this was a nuclear facility where a breach of security could mean a Chernobyl-like meltdown. However, if what she suspected was true, and a mistake had been made to use the reactor while bypassing the flushing tank, there could be toxins being released into the river.

Sabrina's clothes stuck to her and she shivered in the air-conditioned lab. She couldn't imagine what it meant if, in fact, Grade 2 garbage was being processed. No way could that happen without EchoLab's knowledge. They'd be drawing samples, testing combinations, adjusting coke temperatures. It simply wasn't possible and certainly not possible without using the flushing tank. Grade 2 garbage usually included unrecyclable mixtures of over twenty-five kinds of plastic, nylon, rubber, metals, wood and fiberglass, and that was just for starters. Unlike slaughterhouse waste, processing this mix of garbage could give off residue such as PCBs and dioxin, which would be very toxic. The hydrogen in water worked to stabilize and break it down. Bypassing water would not only be a mistake, *it would be deadly.*

But as O'Hearn had told her, they weren't processing Grade 2 garbage.

O'Hearn. Sabrina had told him about the reactor yesterday afternoon. Could he have changed the access as a safety precaution until Lansik returned? And why would he change it? Unless there was a problem, a mistake, and O'Hearn didn't want anyone else to notice it.

Sabrina grabbed the wad of scratchy paper towels she had gotten from the employee restroom and wiped her face and arms. This was silly. She prided herself on being logical and levelheaded. There were always explanations. Sometimes you had to dig for them.

Another burst of lightning sent the electricity in the lab flickering. The fluorescents blinked. The computer screen went black. The hum of the machines sputtered. A crash of thunder left the entire lab dark and silent.

Sabrina sat still, willing herself to calm down, to breathe. It was a typical Florida thunderstorm. It would soon pass over. She watched shadows of tree branches dance on the lab's walls. The rain continued to pound the windows. Then from somewhere down the hallway, outside the lab's door, she heard footsteps.

The middle of the morning and it looked like twilight in the lab. The wall of windows that overlooked the back park became picture frames of spidery lightning and animated branches. But most unnerving was the silence. Without the rattle and hum and vibration of machines, the footsteps echoed on the tiled hallway floor, and Sabrina sat perfectly still, paralyzed in front of the dead computer screen.

She saw the tunnel of light lick up and down from the window of the door to the bottom, slipping under. A flashlight, she told herself, and began to breathe again. She could almost fake normal by the time the door slid open and a security guard poked his shaved head into the lab. He ended up being the one who jumped, startled at her presence, but he turned it into a cough and a high step into the lab like he meant to do that.

"Everything okay, ma'am?"

He pointed the flashlight in her eyes. Whatever his intent, Sabrina found it more annoying than intimidating.

"Just trying to get some work done."

"Generators should kick on in a little bit," he said, this time revealing a slow southern drawl. He moved the flashlight off her face to inspect the lab, swiping the light over shelves and into corners, even though unlike the hallway it was light enough in here to see without the spotlight.

That's when Sabrina saw a gun in his other hand, up and ready as if he expected someone to jump out at him from the shadowed corners. She tried to remember if EchoEnergy's security guards were armed. Other than having them check her credentials at the guard hut, she hadn't ever met up with one. She watched the way he handled it. In the flashes of lightning he looked as though he was moving in slow motion, a blue-haloed character in a video game.

"Are you the only one in here?" he asked without glancing back at her, focused now on Dr. Lansik's half-opened door.

Suddenly there was something unsettling in his intensity. The electricity had been knocked out by the storm. That was it. Why would it warrant a SWAT-like search?

"There are usually several of us here on Saturday mornings," she answered, not wanting to admit she was alone with this Robocop.

As he reached Dr. Lansik's office the lights blinked twice before staying on. The lab rustled and choked, coming back to life. It was enough to break his spell. Like a sleepwalker he stood up straight, his head jerking around as if seeing the surroundings for the first time. Settling on Sabrina's eyes, he holstered his weapon and clicked off his flashlight.

"Back to normal," he said, and Sabrina couldn't help wondering if he meant the lab or himself.

22

Washington, D.C.

Jason Brill stood over his desk, glaring at the open file folders scattered across the surface alongside the legal pad with his own messy notes. Then he looked up and focused on the dartboard attached to the far wall. Without taking a step closer, he tossed two darts, one right after the other—*pop, pop.* He should have been pleased—both darts struck the bull's-eye—but the exercise was an absentminded stress relief. Not at all a competition. Tossing the darts and having to focus on the bull's-eye helped him think. That he was good at it, a dead-on shot, didn't really matter to him. What did matter was finding a way to get the Appropriations Committee to authorize EchoEnergy the $140-million military contract. Somewhere in this pile he had to uncover information that would make that happen.

Jason had been in D.C. long enough to know there was no such thing as a sure thing. He didn't need Senator Allen to remind him.

But the measure had already passed the subcommittee where Senator Allen was the chairman. That was half the battle. Somewhere on the full committee there was opposition that Jason hadn't anticipated. Opposition that Senator Allen evidently thought he couldn't overcome. If Jason could get an overriding majority they wouldn't need to worry about one or two opposing.

Jason flung another dart across the room, turning away just as it hit the bull's-eye. He continued to stand over his desk and he flipped through several pages from one of the folders. He scanned every other line, not sure what he was searching for. He figured he'd know it when he saw it. His upbringing may not have taught him which fork to use at a formal dinner—the people he came from might say "crick" when they meant creek—but one thing Jason had learned, and learned well, was where to look and how to find dirt on anyone who happened to get in the way. And how to use that tidbit of information to its fullest capacity. In other words—or rather in the words of his relatives—*to put the screws on.* He had learned valuable lessons in how to milk a grudge, win and manipulate trust and not only figure out a person's weaknesses, but more important, discover what it was he or she held most dear. All were lessons that had equipped him for dealing politics in D.C., much better than any degree from some university.

Jason tossed that set of papers back in the folder and pulled out a neatly stapled set from the next folder. He knew Senator Sherman Davis of Louisiana's pet project was to rebuild medical facilities that had been ravaged by Hurricane Katrina. A noble cause, but Jason smiled as he read one of the last pages in the thick, stapled proposal. There, at the bottom, after an exhaustive read, was a paragraph that the largest facility, a state-of-the-art medical center—one that would rival the likes of the Mayo Clinic—would be called the Sherman Davis Medical Center.

That was Washington, D.C., or at least the D.C. Jason saw. At the heart of even the grandest and most generous ventures Jason could usually uncover the true motivation and too often it included either pride and ego or old-fashioned greed, sometimes both. But Sherman Davis was the least of Senator Allen's worries. Or in "D.C. talk," Sherman and John Quincy were even in the exchange of favors and both were content to stay that way. No, Sherman Davis wouldn't be a problem when the contract came to a vote.

Jason put down that stack and picked up another. Senator Shirley Malone, the senior senator from Indiana, seemed harmless at first glance. A tall, graceful woman who wore tailored suits and salon-coiffed hair, she looked nothing like Jason's perceived stereotype of a beef-eating, polyester-wearing Midwest housewife who had only gotten into politics in order to finish out her deceased husband's senate seat. However, after several elected terms of her own, Senator Malone had become a force to contend with.

When Jason first started looking for opposition he immediately thought, competition. It would make sense that any of the senators from oil-producing states would oppose—maybe even want to trip up any contract, and therefore, any success EchoEnergy might enjoy. He set aside Texas senator Max Holden in his "problem" pile, but eliminated Louisiana Senator Davis. And as he separated the piles, he remembered to include alternative competitors like ethanol. Senator Shirley Malone and the great state of corn-producing, ethanol-manufacturing Indiana immediately went into the problem pile.

So far Jason had five senators in the problem pile. Five out of twenty-eight members on the Appropriations Committee was not a bad start, definitely one he could work with.

Jason checked the time and stuffed his problem pile into his leather briefcase. More than anywhere around the hallowed halls of Congress, the place Jason learned the most was Wally's Tavern. And if he wanted information, or rather to find some dirt, Wally's was where he could find it. He flung the last dart, slipped on his jacket and headed out the door, not even bothering to look at his last bull's-eye hit.

23

Sabrina snapped off her car's air-conditioning, if only for a few minutes before the windshield fogged up again. The rain had stopped. The storms had moved through, leaving behind a freshly scrubbed blue sky and a short break from the last several days of torturous heat and humidity. It was Florida brochure-beautiful and yet Sabrina couldn't stop shivering.

Back at her office she had changed out of her wet clothes into a pair of running shorts, running shoes and a baggy T-shirt she kept in her locker. One of EchoEnergy's employee benefits was the use of a state-of-the-art fitness center with indoor track and an Olympic-sized pool. But Sabrina always felt there was something counterproductive about running indoors, breathing regurgitated air.

Even with the sunlight Sabrina felt on edge. Dwight Lansik was missing. She was sure of it. Reactor #5 seemed to be processing

Grade 2 garbage without anyone in the lab knowing about it. Maybe Lansik had approved it, but Sabrina doubted he would agree to bypass the flushing tank. If all that wasn't bad enough, the thunderstorms and Robocop security guard had frayed the last of her nerves. Ironically, the fiasco had kept her mind off her father.

She managed the pitted two-lane highway with ease, no tanker trucks to battle on the weekends. She rolled down the car windows when the windshield started to fog again. Then she breathed in the fresh air, crisp with pine and wet dirt. Despite the deluge, the air was now lighter, no longer the hot, thick blanket that wrapped around you like a wet Turkish towel.

Sabrina had chosen to stay at the university for her undergraduate and graduate studies when her mother, who grew up in Philadelphia, suggested she give the East Coast a chance. She barely left the city except for one or two yearly conferences where she saw more of the luxury hotels than the designated host cities. She couldn't remember the last time she had taken a vacation, at least not one that didn't include a conference, a workshop, a presentation or a guest-teaching session.

She didn't mind. Her main goal for the last ten years had been to make tenure. It had superseded everything else in her life, including, some might say, a life outside her career. Even Daniel claimed she treated him at times like a distraction or obligation. He hated coming in second behind her career, sometimes third behind her family. Her only defense was that she just wasn't good at relationships. People, in general, were illogical, prone to mistakes, too unpredictable. She was used to dealing in resolutions and equations that, despite the complex factors involved, could always be solved with logic and patience.

The truth was she never once—not even a little bit—felt the kind of passion that she watched and observed in her parents' relationship. Maybe she simply didn't want to settle for anything less. And maybe that was why her family still came before Daniel.

When Sabrina decided she needed to leave Chicago to be closer to her father she didn't even discuss it with Daniel. She simply told him her decision. He assured her it wouldn't change things between them. Likewise, even her dean insisted she take a sabbatical from the university rather than resign her post.

"How much time do you need?" both men had asked her separately, both with genuine concern.

Six months. She wouldn't need more than six months, a year at the most. Her father's condition remained unchanged, perhaps a slight decline if anything. In another month her year would be up and she'd need to ask for more time from her dean. She already knew she wouldn't be asking for more time with Daniel. Now it was just a matter of how to tell him. What initially seemed to be a temporary glitch in her disciplined, orderly life had become a limbo in too many ways.

Sabrina thought of her brother, Eric. She approached I-10 and noticed the sign: Pensacola, 190 miles. Why would her father hallucinate a visit from Eric? Wishful thinking seemed possible, but why such an elaborate story?

She hadn't seen Eric since their mother's accident. As far as she knew, her father hadn't seen Eric, either. Funny how the same event could change people in such different ways. One day you're arguing over turkey or ham for the traditional Christmas feast. The next day you're taking sides over whether your mother's battered remains should be cremated or buried.

It had been an accident. Slippery Chicago streets. A car spinning out of control and slamming into their mother's car. When her father called and said, "Your mother's been in an accident," Sabrina had grabbed a pen and notepad from her office desk ready to scratch down the details and which hospital. Nothing had prepared her for her father's follow-up. "She's gone."

Sabrina still remembered her hand with the pen hovering over the notepad. Her breathing stopped. Every buzz and hum around her came to a sudden halt, replaced by the banging of her heart. She waited for what seemed an eternity for the words to register, for her father to continue with something, anything that would erase what he had just said. Instead, she had heard his sobs. She had never heard her father cry before, and a sudden lump in her throat obstructed any hope she had of breathing. She remembered gasping for air, not sobs, not a cry but a primal struggle to catch her breath. How could she be gone, just like that? Yes, life was funny that way. One day you're splurging on red and white poinsettias and a few days later you're arranging them in front of your mother's casket.

Eric blamed their father. How could he let her go out in the snow to deliver one of her sculptures all by herself? He knew she hated driving on slick streets. The arguments were ridiculous and painful. A hurt and stubborn father and an angry son throwing down a gauntlet neither would retreat from. One man running as far away as possible, the other turning deep inside himself. And a daughter and sister left without either.

As Sabrina entered the outskirts of Tallahassee, she decided the lousy day called for a drastic pick-me-up measure. Instead of heading to the condo, she'd treat herself to lunch. She'd already failed her gradual withdrawal from caffeine; she might just as well give in to a cheeseburger at the Club Diner, greasy but cheap therapy.

24

Washington, D.C.

Jason ordered his second Jack and Coke. The first one had gone down a bit too quickly. He'd slow it down, not because he had to, but because he wanted to be sharp. He wanted all his reflexes firing and on alert.

He stayed at the end of the bar, swiveling the stool to survey the tavern. The lights were dim. Cigar smoke prevailed over cigarette, but the clouds stayed mostly over certain booths in the corner. Jason hated the stink, hated how it would cling to his clothes and stay in his hair when he got home tonight.

He recognized a staffer for Texas senator Max Holden. Zach was tall, blond and lanky with a pedigree that insured handsome be used in his description. He had elbowed Jason into the wall at a charity basketball game they had both participated in. Thing is, they were supposed to be on the same team at the time. The asshole had shoved

Jason out of the way just so he could hog the ball. He couldn't remember Zach's last name. Probably something short of Kennedy. It didn't matter. Mentally, Jason crossed him off the list, dismissed him. Zach didn't play well with others. It'd be too much work to pry any information out of him. Nothing there. Or was there?

A messenger for the same service Jason used to work for, a messenger who Jason recognized but couldn't name, put a hand on Zach's back. Jason watched the hand trail down a bit too far south to be anything less than an advance. Ordinarily it wouldn't mean much. What's a little flirting in D.C.? Except the messenger was male. Jason wondered what Senator Max Holden would think, especially since Holden was the strapping cowboy of the John Wayne era much more so than the *Brokeback Mountain* type.

Jason tucked the tidbit away for further consideration. Right now he was more interested in the brunette across the room, the center of attention for a group of probable staffers. They were holding their glasses up, toasting her. Jason was pretty sure he had seen the brunette with Senator Shirley Malone. If he remembered correctly, she had been feeding the senator notes and briefs at the last session of Congress.

Jason took a sip of his Jack and Coke, a long, satisfied sip. This was more like it. He could be charming. Okay, he was out of practice, but he was capable. Where better to get information, to find out Senator Malone's weaknesses, than one of her own. It was like infiltrating the enemy camp. Talk 'em up a bit. Have a little fun, a few drinks. Loosen up the tongue. Who knows what else.

Jason didn't realize his attention had been so obviously focused until he heard someone behind him say, "She is something else, isn't she?"

He glanced around, half hoping the comment hadn't been meant for him, that he hadn't been caught. No such luck.

"Excuse me?" he said, knowing it was too late to play dumb.

The tall, attractive woman came around him and hiked herself onto the stool beside him without effort, not in the least concerned that her skirt had also hiked up to reveal the promise of shapely thighs. She didn't seem to mind that he noticed, his eyes no longer paying attention to the younger woman across the room. Jason only hoped that his jaw hadn't fallen, because that was exactly how it felt.

"It's her twenty-eighth birthday," the woman said, setting her wineglass on the bar. "A worthy cause for celebration and a very worthy young woman. Are you a friend of Lindy's?"

So much for charm. Jason couldn't even find his voice. Instead, his brain was screaming at him, *I can't believe I'm sitting next to Senator Shirley Malone.*

25

Leon signed the receipt, proud of the one-line scribble that started with an *L* and then flatlined. By now the signature was second nature though Leon wasn't his Christian name. He had given himself the nickname years ago when he decided to go into business for himself. It was something he picked up from a book about chameleons.

He'd actually bought one of the lizards from a guy who ran an exotic-animal store in Boca Raton. Well, it wasn't so much a store as the back dock of a warehouse. The guy had all kinds of lizards, pretty much any size and color you could imagine. The chameleons fascinated Leon, changing colors right before his eyes, half the lizard green on a leaf and the other half still brown as the bark. How cool would that be if people could do that crap? But Leon didn't bother with disguises like so many of his colleagues. He didn't need to. He already had the best one of all.

The waitress picked up his receipt while she filled his coffee cup.

Not a word. Barely a glance. If someone stopped her later and asked about him she'd never be able to describe him. She'd hardly remember him. That was the beauty of being plain and ordinary. No one ever noticed Leon. He couldn't buy a better disguise if he tried. And he didn't ruin it by wearing bright colors or anything trendy. No stripes. No patterns. No cute designer logos. He wore short-sleeved, button-down shirts, the kind that didn't need ironing and were easy to pack. Same with the sport coats and trousers. Even his sunglasses were off the rack at Walgreens. Absolutely nothing to draw attention to himself.

So yeah, he may have gotten Leon from "chameleon," but not because the lizard could disguise itself and change colors. The book said the word *chameleon* meant "earth lion." Lions were the king of the jungle. Life was a freaking jungle. Leon liked thinking of himself as a lion.

He sipped the coffee. No use wasting the warm-up. He fished out a couple of Tums from his pants pocket, checked them for lint and separated them from a bullet, a nail clipper, three dimes and a quarter, then popped the Tums into his mouth. *Fucking indigestion.* In the past two years he'd survived a box cutter slitting his throat, a gunshot through the shoulder and more broken bones than he cared to count, but in the end it'd probably be his own fucking gas that did him in.

He took another sip of coffee to wash down the crumbs of antacids, wishing for a beer instead of the cup of joe. But then he didn't choose this two-bit diner. One of those occupational hazards. And from the looks of it, Leon knew he wouldn't be frequenting any bars or clubs on this duty call. Although she'd surprised him earlier, stopping by a liquor store and picking up what looked like a bottle of whiskey. Maybe she wasn't as straitlaced as she looked. 'Course, it could have just been that freaky lightning storm and the even freakier security guard. Leon still wasn't sure what the hell that was all about, but it certainly kept him in the shadows when he could have taken advantage of a prime opportunity. All kinds of weird accidents happen when the electricity goes off.

He sat in the far corner of the diner with his back to her, but he could watch her in the plate glass mirror above the soda fountain. For a small woman she could sure put it away—cheeseburger, onion rings smothered in ketchup. But just one cup of coffee that she'd been nursing for the last half hour—the burger and rings devoured long ago. He'd watched her wave off the waitress three times, nursing the original brew while absorbed in the contents of a plain manila folder. Probably the same stuff that got her into trouble in the first place. He didn't care what was in the folder. It wasn't his job to figure out what the trouble was. Nope, his job was simple—*stop the trouble*.

He waited for her to get out the door, and then he left the three dimes and a quarter for a tip, pocketed the bullet and nail clippers and followed.

26

Jason offered to buy her another glass of wine. She let him. Kendall Jackson. Chardonnay, not cheap, but not pretentious. He filed that tidbit away. He ordered himself another Jack and Coke, but left one half-full on the bar when they moved to a small booth in the corner. More than ever he needed to keep a clear head.

When he admitted he'd never met her staffer, Lindy, Senator Malone offered an introduction. From somewhere he'd been able to pull out enough charm to decline by saying he'd much rather talk to her. That's when he asked if he could buy her another wine. She floored him. He didn't expect her to say yes. Now he wasn't sure what to do. She obviously didn't know who he was, but how the hell could he pull off pretending not to know who she was? He had seen her in the halls of Congress. As a staffer he had been invisible to her. But after tonight she'd start to see him.

"I'm Jason Brill," he decided to tell her straight out and extended his hand. He smiled, as if a formal introduction was called for, but then held her hand long enough to relay that it certainly wasn't all he intended.

"I'm—"

"Senator Shirley Malone," he cut her off. "Senior Republican from the great state—a red state—of Indiana."

"Now I remember you. You work for John."

He didn't even try to hide his surprise.

"From the other side of the aisle," she continued, but she was smiling. "An enemy?" And she arched a graceful eyebrow as she sipped her wine.

"Enemy?" He feigned his best hurt look, even throwing back his head a little, pretending to take her sucker punch in the jaw. "No, not an enemy. Let's say an admirer."

"Oh, really?"

Too much sarcasm and Jason was worried he'd laid it on way too thick, but they were playing with each other, weren't they? Maybe he needed to sit back and let her set the rules.

"Yes, really," he said, his mind flipping through stored data, trying to access and retrieve information. "I thought you did an excellent job chairing the commission on federal disaster relief for last summer. You were objective and fair in spite of the fact that Indiana suffered through fifteen tornadoes last year."

She met Jason's eyes over the rim of her wineglass as she took another sip. *Was it too much?*

"Sixteen," she said with another smile.

And Jason felt the surge of adrenaline like he had just sunk a three-pointer from half court. He was better at this than he thought. He'd have to thank his uncle Louie, who had taught Jason the art of bullshit at a very young age.

"Go tell your aunt I said how pretty she looks with that new hairdo." Jason remembered that one was worth a buck to him, but Uncle Louie probably got laid.

Senator Malone sat back in the booth obviously more relaxed and, more important, comfortable with him now.

Jason sipped his Jack and Coke, trying to retrieve other data. In this dim light she looked younger, softer, and actually pretty. Learn your enemy's weaknesses, but also what they care most about. Discover someone's passion and usually you can discover that person's greatest vulnerability. Or as Uncle Louie would say, "Figure out what a guy gives a shit about. Take it away or just pretend to and you'll have that guy on his knees, beggin' and crying for his momma."

Jason didn't exactly want Senator Shirley Malone on her knees, begging. Or did he? Jesus! He shook the sexual innuendo out of his head. It'd been too long, way too long.

Then without warning she leaned forward almost as if she had read his mind. "So what's a smart, good-looking guy like you doing working for John Quincy?"

He may be able to get an invitation to her suite if he played his cards right. Unlike other senators who bought extravagant homes or condos in D.C.'s finest neighborhoods, Jason knew Senator Malone simply rented a suite at the Mayflower. Rumor had it her room service was always just for one. But she was definitely flirting with him and he used to be good at this. That she was older, classier, way out of his league should have made the challenge all the more appealing.

Yet his attraction to her unnerved him. He wasn't quite sure he understood it. He liked her. He hadn't expected to like her. Somehow it made the game unbalanced, not fair, his weakness exposed when he was supposed to expose hers.

After about an hour of what he could have called mental foreplay, he offered to walk her to her car even though her driver was out front waiting. Then he watched her get in, still smiling at him as she waved goodbye.

He decided to walk back to his place. The night air felt cool for June. Maybe in the morning he'd be kicking himself. But for now if he wanted to manipulate the Appropriations Committee vote, he decided he'd need to take another look at Senator Max Holden's gay boy, Zach.

He hadn't gotten far when he heard his name being called. Jason turned to find the birthday girl, Lindy, running to catch up with him.

27

Tallahassee, Florida

Sabrina actually looked forward to her Saturday movie nights. She had read somewhere that the major difference between extroverts and introverts was how they got their energy. Extroverts needed to rejuvenate themselves by being around people, bouncing their ideas off someone else and being able to discuss their thoughts and feelings.

Introverts, however, required time alone with their thoughts, having time to themselves to recharge without needing to explain or talk to anyone. Sabrina knew she fit comfortably with the latter and accepted it. Though it was oftentimes difficult to explain to extroverts that she enjoyed her Saturday-night rejuvenation sessions. She needed her Saturday-night alone time. So tonight she was home alone with Alfred Hitchcock.

She had chosen one of her favorites, *Rear Window,* with Jimmy

Stewart and Grace Kelly. It didn't matter how many times she had seen it, it still made her jump.

When she and Eric were kids they were allowed to stay up late in the summertime to watch classic movies. Lewis and Martin were Eric's favorites. He was a sucker for comedies, even the romantic ones, especially with Cary Grant, which wasn't much of a surprise looking back. Sabrina guessed Eric thought himself a bit of a Cary Grant, maybe with a little James Bond mixed in.

She, however, loved psychological suspense, classics like *Gaslight; Sorry,Wrong Number,* and of course any of Alfred Hitchcock's films. Over the years she had built up an extensive video library and she and Eric had gotten together at least one Saturday a month to watch a favorite. Sabrina would order pizza, half veggie and half Italian sausage with green pepper. Eric would bring the cold beer, always some kind of expensive ale for the two of them to try. Tonight she settled for popping a frozen pizza into the oven and a Bud Lite.

Nights like this she realized how much she missed her brother and how much she missed her old life. The old saying that you never know how good you've got it until it's all gone couldn't be truer.

Sabrina heard a noise outside her condo and paused the movie, leaving Jimmy Stewart with his binoculars and his broken leg. He was just starting to believe that his neighbor may have actually killed his own wife.

She listened and waited, taking a slow sip of the beer. Maybe the movie had kicked her imagination into high gear. The whole day had been like that, with Lansik's disappearance and the thunderstorm knocking out the electricity. The movie was supposed to be her escape from reality, not a reminder of it. Maybe tonight one of Eric's favorites would have been a wiser choice.

She turned the interruption into an intermission and decided to get more pizza from where she had left it on the counter that separated her kitchen from her living room. She reached for a slice and out of the corner of her eye she saw a shadow move outside her kitchen window.

Sabrina froze. She held her breath and listened again. She hadn't left a light on in the kitchen. Didn't think she needed one, depending instead on the glow of the TV. But now the room seemed too dark.

In the tinted blue light her eyes found the back door's knob. She had locked the dead bolt. She was sure she had. Still, she listened and watched.

She heard a rustling sound outside the door, but the knob didn't move. She held her breath again. Her eyes darted around the kitchen, searching for a weapon. She eased her way around the counter and grabbed a cast-iron skillet hanging above the range.

A scrape against the outside wall stopped her so suddenly she thought her heart had also stopped. Then a high-pitched screech made her jump. She almost dropped the skillet. A *thump-thump* followed before Sabrina realized the screech belonged to an animal. Of course, Lizzie.

Relief instantly washed over her, but she stopped at the door's peephole. The fish-eye view of empty sidewalks and an empty street satisfied her. She unlocked and opened the door just enough to look out.

Sure enough, Sabrina saw the last of Lizzie, a white tail disappearing into the crepe myrtle. Before she closed the door she glanced at the area under the kitchen window. Nothing there. Absolutely nothing, including no bush, no flowerpots, no ledge, nothing that would explain that the shadow she had seen could have been a cat's.

Light refracted in a lot of different ways, from a lot of different sources. There could be a number of reasons a prowling cat's shadow could appear three feet higher in front of Sabrina's kitchen window. This is what she told herself as she closed and locked the dead bolt on the back door.

28

Jason left a note and passed through the lobby before the concierge's desk was even open. He didn't stop for a receipt of the charges. He didn't stop, period, afraid someone would recognize him.

Last night the Washington Grand Hotel had been the first to come to Jason's mind, in fact, the only one he could think of while in the cab with Lindy's tongue probing his ear. He'd never even been inside the hotel's lobby before last night. He had, however, reserved rooms many times for Senator Allen when the senator had friends or colleagues in town who needed a discreet and luxurious place to do business. Jason knew the senator didn't actually mean business. It was a sort of code between them. Maybe that's why it was the first place to come to Jason's mind when he decided he needed a discreet place.

God! He couldn't believe he'd left a note. How lame was that? But all he could think about was escaping.

He waved down a cab though the morning air and the quiet would have done him some good, especially with the fog that capped the city. At four o'clock in the morning no one was out on the streets of Washington except the homeless. Those who made their living on the streets were finished conducting business and tucked away somewhere.

The cabdriver kept glancing at Jason in the rearview mirror. Maybe he had schmuck written all over his face. He resisted the urge to defend himself, to tell the guy that she wanted it as much as he did. Maybe more. She was the one who'd approached him. Jesus! She'd rubbed against him and fondled him right there on the street in front of the restaurant. And he had already been charged up by Senator Malone.

A sudden chill skidded down Jason's back as he remembered Lindy on top of him and the whole time he kept seeing Senator Shirley Malone. The thing is it didn't stop him. Instead, it...hell, it propelled him.

God! He was fucked up. He shook the thought and the image out of his head, especially since it started to turn him on again.

He glanced up. The fucking cabdriver was watching him again, only this time he had the decency to avert his eyes when he got caught. Jason checked for the guy's ID and took a good look at it. He committed the name and cab number to memory. Not that it would do any good. After all, what the hell could he do with the information? Turn the guy in because he recognized Jason's guilt? He couldn't just have him fired like Senator Allen had done to that limo driver.

That's when it hit him. *He* could actually get fired for sleeping with another senator's staff member. Senator Allen had made it clear when he hired Jason that he wouldn't tolerate any "intimate encounters"—that's what he called them, "encounters"—between any of his staff members.

He leaned his head back against the seat and closed his eyes. What the hell had he done?

The cab jolted to a stop.

"That's seven-fifty," the guy said.

Jason handed him a ten.

"Keep it," he told the driver. And on his way out Jason took one last look at the ID badge on the sun visor to make sure he had it memorized, just in case. Cab number: 456390; and driver: Abda Hassar.

29

The Washington Grand Hotel

Natalie Richards knew this was a courtesy call. No matter who she worked for they didn't call her because they had to. She'd owe someone big-time and not just Colin Jernigan.

He met her at the door to the hotel suite—the presidential suite. Damn, the bastard—whoever he was—had a sick sense of humor. No way that was some mere coincidence.

"How'd they know to call you?" she wanted to know, whispering to him even though no one else paid attention.

"I was his I.C.E."

"His what?"

"In case of emergency," he said matter-of-factly. When the confusion didn't leave her face he added, "On his cell phone under I.C.E.—in case of emergency. He had my number programmed in."

Natalie shook her head. So they'd simply lucked out. She didn't like that.

"It's not pretty," Colin told her, shifting her attention, but standing in front of her, maybe giving her a second chance to change her mind.

"I've seen not pretty," she said. "You don't think I've seen things?" Little hard to change her mind now and not look ungrateful. Someone was risking his neck letting her and Colin be here. "You think I grew up in some lily-assed neighborhood?"

Colin wouldn't buy her bravado, but she could pretend for the rest of them.

She stomped her way past him, determined to make this look like no big deal. Her reputation of being a hard-ass depended on it. But then she stopped cold in the middle of the room. She hadn't seen anything quite like this. She made herself look at him and hoped to God almighty she didn't lose her breakfast.

She'd only met the young man once. Now she couldn't remember exactly when that was. But she did remember it was a State Department dinner for some visiting dignitary, because she remembered the tux. Been a long time since she'd seen a man that comfortable in a tuxedo. As if he'd been born to wear one. Zach Kensor had introduced himself to her like he was some kind of royalty, all cocky and sure of himself. And the kid certainly looked the part, like a tall, blond and bronze Adonis. He could have easily passed for a Hollywood actor. Maybe that's why Natalie believed he'd do such a good job running a few errands. No one would have pegged him a simple messenger. Or so she thought.

She kept her hands at her sides, resisting the urge to bring them to her face, to cover her eyes. He looked nothing like a messenger now. Nothing like an Adonis, either.

His wrists were tied to the bedposts with what looked like neckties or silk scarves. Blood had splattered everywhere and on everything—the wall, the headboard, the bedsheets, even the room-service tray left on the nightstand. She could smell it, sweet yet rancid like spoiled fruit. She wasn't sure if it was the blood or the leftovers. It didn't matter. She'd never be able to order room service again.

It was his eyes that Natalie Richards knew would forever haunt her, blue marbles staring out of a bloody, swollen, mashed and ripped face.

"Definitely personal," one of the detectives said in reference to her staring.

"Excuse me?"

"The face." He pointed with his chin. "Nobody makes mincemeat out of the face unless it's personal."

This time Natalie's stomach lurched and she did have to look away.

"The killer wiped everything down," the detective continued, now addressing Colin.

"How about the room-service menu?" Colin asked, pointing to the leather-bound booklet on the desk across the room.

"Wiped down," the detective told him.

"Even inside? He may have left prints on the inside cover when he opened it. Looks like the pages might be laminated, too. Sometimes they forget about the inside when they're wiping things down in a hurry."

The detective didn't answer. Instead he went back to the desk and waved over a crime-lab tech, pointing to the menu.

Natalie glanced up at Colin, surprised at the impatience in his tone. It unnerved her to see that usually calm exterior showing frustration. He shifted his weight and dug his hands deep into his trouser pockets. Only now did she notice that he was wearing tennis shoes and had on a T-shirt under his suit jacket. A restless energy bounced off his body. Even his eyes darted around the room as if he didn't want to miss anything.

"It was me," she said to him. "Not you." Meaning she was the one who'd decided to use this young man as their messenger even though Colin had been his liaison. When he didn't respond, she thought she needed to elaborate. "I'm the one who hired him. Not you."

He nodded, but didn't give her his eyes, and she knew it didn't matter what she said. He would still blame himself.

"Wait a minute," she said, the thought only now occurring to her. "You think his killer was the same person who had room service with him?"

The detective glanced back at them like he expected Colin to answer.

"There was no forced entry," Colin told her. "And no signs of a struggle. I'm guessing whoever he met here ended their evening together by taking the room-service knife and carving him up. I don't think Zach even saw it coming."

30

Abda was supposed to pick up the fare he had dropped off just after midnight at the Washington Grand Hotel. He had told Abda to be at the front door at three-thirty but the young man was already thirty minutes late. What could Abda do when another man came out waving for him?

At that time of the morning there were no other cabs waiting. He probably could have told the other man he was off duty, but then why would he be there at four in the morning? And if he had told him he was waiting for a fare who had already booked him, the man would have continued waiting and seen his fare leave the hotel. Abda knew that also would not be good. So he chose to take this man to his destination and hurry back. It was better, Abda had decided, to make his fare wait than to expose him.

Now as he approached the Washington Grand Hotel he could see the front blocked off by police cruisers with flashing lights. An ambulance took up the valet drive-up space. There was nothing Abda could do but park in the next block and walk back to get his fare. He couldn't keep driving around until the man saw him. It would be impossible. A small group had started to gather, pushed back with yellow crime-scene tape and police officers with ear-piercing whistles and little patience.

If only the other man had waited to hail a cab. If only Abda's fare had not been late then Abda could be off getting some much-needed sleep instead of trying to politely shove and make his way through this early-morning odd menagerie of street people and churchgoers. Didn't they have better things to do?

Abda recognized one of the doormen, a Pakistani named Okmar, who had been kind to him several times when Abda had waited to pick up this same fare at odd hours of the morning. He was beginning to think this exchange of favors was getting a bit out of hand with these absurd petty errands.

Abda squeezed past a smelly old woman in a long skirt and a dirty white T-shirt with yellow stains. The woman shot him a look and pulled her bulging black garbage bag closer to her as if worried he might try to grab it. Abda walked on, keeping his anger inside. He grew tired of simpleminded, filthy street bums treating him like a criminal because of his obvious Middle Eastern heritage. Instead, Abda waved at his doorman friend when he looked his way.

Okmar only nodded at him, but came over to the edge of where the crime-scene tape began.

"Did someone fall ill?" Abda asked though he knew very well that it would need to be someone important to get this kind of attention. But in Washington, D.C., it wouldn't be unusual.

Okmar leaned closer to Abda and in a low voice just above a whisper he said, "Someone got himself murdered."

Abda was taken aback. His eyes darted around the small group and then he looked to see if he recognized his fare inside the lobby through the windows. All the police activity may have simply made him take another exit.

"Any idea who the poor bastard was?" Abda asked Okmar, only because he looked anxious to tell someone.

"A young man. Rumor is he worked for a senator."

Abda nodded, feigning surprise though he wondered why anyone would be surprised. It was impossible to go anywhere without meeting someone who worked for a senator or congressman.

"Do you know how he was murdered?" Abda asked, only slightly curious. But Okmar's eyes widened and he glanced around.

"They haven't said. But I heard one of them say something about it being...what is the word?" Okmar said, struggling to remember then brightening when he did. He whispered, "*Kinky.* That was what he said." And he looked at Abda to see that he understood, so Abda raised his eyebrows to show he knew indeed.

They heard a whistle blow and Okmar jumped to attention, returning to his post as the hotel doors opened and they brought out the stretcher. Abda noticed there was no black body bag, only a sheet wrapped tightly from head to foot. He wasn't sure what he'd expected. Maybe he had watched too much American TV.

He had a perfect view of the back of the ambulance, so he stayed and watched, his fare probably long gone as soon as he saw the commotion. Just as the stretcher jerked and slid into the ambulance the dead man's wrist slipped out from under the sheet. There was a gasp from the voyeurs, the vultures pressing over the crime-scene tape to get a better look. Abda started to turn away when he saw the flash of something metallic hanging from the dead man's wrist. He recognized the gold bracelet.

He may have been mistaken. It was absolutely possible. But this would explain why his fare who had never dared to be late before had been late this morning. Abda had a feeling—what the Americans called a gut instinct—that there would be no more favors for a while.

No, Abda knew it was time for them to move on to Florida.

31

Sabrina spent most of Sunday afternoon running errands, including another trip to visit her father in Chattahoochee. Without realizing it she had lumped him in with the rest. When had her father become another errand?

This time she found a Whataburger restaurant and bought him a cheeseburger with pickles and onion, remembering the fries and adding a chocolate shake. The charge nurse just shook her head at the bag Sabrina pretended to hide inside her tote. There was no pretending or hiding. The scent of French fries and onions overpowered the sterile hallway and admitting area, but instead of getting reprimands she got requests for orders.

"Next time," she promised and received smiles, none of the usual frowns and scowls. She'd remember to keep this promise. She wasn't beneath buying her father some compassion with a round of cheeseburgers.

He sat quiet and calm this time, arms stretched out on the recliner's armrests, head lolled onto his shoulder. His eyes were glassy, but still looking everywhere. Now, instead of darting around they moved in slow jerks like images in an old-fashioned movie.

She hated when they did this to him. She almost preferred the fidgeting; at least there was some energy, some hope of life captured and trapped, but fighting its way to the surface. Like this, he reminded Sabrina too much of a zombie, an empty shell. It took everything she had inside to keep from grabbing him by his shirt collar and screaming into his face, "Dad, are you in there?"

She sat in front of him on the edge of the chair, holding the fast-food bag in her lap. She waited for his eyes to find her. They flitted across her face but didn't stop, didn't even hesitate. She already had allowed herself too high of hopes. How could she expect to bring him a cheeseburger and fries and make everything okay again? Although it had worked for her when the tables were reversed. How many times had her father brought her a hot-fudge sundae or a cheeseburger when he knew she needed cheering up? Once when she came in second in the state science fair and they both knew she should have taken first. Again, after a fender-bender that smashed up her car. Time after time he was there to make it all better with some fast-food treat that took the place of the words he couldn't come up with.

Sabrina unwrapped the cheeseburger and set it out with the fries and shake on a tray table between them. Then she sat on the edge of her chair and watched and waited. Two hours later when she kissed him on the forehead and left, the food remained untouched.

The sun had already begun to sink behind the forest of tall pines.

This time Sabrina tried to pay close attention so she wouldn't miss her turnoff and end up on Highway 90 instead of Interstate 10. Otherwise, as soon as the sun went down, she would lose her sense of direction. Not much of a scientist when it came to navigation.

The two-lane blacktop was missing the white center guidelines. It didn't help matters that several road signs had been pushed over by tropical storms from the season before and were still not repaired. Last time Sabrina had taken a right turn when she should have taken a left, and she ended up alongside Lake Seminole. This time she vowed to keep her mind on the road and not on her disappointment.

When she first made the move to Florida she had been confident her presence alone would bring her father back. She could get him to snap out of it with the sound of her voice and tales from happier times. But as the weeks dragged into months, the realization tugged at her optimism, weighing it down. She functioned by rote rather than by reason.

After her mother's death, Sabrina walked around in a fog. She found solace in her routine. Her predictable, boring life—as Eric had labeled it once upon a time—had ended up saving her sanity. She put herself on autopilot, which was exactly what she needed at the time—reason had become too painful. Her father hadn't been as lucky. Just when the three of them needed each other the most they split apart.

Sabrina had done exactly what she had promised herself she wouldn't do. She let her mind and eyes wander off the road. She didn't even see the black sedan until it roared up behind her. The car's tinted windows and the escaping sunlight made it look like a driverless machine out of control. Something right out of a Stephen King novel.

She pulled as far over as she could to the side of the narrow two-lane back road. There was no oncoming traffic, but too many curves to be certain. She started to slow down and the sedan rammed into her bumper, slamming her body against her seat belt.

What the hell is wrong with this guy?

She skidded to the shoulder, trying to ease her car over the steep drop-off from the blacktop to the dirt shoulder. One tire, then two, but it was more mud than dirt and the car started to slide. Finally the sedan veered into the other lane, roaring up alongside her. Sabrina kept a firm grip on the steering wheel and glanced over at the shiny black car. It was still impossible to see beyond the tinted glass. She expected it to pull ahead just as it jerked toward her.

There was a scrape and crunch of metal. Another violent punch sent Sabrina's car hurtling out of control despite her twisting the steering wheel. Steering didn't matter. The tires were no longer touching blacktop or dirt. Her car flipped sideways over the rain-filled ditch. All she saw was water and sky.

32

Sabrina waited for the car to stop rocking and her head to stop pounding. The headlights shot at an awkward angle, illuminating the tops of the pine trees. Out of her side window she could see grass and water. The air bag hadn't deployed, but her shoulder belt trapped her against the seat. She reached to unbuckle it. As soon as she heard the click, her body slid to the driver's door, igniting a pain in her shoulder and sending the car rocking again.

She tried to be still, listening for the sound of a car engine, straining to hear over the cicadas. Certainly the driver of the sedan had turned around when he saw what happened.

Instead, all Sabrina heard, other than the twilight insects, was the hissing and sputtering from her own car.

She examined her predicament. Maybe in his hurry he hadn't

noticed her going into the ditch. How could he have not noticed? His car had rammed against hers.

Despite the pain in her shoulder—she knew it was bruised—nothing broken, she strained and reached for the tote bag that now hung from the gas pedal. After a gentle tug-of-war trying to free it, she stretched and rummaged inside. Her fingers found the cell phone just as she noticed the scent of gasoline. She had filled the tank just before leaving. Until now she had been calm.

Suddenly the panic rushed into her like an injection, making her nauseated. A chill accompanied the panic as soon as she noticed how quickly darkness swallowed up the last shadows of twilight. She needed to get out of the car and *she needed to get out now.*

Sabrina twisted her legs out from under the steering column. From what she could see, the car had gotten caught on the splintered remains of a fence. For now it kept the car from rolling over completely into the rain-filled ditch. Maybe she should try and force it to roll into the ditch? Would the water keep the car from igniting? Probably not. She tried the driver's door, not surprised to find it trapped against the slope of grass and dirt. She'd need to climb up and out the other window. Halfway into her gentle maneuver, the vehicle groaned. She stopped, but it was too late. The shift in balance sent the car into a slow-motion roll, screeching metal silencing even the cicadas.

This time Sabrina didn't wait for the rocking to stop. On hands and knees she crawled across the car roof that was now her floor. She pulled and pushed at the door, relieved to feel it give without much struggle. She half crawled, half fell into the wet grass and mud. She didn't stop. She was breathing in gulps, driven by the burning in her lungs and the taste of gasoline in her mouth.

She reached the road and was able to get to her feet. That's when she remembered her tote bag still stuck on the gas pedal and suddenly her mind tried to retrieve the list of contents: credit cards, driver's license, condo keys. This was ridiculous. She need to get a safe distance away. But only when she realized she was still clutching the cell phone—though it was now encrusted in mud and grass—did she allow herself to hurry farther up the road into the dark.

She didn't look back when she heard the strange sizzle and the faint pops like a skillet full of bacon. The explosion blew her off her feet. Sabrina scrambled again on hands and knees into the wet grass as the fiery debris filled the night sky.

Everything would be okay, she tried to tell herself in a useless attempt to stay calm. Her fingers were shaking so badly it took three tries before she could successfully punch in 911.

33

Washington, D.C.

Jason had avoided Lindy's phone calls all day. He could tell her he was at the office, at the gym, visiting friends. Or just admit that he was an asshole. But damn, he had to hand it to her, she was persistent, leaving three messages for him to call as soon as possible. Last night she hadn't come across as a hanger-on. But then how would he know? He didn't know her. He was sure he'd regret the whole thing. He just didn't think it'd be this soon. He had hoped not to think about it at all.

He paced his studio apartment, not an easy thing to do. The place was one room with a sofa sleeper, flat-panel TV, minifridge and a view of the Dumpster. It wasn't usually a problem. He spent little time here except to change clothes and sleep. Besides, for Jason an apartment was only as good as its building's amenities. There was a dry cleaner down on the first floor along with a small deli where he'd pick up a bagel, some fruit and a Red Bull for breakfast, sometimes a sandwich, too, if he knew he wouldn't be able to leave the office for lunch. A newsstand sat right out front, so he had access to all the headlines of the day before he got to work.

He could pace all night, but it was inevitable. He needed to call Lindy. Otherwise she'd track him down tomorrow at work. Senator Allen would fire him for sure if Lindy kept calling him at the office.

Jesus! What the hell was he thinking?

He flipped open his cell phone and punched through the "missed calls" list, stopping at her last one. He let out a deep breath, punched Talk and waited for it to dial her number.

Three rings—could he be lucky enough to get her voice mail?

"Hello?"

"Lindy, hi, it's Jason."

"Oh, thank God."

Jason caught himself cringing and swallowing hard. Not exactly the reaction he wanted. *Be cool,* he told himself. *You don't have to apologize.*

"I've been kinda busy," he said and before he could stop himself added, "Sorry I didn't call you back sooner." He winced and wanted to bite his tongue. He was so preoccupied in gauging his next response that he thought for sure he must have heard her wrong when she said, "Zach's dead."

"What?"

"He was murdered."

"Wait a minute. Who was murdered?"

"Zach Kensor. You know Zach. He was there last night with us at Wally's."

"Murdered?"

"Oh, my God, Jason. It gets worse. He was at the Washington Grand Hotel, too. It had to have happened while we were there."

Jason stopped pacing and sat down on the arm of the sofa sleeper. "Was it some random-violence…thing?"

"He had a room. I know he was meeting someone. They were…" Lindy paused and in almost a whisper added, "You know, like we did."

There was that automatic cringe again. Jason had spent the better part of the day wishing he could just forget about last night, hoping that Lindy would do the same. Now hearing her whisper it as though it might be something she regretted, he wanted to call her on it. Instead he tried to focus on what she was telling him. Zach had been murdered.

"Any idea who he was meeting?"

"Yeah, sort of. In fact, I'm wondering if maybe I should contact the police." Her voice suddenly sounded small like a little girl who was asking permission. Definitely not like the Lindy of last night who had been sure and confident. "I mean, I don't know who it was exactly," she clarified in a stronger tone. "But Zach told me last night that he was…maybe I shouldn't say anything. He said he was having an affair with someone high-level. I think it might have been a senator."

34

Sabrina left the homemade icepack on her knee though her whole body felt bruised and battered. Miss Sadie insisted she was still in shock. Evidently that was what the Gadsden County sheriff had thought, too. He brought her home himself, all the way back to Tallahassee. Sabrina had watched his eyes the entire time he took the report. She could tell he didn't believe her, interrupting her twice to offer her an out by mentioning how bad that two-lane blacktop had become.

"I could certainly understand someone losing control, especially right at twilight. Someone who wasn't familiar with the roads." He said it like a father coaxing the truth out of his teenage child.

Sabrina stuck by her story even as she wiped mud from her elbows with the towel he had given her. She described the black sedan as best she could, but when the sheriff asked her for a description of the driver, her explanation that the car's windows were tinted too dark sounded a bit fantastic even to Sabrina. He looked up at her and said, "Uh-huh," and he could just as well have said, *What movie did y'all pull this from?*

Once he deposited Sabrina at her condo, she no longer cared what the good sheriff of Gadsden County thought. She just wanted to forget the whole night, scrub it off and rinse it off in a nice warm bath.

Sabrina had to go around to the back of the condo where she kept a spare key hidden underneath one of the terra-cotta planters— hopefully one of the few Lizzie Borden hadn't destroyed. That's when Miss Sadie caught Sabrina.

"Girl, I thought someone was breakin' in," she scolded Sabrina, her voice coming out of the darkness, surprising Sabrina.

She never thought of Miss Sadie as a small woman, but coming around the corner in her long, hot-pink chenille robe that made her coffee-brown skin look smooth as silk, wielding a baseball bat that appeared oversized in her small, arthritic hands, Miss Sadie suddenly looked like a vulnerable, eighty-one-year-old woman. That is, until Sabrina saw that she was choked up on the bat like an expert.

Miss Sadie snapped on the patio light, took one look at Sabrina and turned the light off. Sabrina just stood there with the key in her hand, exhausted but waiting for the string of questions. She was in no mood to tell the story all over again. But the old woman surprised her. Instead of a barrage of questions, she pointed at Sabrina's blood- and dirt-caked kneecap exposed by the rip in her jeans and the old woman gently said, "You'll need some ice for that. Come sit down."

Before Sabrina could protest, Miss Sadie had disappeared back into her condo. Sabrina didn't argue. She didn't want to. She eased herself into one of Miss Sadie's wicker chairs and she took comfort in the familiar scent of lavender and the screech of night birds. She had for-gotten how good it felt to have someone care. It was impossible to understand what an absolute luxury it was to have someone care about you until you no longer had it.

Minutes later Miss Sadie emerged with an economy-sized bag of frozen peas wrapped in a bright yellow Home-Sweet-Home kitchen towel. She also had a tray with a steaming mug and a plate of food.

"Hot toddy," she said, placing the mug in front of Sabrina. "My special recipe. It'll calm your nerves." Then she put the plate before Sabrina, laying out her good silver and a cloth napkin. "And a little something to calm your soul."

Miss Sadie took her place beside Sabrina and sat quietly while Sabrina ate and sipped and told the story again.

35

Jason Brill had already rifled through the *Post* and the *Times*. All he had found about Zach's murder were a couple of paragraphs at the bottom of page three and Zach was an unidentified male at the Washington Grand Hotel.

Now Jason flipped between cable-news channels on the small portable TV he kept in his office. He'd gotten here earlier and practically locked himself away, looking and listening for anything about Zach. He'd gone through three Red Bulls to keep him charged for the rest of the day. But so far he couldn't find anything more in the newspapers and not even a phrase on the crawl of any morning-news station. He expected more in a city where reporters gobbled up this sort of stuff. He thought it was odd, but at the same time found himself almost relieved and hoping Lindy hadn't called the police.

While he didn't find anything much about Zach, he did find an op-ed piece about Senator Allen and the upcoming energy summit. He'd already made several copies and highlighted key phrases that called his boss "a progressive thinker," "a liberator from foreign oil" and one of the few on Capitol Hill who "genuinely gave a damn about the environment."

It was the kind of piece that Jason considered a personal success after months of sending out press releases and repeating those key phrases anywhere and everywhere. It was good news and the boost they needed to get the EchoEnergy contract approval by the Appropriations Committee. Most of all, it was a relief that Friday's vomit fiasco hadn't found legs to last through the weekend.

There was an unexpected, gentle tap at Jason's office door. It startled him so much he almost jumped out of his chair.

"Come in."

A pause, then the door opened just enough for Senator Allen to peer in around it. Immediately Jason thought it a bit odd, or maybe his boss was trying to do something he didn't want to do—like fire Jason. Could the senator have already heard about Jason's extracurricular activity with the enemy camp?

"You're here early," Senator Allen said. "Everything okay?"

"Everything's fine. Just wanted to get a jump start on the week," Jason told him, glancing at this watch, pretending he didn't know exactly what time it was. He was always here early. The senator would know that if he was here early.

"I could ask you the same question," Jason said, using one of the senator's favorite phrases. "Everything okay?"

"Oh, sure." He opened the door wide enough to wave a hand at him. "I decided to do some old-fashioned arm-twisting instead of sitting back and letting the chips fall where they may."

Jason was relieved, but also pleased. Without asking, he knew the senator had seen the op-ed piece. Positive media coverage motivated him beyond anything Jason could say or do.

"That sounds like a great idea. What do you need me to do?"

"Lunch. I'll need you as backup. Make reservations at Old Ebbitt's. Get my regular table."

Jason wondered if he should tell Senator Allen to exclude Senator Holden for a day or two. But then how could Jason tell his boss without explaining how he already knew that one of Senator Holden's top staffers had been murdered?

"You got it," he said and left it at that.

36

By Monday morning Sabrina's accident had become an annoying in-convenience rather than a dramatic brush with death. Her shoulder ached and her knee looked like a miniature Jackson Pollock painting—splashes of purple and blue with streaks of red. It had taken two frozen bags of peas and one bag of okra to take down the swelling and to get her through the night. Otherwise all she was left with was the inconvenience of having her car and wallet torched.

She tried to call the lab to let them know she'd be late. No one answered the lab's main line and instead her call kept getting bounced to Dwight Lansik's voice-messaging service. She left a message, but after finding Lansik's duffel bag in his closet and his car still in EchoEnergy's parking lot, she wasn't hopeful that he would be picking up his messages.

Thank goodness the rental car agency had her driver's license on file, one of the perks of online membership. It didn't, however, seem to make a difference when choosing a car. They had already delivered a subcompact when she specifically had requested a four-door sedan. Her mother's accident had left Sabrina with an irrational phobia of traveling in anything smaller than a four-door, but the agency's representative said this was it, if she wanted a car before noon. That was just one of her problems.

Since she hadn't gotten her driver's license switched yet from Illinois to Florida, the local Department of Motor Vehicles couldn't help her with a replacement.

"This move was supposed to be temporary," Sabrina tried to explain to the clerk over the phone.

"And I'm sure the state of Illinois can help you get a temporary replacement."

She called the Cook County DMV for the city of Chicago. Of course they could issue a replacement driver's license. All Sabrina needed to do was present a birth certificate and one other form of identification at any one of their county offices.

"There's no way it can be done over the Internet or by mail?" But even as Sabrina asked, she knew it was a ridiculous question. Before the woman finished her string of disgusted sighs, Sabrina tried to redeem herself. "Okay, what about getting a new license in Florida? I've been a resident for almost a year."

"Usually you can present your license and simply apply to the new state according to their rules and regulations." The woman sounded like a recording only not as friendly. "But in your case, where you don't have your current license to surrender…" She went on to explain a long-drawn-out process that included letters of request and verification that would take weeks.

Sabrina was beginning to think it would be faster to fly up to

Chicago, but then how could she do that without a driver's license and a credit card for identification?

Damn! She hadn't even thought about the credit card. She had only one and used it for everything. The credit card doubled as her ATM card.

However, the credit card company renewed Sabrina's faith in the world of technology. After about a half hour of transfers and verifications that included her mother's maiden name, Mrs. Jones, the company representative, assured Sabrina a new card would be on its way within twenty-four hours and express delivered to her Florida home.

By now Sabrina was pulling into EchoEnergy's park, thankful she had forgotten her badge on her lab coat and her security key card in the pocket. At least there were two items she wouldn't need to replace. She punched in her pass code at the guard hut. Before she found parking for the small tin can of a rental car, she drove to the back lot closest to the river. Sabrina made two trips around and through the aisles of cars, but there was no mistake. Dwight Lansik's white Crown Victoria was gone. She hoped Lansik was back and had simply moved his car.

Sabrina had missed most of the morning, but her colleagues worked independently of each other. She expected them to hardly notice her absence. After all, they hadn't noticed their boss had been missing since Thursday. And yet when Sabrina walked into the lab she seemed to surprise all three of them, catching them huddled together as if they were waiting.

"There she come," Pasha said in a tone that registered somewhere between urgency and relief.

"Your message said something about an accident?" O'Hearn said.

Anna came out from behind the table the three were gathered around. She put her hands on her hips and looked Sabrina over. She couldn't help thinking Anna could at least try to hide her disappointment that Sabrina was okay. In fact, Anna sounded a tad too smug when she announced, "Here she is, Mr. Sidel."

William Sidel came out of Dwight Lansik's office with his cell phone pressed to his ear. The others had looked surprised to see Sabrina, but Sidel did a double take. His eyes met hers, but it wasn't surprise as much as astonishment. He clicked off the phone without saying goodbye. His boyish, ruddy face turned a bit pasty. If she didn't know better, Sabrina would have said that William Sidel looked at her like he was seeing a ghost.

37

Washington, D.C.

Natalie Richards waved Colin Jernigan into her office from where he hesitated at her door. She shifted the phone into her other hand and pressed it against her opposite ear. She hadn't been able to get anything done this morning. The phone calls had been relentless, all of them so-called "emergencies" or "urgencies" that supposedly only she could handle. Her assistant handled all the details, but Natalie still had to be the voice—or rather her boss's voice—of reassurance.

Colin stood by the window, leaning against the wall and watching the street below. Natalie watched him as she listened to the rants and ramblings of the person on the phone. She knew the folder tucked under Colin's arm was the reason he would dare to bother her without an appointment. He was the only one, other than her boss, who got away with a drop-by. This was only the second time he had used the privilege, which meant it wasn't good news. What the hell more could go wrong?

Finally the man on the phone took a breath and Natalie jumped in. "We are well aware of the concern, but I assure you every detail will be handled."

"Of course, that is all we ask."

They exchanged goodbyes and Natalie hung up, letting out an exasperated sigh.

"Paranoid bastards," Natalie said more to herself than to Colin, who stood at the other end of her office. When he raised an eyebrow with interest, she offered, "Another oil sheikh worried about security for landing his private jet."

"They're used to having their own airstrips," he said.

"They're used to having their own way." Her hands went to her hips. "If it was my party they wouldn't even be invited."

That drew a smile. Satisfied, she was ready to get down to business though she wasn't quite ready to get to that folder tucked under his arm.

"By the way, how are we situated for all these flights coming in?" she asked as she pointed to one of the chairs in front of her desk. She liked being the only one standing in her office while she talked. At five foot three with what she liked to call a generous figure, she knew she didn't have the physical presence to back up her authority.

"I'm told Tyndall Air Force Base is ready and more than capable." He sat down, crossed his legs, made himself comfortable or at least pretended to. She knew him well enough to see the tension on his face that he thought he could disguise—the tightness around his mouth, the squint of tired eyes. "Secret Service, of course, is in charge of background checks," he continued, "along with lining up limos and routes for the VIPs. Homeland Security has its own group, including the Coast Guard taking care of security in, around and on the estate."

"I don't know why we didn't have it here in Washington." Natalie shook her head. "I don't like what I don't know and I don't know the Gulf Coast of Florida."

"Believe it or not, from a security point of view, a private estate is less work than a major city. When Bush 43 held his energy summit in Crawford, everybody laughed, but it was probably the smoothest summit I've seen."

"You were around back then?"

He nodded. Maybe someday they'd get around to exchanging stories about their past political lives.

"Then you won't mind being there for this one," she said, picking up and waving an envelope, this one bulging. "I'll need you to be my eyes and ears down there."

"You don't want to take a quick trip to sunny Florida?"

"Sweetie, this hair doesn't do Florida." She put the envelope back on her desk and crossed her arms over her chest. "Besides, something tells me I'll be busy here with whatever that problem is you have in your hands."

He let out a sigh and tapped the folder against his leg, shifting in his seat. He handed it to her as he said, "We weren't expecting anything like this."

"I don't like the sound of that." She searched his eyes, trying to discern how big a problem "this" was. She left the folder dangling in the air for a second or two. Then she snatched and opened it in one swoop like ripping off a Band-Aid to reduce the sting.

At first she didn't recognize what she was looking at. The form resembled something ancient, poorly printed and filled in with blue ballpoint ink. She could even see the indents in the paper from the pressure of the pen. Her eyes caught phrases: "throat slashed," "multiple wounds." That's when she realized she was holding a police report—the original report, not a copy—for the murder of Zachary Kensor. Stapled to the form was a printout with a set of fingerprints. She recognized this document. All federal employees were required to have their fingerprints on file with the Justice Department. Somewhere there was an exact document with a set of hers.

"So they did find some fingerprints at the crime scene?" she asked, her eyes not able to leave the space that identified the owner. If she dared blink, would it be possible this might all be some bad dream? She needed to sit down. She leaned against the desk instead.

"On the inside cover of the room-service menu," Colin said, but there was no satisfaction in his voice that he had been right. "Everything else was wiped clean, but it's easy to miss, to forget the inside pages."

"And there's no mistake as to who they belong to?" She wasn't sure why she even asked. Wishful thinking, perhaps. She tried to correct it before he answered. "I'm just asking how solid is the source they're matching these up to?" She already knew the answer.

"Justice Department records."

"That's what I was afraid you'd say." She eased herself around the desk and dropped into her leather chair. She didn't let up on the viselike grip she had on the folder and its contents. She met his eyes and she could see he was thinking the same thing. That it was as much a curse as it was a blessing. "How long are they willing to sit on this?"

"I can probably get us a day or two."

The energy summit started in three days.

"Forty-eight hours," she told him. "All I need is forty-eight hours."

38

Sabrina would never have pegged William Sidel for a man who bit his fingernails. Maybe a little dirt behind them, but certainly not chewed to the quick. She found herself focusing on his hands; the huge knuckles and pudgy fingers dwarfed two rings, a wedding band and a gaudy pinkie ring. He used his hands as extensions of his words, emphasizing a point with a chop here and drawing out a sentence with a slide and an open palm. He was telling them that Dwight Lansik had resigned, "just up and left" without notice or an explanation.

"But I don't want y'all to worry about it," he told them with a charming southern drawl. Sabrina had noticed the other day that Sidel brought out that same drawl when the investor from Omaha started questioning the plant's use of energy to operate.

"I like the job y'all have been doing. I know I have a great team in place," he continued. "And I'll already tell you that's why I'm not bringing in somebody from the outside to replace Dr. Lansik."

Sabrina stole a glance at Pasha, who was nodding his agreement, but Anna Copello's smile was tight-lipped. She kept her arms folded over her chest. When Sabrina glanced at O'Hearn he caught her eye and raised his brows just enough as if to say, *Can you believe this guy?*

"I want you to know I'm not going to rush into making my decision," Sidel was saying and Sabrina watched his hands come together, fingers intertwined as he rested them just below his paunch. "You're all more than qualified to lead this team."

Sidel sidetracked to one of his stories and Sabrina's mind went back to Saturday—Lansik's car still in the parking lot, his duffel bag stashed in his office closet. She wondered when he had given his resignation. No one had seen him all day Friday and yet Sidel had known ahead of time that Lansik wouldn't be available to lead the tour. Perhaps the resignation happened Thursday, and Sidel had simply given Lansik the weekend to come in and clear out his things.

That seemed unlikely. In most corporate settings if a director resigned or was fired without notice he or she would be asked to pack up that day. And then, oftentimes, escorted off the premises by security. Something wasn't right about all of this.

She waited until Sidel finished and left the lab, then she caught up with him halfway down the hall so she wouldn't have to ask her questions in front of the others.

"Mr. Sidel," she called out and hurried up alongside him.

"Now, Dr. Galloway, I'm sure you're not expecting any favoritism in exchange for saving my hide on Friday."

He forced a laugh while he looked around the hallway. Sabrina saw Anna Copello jerk back inside the door to the lab. Sabrina wanted to tell him to keep his voice down and at the same time she wanted to bellow out that she wasn't interested in taking Lansik's position

Instead, she kept her voice hushed when she said, "I noticed something on the tour." She decided to choose her words carefully. "It looked to me like the valve to Reactor #5 may have accidentally been opened."

His otherwise animated hands went into his trouser pockets. "Well, I can tell you without a doubt that we're not set up yet to use Reactor #5."

She waited, then realized that was it. That was his explanation. She almost blurted out that she had been inside and the reactor was, in fact, running at full throttle...except for the flushing tank. She caught herself. He had selected his words just as carefully as she had. Instead of answering whether or not the valve was open, he gave her the same line O'Hearn had used. Sabrina decided to try again. She stood her ground, looking up at him.

"It sounded like there might be material flowing into the reactor."

"I don't know what you thought you heard, Dr. Galloway. Hell, it's so loud down there it sounds like everything's echoing off the walls."

Was it possible William Sidel had gotten so caught up wooing investors and lobbying members of Congress that he didn't have a clue whether his processing plant was using four reactors or five?

Sabrina knew she heard pinging in the pipes. She knew the consistency and density of the input feedstock and the output. She had been instrumental in devising the current formula that separated bones from the chicken guts and blood by a unit weight before the mixture even entered the depressurization stage. The bones were forced into a tank ready to use for fertilizer products, while the guts and blood were pushed through to the next reactor. Had William

Sidel told her they were processing something, anything, through Reactor #5 she would have sooner believed him. She had hoped for a simple, rational answer. Instead, his evasiveness made her stomach twist into knots.

He was lying.

The doubt must have shown on her face. Suddenly Sidel smiled at her, his boyish face relaxed. His hands came out of his pockets.

"Tell you what, Dr. Galloway, why don't I have our plant manager, Ernie Walker, meet you later today over at Reactor #5. Why don't we say around four. Maybe the two of you can check it out together. Hell, I can't afford to have something else throw us off track."

39

Washington, D.C.

Jason walked into Old Ebbitt's Grill and waited for his eyes to adjust to the dim lights of the restaurant. The senator's secretary had called earlier and told Jason that Senator Allen would meet him there.

It had been a crazy morning. Jason had a dozen details to take care of for the energy summit's reception. Somehow he had missed a phone call from an ABC producer who wanted to schedule an interview with the senator for *Good Morning America*. He had been on the phone with the Florida catering company and his secretary hadn't interrupted.

He shook his head while he waited for the host to guide him to the senator's table. He still couldn't believe her. He wasn't good at firing people, but missing a stint at *GMA* would give him enough reason. He left her with strict instructions on how to get hold of him. As he followed the host he flipped open his cell phone just to double-check that it was on.

So with things as crazy as they were he probably should have asked Senator Allen's secretary for more information when she called. Yeah, he should have asked, then he wouldn't have felt his stomach slide down to his well-shined shoes when he got his first glimpse of Senator Allen already seated with Senator Shirley Malone and Lindy.

Maybe because he had firings on his mind his first thought was that both he and Lindy would be fired. Of course, it seemed a bit crazy to do it in public, but Jason remembered his cousin, Renee, using her wedding-rehearsal dinner to announce that her fiancé, Greg, had banged her maid of honor the weekend before.

Senator Allen looked relieved. "Jason, this is Senator Shirley Malone."

Jason reached across the table to shake her hand and nodded. He remembered and liked the feel of her hand, a real handshake, not too soft and wimpy, but not a ballbreaker, either.

"I've heard nothing but good things," she said as their eyes met, and Jason thought he recognized a knowing smile while she neither acknowledged nor denied they'd met before.

She wore a copper-colored suit that brought out the highlights in her hair, and a scarf of oranges and browns that complemented her eyes. She had friendly, gentle eyes. Eyes, he found himself thinking, that couldn't lie.

"And I'm sure you know her chief of staff, Lindy Matthews," Senator Allen said, snapping Jason back to attention and back to paranoia.

Was Senator Allen saying he knew Jason and Lindy knew each other or simply that they should probably know each other? Jason tried to read Lindy. She, of course, looked beautiful. But her limp handshake and refusal to meet Jason's eyes only drove him to wonder if she had told. Maybe he was the only one getting fired.

The senator ordered a Chivas on the rocks. Another signal that usually put Jason on alert, because Jason always had to monitor the senator's words whenever he drank. One cocktail at lunch shouldn't matter. Quickly Jason realized the senator had an agenda. And the cocktail was liquid bravery.

Before the entrées arrived, Senator Allen began throwing down the gauntlet.

"Shirley, I know you're looking out for Indiana, same way I'm looking out for Florida." Senator Allen talked while he picked up his flatware piece by piece and moved it a quarter of an inch. Jason had seen him do this at other lunches and it reminded Jason of a chess player lining up his pawns or a general setting up his front line.

"When hurricanes hit Florida two years in a row and we needed some bridges repaired and replaced, it was quite helpful that we could include expert construction companies all the way from Indiana."

Jason wanted to cringe. This would not have been his choice of opening and now he wondered if the Chivas had not been the senator's first drink of the day. If Jason remembered correctly, the contracts to those expert construction companies came after Senator Malone agreed to vote in favor of a controversial gun-control bill that Senator Allen had cosponsored. She hadn't asked to be rewarded, but even so, Jason remembered Senator Allen calling the multimillion-dollar earmark to those Indiana companies as "insurance."

No, as Jason watched the color rise in Senator Malone's cheeks, he knew this was not a good start.

"Unfortunately we have lots of experience in Indiana rebuilding after disastrous tornadoes," she said in a tone that set Jason at ease. The lady could take care of herself.

"Of course you do. And if we play our cards right," the senator continued as if he had just gotten the thank-you he expected, "there's more than enough for both our states in this $140-million energy contract."

"Ethanol has a proven record in delivering," Senator Malone countered between delicate bites of her salad. "I'm not convinced EchoEnergy can make that claim."

"Yes, that's right. Ethanol can deliver." Senator Allen nodded and smiled. "But only with an awful lot of help from government subsidies."

Jason glanced at Lindy. From where he sat he could see her hand in her lap, twisting her cloth napkin, but her eyes were on her senator.

Jason was wrong. This had nothing to do with their illicit one-night stand. For one thing, Senator Allen would never be this cocky about a military contract if he knew his chief of staff had boinked Senator Malone's chief girl. Or maybe that was exactly why he was so cocky.

"It's not up to me, John," Senator Malone was saying.

"We'll cancel each other out if we go up against each other," Senator Allen said, moving the salt and pepper shakers a quarter inch from their original position. And then his fingers retreated to his now-empty glass of Chivas. "That happens and you know who wins."

He lowered his voice and leaned forward to add, "Those fucking Arabs win, that's who."

Jason shifted in his chair, staring at the remnants of his own salad. He should feel relieved this lunch had nothing to do with him. That's when the waiter chose to bring their entrées and everyone sat back. Intermission, Jason thought, avoiding Lindy's eyes and especially Senator Malone's. He heard Senator Allen praise the young waiter, but Jason kept his eyes on the sirloin tips and roasted potatoes on the plate in front of him. It looked delicious, but Jason had absolutely no appetite.

40

Tallahassee, Florida

"That's impossible," Leon barked into the cell phone, pulling it away from his ear and smacking the piece of crap phone against the wall as if that might help him get a different answer. He had to stop lifting these flashy, razor-thin, worthless pieces of technocrap.

He pressed the phone against his ear just in time to hear the voice on the other end say, "...today. Take care of it."

Leon slammed the phone shut. He wanted to put his fist through a wall. Instead, he looked around the restaurant, trying to find his waitress to wave her down. This was fucking incredible. He pulled out a miniature pack of tissues and his stubby, clumsy fingers tugged one out so he could wipe the sweat from his upper lip. He took out a second and dragged it all the way from his forehead, over his widow's peak to the back of his head.

Jesus H. Christ! How the hell could she have made it out? He knew he'd given her car a good shove. He'd seen it take flight over the ditch. And he'd seen the fireball. No way she survived that. Maybe he should have stuck around, but the angle that the car took off, no way she was getting out.

Son of a bitch. What a fucking streak of bad luck he was having. It all started with that incident that put Casino Rudy in the psych hospital instead of six feet under. Leon was hoping to cash in on this job before that recent little mishap got out. Truth is, he about pissed his pants yesterday when he realized that's where the Galloway lady was going, even though he knew damn well it had nothing to do with Casino Rudy. Fucking coincidence that she'd be going to Chattahoochee. But she was there to see some other old guy. Being in that place for crazies gave Leon the major creeps.

That's also why he was in a hurry to knock her off. He was fucking tired of trying to figure out some accident. Mistakes happen when you're in a hurry. Then to find out her old man was in the same kookhouse as Casino Rudy. What the hell was he supposed to do? But nothing right gets done when you're in a hurry. That's exactly what happened with the hit on Casino Rudy in the first place. Leon would rather believe that than remind himself of that batty fortune-teller who claimed to have put a curse on him.

Who the hell believed in curses? Leon certainly didn't. Or at least he never used to.

About a month ago, he was trailing a schmuck from New Jersey, an accountant stupid enough to think he could embezzle over two hundred thousand from his employer and not get caught. Leon had followed him to Coney Island. What a prime spot to knock the guy off. Just when Leon decided he'd pop the son of a bitch during the fireworks, the schmuck meets up with a woman and her little girl. Even Leon had standards. He wouldn't off some guy with a little kid tagging along.

Instead of wasting the night, Leon bought a beer at the freak bar, thought he'd check out one of the freak shows, but there was nothing to compare with when he was a kid. Nothing even close to JoJo, the dog-faced boy. Only tattooed freaks and sword swallowers. Hell, he'd seen enough knives inserted into body parts more interesting than mouths.

He was about to leave when a fortune-telling gypsy with black eyes and a decent cleavage waved him over, her index finger giving him that come-hither twitch like she was reeling him in. With an approach like that how was he supposed to know it pissed off fortune-tellers when you propositioned them? Maybe they should have a sign or something posted. Didn't stop her from taking his twenty, and then spitting in the palm of his hand and declaring "upon his head" some "curse of a dead ancestor."

Leon laughed about it that night, but now it was starting to spook him.

He paid his tab and left the restaurant without even getting a piece of key lime pie like he wanted. He noticed the three-level parking garage across the street. He'd need another ride if he was sticking around. He couldn't just dump the black sedan at the airport and leave like he intended. Originally he'd planned to wait for the two o'clock electronic transfer to be made into his account, then he'd book a flight home. In ten years he'd never had so much trouble. Maybe he'd stay away from fucking Florida for a while. Curse or no curse, nobody should push their luck. He should have known he couldn't do three hits in the same area without something going wrong. Not that he expected all of them to be as easy as shoving a guy into a tank of chicken guts.

41

Sabrina shut herself away in her office. O'Hearn had disappeared. Pasha had returned to his files and test tubes. Anna shot Sabrina a series of dagger looks, once even mumbling something that sounded like, "I know what you're up to."

Sabrina just shook her head. Sidel wanted to create some competition among them, maybe even keep them distracted from asking any more questions. His evasiveness had set Sabrina on edge. Something was going on and she had a feeling Dwight Lansik's resignation was somehow part of it.

She punched a security code into the computer and unlike Saturday's unsuccessful attempts, this time it allowed her access. Maybe the thunderstorms had screwed things up. She didn't care what the reason was. At least now she could check the system.

She brought up the software program that showed the entire

process from pipelines to tanks to filters to depressurization process, pumping and flowing, opening and closing valves and all in real time. Lansik had designed an ingenious system. Using this software he had been able to control the entire process, simply punching a computer key if the cooking temperature needed to be adjusted.

Lansik's security code allowed him to make changes. Sabrina's allowed her only to view the process. It was a digital video screen, calling up various sections according to what stage the process was currently going through. And although it was impossible to see inside the pipes or the tanks, obstructions showed up on the screen like glowing green globs on radar. Feedstock showed up in liquid red so Sabrina could track its flow from one reactor to another, then to the depressurization tank. She could even watch the separation of the oil, all pushed out to one tank.

What wasn't depressurized went into a separate tank where it would be mixed with the crushed bones and made into fertilizer products. The third was leftover water, which flowed into a flushing tank that rinsed it one last time and brought down the temperature before releasing it through a pipeline that led to the river. So without leaving her computer Sabrina could watch the entire process.

All she was concerned with was Reactor #5. She called up one screen and then another, punching computer keys, dismissing each stage, each level, running through the entire process twice before she finally stopped. Sabrina sat back and pushed her hair behind her ears. She couldn't access Reactor #5, which should make sense if, indeed, it wasn't being used. Maybe she was making too big a deal out of nothing. It could have been a mistake that was already corrected. And if it had already been corrected did it matter whether or not anyone admitted to it? Besides, she would find out soon enough when she met with the plant manager.

Sabrina started to close down the program when something caught her eye. She clicked back through the screens until she found it, a glowing green mass in one of the pipelines. She tapped through the menu and double clicked on the location to see exactly where it was. The computer took a few seconds, then flashed STAGE: FLUSHING and LOCATION: FINAL PIPELINE.

Sabrina checked the screen again. There had to be a mistake. If this was the pipeline flowing from the flushing tank and leaving the building to the rear, it would be only water. She pressed several computer keys and zoomed in. She could see exactly where the obstruction was. The pipeline ran along one side of the back parking lot. The elbow that glowed was the final angle down into the river. If she was right, it probably sat back in the trees just three or four yards from the edge of the parking lot.

Lansik had constructed traps into most of the angles and elbows of the pipeline so clogs could be easily cleaned out. But since this was a water-only pipeline he may not have added one to this pipe.

Sabrina glanced at her wristwatch. She had time before she needed to meet Ernie Walker. Maybe she'd take a bit of a detour.

42

Jason started to get a little antsy. He wanted to get out of the limo and stretch his legs. They'd been driving around D.C. for at least an hour, maybe an hour and a half after leaving Old Ebbitt's. Jason knew exactly why the senator didn't want to go back to the office. He'd limited himself to one Chivas during lunch, but needed the extra two in the limo to convince himself that he had Senator Malone's all-important vote for EchoEnergy.

"Worst-case scenario," Senator Allen was telling Jason for the third time, "we have to split it. I'd rather split it with Malone and ethanol than those blood-sucking Arabs."

When Jason's cell phone rang he reached for it quickly, relieved at the interruption. He punched Talk before the senator could protest.

"Jason Brill here."

"Mr. Brill, it's Lester Rosenthal with *Good Morning America*."

The call took Jason by surprise. He'd given up on hearing from *GMA*.

"Mr. Rosenthal, what can I do for you?" It was another tactic the senator had taught Jason. Even when you want something badly from someone never let them know. Let them think you're the one doing them a favor.

"Robin Roberts met Senator Allen back in 2005 after Katrina hit the Gulf Coast. He was one of the few senators in the area immediately after even though he had a mess of his own down in Florida. He made an impression."

Jason couldn't help but smile and nod, indicating to the senator who sat across from him that it was something positive. He could relax. Going to the devastated gulf areas had been Jason's idea. When he realized Hurricane Katrina would certainly steal the media spotlight, he convinced Senator Allen to be one of the first senators surveying the damage. At every opportunity Jason had stressed that the senator's experience with the aftermath of hurricanes and his position on the Appropriations Committee made it impossible for him to not come and lend a hand. When, in fact, Jason had to bargain with Senator Allen, promising it would be only one day and he would not have to go near New Orleans.

Instead, Jason had chosen Pass Christian, Mississippi, on purpose, when he discovered *GMA*'s Robin Roberts was from the area. He figured Shepard Smith with Fox News, who was also from the Mississippi area, would be a great backup.

He didn't have to worry. The media coverage had paid off bigtime, and for a few months—not much more, it was D.C., after all—Senator Allen became a sort of hero given permission by the taxpayers to rubber-stamp whatever he saw necessary through the Appropriations Committee.

"I'm glad to hear that," Jason said. "Senator Allen simply tries to do the right thing."

Jason glanced again at Senator Allen, who was now looking out the window of the limo. His complexion was pasty with the exception of a red nose. The bags under his eyes seemed a bit more pronounced today. He had his suit jacket off and his signature red suspenders held up baggy trousers. Jason hadn't noticed the senator had lost weight. He was a small-framed man, wiry, with a nervous energy that Jason called passion. Other than the overindulgence in alcohol now and then he took care of his body. At the moment, however, Jason couldn't help thinking his boss looked like hell.

"We'd like to do an interview before the summit," Rosenthal explained. "This oil from chicken guts is fascinating stuff, just fascinating."

Jason could no longer contain his grin. This was great news. Exactly what they needed. Senator Allen noticed, setting his glass aside. He actually sat forward, elbows on his knees, waiting, looking anxious and sober.

"We can do a live satellite feed on Thursday's show with Senator Allen in Washington and Mr. Sidel in Tallahassee. I'll call with details tomorrow. How does that sound?"

"Perfect," Jason said, trying to keep the smile from sliding off his face. Why the hell did they have to include Sidel? "I'll look forward to your call tomorrow."

He flipped his phone shut. Senator Allen was waiting.

"Great news," Jason began, trying to figure out how to word it. "*Good Morning America* thinks thermal conversion is a fascinating idea."

Senator Allen started to smile just as Jason added, "They want to interview you and Sidel."

The smile immediately disappeared, and he stared at Jason as if he had heard him wrong.

Then finally Senator Allen slumped back and said, "Well, that's just fucking peachy."

43

At least Leon couldn't say his job was ever boring. He had worked his fill of crappy jobs, including construction one summer in Arizona. Son of a bitch! You wanna know what hell feels like? Go to fucking Tucson in August. One hundred and sixteen degrees. No shade. Everybody says it's a dry heat like that means something. Leon could still remember what it felt like after two or three hours in that scorching heat. At the time he swore he could smell his own skin baking, peeling back from the bone all red and crisp. It's just not natural.

No, he couldn't really complain. He traveled first-class, stayed in luxury hotels. He now had a stock portfolio worthy of any of those Wall Street big shots. Oh, and plenty of real estate. Leon liked the idea of owning land.

And Leon liked the idea of branching out, trying new things—bettering himself. He started reading mystery and suspense novels, mostly serial-killer ones 'cause those guys were really fucked up. He read Hiaasen and Evanovich, too, because they made him laugh out loud. He was trying to drink ale instead of beer and learn a thing or two about fine wines. Last year Leon had even taken up chess, at first sitting and watching the old men who played in the corner café a block up from Leon's little square house in Wallingford, Connecticut.

That was just one of Leon's houses. He owned a half dozen across the country in small, unpretentious cities like Wilmington, North Carolina; Terre Haute, Indiana; McCook, Nebraska and Paducah, Kentucky. Most of them he rented out, usually to little old ladies with a cat or two. Not like they'd ever run out and stiff him for the rent. And he never had to evict a single one…yet. Yeah, old ladies with cats were about as sure a bet as you could get.

No, it wasn't a bad life at all. A long way from where he'd come. His first paycheck at fifteen came from repairing and replacing roofs. Nothing worse than sitting your ass on hot asphalt in the summer heat. No, compared to that this life was pretty good. This job, this business afforded him not just luxuries but time. So he couldn't complain despite his current state of affairs, the string of unfortunate events. He decided that sounded much better than calling them bad luck or some fucking curse.

He pulled up to the guard hut. Before he punched in the pass code, one of the guards inside waved at him. They knew him by now. He wasn't sure he liked that even if they were led to believe he was some head honcho in the security department. He gave the guard a nod and drove on through.

He liked this SUV. Too bad he didn't have the son of a bitch four-wheel-drive V8 yesterday—he'd be on a flight home with the money in his bank account by now if he had been driving this machine. He shoved the previous owner's one-eyed teddy bear back under the seat and tried not to concentrate on what coulda, shoulda been if only he had given that lady scientist's car a better shove.

It only gave him heartburn. He didn't like being back here, either. Returning to the scene was also bad luck. Leon didn't need to be a rocket scientist or a fortune-teller to know that. But he'd been successful last time he was here and besides, he was told it would be all set up for him again. All neat and simple. Yeah, Leon thought, if it was so neat and simple, why the fuck didn't they do it themselves?

He parked in the far-corner lot, away from most of the park activity. He pulled out the map they'd sent to him. This place was like a fucking town of its own and there were too many catwalks and too many doors with security key card boxes. They must've given him a master code because he hadn't had a problem getting in anywhere...*yet.*

Leon turned the map around, trying to match whatever corner of the processing plant he could see from this angle of the parking lot. They had sent the map weeks ago before he arrived in Florida and at the time he had studied it over and over again. The thing was stained with remnants of his study sessions and he even recognized the hot mustard from pastrami on rye at Vinny's Deli. That was the first thing on his agenda when he got back home, stop in and see Vinny and the gang.

Damn! He hadn't had a decent sandwich since he got to Florida. Leon had always heard Florida was full of retired New Yorkers, but evidently not a single one of them thought to bring down a decent deli with them.

The mustard stain actually covered the entrance to the fucking room he needed to get into. He scraped off the dried mustard with a stubby fingernail. Yup, there it was, Reactor #5.

172

ALEXALEX KAVA

As Leon left the SUV he noticed the white pipeline that ran alongside the edge of the parking lot. The pipe was about six inches wide and it stretched all the way from the side of the building down around the parking lot and into the trees. On the map it went all the way to the river and was labeled Flash Off.

As he made his way through the rows of cars, he found himself glancing back at that pipeline and wondering how much of that guy he shoved into the chicken guts had ended up making his final trip out that pipeline.

44

EchoEnergy

The heat and humidity had returned full force as if making up for the weekend reprieve. Sabrina's linen shirt was already sticking to her as soon as she left the air-conditioned building. Though rarely without her lab jacket, she was grateful to have left it behind. She had snatched her security key card from the pocket and grabbed the rental-car keys, debating whether a quick drive to the back lot would attract less attention. Now, as she wiped the sweat from her forehead and pushed back her damp hair, she wished she had driven the car across the park.

She avoided the sidewalk along the plant where the last tanker trucks of the day hissed and rumbled while hoses emptied or filled them. Instead, Sabrina took a path through the landscaped courtyard between the large sprawl of corrugated-steel buildings and catwalks that made up the administration buildings and the processing plant.

The courtyard included benches, stone paths and a well-irrigated array of blooming landscape that had been Sidel's attempt to complete his small-town vision for the industrial park. But Sabrina had never seen any employees eating lunch or holding meetings as Sidel may have hoped. She suspected the courtyard was still too close to the noise and the smells—a combination of bio diesel fumes, and on the hottest of days, fried liver.

Lansik had told Sabrina that within the last year EchoEnergy had installed a million dollars' worth of equipment to tackle the odors after several ex-employees threatened to file lawsuits. At the time Lansik seemed annoyed by the complaints, telling Sabrina the odors were a nuisance but not a danger to anyone's health.

"If I knew there was a risk I would have taken measures immediately," Lansik had said, genuinely offended. The entire process, and thus the plant, had become for Lansik an extension of himself. It wasn't unusual. Sabrina had recognized the occupational hazard with her father every time he invented something.

Which gave Sabrina all the more reason to believe Lansik would never have allowed a mistake to go unchecked or uncorrected. Nor would he resign and leave without a word to his team. Sabrina knew that EchoEnergy's vision was as much Dwight Lansik's as it was William Sidel's. Maybe that was what bothered her so much. She wouldn't expect Sidel to share with them a falling-out that the two men may have had, but it didn't seem right that Sidel would be so nonchalant about it, either.

She left the courtyard and also left any hint of shade. No one dared to venture out in the afternoon heat so close to quitting time. It looked like Sabrina would have the whole parking lot to herself. Even security would be staying in their air-conditioned outposts.

She followed the pipeline along the concrete edge of the lot. The pipeline continued and disappeared into tall scrub grass and thick pine forest. Maybe she was being a bit ridiculous. She wasn't sure what she was expecting or even what she was willing to do. Her face and bare arms were slick with sweat and she could feel trickles sliding down her back. She glanced down at her leather flats, black trousers and white linen shirt. She had six identical outfits in her closet. She could spare to ruin one. Though in the back of her mind she could hear her mother's voice, scolding her for not taking better care of herself or her appearance. There were too many more important decisions to be made. And finding out why a clean-water pipeline had become clogged was one of those.

Except that her mother's memory distracted her. She was thinking of her mother more often the last several days, brought on, of course, by her father's hallucinations and her own car accident. Neither was a pleasant reminder. Remembering her mother's lecture about clothing was actually a welcome change.

Even if she wanted to, Sabrina could never duplicate her mother's fashion extravaganzas. For one thing she didn't have her mother's silky dark hair and dark brown eyes with a bronze complexion that certainly helped to make lime green and pink work well together. Eric had inherited their mother's looks and the charm that went along with them. Sabrina favored her father—fair skin, blue eyes and light-colored hair that couldn't really be called blond or brown. Even the way Sabrina wore her hair—carelessly down and straight with no attention to style—would cause her mother to shake her head and sigh. Once when she saw Sabrina getting ready for a run, pulling back her hair into a tight ponytail and plopping on a baseball cap, her mother almost refused to let her leave.

"You certainly can't go out in public like that," she had told Sabrina in her dramatic manner that gave meaning to too many things that should not justify such theatrics. But that was her mother and as if in tribute to the woman she missed with an ache that felt as physical as mental, Sabrina bent down to roll up her pant cuffs. She wasn't sure that it would save them from ruin, but she knew that to bother would please her mother.

Her leather flats were history. Sabrina was certain of that after only a few steps into the marshy scrub grass. She followed the pipeline, navigating carefully. She searched for the ninety-degree angle that shifted the pipe's flow directly down to the river. Not an easy search. Grass and vines had grown up around it so that only pieces of white showed through and it became like hunting for broken fragments. Sabrina checked the time. This was taking longer than she expected. She'd be late getting to Reactor #5 to meet Ernie Walker.

Finally she heard a gurgling sound. And before she saw where the pipe turned, Sabrina could see a puddle where the clogged elbow was leaking. She felt her stomach twist into knots. The puddle was a murky orange, not clear.

She pulled away vines, fallen twigs and pine needles, revealing the muddy elbow. Suddenly she didn't care about dirty pant cuffs or sludge on her hands. She pried and tugged at the release hatch, breaking a fingernail, but not stopping until she felt the metal trapdoor swing open. The spray made her jump back, but it was too late. Her white shirt blossomed with a rust-colored stain. She wiped at her face as she came back for a closer look, relieved to see that opening the latch had been enough to disengage the clog. Clear water now flowed out of the elbow and Sabrina used the heel of her hand to slam the latch against the force of the water. Her fingers were shaking when she secured the release lever.

Even at a glance the contents of the clog made her knees weak.

She found a stick to poke at the glob that glittered with chunks of metal embedded in pieces of what Sabrina could only imagine must be unprocessed feedstock.

Sidel was wrong. This looked like Grade 2 garbage. Sabrina fumbled through her trouser pockets, coming up with only an empty plastic sandwich bag from lunch. Using the stick, she scooped up a sample of the sludge into the bag. She stopped when she dislodged a disk of metal about the size of a quarter. There was no way Sidel could deny Grade 2 garbage when she showed him this. Sabrina shoved the metal disk into the bag.

She cleaned her hands on the grass and made her way back to the parking lot. She was a mess and she was late.

45

Leon watched from below the catwalk. Down under the massive pipes and valves the sound was deafening. Stuff clanked and hissed as machinery overhead turned on and off. It sounded like water spraying and shooting through the maze of twisting white pipes, some of them as small as Leon's arm, others big enough to swallow him whole. All of them snaked in from the walls. Most of them, especially the massive ones, were connected to the huge tank in the middle of the room.

This tank was different from the one outside—no floating chicken heads. That had freaked Leon out. All those bobbing chicken heads with their eyes wide open, witnessing him toss that poor sucker in. Maybe it wouldn't have bothered him so much, except for that stupid fortune-teller. She had him looking over his shoulder, scrutinizing stuff, examining it like it mattered. The same stuff he wouldn't ordinarily think twice about.

The place was a sauna. He could feel the steam and heat radiating off the pipes. He had gone through his packet of tissues waiting for her. Now a river of sweat ran down his back and sides. His shirt stuck to his skin. His forehead dripped. But he tried not to rush it this time. Being in a hurry had made him screw up twice. Instead, he stayed put and watched her up on the catwalk. He'd wait for her to settle down.

She looked different somehow, but Leon couldn't decide what it was. He had scoped out the place before she got here. No one else had been around in this entire area, not even in the hallways that ran along the upper floor, so he didn't have to worry about her bringing anyone along. As far as he could tell, there were only two doors into this place, the one behind him that led outside to the parking lot and the one she had used on the second level that connected the catwalk into a series of hallways that led to the rest of the plant.

She paced the length of the catwalk, shoving her hands into the lab coat and then taking them out to check her watch. She kept glancing at the door as if expecting someone to come through it.

Leon wiped the sweat from his eyes again. She appeared jumpier today, on edge, impatient, like she wanted to get this over with. Leon smiled, thinking, *You aren't the only one, lady.*

He started up the metal ladder on the back wall. He had already checked it out. An easy four-foot drop got him to a platform that was connected to the back end of the catwalk. She'd never see him coming. Leon reminded himself he didn't need to waste any energy trying to be quiet. No one could hear a damn thing in this place with all the clanging and hissing.

He'd brought along a two-foot length of galvanized pipe. He'd used it the last time. It felt good in his hand—just the lucky charm he needed.

Not that Leon was superstitious. He wished he could use a fucking .22 and get it over with. This accident crap was bullshit. He was much better with a simple double tap to the back of the skull, letting the bullet ricochet inside the skull. No mistakes with a .22.

He was still sweating like a son of a bitch, but he climbed up the ladder with ease despite that fucking ringing in his head and the throbbing beat of the clanging pipes.

He dropped onto the platform and stayed in a crouched position, hidden behind a square metal box that vibrated. She didn't turn around, didn't break her pace. He was safe. That metal box shimmied and rattled the catwalk enough that Leon's added weight didn't matter.

Leon caught his breath. Adjusted his grip on the pipe. This was almost too easy. Just like the last time they had brought his prey right to him. He could have saved himself a car trip clear out to that loony bin had he taken care of her here on Saturday. Stupid security guard got in the way. And then he freaked over Casino Rudy. After all, what were the chances of your botched hit being in the same loony bin that your next hit includes on her Sunday-afternoon drive?

He pulled himself up to his full height and began his stalk. He kept his eyes on her back. One slow step then another like an animal stalking its prey. Steady and focused, ready to attack. If she turned, he'd pounce and be there swinging before she had a chance to react.

She pulled her fingers through her hair and he knew she had no idea he was there. He almost wanted to call out to her, at least let her know what was coming. Then he reminded himself that she had survived his first attempt. He had already given her a second chance. He told himself he could be on a plane right now, headed home if it wasn't for this lady. He deserved a break.

Leon swung the pipe from right to left, smashing it into the side of her skull. Despite the machinery noise he thought he heard a distinctive crack. The blow was enough to send her flipping over the catwalk railing, her white lab coat making her look like a broken-winged bird. She splashed facedown and he waited for movement.

Nothing. Finally a dead hit.

He took in a generous gulp of hot, stagnant air. In seconds he could see blood from her head wound beginning to pool into the clear water. And just as Leon turned to leave, a red light started flashing above him. A screeching siren pierced through the hum and rattle and clanking noises.

Goddamn it! Something had tripped the fucking alarm.

He didn't remember sliding down the ladder, but his left knee would. He rushed through the same door he came in. Then made himself walk, not run, across the parking lot.

46

Sabrina ran, stumbling every time she looked over her shoulder. Was it possible he hadn't seen her? She knew she had screamed out loud when Anna Copello's body plunged into the tank. He had to have heard. Maybe because she was underneath the catwalk the noise of the engines and pumps had drowned out her scream.

She took a sharp left around the corner of the building, slamming her body against the corrugated steel. She stopped to catch her breath. And to listen. The hydraulics of tanker trucks hissed and whined. An air-conditioning unit hummed. The alarm siren could barely be heard outside. It wasn't necessary since the monitors in every security post would be flashing codes and location. They might not even hurry, Sabrina realized. After all, Reactor #5 wasn't online. And the code wasn't a breach of security. Sabrina knew exactly what had tripped the alarm. Lansik had installed alerts on every clean-water flushing tank so that when an oversized object fell in, an alarm would go off. Anna Copello's body definitely constituted an oversized object and had tripped the alarm.

Sabrina wedged herself between the building and a scrawny line of crepe myrtles. Her heart banged against her rib cage. She couldn't think. Instead, her mind sounded its own alarm, drumming over and over again. Why the hell was Anna even there? Did she really believe she could gain something by honing in on Sabrina's meeting with Ernie Walker? One thing was for certain, Anna could not have been the target. And that man, whoever he was, was not Ernie Walker, the plant manager.

Sabrina contemplated what to do, where to go. If the man realized his mistake, if he heard Sabrina's scream or saw her down below, would he check the lab? Would he find her office? Should she go to one of the security outposts? Would they even believe her? What would she tell them? She wasn't even sure what had happened.

She made her way along the side of the building until she could cross between the tanker trucks, using them for cover. One of the drivers waved her out of the way. She found relief in the organized chaos despite filling her aching lungs with diesel fumes. She continued to glance over her shoulder, suddenly aware that the noise would camouflage his following her. But he couldn't attack, not here, not out in the open.

She wanted to run again, but instead quickened her pace and wove her way under catwalks and behind tanks. Two men in hard hats looked up at her while they struggled with a lever on what Sabrina knew to be a shutoff valve. She checked their faces and wondered if she'd even recognize the man. That's when she realized she must look a mess, her shirt stained and clinging to her, her shoes and pant legs muddy.

She stayed away from the administration buildings, circling to the parking lot. Her fingers grasped and held on to the car keys in her trouser pocket. Her heartbeat throbbed in her head and she stepped to its rhythm, hoping it would keep her from panicking and running. She didn't need to think beyond getting across this parking lot and finding her rental car.

What the hell color was it? Why couldn't she remember?

Before the panic dismantled her, she saw the corner space where she always parked. Thank God for routine. Now all that was left was to get inside, start the engine and get the hell away from there.

47

Washington, D.C.

Natalie Richards poured herself a second glass of wine. She needed to sip, not gulp, this one. Her boss would certainly understand, but Natalie knew her own limits. She'd wait until after their phone call before she had a third. She checked her cell phone to make sure it was turned on, then she set it aside and dropped onto the sofa.

She had kicked off her shoes at the door and peeled out of her panty hose. The tension in her shoulders and at the pit of her stomach wouldn't leave, though she was determined to get both under control. This was the earliest she had gotten home in months and thankfully it was peaceful for a change. Her sons and ex-husband were somewhere in Michigan at a campground on a lake in the middle of nowhere. It was supposed to be a three-week vacation. She'd give them three days, maybe four, and they'd be begging and bargaining for a PlayStation or an Internet connection. As nice as the silence was, she missed them—all three of them.

Ron had offered to take the boys when Natalie thought she'd be accompanying her boss to the energy summit in Florida. "You go to Florida and treat yourself to a few extra days. You never do that," Ron had told her. "The boys and I have been talking about fishing with my dad for over two years. We'll just do it."

He'd say things like that and she forgot why she divorced the man, especially since Natalie knew how much of a sacrifice it was for Ron Richards to spend three weeks in the wilderness, no matter how much he loved his boys. And despite what Natalie told anyone, she had liked the idea of going to Florida and possibly tacking on a few extra days so she could enjoy an afternoon at the beach. The Reid Estate sounded like a paradise retreat, fifteen acres overlooking the Gulf of Mexico with a private coastline of sugar-white beach. But now for sure she'd be staying in Washington, D.C.

Her boss had called Zach Kensor's death "unfortunate" and "collateral damage." "Sometimes it takes sacrifice and loss for a greater cause," was another phrase. Natalie knew all that. It was exactly the sort of thing she had tried to use to reassure Colin Jernigan. It hadn't relieved Colin's guilt, nor would it relieve Natalie's. And for a man like Colin who had seen more crime scenes and collateral damage than Natalie watched on TV, guilt was a frivolous emotion and definitely one she didn't expect to see in him. Of course, all that guilt was before the fingerprint match. Either way it didn't really matter. It was a mess and it would be up to Natalie to figure out how to clean it up. And do it in forty-eight hours.

Her cell phone startled her. She jerked enough to spill merlot on her white carpet. She cursed under her breath and grabbed for the phone, sitting up and gathering her thoughts, then finally hitting Talk.

"This is Natalie," she said only because she knew her boss hated to ask.

"You're not gonna believe the size of the fish I caught."

It took Natalie a second or two before she sighed and sank back into the sofa.

"My baby boy caught a fish?" And she smiled at his groan. Oh, how he hated when she called him her baby boy, but he was and always would be.

Maybe it was only the wine that made her a bit teary-eyed as she listened to Tyrell tell his fish story. She smiled at the excitement in his voice and suddenly she couldn't help wondering about Zach Kensor's mother.

She bit down on her lip and that was when she decided. Her boss would approve, of that she was certain. Yes, Natalie knew exactly what she was going to do in the next forty-eight hours. What she had to do.

48

EchoEnergy

William Sidel had almost escaped his office for a late round of golf when Van Dorn, his head of security, called. He was tempted to have his secretary tell the man he was already gone, but this was what he had hung around for, anxious and curious. He waved his secretary to take off for the day. It was after five.

"Hey, Van." Sidel used it like a nickname only because he could never remember the guy's first name.

"We've had an accident. A worker in one of the tanks."

That's what he liked about Van Dorn, quick and to the point.

Sidel was alone in his office. He allowed a smile, but kept his voice concerned. "What are you talking about? What kind of accident?"

Finally Dr. Galloway wouldn't be interfering. This close to the vote and to the energy summit, it was better this way. They couldn't take any chances.

"I've gone ahead and called the county sheriff's department."

Sidel's smile disappeared and he gripped the phone. "I'm not sure I understand," he said when he wanted to yell, *What the fuck did you do?* "I thought you said it was an accident?"

"Just following procedure, sir."

"Of course," Sidel said. He'd fire the bastard next week. "I have a previous engagement," Sidel continued, glad the golf clubs were already in his Beemer. "I trust you to handle things. Make sure I get a report in the morning."

"Yes, sir."

Sidel had barely hung up the phone when it started ringing again. He was going to ignore it then noticed it was his direct line.

"Sidel."

"We've got a problem."

"I just heard. I'm letting Van Dorn talk to the deputies. He called them, let him deal with them."

"We have a bigger problem than that."

"What are you talking about?" Sidel stood at his wall of glass, looking down as if he might be able to see what was going on.

"It's the wrong scientist."

"How is that possible?"

"Copello was jealous of Galloway. Maybe she thought she'd get a heads-up on what was going on."

"I thought scientists weren't supposed to get jealous." Sidel delivered the dig and let it hang there a second or two before he added, "It wasn't supposed to be this complicated. Was Galloway even there?"

"Yes, her security key card shows her entering and leaving the building through the rear door that goes directly to the outside."

Sidel hated silence in conversation, but this time he needed to shut up and wield it to his advantage.

"I'll take care of this."

"No," Sidel cut the caller off. "You had your chance. Now we'll play it my way."

He slammed the phone back on its cradle and yanked open his desk drawer. Under a spilled bag of peppermint candies he found his little black book. It was an insurance policy he added to on a regular basis, but used only in extreme circumstances. The pages were filled with private phone numbers and coded names so that only he knew who they belonged to. He easily found the first of the numbers he needed under LCS and punched it.

"Hello?"

"Lyle, it's William Sidel."

"Mr. Sidel, what can I do for you?"

"A couple of your deputies are on their way out here."

"I heard about that. Sounds like a god-awful accident."

"I wish it were an accident, Lyle, but it looks like you'll need to call out the boys from the State Patrol. One of my scientists just killed her coworker."

49

Sabrina must have relied on instinct. It was the only explanation since she certainly didn't remember the drive from EchoEnergy to her condo.

She parked the rental car in the garage, and once inside the condo, locked all the doors and pulled every blind and curtain. Several times she picked up the phone, pacing from room to room. She didn't know who to call. *The lab? The police? Daniel? Her father?*

Her mind was stuck in a loop, replaying Anna's body plunging into the flushing tank. Each time the arms flayed a little bit more, the white coat floating, soaring like a parachute that didn't open in time. Poor Anna.

She had to tell someone. She picked up the phone. The panic twisted a tight knot inside her chest. She had to sit down. She thought she might be having a heart attack. No, it was probably shock. She tried to concentrate on breathing. That the breaths came in gasps only panicked her more. There had been nothing in her life until now to prepare her for this.

The pain continued, a dull ache. Sabrina slipped from the chair to the floor, hugging her knees to her chest and closing her eyes. She knew too well that there were moments you remember all your life, moments that change things forever, that change you. Her mother's car accident had been one of those moments. At the time, Sabrina didn't think anything could hurt as bad. For days afterward her entire body had felt bruised and battered so much so that it physically hurt to get out of bed. The pain was replaced by a numbness, not much better but easier to ignore.

This pain, this panic felt like only the beginning and that made it almost more unbearable. She wasn't sure how long she sat there, staring at the wall, concentrating only on breathing. The room grew dim, but none of her timers had switched any lights on yet.

There was a knock on the window. Sabrina jerked up as if it had been a gunshot. Then frantically she scooted herself into a corner between the chair and a wall. How had he been able to find her so quickly? This time there would be no alarms, no escape. Her eyes darted around her in search of a weapon, but everything looked blurred. She hardly recognized the room.

She heard it again, a faint tap on glass, not a knock. At a window, not a door. Like he was teasing her in her own home— no, not her home. Chicago was home. This place was supposed to be temporary.

"Sabrina, dear," came a whisper accompanied by another tap. At first she thought she was hearing things. *Her mother's voice? Was she that far gone? Had she gone over the edge just like her father? Did it run in the family?*

"Dear, are you in there?"

It was Miss Sadie. She could see the woman's small silhouette at the patio door, the last of the sunset pasting her shadow to the vertical blinds.

Sabrina used the wall to steady herself as she stood up. She felt a bit wobbly like she had had a couple glasses of wine. She was in shock, she kept telling herself. Funny how she could know and still not control it. Her chest still ached, that knot still tight and pressing against her lungs. She wanted to tell Miss Sadie to go away, that her hot toddy remedy wouldn't soothe this over. She'd need more than a couple bags of frozen vegetables. This wasn't a bruise that would go away in a few days. And yet Sabrina rushed to the patio, relieved to have someone.

Sabrina pulled the door open without pulling back the blinds. The hot humid air slapped her in the face. Before she could say a word, Miss Sadie's long, thin fingers wrapped around her wrist.

"Come on over to visit with Lizzie and me for a spell," she said, giving Sabrina's arm a tug.

Sabrina wanted to laugh. "A visit?" Even her voice sounded on the edge of hysteria.

"Come with me," Miss Sadie insisted, her voice as calm and soothing as ever. But then one look into the old woman's eyes and Sabrina realized that Miss Sadie already knew, just like last night.

50

Washington, D.C.

Lindy called before Jason left his office. She wanted to meet. Said they needed to talk. He suggested Wally's, thinking everyone went to Wally's. If someone noticed them together it'd be difficult to know whether it was planned or a coincidence. But as he walked through the door and saw her wave with an enthusiastic smile, he wanted to kick himself. Hell, what if she thought he was being romantic, suggesting the place where they'd first met?

That wasn't the worst of it. Lindy had chosen the exact booth where Jason and Senator Malone had exchanged what Jason classified as a hot game of mental foreplay. He was almost embarrassed that the memory triggered more of an immediate physical reaction than the memory of sex with Lindy.

She had a huge margarita in front of her, half of it already gone.

He slid into the booth opposite, not even settling into the corner when she said, "What? Not even a peck on the cheek?"

He stared at her. He hadn't even considered it. He'd always thought signs of affection like that were signs of possession. He wanted to say, *It was only one night.* Before he defended himself she let loose with another smile.

"I'm kidding," she said. "Really. You can unclench your jaw."

He attempted a smile, but he didn't think it was funny. He felt that he'd been summoned and he didn't like it. He wondered if women realized how much power they had over guys like him, guys who felt obligated every time they were given something of great value like sex...or trust. There were three things his uncle Louie used to say that a man can't live without: having someone trust him, taking pride in himself and getting laid.

"It's been a long day." He sighed and offered it as an explanation.

"That lunch wasn't much fun, was it?"

He nodded, but said nothing more. Jason was always careful what he said about work, even in jest. There were too many vultures waiting to report anything they could use—even out of context—and make it the next D.C. scandal. He worried that Lindy wasn't as careful.

She leaned forward. "I'm having a tough time with this Zach thing."

Okay, Jason thought. Her version of careful was substituting "thing" for murder.

"There's nothing we can do."

"You keep saying that." She said it like a slap.

Jason hadn't remembered ever saying it, maybe once. If this was what she thought they needed to talk about, he had no idea what to say. He almost wished it had been some relationship crap.

"I have to go to the police with what I know," she whispered this time, looking up at him through long eyelashes, reminding him of a little girl.

"Why do you think you need my permission?"

"We were both there."

He started to ask what being at the same hotel had to do with what she knew about Zach, but a waiter interrupted. "What can I get you?"

Jason saw Lindy slide back against the booth, her full lips pouting, only emphasizing his image of a girl.

"Jack and Coke," Jason told him, then watched him leave.

Jason looked around the tavern, searching for excuses not to give Lindy his eyes or his attention just yet. He noticed another celebration like the other night's, this one several tables away. There were balloons and flashes from a camera. It left him feeling hollow and ill prepared for a girlfriend who didn't really seem to want to be his girlfriend. A girl…a woman he barely knew but now would forever be connected to.

Finally he turned his attention back to Lindy. As he pulled out his wallet and laid a ten-dollar bill on the table, he said, "You do what you think is right."

Then he got up and left, acting more casually and less stressed than the first time she had fucked him.

51

Tallahassee, Florida

Sabrina had never been inside Miss Sadie's condo. The floor plan was exactly like Sabrina's, but Miss Sadie's home was decorated with colorful afghans and elegant, dark-wood antiques, framed oil paintings—original seascapes on canvas, some with fishing boats, others just the ocean—and a scattering of small charcoal drawings of ballerinas. Everything had a place, neat and clean and orderly even though the shelves and surfaces were full of exotic things, from tiny blown-glass animals to brass elephant bells and ceramic ginger jars, to leather-bound books and handcrafted African masks.

Sabrina found herself fascinated and charmed and momentarily distracted, but most of all she felt safe. It was a false sense of security. She knew that, but for the first time in hours she could breathe.

Miss Sadie had led her to the kitchen without stopping or slowing her pace, her fingers still gently wrapped around Sabrina's wrist. The old woman guided her to take a place at the small kitchen table where Sabrina could see dinner had been interrupted. Lizzie looked up at her from her corner by the back door, then continued her own dinner as if Sabrina's presence had become a routine distraction, nothing more.

"We have supper every evening while we watch the six o'clock news," Miss Sadie said, pointing to the small TV tucked under the cabinet. She poured a glass of water from a jug on the counter and set the glass in front of Sabrina.

Sabrina half listened and sipped the water only because Miss Sadie made a motion for her to do so. The pain in her chest had eased a bit. So had the banging in her head. But now exhaustion swept over her, making it an effort just to lift the glass to her lips.

Suddenly Miss Sadie scurried across the kitchen, grabbing and putting on a pair of reading glasses while she pushed at buttons on the TV, stopping when she filled the room with the local news anchor's singsong voice.

"Here's more," Miss Sadie said, waving her hand, the palm open, reminding Sabrina of a TV game-show hostess telling her what she'd won.

Sabrina jolted, sitting up straight. She grabbed the edge of the table to steady herself as she stared at a photo of herself on the TV screen. The photo was three years old, taken from a science journal that had published one of her articles. She was so startled she missed the news anchor's words, tuning in to hear only the last part…"for now calling her a person of interest in connection to the murder."

Sabrina's eyes found Miss Sadie's. "They think I did it?" She couldn't believe it. She had to have misunderstood.

Instead of asking for an explanation, the old woman turned down the TV's volume and sat in the chair across from her. She took both of Sabrina's hands in hers.

"We need to get you away from here, dear. And we don't have much time."

52

Leon had chosen a table in the corner of the airport café where he could watch the local TV news. His flight didn't leave for three hours but he considered himself lucky that there was even another one. He ordered a cheeseburger with extra onions and home fries. Then told the waitress to bring him a slice of key lime pie when she brought the burger. No way he was leaving Florida without a piece, especially since his last meal was so rudely interrupted.

Leon sipped his Samuel Adams from the long-neck bottle, having shoved aside the frosty mug the waitress served him. She'd offered it up like it was something special. Wasn't her fault. Young girls these days didn't know what was sissy. Hell, they put up with guys drinking stuff called "hard lemonade."

She brought him dinner and Leon was pleased. The home fries looked like they might actually be homemade. He covered them with salt and ketchup until they were almost swimming. Before he took a bite of the burger or one fry, he scooped up a mouthful of key lime pie. Not the best he'd tasted, but by this time damn near close. Leon had spent half his life disconnecting himself from his southern roots except when it came to food. Oh, he loved it all—Chicago dogs and New York delis—who didn't love that stuff? But he couldn't be in the South for long without craving hot-boiled peanuts and cheese grits, sweet tea and fresh, hot, pan-baked corn bread. He should have his fill 'cause this would be his last trip south for a while.

He filled his mouth and could barely hear the TV's volume over his chewing. It had NEWS ALERT in the corner. They flashed pictures of the processing plant and Leon stopped with a wad in his cheek, trying to listen to the report. They were calling it an accident. No shit, Leon thought, allowing himself to chew and swallow. That fucking alarm almost gave him a heart attack. They easily coulda had two "accidents" on their hands. It still pissed him off that he wasn't told about the alarm.

Leon took another bite, wiping off strings of onion and ketchup with the back of his hand. Just as he took a swig of beer to wash it down they showed a picture of the victim, Dr. Sabrina Galloway. Only they weren't calling her a victim. He stopped again in midswallow, trying hard not to choke.

"...wanted for questioning in the death of her coworker. That coworker's name is being withheld pending notification of the family. A reliable source has told News Watch 7 that when the victim was found she was wearing Dr. Sabrina Galloway's lab coat and name badge. No information is being released, however, as to what may have happened to cause such an accident. Again, police are calling Dr. Galloway a person of interest for the time being. Anyone who sees her should contact police at the number on the screen."

By the time the newscaster got to explaining what and where EchoEnergy was, Leon had shoved back from his half-eaten dinner and was popping antacids.

53

"I saw it happen," Sabrina said. "As soon as I explain it to the police I'm sure they'll see there's been a misunderstanding."

Miss Sadie nodded and listened while her small frame glided around the kitchen, cleaning up any remnants of supper.

"I knew I would need to call the police." But even as she spoke the words Sabrina wasn't sure why that alternative didn't feel right. Only now did she notice the small cooler on the counter that the old woman passed by, slowing to put things inside but never breaking her stride.

"Seems to me the po-lice should be calling you a witness, not a person of interest," Miss Sadie said as she continued her constant motion, wiping, washing, wrapping and nodding. She had done the same thing all the while Sabrina described what she had seen take place in Reactor #5.

Sabrina was exhausted, but the effects of the shock were slowly fading. Now the questions came, although none of them concerned her story or whether she was guilty.

"Do you have anyone away from here who you can stay with for a few days?" Miss Sadie's voice remained low, calm and soothing as if she hadn't heard Sabrina's tale of murder.

"I…I, ah, have friends in Chicago." She hesitated, but Miss Sadie shook her head.

"That would be the *first* place they'd look." The old woman began gathering the makings of a sandwich on the counter, pulling out mayonnaise, bread, deli-sliced wrapped ham and cheese and a jar of pickles. Sabrina didn't ask though it seemed odd; she had just cleaned up from supper.

"But eventually won't the police find me no matter where I go?" Sabrina asked, her eyes riveted to Miss Sadie's precise swipes and layering, the making of sandwiches no different than creating a work of art.

"I don't mean the po-lice," she said, looking over the wire-rimmed glasses at the end of her nose. She had even stopped in midspread of the mayonnaise.

It hadn't occurred to Sabrina until that moment that Miss Sadie was right. The police were searching for her, but someone else wanted her dead.

She tried to remember what the man looked like. From below she hadn't been able to see his face. He had on plain navy-blue trousers and a white short-sleeved shirt almost blending in with the white pipes and steel-blue gears and valves and metal grates.

"What about your brother?" Miss Sadie asked, jerking Sabrina's head and attention back to the kitchen.

She tried to remember what she had told Miss Sadie about Eric. Had she told her anything at all?

"My dad said Eric was living on Pensacola Beach. But I'm not sure where he is. The last I knew he was living somewhere in the Northeast, New York or Connecticut."

Miss Sadie cocked her head, a look of confusion, but she waited for an answer rather than ask any questions.

Sabrina leaned her head back against the chair and closed her eyes. Launching into the whole story seemed too exhausting, so instead she said, "Eric hasn't been in touch with me or my dad since my mom's funeral. I think my dad wanted so badly to see Eric he hallucinated him visiting."

When she opened her eyes, Miss Sadie was still watching her, studying her. Maybe, Sabrina thought, she was trying to figure out what the hell to do with her.

"It's been my experience," the old woman finally said, "that there's an awful lot of truth in every lie. Maybe that's also true of hallucinations."

She wrapped the sandwiches using wax paper and slipped them into an empty plastic bread bag, then put them inside the cooler. She added cans of cat food to a brown paper sack that Sabrina only now noticed sat next to the cooler on the counter. The woman was back at the refrigerator, pulling out a plastic container from the freezer. Sabrina couldn't imagine what more she thought was needed.

Miss Sadie plucked out of the container something wrapped in foil and began peeling it open. Sabrina's eyes widened at the contents, a three- to four-inch stack of bills. Miss Sadie handled it like a deck of cards, counting off a layer of twenty- and fifty-dollar bills, then rewrapping the rest in the foil, snapping it into the plastic container—with a label on the lid that Sabrina could now read—PORK CHOPS—and returning it to the freezer.

When she noticed Sabrina's look of surprise she said, "My previous employer was very generous to me. When she passed..." She lowered her head with respect and continued, "God bless Miss Emilie's soul." She looked back at Sabrina. "She left a third of her estate to me. I'm a logical woman and I've invested well, but I just don't trust banks with all of it. This here's my little personal stash for a rainy day. My own savings vault." She patted the freezer door.

Then just as matter-of-fact as ever, she turned to Sabrina and said, "I think we should take a drive over to Pensacola Beach."

54

Tallahassee Regional Airport

Abda Hassar arrived at the airport first. Though the other two weren't with him he had dressed according to Qasim's detailed instructions. Now, as he walked through the crowds of tourists and business travelers, he was grateful for his young friend's attention to popular culture. No one appeared to notice Abda. Though he felt ridiculous carrying a leather briefcase while wearing cargo shorts, sandals and what Qasim had called a Tommy Bahama shirt, amazingly he blended right in.

As much as Abda hated to admit it, Qasim had been correct about the gold rings, too. He had insisted all three of them buy and wear simple gold wedding bands.

"Married men, family men," Qasim told them, "are looked at with less suspicion. They will treat us differently if they believe we have families. They will think we are less likely to do something reckless like blow ourselves up for the promise of virgins in the afterlife."

Abda despised any comparisons to what he considered religious zealots who knew nothing of national pride, who cared little about a greater good beyond their selfish desires. He despised the comparisons, but he also wasn't surprised that Qasim was right again. Back at Reagan National, Abda had caught an airport security officer glancing at his fake wedding ring right before he waved Abda through the security checkpoint without pulling him aside for a more thorough search. Small details, but Abda knew each one could be the difference between success and failure.

He bought a drink and a sandwich and found a table by the window of the airport restaurant. He glanced at his watch as he pulled out his laptop. Qasim's flight from Dallas would be in shortly. Khaled's flight from Baltimore would be another hour. He would wait for them as planned. Three Middle Eastern men flying together raised eyebrows. Three Middle Eastern men eating together at an airport restaurant was much less interesting.

Abda turned on his computer and plugged in the small jump drive he had kept separate in one of the many pockets of his cargo shorts. If airport security had confiscated his computer, at least they would not have gotten his files. Now he accessed the file folder named CatServ.

The week before, the young, blond-haired man had left an envelope on the backseat of his cab. That envelope had contained what looked like three ID badges but was in fact worth more than gold. They were for three employees of JVC's Emerald Coast Catering. There were no photos on the badges. There was no need because there was something better. Each badge had a computer bar code printed across the bottom in special ink that according to Khaled was similar to other government documents that made them almost impossible to duplicate. Which also meant, again according to Khaled, that each employee had already passed a security background check.

Abda clicked through the file folder until he found the one he wanted, a page he had downloaded from the Web site for JVC's Emerald Coast Catering. All he needed was to see their employees' uniforms. He already had three free passes to the energy summit's reception banquet. Now he just needed to see what to wear.

55

Tallahassee

The car reminded Sabrina of a tank, huge and army green, though Miss Sadie called it Shenandoah green. Sabrina had never seen the old woman drive. Come to think of it, Sabrina hadn't seen her do much of anything but putter around her patio garden. She had no idea the car existed, stashed inside Miss Sadie's garage under a cover.

She packed the trunk with the few things she'd managed to gather in the small amount of time they decided they had. Sabrina estimated they had an hour at best before either the police or the man trying to kill her found her condo.

The car's trunk was enormous and deep. So was the backseat where Miss Sadie spread out her colorful afghans and threw in three plastic garbage bags she had filled with sweaters and blankets. She explained to Sabrina that she could hide under the afghan and if they were stopped, the police would simply think she had old bundles of clothes. It was as though Miss Sadie eluded the police on a regular basis. The whole time she was saying it her voice remained calm and soothing. She made it seem as though they were packing for a summer vacation instead of a last-minute escape.

Lizzie shared the front seat with Miss Sadie and the cooler. The old woman could barely see over the steering wheel though Sabrina had noticed pillows already in place, one for Miss Sadie and one for the cat. From the way Lizzie settled into her spot—the huge white cat curled up into the passenger seat—Sabrina knew the two of them had taken many trips together.

The air inside the car was suffocating even with the windows rolled down. There was no air-conditioning, no radio, but the pristine seats smelled like new and the engine turned over immediately.

"Miss Emilie's husband bought her this car, brand new in 1947 even though she didn't like to drive," Miss Sadie told Sabrina, without looking back at her. Both hands were on the wheel, and she raised her voice so she could be heard over the engine's hum and the wind through the windows.

"I went to work for Miss Emilie when I was twenty-two years old. Several years later her husband's fighter plane went missing shortly after the beginning of the Korean War. She didn't drive this car much after that but she'd never part with it. Made me promise I'd never sell it, either."

Miss Sadie's eyes met Sabrina's in the rearview mirror. "I took good care of Miss Emilie and her girls. Three beautiful girls, all accomplished, successful women now. They still visit with me from time to time, less and less now that their momma's been gone. Yes, I took good care of Miss Emilie for forty years and in turn, she made sure I was taken care of."

Sabrina had never heard the old woman talk much about her past. And Sabrina had never asked how she had been able to provide so well for herself. She knew Miss Sadie hadn't married and had no children. Now Sabrina realized why. She had spent a lifetime taking care of another family and in that brief explanation Sabrina thought she could see absolutely no regret in Miss Sadie's eyes. It had been more than a job. That was easy to see. Miss Emilie had not only been Miss Sadie's employer, she had been her family.

Maybe that was what had brought them together. They were two women looking to replace the families they missed. It also helped explain why Miss Sadie was used to taking charge and taking care.

Sabrina had seen signs for Pensacola on Interstate 10, but Miss Sadie evidently wasn't planning on taking the interstate. Sabrina didn't recognize any of the surroundings, not that she expected to, but as soon as they started putting miles between themselves and the city, the darkness of the countryside renewed her sense of panic. Panic and also guilt for involving Miss Sadie. She still wasn't sure what or who she was running from. Or whether running was even the safest decision.

Suddenly, Sabrina felt the car slow down. She saw flashing blue and red lights up ahead just as Miss Sadie started rolling up her window. Even Lizzie left her perch and jumped on top of the cooler that sat between her and her owner, tail swishing from side to side.

"Is it a roadblock?" Sabrina asked, already convinced that the police were stopping traffic, searching for her.

"I don't believe so," Miss Sadie said in such a whisper Sabrina thought she might simply be humoring her.

Even though they could see an officer in the road, there was a long enough line of cars that Sabrina found herself wondering if they could just turn around and go back. How serious were the police? Would they send a cruiser after them? There was no way she could ask Miss Sadie to go on a high-speed chase. Miss Sadie with her ten o'clock–two o'clock grip on the steering wheel was having a hard enough time keeping to the speed limit.

As they crept closer and closer, Sabrina could see she was wrong. One car had crashed into another and a third lay on its side in the ditch. There was no search, no roadblock. But as they inched their way around, Miss Sadie following the gestures of the officer patrolling the road, Sabrina felt no sense of relief. Instead, her panic washed over her again. She thought about her car accident last night. For the first time she realized it was no accident.

56

Leon figured it'd be a waste of time, but he drove to the Galloway woman's condo anyway. He had trolled the airport, half expecting to see her there. As soon as the cops started moving in, Leon moved out.

Now a couple of blocks away from her condo he got distracted by a '47 Studebaker rolling through the intersection. He thought about following it just to check it out. It was a beaut.

Two State Patrol cars were parked in front of Galloway's condo. Leon drove by and pulled in to the driveway of the only house that wasn't lit up like some block party. Flashlights lit up Galloway's front yard. At least they wouldn't be tripping over any fucking cats like he had the other night. Looked to Leon like there were three of them, but none of them were breaking down the door. They probably didn't have enough for an arrest warrant.

So where the hell was Sabrina Galloway? And what the hell went wrong? Why wasn't she there on the fucking catwalk?

The State Patrol hadn't paid any attention to him, so he backed out of the neighbor's driveway and headed back toward Tallahassee. A few blocks away he pulled in to a convenience-store parking lot. He'd been so pissed off at the airport that he wound up stealing a cheap-ass Taurus left in long-term parking with less than a quarter of a tank of gas.

Leon filled up and paid with a credit card the asshole owner left in the glove compartment. That's when it occurred to him that he knew something the State Patrol probably didn't...*yet*. If anyone had an idea where the hell Galloway had taken off to, it'd be her father. Sane or loony, Leon figured he knew a thing or two about getting someone to tell him what he wanted to know.

He'd make the trip first thing in the morning. For now he'd find an expensive hotel and order some room service, maybe a Pay-Per-View movie, too. No sense wasting a perfectly good credit card.

57

Exhaustion and the steady rumble of the Studebaker's engine made it difficult for Sabrina to keep her eyes open. Miss Sadie insisted she lie back and get some sleep, that she was wide awake and perfectly fine driving at night, so Sabrina tried to doze while her subconscious skittered over the events of the past few days. It was like miniature film clips, from memory to reality to imagination. Soon all three would be indistinguishable from one another.

She heard music and for a moment thought she had been mistaken about the car not having a radio until she realized it was Miss Sadie humming. The melody was familiar and soothing, as comforting as a mother's fingers caressing her forehead, petting her hair. She gave in and lay down across the backseat. The afghan smelled good, clothesline fresh, reminding Sabrina of her mother's attempt to dry clothes on their balcony, ten stories above Chicago traffic, waving against the skyline. At thirteen, Sabrina was horrified to come home from school and find that her mother had hung out their underwear for the world to see. "But they'll smell so good," she told Sabrina. The next month her father had found them a cute little house in the suburbs with a backyard big enough for a garden and a clothesline— hidden from view. Sabrina wondered if her father had been equally embarrassed about his Jockeys flapping over the city streets.

She startled at the reminder of her father and fought her way back to consciousness. She sat up so suddenly she even startled Miss Sadie.

"Are you okay, dear?"

"I was just thinking about my dad," she said and Miss Sadie nodded.

Sabrina wiped the sleep out of her eyes. Her hair stuck to her forehead and the back of her neck. She rolled down the back window and she could smell the saltwater. Somewhere beyond the black night was the Gulf Coast.

"We'll need to stop for gasoline," Miss Sadie said softly. "It'll be all right. No one's followed us."

Sabrina spun to look behind them. Most of the cars had passed them since Miss Sadie seemed determined not to exceed the speed limit. Sabrina saw only small beads of headlights in the distance. She hadn't even thought of being followed. But if her car accident had not been an accident, then she had certainly been followed from Chattahoochee. Which made her think of her father again. If they were capable of driving her off the road and shoving her into a water tank, were they capable of hurting her father?

"You haven't eaten, dear. Would you like a sandwich?"

"No, thank you." Sabrina scooted up so she could put her arms on the seat back, behind Miss Sadie, close enough to smell the lemon rinse she knew the old woman used on her hair.

"I should call my dad...or the hospital."

Miss Sadie looked up at her in the rearview mirror, eyes meeting eyes. "You're worried they might hurt him?"

"In order to find me, yes." Sabrina hesitated, not wanting to say it out loud, like somehow that would make it real. "My car accident yesterday…"

"Wasn't an accident," Miss Sadie finished for her.

They rode in silence, staring out the windshield. With her arms leaning on the front seat, Sabrina rested her chin there, too. With every oncoming flash of headlights she tried to catch a glimpse of Miss Sadie's face, hoping to read her thoughts. The old woman's face remained expressionless, eyes straight ahead, focused only on the road. Sabrina knew the shock and emotion had exhausted her ability to rationalize. But maybe she was depending too much on the solid and wise counsel of her friend. She was, after all, an eighty-one-year-old woman.

What seemed like minutes later, Miss Sadie finally said, "Your daddy would want you to be safe. You're no good to him walking into a trap. And going to him or contacting him right now might be just that."

58

Tuesday, June 13
Pensacola Beach, Florida

The sun was just coming up when Eric Galloway made his way back to his apartment. He took the long way around the marina though he was tired. Most everyone was still in bed, which made it one of his favorite times of the day. No traffic. No car horns. No giggling teenage girls or their show-off counterparts. The beach remained quiet except for the crashing waves and the screech of the feeding seagulls, just the way Eric figured it should be.

Eric had grown up in Chicago alongside Lake Michigan, so he was used to having seagulls, beaches and boats around him. But in Chicago you tucked it all away for the winter. Here, it was a way of life. He could get used to this life. Funny, he didn't think he'd ever say that about any one place, blaming his restless soul and his sense of adventure.

He had his deck shoes in his hand, preferring to enjoy the white sand between his toes. At this time of the morning it was still cool. He avoided looking in the distance where too many steel cranes and wrecking balls hovered over storm-damaged businesses and homes. Several years had passed, and yet roofs were still covered in blue tarps and sand stood ceiling high in many of the homes. Too many owners weren't quite ready to repair and remodel in time for yet another season that might be disastrous.

Eric's boss, Howard, liked to remind people that Pensacola Beach was just a barrier island, possibly formed years ago by hurricanes shifting sand and shorelines around. Howard, the philosopher, would often say, "That which had created the barrier island was continuously threatening to destroy it."

Eric hadn't been around for Hurricanes Ivan or Dennis, but he sat patiently in awe and listened to the stories, feeling a bit like a war correspondent trying to empathize and take it all in, but never really being able to know the fear, the hardship and loss of those who actually experienced them. He'd heard of looting on the beach. And owners not being able to get to their homes for months. He'd also heard about the goodness of neighbors, coming together from every-where to cut down trees, clear roads, remove piers out of front yards and pull boats from living rooms.

The true-and-tried locals, who had been on the beach for the long haul, had claimed the storms brought a lot of strange characters onto their barrier island, most of them either cleanup workers or con-struction crews, but also some real con artists. Little did the locals know Eric probably fit into that last category. Come to think of it, most of the people he'd become friends with since he arrived on Pen-sacola Beach probably fit into that category.

Eric watched the sky light up over the bay toward Gulf Breeze. It looked like only the regulars were out on the water, the working stiffs. Howard was expecting some friends from Miami, although the way Howard said it, it didn't sound as though they were really his friends. Seemed he had no idea how many days it would take them to come up the coast. He'd asked Eric to keep an eye out for their arrival, but when Eric asked what to look for, Howard just shrugged and said, "You'll definitely know them when you see them."

He liked Howard. He hadn't been prepared to. He really didn't want to. He was used to having bosses who threw around their authority, who seemed to enjoy telling others what to do. That definitely wasn't Howard's style. He still possessed the laid-back attitude of the surfer boy he had been years ago. He seemed content, having made his fortune and now enjoying it in a simple, genuine way that included working when he wanted and closing shop when he felt like it. Eric looked for a temper, figuring every Vietnam vet had to have one brewing somewhere even deep beneath the surface, but he never saw it. Not even close. Sometimes Eric wished Howard would push him around. It'd probably make what he was really doing here a lot easier.

Eric heard the noise before he realized what it was. The scrape and clop came from around back of Howard's Deep-Sea Fishing Shop. On the water side was a boardwalk with a half-dozen small bistro tables and chairs that separated Howard's shop from the boat slips. There was an adjoining oyster bar and around the corner was a set of narrow stairs leading to Eric's second-floor studio apartment. The only thing next to it was the fenced-off Dumpster area and that's where the noise was coming from.

He saw the yellow-gloved fingers hanging over the top of the Dumpster, someone gripping the edge from inside. Now Eric could hear the shoving and flipping of garbage being moved against the metal. The top of a shaved head popped up and just as quickly went back down. Another yellow-rubber-gloved hand came up. The metal screeched a bit from the extra weight climbing up over the side, and Eric could hear the scrape and clop of feet trying to get traction as the hands pulled.

The young man lifted himself until he could fold over the side, allowing his stomach to hang on as he swung one leg over, straddled the Dumpster edge like a gymnast on the vault. He swung the other leg over and made a professional dismount, unencumbered by the black hip boots. He took his yellow gloves off, pushed his goggles to the top of his head and pulled off the air filter from his nose, letting it hang by its rubber band around his neck. Other than the strange gear and the bright yellow rubber gloves—the kind for dishwashing, not surgery— the man looked like a college kid. He started going through the deep pockets of his cargo pants before he even noticed he wasn't alone.

"Oh, hey, Eric."

"How's it going, Russ?"

"I struck gold." He smiled at Eric and showed him a wad of what looked like wet and stained unopened envelopes. "Real gold." He pointed to the streaked preprinted envelope. "Preferred card holder," he read it to Eric. "You know what this means."

And Eric did. He knew it meant there were preprinted bank checks with the credit-card holder's account numbers all ready and waiting to be filled in and the signature forged. He knew this only because Russ had educated him. The kid made a science out of Dumpster diving. It was supposed to be a hobby.

Eric knew Russ had served some time for identity theft. But nobody ever questioned Russ, at least not among the group that hung out at Bobbye's Oyster Bar. They were a select group that had gravitated to each other because of their past indiscretions. A little credit-card fraud seemed minor when any one of the others could easily toss up much greater sins. And that included Eric.

59

Washington, D.C.

Jason turned on the TV as he finished dressing. He'd decided to go for a run this morning instead of getting to work early. Usually he ran in the evenings, but lately he'd been staying at the office. He didn't mind. He liked his job, but his job was consuming his life.

Jason stopped in the middle of knotting his tie and glanced around the small studio apartment. Who was he kidding? The job had become his life. He couldn't remember the last time he'd stopped at theY for a game of pickup basketball. He quit going out with coworkers for drinks or pizza when he became chief of staff. Even his buddies from his messenger days had written him off as soon as he moved up to the big office with a secretary and an expense account. No, that wasn't right. It was Jason who had put the chill on them, only because that's what was expected.

He flipped TV channels, looking for anything more on Zach's

murder. He left it on ABC and *Good Morning America* while he checked the newspapers. Earlier when he was getting back from his run he'd bought copies of the *Post* and the *Times*. He sipped orange juice straight from the gallon container and searched headlines. How could a member of a congressman's staff be murdered in a D.C. hotel room and not make the front page? Maybe it wasn't a big deal. Or maybe someone was working to keep it out of the headlines.

He wondered what, if anything, Lindy had told Senator Malone about being at the hotel, about being with him. It didn't matter. It shouldn't matter. Christ! He just realized it did matter what Senator Malone thought of him.

He emptied the orange-juice container in two final gulps and tossed it in the trash can under the sink. That's when a voice on television stopped him dead in his tracks.

He made his way to the TV, grabbing the remote and punching up the volume. The whole time he looked for signs that it could be film clips from something previously recorded. But no, it was live, today, happening right now. On *Good Morning America* via a live satellite feed, Robin Roberts was interviewing William Sidel.

60

Pensacola Beach, Florida

Sabrina didn't think sleep was possible. She had had problems ever since she moved to Florida. When sleep came it came in restless fits, an hour or two of dreams. And even her dreams exhausted her. In them, she constantly packed for trips she hadn't planned or she kept getting dressed for an appointment she was already late for.

Sometimes her mother came to her, inviting Sabrina into a house Sabrina didn't recognize. Her mother stood in the doorway, waving to her, smiling, but when she turned, Sabrina could see the side of her face still mangled from the car accident. It woke her every time, sometimes with a gasp, sometimes with tears. The tears always surprised her because she hadn't cried about her mother while awake. She hadn't allowed herself.

This sleep was different. Light, almost weightless, she floated on a breeze of ocean mist. She felt relaxed. She felt safe. She could smell the saltwater with a combination of coffee and bacon. She thought she heard seagulls...and singing. Her eyelids were too heavy to open. She didn't want to leave this place. Somewhere on the other side was a man with a baseball bat, his shirtsleeves rolled up, the bat slung over his shoulder ready and waiting. Then suddenly she saw Anna, a white parachute billowing out as she plunged and fell right on top of Dwight Lansik in a tank of chicken guts.

Sabrina woke with such a jolt she felt the car move. Miss Sadie jumped, too. Even Lizzie gave a hiss. Sabrina woke them all from their respective places inside the Studebaker.

"Are you all right, dear?" Miss Sadie twisted up and around to get a good look at her, grabbing for her eyeglasses at the same time.

Sabrina could see several strands of hair had come loose from the old woman's meticulous bun, and the bags under her eyes were swollen from driving most of the night.

"Where are we?" Sabrina sat up slowly, taking in the surroundings of the parking lot.

"Pensacola Beach," Miss Sadie announced, pointing over the hood of the car at the colorful water tower across the street that looked like a giant green, blue, yellow and orange beach ball in the clear morning sky.

Beyond the water tower was the beach and water, lots of it, the emerald green waves of the gulf and the sand as white as sugar. Miss Sadie had pulled the Studebaker into a restaurant's empty parking lot. The sun was coming up in one direction and the moon still hung bright in the opposite sky, almost full. It was that time of day her mother used to call the moonraker hour, when she claimed the muses guided her hands over the clay or directed her paintbrush, depending on what medium she chose. Sabrina's dad used to laugh and say her mother was the only artist he knew who bothered to get up before noon. But her mother's obsession or compulsion—because Sabrina was certain her mother's love of drama would have insisted on calling it one or the other—had rubbed off on her. It was the time of day when Sabrina usually ran because she enjoyed watching the sky go from purple to blue. And it was the one time of morning when she could think without the noise of the day interrupting.

The restaurant looked closed, but Sabrina could smell fresh coffee and bacon coming from the vents on the side of the building. So she hadn't been dreaming entirely. The screeching seagulls were real, too.

The smell of coffee and sweet vinegar filled the car. Stronger now. It definitely wasn't just the restaurant vents. Sabrina leaned up against the front seat to find Miss Sadie rummaging through the cooler.

"You must be starving, dear," she said as she handed Sabrina a wax-papered sandwich that included the sweet pickles Sabrina could smell. She watched the old woman's arthritic fingers wrap around the stainless-steel thermos and pour a second cup of coffee. Then she took the offerings and sat back, trying to eat slowly when she wanted to gobble. A sandwich had never tasted so good.

They sat separately, Miss Sadie and Lizzie in front, Sabrina in the back. They ate in silence, watching the first arrivals across the street on the beach.

"I don't know if he's even here," Sabrina finally said, realizing for the first time that she wanted him to be. "We may have come all this way for nothing."

"I wouldn't say that," Miss Sadie said without looking back at her. "I haven't been to the beach in a very long time."

61

Leon wasn't happy about returning to the Florida State Hospital. The place gave him the creeps. Didn't help matters that he knew Casino Rudy was here somewhere with a bullet lodged in his head, a bullet that so far, almost everyone thought he had put there himself. Last Leon heard, Rudy was conscious but talking out of his head about a janitor named Mick slipping into his Biloxi hotel room and popping him. Sounded like total nonsense to everybody...everybody except Leon. Who knew a plain gray jumpsuit with just the right name badge could save Leon's ass. At least for the time being. If he could figure out a plan, he'd take care of Casino Rudy while he was here, too. But with the way his luck was going, he knew better than to push things.

He still couldn't figure out what went wrong. Maybe the Galloway woman knew she was being set up. But it didn't make sense to Leon that she'd let her coworker take a fall for her. 'Course, Leon had worked with a few assholes he wouldn't mind seeing take a death plunge. Still, it nagged at him like a hangnail.

Whether she knew she was being set up didn't really matter. What did matter was that she had been there, according to his client, whom Leon had finally given in and talked to an hour ago. She was there someplace, hiding in that shitload of pipes and gears and noise.

His client told him Sabrina Galloway's security key card had been used at 4:06 p.m. to get in the same door that he had entered. It was information they had given to the State Patrol in order to put suspicions on her as the murderer. Leon didn't ask how they managed to explain his key card's entrance. They didn't seem concerned about it. The magic of computers, Leon figured. They could hand over whatever they wanted. Maybe they could even make his master key card entrance disappear. He didn't really care. What he cared about was that if Sabrina Galloway was there at 4:06, then she saw him.

His client had taken advantage of what he thought was an opportunity to make the best of a mistake. His client probably thought Leon should be grateful, like he was making Leon's job easier for him.

"In less than twenty-four hours there'll be an APB out for her. There won't be anywhere for her to hide."

What could Leon do? He'd screwed up, again. How could he complain about having cops all over the place looking for the same mark he was looking for?

At one point the client sounded as though he didn't mind if the State Patrol took her into custody, like that would be enough to solve his problem.

"Who's going to believe her?" he'd said. "Her version of the truth will never hold up now that she's a suspected murderer instead of a victim."

Cocky son of a bitch, Leon had thought, but said nothing. He hated this guy's type. Too much arrogance and too little common sense. Not that he was complaining. He made a decent living because assholes like this guy thought they should be able to control their own world, including all the schmucks that came into that world. The one thing these assholes didn't respect was that human nature was a fickle thing. It was something that Leon had even forgotten, and now he realized that more than luck, or more than some fortune-teller's curse, the simple unpredictability of human nature had probably caused his mistakes.

Take nothing for granted. There is no such thing as a coincidence. Look ahead and expect the unexpected. Figure out what's predictable, then do the exact opposite. He'd gotten lazy. Maybe even cocky. He needed to remind himself of the basics, follow the rules he had lived by and survived by. And that's why even though the client sounded content to let the police take care of Sabrina Galloway, Leon could not. His last and most important rule had always been cover your ass, no matter what it takes.

After all these years his face had never been seen by a mark, or at least, as in Casino Rudy's case, not by one who had and lived to speak about him. If Sabrina Galloway had seen him, he needed to take care of her before the State Patrol got to her.

62

Pensacola Beach, Florida

On the second drive-by, Sabrina agreed it wouldn't hurt to check it out. Her father had told her that Eric was living above a boathouse on Pensacola Beach and worked for a man named Howard Johnson. So here was a boathouse, a small business named Howard's Deep-Sea Fishing. The small shop included Bobbye's Oyster Bar on the side of the building. Miss Sadie parked the Studebaker in such a way that Sabrina could see small bistro tables on a boardwalk, positioned for a view of the charter boats coming and going from their slips in front of the building. On the other side there was even a set of steps leading to a second-floor apartment with a small deck and an old-fashioned red neon No Vacancy sign above the door.

Sabrina told herself not to get her hopes up. If Eric was here it would mean her father's mind was more lucid than she or his doctors believed it could be. She felt the familiar knot twist in her stomach and she wished she could call her dad to make sure he was all right. But how could she call to warn him when he probably wouldn't even recognize her voice?

Miss Sadie tidied herself up. She stretched her small frame over the steering wheel so she could get a close-up look in the rearview mirror. Sabrina watched the old woman poke and smooth crinkled strands of hair back into her meticulous bun. Before she replaced her glasses Sabrina noticed again the swollen bags under her eyes. She had to be exhausted and yet she was still calm and in charge, taking care of Sabrina as if...as if she were family.

She hadn't had anyone like Miss Sadie in a long time. Someone who only wanted what was best for her. Certainly not Daniel. Not even Eric. There hadn't been anyone since her mom died. Though her mom never really fussed over her, or tried to still take care of her after Sabrina became an adult. In fact, while most women had empty-nest syndrome, Sabrina's mother embraced her time alone and flourished. Especially when she immersed herself in her "marathons of creation," as she liked to call them. Between her mother's commissioned art projects and her father's mad-scientist inventions, it wasn't easy to get their attention. Or at least not for Sabrina. She was the independent one whose life was planned and plotted with timers and day planners to keep her on track. Sabrina's mother used to say her daughter had been twelve one day and thirty-three the next.

Eric on the other hand lived on the edge—whatever that meant. Sabrina often thought it was simply a way to make being irresponsible and undependable sound romantic. He had a law degree and had been a ski instructor, bartender, road-crew boss, insurance salesman, repo man, short-order cook, security guard and limousine driver, but never a lawyer. And that wasn't counting the last two years that they'd been out of touch.

But for as much discipline and consistency that Sabrina had gathered within and around her life, there were times—this one in particular—that she'd trade it all for just one ounce of Eric's street smarts.

Miss Sadie was waiting, watching her.

"Why don't I go in alone, dear." She petted Lizzie, who stretched and yawned, turning around and curling up for another nap. At the restaurant parking lot Miss Sadie had let the cat out of the car and Lizzie raced behind the building to find a bathroom sand pile. Sabrina didn't think they'd ever see the cat again when she disappeared between the building and a Dumpster. Even Miss Sadie looked ready to bolt from the car just as the white cat came slowly meandering back, discovering all too quickly, Sabrina imagined, what a big, dangerous world it was out there.

"Sabrina, dear?" She reached over the seat and took Sabrina's hand.

Only then did Sabrina realize she was shivering. It was probably eighty degrees in the car and she was shivering. What the hell was wrong with her?

"I'll be fine. I just need a few minutes."

"Why don't you stay here, dear. I'll be right back."

Before Sabrina could argue, Miss Sadie had left the car. Sabrina wanted to kick herself for feeling like a scared little girl. She watched the old black woman climb the steps to the boardwalk and she realized how very lucky she was to have her very own Merlin ready to provide and protect.

63

Eric turned down the sound on the TV that Howard kept behind the counter and insisted the channel stay on Fox News. It had nothing to do with politics. Howard didn't have any, or at least he kept them to himself. No, it had nothing to do with politics and everything to do with the pretty brunette who did the News Alerts. Howard had a huge crush on her, said she was the spitting image of Bobbye, the only woman he'd ever loved. Eric wasn't quite sure if seeing her every half hour was Howard's way of paying tribute to her or just some odd punishment, a daily reminder that he had let her get away. Either way, Eric didn't change the channel. Howard had few requests and no demands.

Eric minded the store while Howard took out that day's fishing customers. He was tired from being up all night, but he knew Howard wouldn't mind if he closed up for a few hours to get some sleep. It would be a late night again preparing oysters, grilling fish and serving drinks to the Texans. This was a group Eric didn't look forward to serving. And although Eric loved being on the water, he didn't envy his boss today.

The five businessmen from Dallas looked like executive desk jocks. One insisted on wearing his Stetson and fancy boots. Eric was betting the cocky cowboy with the big mouth and "shit wit" would be the first one to hurl those chocolate doughnuts he was hoovering down. Nothing more humbling than a guy hanging over the railing puking up everything down to those fancy boots. And there was nothing worse than motion sickness with no cure once they were in the gulf. Eric was willing to bet Mr. Chocolate-Doughnut Stetson would be a much different man when they returned.

Eric was on his knees stocking the front-counter shelves with impulse-buy items when something caught his attention on TV. The photograph in the corner of the screen looked like…no, it couldn't be. He scrambled to his feet to get a closer look and punch up the volume to hear the Fox News Alert as Howard's pretty news anchor came on.

"What was called an accident last night at EchoEnergy outside of Tallahassee, Florida, is now being considered a homicide by State Patrol investigators. This morning an arrest warrant was issued for Dr. Sabrina Galloway. Anyone with information on the whereabouts of Dr. Galloway is asked to call the number at the bottom of the screen. We'll have more on the hour."

Eric sat down on the bar stool behind the counter. It was ridiculous. It had to be a mistake. Sabrina couldn't kill anyone. She was the levelheaded one. He was the hothead.

Staring at the phone on the counter, he thought about who he could call. His mind raced through options, eliminating all of them quickly. Another time, another place and all he would have had to do was pick up the phone and make a couple of calls, call in some favors.

He was beating himself up when the bell above the entrance tinkled.

"Good morning," he said over his shoulder with no enthusiasm and without even looking around. He bent down to pick up the empty boxes he had left in front of the counter.

"Excuse me." A smooth, deep woman's voice came from directly behind him. "I wonder if you could tell me—" She stopped as he stood up and turned to look at her. She stared at him instead of continuing.

She was a small, old black woman, dressed very nicely in a purple shirt dress and carrying a black leather handbag—definitely not a typical customer at Howard's.

"Sure, what can I tell you?" He smiled, a bit unnerved that he seemed to have rendered her speechless. He felt her examining his face as if she had seen it somewhere before, as if she might know him from another place.

Finally she smiled back at him and said, "I think you may have already told me."

"Excuse me?"

"I can see the resemblance plain as day," she said. "You're Eric, aren't you?"

64

Leon parked the white Interstate Heating and Cooling van in the hospital's loading zone right in front so it could be seen from the reception desk. He figured he had an eight-hour shift before the company discovered it missing from their fleet in the parking lot back in Tallahassee. Even then, the last place they'd start looking would be Chattahoochee.

His gray jumpsuit fit a bit tighter through the chest, the result of too many burgers and bottles of Sam Adams since he popped Casino Rudy. He kept the same name badge, deciding it was not tempting fate, but instead going against human nature. After all, human nature would dictate doing the opposite, staying as far away as possible from duplicating a botched plan. Besides, he was pretty sure he looked more like a Mick than a Leon.

He grabbed the duffel bag, pleased that the clanking made it sound full of tools. When he walked through the automatic front doors, he remembered to lean just a little as if the weight of the bag strained him.

The receptionist had already noticed the van. He could tell from her tight-lipped pout that she was trying to decide whether or not to tell him he couldn't leave it there. Before she could make up her mind, Leon shot her a look of impatience as he passed her desk on the way to the locked security doors she controlled.

"Someone said there was a problem," he called over his shoulder.

"I don't have any record of that." Her voice was high-pitched as she flipped through several piles of memos, phone messages and written authorizations.

"I don't have all day," he told her, glancing at his watch. "If I don't check it now I won't be able to get back this way until tomorrow. I have four calls in line after this one."

He could see she was getting flustered. It would take too long to find out who'd made the request. Maybe she'd have to admit she overlooked it. And if she turned him away and there was a problem she could lose her job for making some poor patient—or worse, a doctor—wait until tomorrow when the temperature would be in the high nineties all week.

"You have to sign in," she finally said, pointing to a clipboard and pen in front of her.

Leon shook his head and stomped back to the desk. He made sure the duffel bag clanked out his impatience. He scribbled an indecipherable line of ink in the place she pointed to. But it seemed to satisfy her and she waved him on. This time he heard the click of the lock before he even reached the door.

Now inside, things were a little easier. Everybody who made it past the locked door surely belonged and knew where they were going. Leon ducked into a linen closet he'd found Sunday evening. He plucked off the name badge and slipped it into the duffel bag. Then he pulled out a lightweight cardigan and a pair of horn-rimmed glasses and put both on, shoving the sleeves of the cardigan up to his elbows. He dropped a pair of pliers into his pocket. Then he stuffed the duffel bag behind a pile of towels and headed back out.

Leon didn't spend much time on disguises. Why bother when it was this easy to go from repairman to visitor or resident of the loony bin?

65

Jason didn't believe him.

"Don't worry about it," Senator Allen said for a second time. "It's not that big a deal. There'll be other interviews." He paced behind his desk, arms crossed over his chest. Once in a while he rubbed at his jaw and Jason couldn't help thinking it looked like he was trying to rub away the sting of being sucker punched.

Jason sat in the leather guest chair on the opposite side of the desk. He had hoped to garner a separate interview for the senator before he found out. Who knew Senator Allen watched *GMA*? In fact, Jason had spent most of the morning trying to get in touch with Lester Rosenthal, the ABC producer. Though he wasn't sure what he'd say. He knew what he wanted to say: *Why the hell didn't you include Senator Allen?*

"Most of the interview was spent on questions about that murder. I almost felt bad for Sidel, trying to spin it like some terrorist plot to knock him out of competition." The senator shook his head to emphasize how pathetic he thought Sidel's effort was.

Jason kept it to himself that he believed it was far from pathetic. It was brilliant. Only Sidel could turn a catfight between two women scientists into a Middle Eastern terrorist plot to derail his chances at the upcoming military contract and his deserved spot at the energy summit. Yeah, it sounded farfetched, but Sidel made it convincing. There was a reason they called this guy "a wizard."

Jason watched Senator Allen continue to pace. He hated seeing him like this. He *had* lost weight. Jason could see that now. The senator's normally lean, athletic frame looked too angular. His cheeks and eyes seemed a bit sunken. Jason couldn't help noticing the contrast between the senator and the framed photos on the wall behind him. The photos displayed a vibrant, energetic statesman with his arm around leaders like President Putin or Hollywood celebrities like Tim Robbins and Susan Sarandon. Jason had never met a politician—and as a simple messenger he had gotten a behind-the-scenes look at too many of them—who couldn't make anyone, within minutes of an introduction, feel like he understood and could empathize with their agenda. And not just a Democratic agenda but Republican, as well.

Jason had grown up with few male role models in his life except his simpleminded but well-meaning uncle Louie or maybe Michael Jordan. Senator Allen had entrusted him with his entire office, his image, his reputation. That was huge. Jason, in turn, gave him his loyalty and respect. Now he wished there was something more he could do for the man.

The senator's desk phone rang, two short rings then silence. Jason recognized the signal from the senator's secretary that indicated he had a call he wouldn't want to miss.

Jason thought Senator Allen looked almost relieved—here was something to divert his attention.

"Yes," he answered. He glanced at Jason and raised his eyebrows. "Put him through," he told his secretary. A pause then a sarcastic greeting, "Well, speak of the devil."

Jason thought for sure he'd finally witness Senator Allen reading Sidel the riot act. But his greeting was the most the senator said for the next several minutes other than an "uh-huh" here and there. At one point he turned, giving Jason his back.

"I'll take care of it," he said and hung up.

Jason stayed quiet. He didn't dare risk a joke.

Senator Allen dropped into his leather swivel chair and leaned forward. His fingers started rearranging everything on his desk— piece by piece, a quarter inch—no more—to the right. Jason recognized the familiar gesture and waited for his boss to put his thoughts together, to calm himself. The whole time Jason kept thinking, *Why does he let that guy do this to him?*

As if the senator could hear Jason's question he looked up, leaving his elbows on his desk, his fingertips arched together, his hands creating a neat little tent that told Jason he was back in control. "It appears this woman, this scientist, does pose a threat. Sidel's worried she or her father might try to disrupt the energy summit."

"Has he alerted Homeland Security?"

Senator Allen put up his hands to slow Jason down.

"He doesn't want to cause undue alarm and I agree. I told him I'd take care of it." He hesitated, but only a second or two. "I need you to find out everything you can about her father, Arthur Galloway. Sidel seems to think the man could be very dangerous."

66

Pensacola Beach, Florida

"I don't see you for two years and all you can think about is changing me." Sabrina tried to joke more out of exhaustion and nerves than anything else.

Just minutes before she had watched Miss Sadie come out of the fishing shop with Eric behind her. It suddenly didn't matter how long ago she had seen him or even why. There was only relief.

He stared at her from the boardwalk as she stared back, not budging from the back of the Studebaker parked across the lot. Eric looked the same, maybe a bit leaner and his hair a lot shorter. She couldn't say she'd ever seen him in a pink polo shirt, but he looked good, tan and clean-shaven, healthy, strong.

He didn't waste any time, a trait that Sabrina knew had gotten him into as much trouble as it had saved him from it. On the boardwalk he leaned down to tell Miss Sadie something that made her nod and come rushing back to the car. Then they waited while Eric flipped the Open sign to Closed and locked the shop. They had followed him here, a small hair salon next to Paradise Wine and Liquor. Once inside, he had given her a long, silent hug, then taking her by the shoulders he led her to a chair and eased her down in it.

"Miss Sadie says you haven't gotten out of the car since you left Tallahassee?" Eric asked, his brows furrowed. He was more serious than she had ever seen him.

"Except to go to the ladies' room," Miss Sadie said before Sabrina could respond. "At a gas shop in Panama City."

"The best place to hide is in plain sight. How can we do that, Max?" he asked the woman whom Sabrina had not been formally introduced to but guessed owned the salon. "Short and blond?"

"It's not the police as much as the others," Miss Sadie said, and Sabrina was struck by how much she must have been able to tell Eric in a very short time.

She watched the three of them in the wall mirror in front of her. Max was in the middle with short and spiked red hair. She wore a black dog-collar choker, a formfitting black tank top and a black leather miniskirt with bright red flip-flops. There was a tattoo on her ankle and a gold toe ring on her middle toe, tiny studs all the way up one ear and only a small gold hoop in the other.

On Max's right stood Eric and on her left Miss Sadie, an odd three-some with nothing in common except the woman sitting in front of them and their challenge of what to do with her.

"Are they professionals?" Max asked Miss Sadie, who nodded. And Max nodded, too, as if that was all she needed to know.

Sabrina wanted to interject that she might know a little something about all of this, but she was more fascinated by their exchange. She was also exhausted. Who knew panic could drain a body and mind so completely?

"They'll be looking for her to go extreme," Max said with a glance at Eric.

"So, less is best?"

"Keep the same color," she said, running her fingers through Sabrina's hair. "Maybe a few highlights. We can cut it, but not real short. Bangs would be good. Different but not extreme."

"Okay," Eric agreed, making the decision without looking at Sabrina.

Would they even ask her before they started cutting and highlighting? It reminded her of being nine and going to the movies with Eric, who was twelve and thought he knew everything. Their mother always gave Eric the money and as keeper of the money he made all the decisions—deciding which movie, what size drinks, Milkduds or Junior Mints. When Sabrina protested he'd simply say, "Do you want to go to the movies or not?" She couldn't help wondering if she protested now would he say, "Do you want me to hide you or not?"

"She's awfully pale." Max had evidently moved on. "She'll stand out like a sore thumb on the beach. We'll use the spray-tan booth."

"Oh, that's a good idea," Miss Sadie said. "She's so fair skinned and she usually wears black and white. Very classy, but maybe some bright colors would be good. I always thought royal blue would bring out the color of your eyes, dear." And this time Miss Sadie's eyes met Sabrina's in the mirror as the old woman laid her hand on Sabrina's shoulder.

That small gesture seemed to make Eric realize he had been ignoring her. He came around in front of the chair, squatting down to eye level to get a good look at her.

"It's really good to see you, Bree," he finally said with a smile.

67

Leon could be a persuasive guy all on his own without what you might call any professional accessories. Oh, sure, he'd been known to get decent information with only a crescent wrench or a pair of pliers, which was exactly why he had a pair in his pocket, but he could also get people to tell him some of the most unusual things just by asking the right questions.

He found Arthur Galloway in the television room, sitting in the same recliner he was in the other day when his daughter visited. His hair stuck up in a couple of places, his shirt was wrinkled and he wore one white sock and one brown. For a minute Leon wondered if they hadn't bothered to move him since Sunday.

Leon had bought a couple candy bars from the vending machine and now he set one on the tray table in front of Arthur Galloway as he sat down next to him. He had seen the daughter do this with a

Whataburger. The old guy hadn't taken a bite until she left and one of the orderlies tried to snatch it up. Leon sat back and started to unwrap his own candy bar.

The old guy's eyes darted around constantly. Leon had been close enough to notice this the other day, too. That was fine. He could look around all day if he wanted.

"I like Snickers better," Galloway suddenly said without acknowledging Leon's presence.

Leon didn't say a word. Instead, he pulled up the wrapper and put the Snickers bar on the tray table. He picked up the Almond Joy and started again. He had a couple of bites down before Galloway grabbed the Snickers.

"They don't like me having chocolate," he said, stuffing his mouth with about half the candy bar as if he was worried someone would notice and take it away.

"Bossy sons of bitches, huh?"

Leon thought he saw Galloway smile just slightly. It was hard to tell.

"You visiting somebody?" Galloway asked, still not looking at him.

"Yeah, but the schmuck wasn't in his room."

Galloway finished the candy bar in two bites. His hands went to the arms of the recliner and his fingers started drumming. Leon tried not to stare, but the guy's fingers fascinated him. There was rhythm to their movement.

"What about you?" Leon asked casually, trying to sound like he didn't have anything better to do for the time being. "You get many visitors in this place?"

"A few." And that was it, nothing more.

"My buddy doesn't have anybody. His own kids won't even come see him," Leon said, glancing to see if he was pushing any buttons. "They say this place creeps them out." He waited, but couldn't keep his eyes off the guy's fingers. The right hand did something differ-ent from the left hand. "My buddy says he doesn't mind on account of his kids always wanting to borrow money. Says at least he gets some peace and quiet in here. You know what I mean?"

But Galloway was gone. Leon knew. He could sense it. He wasn't making a connection with the guy.

He glanced at Galloway's feet and noticed them both tapping. No, not really tapping, but maybe pumping...yeah, like pumping the pedals on a piano.

Son of a bitch!

Leon shifted his gaze back to Galloway's fingers. The guy's playing the piano, he realized.

And he certainly wasn't listening to Leon. He watched Galloway a little longer, recognizing the gestures, the rhythm and the motion.

"What'cha playing there?" Leon decided to ask.

Without any hesitation Galloway answered, "'When You Wish Upon a Star.'"

68

Eric had acted on gut instinct, pure and simple. Now, as he watched his sister share pizza with her eighty-one-year-old escort while the huge white cat climbed up and down the furniture, he wondered what the hell he was thinking. Being here with him might be more dangerous than sending Sabrina back to Tallahassee. Maybe it'd be safer to take their chances with the State Patrol if they could get them to believe her story. Her story did seem a bit crazy and he had heard some zingers. One thing Eric knew for certain was that unlike him, she couldn't kill anyone.

With the TV remote in hand he paced his small studio apartment, pointing it at the TV in the corner, flipping channels. He should be relieved. Apparently it wasn't a big enough story for national news updates. Finally he left it on Fox News and sat on a squeaky futon, the noise drawing both women's attention.

"What? The place came furnished," he told them with a smile, and the women resumed eating.

He ran a hand over his eyes, then pushed his fingers through his hair. It was way shorter than he was used to and still surprised him a little. It was part of his new look, his new disguise. And that was exactly why he shouldn't have Sabrina stay here with him. But he couldn't just send her away.

He'd been up all night, his usual schedule. But today he hadn't had a chance to take a nap. Damn, he could sure use one, though he doubted sleep would help make sense of the situation.

"So who do you think hired this killer?" Eric asked.

"Mr. Sidel arranged the meeting," Sabrina told him, batting at her new bangs. "Except I was supposed to be meeting the plant manager, Ernie Walker."

"And this wasn't Ernie."

"No."

"So you know Ernie?"

"I know who he is. This guy wasn't any kind of plant manager."

"Wait a minute. How do you know that for sure?"

She gave him an exasperated look.

"I'm not just busting your chops, Bree. I'm trying to figure out if this guy could be someone who works there."

She put her slice of pizza down and sat back in the plastic-resin chair Eric used for his dining set. She wiped her mouth with a paper napkin, slowly, deliberately, but Eric knew she wasn't simply stalling but rather thinking.

"He didn't have any protective gear," she finally said. "No goggles, no hard hat. Just a long pipe or a club, maybe. I couldn't tell from down below."

"Maybe he didn't want to be bothered with all that safety stuff."

"No, there was something more." And she rubbed at her eyes, closing them tight as if that would help her to see the man in her mind.

Eric sat patiently. He noticed the old woman's small black hand cupped over Sabrina's right hand, flat on top of the cheap plastic table. The woman had introduced herself to him as Sabrina's neighbor, but Eric knew in Chicago Sabrina barely let her neighbors know her name and she had lived in the same building for over ten years. She had told him once that she liked the anonymity. Same thing with her students. He knew she kept them at arm's length. Unlike other professors, Sabrina never socialized, no coffees after class, no special-occasion pizza parties.

Eric had always envied her ability to compartmentalize the people in her life, even if he didn't agree with it. In these past two years when he desperately needed to do exactly that to survive, he still found it difficult. His boss, Howard, was a prime example. But Sabrina was either good at it or made it look as though she was, with the exception of Miss Sadie.

"The alarm," Sabrina said suddenly, almost jumping out of her chair as if an alarm had literally gone off. "I knew there was something that didn't seem right. He didn't know about the alarm."

"What alarm?"

"Every reactor has a clear-water flushing tank. It's the last stage in the process. Whatever runoff is left, which should be only water, gets flushed and cooled before it's released through a filter into the river. If there's any solid particles that might clog up or break the filter, anything as big as..." Her voice trailed off and he recognized the look in her eyes. Post-traumatic shock. He'd seen it in Sabrina's eyes before, right after their mother's accident. He didn't like seeing it again.

"Anything as big as a body," he said, finishing her sentence. "Let me guess. It trips an alarm. Any chance he thought he had shut off the alarm or tried to override it?"

"It's all computerized," Sabrina told him. "Only one person can change the process or override or shut off any of it."

Her eyes met his and he watched the realization flood them. It was the same look she'd have when they were kids and she figured out some puzzle for the first time, or discovered the mystery ingredient in Pixie Stix. Only this realization was tinged with a bit of fear.

"What is it, dear?" Miss Sadie saw it, too.

"I was meeting the plant manager because Mr. Sidel wanted to prove to me that Reactor #5 wasn't online."

"So whoever sent this guy must not have known that the reactor and the alarm were on." Eric left the squeaky futon to pace again. "Or they turned it on, wanting him to get caught."

"The only person who can turn anything on or off has been gone since Friday," Sabrina said.

"Forget about on or off." Eric grew impatient. He was tired. It was too easy to lose focus. "More importantly, why the hell would someone want you..." He couldn't bring himself to say "dead.""Why would anyone want you gone?"

Instead of answering, Sabrina pushed away from the table and wandered to her overnight case by the front door where Eric had left it when he brought it in earlier. She went through several zippered pockets before she found and brought back a plastic bag. She set it down on the edge of the table, away from Miss Sadie and away from the pizza. Eric couldn't identify the contents. It looked like an orange and cream–colored glob with bits of metal.

"I think this might have something to do with it."

"What is it?" He picked up the bag and fingered the stuff that felt like jelly with glitter.

"I'm not sure." Sabrina stared at it, but didn't attempt a closer look. "Whatever it is I fished it out of what's supposed to be a clear-water runoff pipe just before it got pushed out into the river."

69

Chattahoochee, Florida

Leon listened. He wasn't quite sure which parts of Arthur Galloway's ramblings were true and which ones were fantasy or hallucinations. He knew Galloway's wife, Meredith, had been killed in a car crash about two years ago. The poor schmuck still talked about her as if she were alive and well, even meeting her for lunch. Leon didn't want to interrupt, afraid he'd derail the flow. And somewhere in the ramblings there was bound to be the information he needed. So he listened.

Galloway stopped playing the piano while he talked about his lovely Meredith.

"She was the prettiest girl on campus," Arthur Galloway told Leon, his tongue flicking in and out and around the inside of his mouth. "I thought I'd have a heart attack the day she noticed me."

Galloway's eyes continued to dart from one side to the other, as if watching an imaginary tennis match. But Leon noticed a glint in them now and there was a smile despite the tongue activity.

"She sat outside in the commons area," Galloway said. "She'd spend her lunch hour doing pencil sketches and sipping Tab."

Leon listened closely as Galloway told the story of a sugar-sweet courtship of romantic picnics and walks in the rain. Leon couldn't really say when it occurred to him, but at some point he realized he had gone from wanting to roll his eyes to envying Arthur Galloway. What was it like, Leon wondered, to love someone so much you didn't want to live in the real world without them?

Leon certainly didn't claim to have any sort of a grip on the human psyche, but he also didn't think it took a degree in psychiatry to see what was going on with Arthur Galloway. This guy wasn't crazy. In fact, if Leon's hunch was correct, Arthur Galloway was crazy like a fox. Leon wondered if the man had simply created his own reality, one that included his beloved Meredith. In his mind she was still real. In his mind he could still see her, and so could Leon as Galloway described her hands slick with wet clay as she plied and shaped her latest masterpiece. To hear him talk about her, even the scent of her—a combination of oil paints and herbal shampoo—it was almost as if she were in the room with them. Leon caught himself looking over his shoulder once when Galloway's eyes flitted in that direction and stayed for a beat longer than usual.

Where better to indulge your fantasies than someplace that expected them? Not only expected them, but fed and housed you while you sat back and lived in the past. Man, the guy had his act down—the flitting eyes, the jittery fingers that weren't really jittery at all.

None of this, however, was getting Leon anywhere. If the guy lived in his own little fantasy world maybe he didn't want anything or anyone reminding him of the real world, like real, breathing kids who only reminded him of the reality he wanted to shut out. The reality that didn't include Meredith. Could be why he hardly acknowledged his daughter the other night. Geez, if that was the case Leon had probably wasted his whole fucking morning. This was the sort of thing where he couldn't even use a pair of pliers to extract what he wanted.

Galloway was quiet again and Leon took it as an opportunity to leave. He stood and waited, but noticed Galloway's fingers already tapping away at his imaginary piano keys.

"So your daughter must favor your wife, huh?" Leon poked one more time. What would it matter? He had come all this way again. "I saw her visiting you the other night. Very attractive young woman. Your Meredith must be a looker."

Leon stood over him, hands stuffed in the pockets of his jumpsuit, jiggling some change like he was in no hurry, fingering the pair of pliers.

"Sabrina. Isn't that her name?" He watched Galloway's fingers, trying to see any indication that he might trip his trigger again. The floodgate had opened so easily about his wife, but the daughter was too real, too much of this world.

Leon considered the pliers. It wouldn't be hard to snap a couple of those fingers. Hell, he could do it without any tools. Push them back until he heard the crack.

He glanced around the TV room. One orderly helped a woman down the hall, otherwise it was a bunch of fucking zombies. He couldn't see the nurses' station. His guess was it'd take a few minutes for any of them to respond. Maybe a little pain would be just the thing to bring this guy back to reality.

"We might have peas for lunch," Galloway said suddenly without looking up at Leon.

Poor, pathetic bastard. Leon shook his head. Maybe he was wrong.

Maybe the man was crazy. Crazy or not, there wasn't a damn thing Leon could do to make him any more miserable than he already was. He checked the time. He'd wasted three fucking hours.

Leon turned to leave when Arthur Galloway said, "Eric favors his mother. Especially with the tan he's gotten from living on the beach."

Leon didn't move, afraid he'd ruin it, break the spell. Was the guy throwing him a bone? Maybe he thought he could trust Leon with his secret. And yet who knew if the old man had seen his son with a tan last month or last year. But it'd make sense the daughter might go to the brother for help, wherever he was. Still, Leon needed to be careful. Treat it as if it was nothing and they usually started singing. Treat it as if it mattered, they clammed shut.

"Yeah, I got a bitch of a sunburn down in Fort Lauderdale last month." Leon threw it out casually, then waited for Galloway to correct him, reveal what fucking beach his son was living on.

"With pearl onions," Galloway said.

"Excuse me?" Leon asked, but was thinking what the fuck was this guy talking about? There was no pearl beach, but Galloway interrupted Leon's thought process with his next words.

"My Meredith loves peas with those little pearl onions."

Leon let out a sigh and rolled his eyes. Either this guy was fucking brilliant or nuttier than a fruitcake. Either way, he had just wasted Leon's entire morning.

70

Jason Brill pushed away from the laptop computer on his desk. He rubbed his eyes and then tried to twist the knot out of the back of his neck. He glanced at his watch, surprised to see that he had been on the Internet nonstop for the last several hours. No wonder his eyes were starting to cross and his stomach was growling.

There appeared to be no secrets in Arthur Galloway's life. Of course, Jason didn't have access to anything on the order of FBI classified. What he did have would certainly not point to or highlight any suspicious activity. One thing Jason had learned from Senator Allen was how to read a bank account. Jason's first assignment with the senator had been to find a leak within the senator's own office staff. "Follow the money," Senator Allen had told him. "A person's bank account can't hide a person's true character." Within days,

Jason had found the staffer, an intern with a sudden passion for Prada and a new secret boyfriend at the *Washington Post.*

After spending hours accessing and analyzing Arthur Galloway's finances for the last five years, Jason had put together a profile that exhibited mostly sadness and defeat rather than anger and revenge. There were paychecks from an accomplished career at the University of Chicago and an alumni newsletter that named him professor of the year. Mortgage payments and property taxes for a two-story home in a Chicago suburb. Then things began to change drastically after a seventeen-thousand-dollar payment to Krauss, Holmes and Sawyer's Funeral Home.

A search of Google easily found the obituary for Meredith Galloway and an earlier article almost five years before in the *Chicago Tribune,* featuring three artists who were making it big on the international level. It included a photo of an attractive, dark-haired woman with an infectious smile despite the brooding brown eyes. It was her face that made it easy for Jason to commit the story to memory.

A large deposit followed by a large payment to the mortgage company indicated the sale of the house in the suburbs. Almost immediately came new paychecks from Florida State University and monthly payments to an apartment complex. All during this time there were no unusually large withdrawals, no paid memberships to suspect organizations, no purchases online of ingredients for deadly terrorist attacks or books from Amazon.com on defaming the president or his administration. Nothing Arthur Galloway bought or paid for seemed out of the ordinary, let alone marked him as a threat to the energy summit or to EchoEnergy or William Sidel. The only thing that connected him at all was his daughter.

Almost a year ago everything stopped. Outside of a onetime payment to a Dr. E. J. Fullerton, Arthur Galloway's financial history—checking accounts, savings accounts, credit card accounts, everything—came to a grinding halt.

Dr. Fullerton's longstanding association, currently as chief of staff, with the Florida State Hospital at Chattahoochee, Florida, seemed evidence enough of where Arthur Galloway was. No one on staff, however, would confirm that he was a patient. Even without confirmation Jason knew Galloway couldn't possibly be a security risk. So why would William Sidel be worried? Whatever the daughter's agenda, the father was hardly in any shape to even help her. Jason wondered if this was really about the energy summit.

Jason's gut said no. He decided he needed to check something that had been nagging him ever since he and Senator Allen left EchoEnergy and Tallahassee after their trip last week.

He found a menu for a Thai place that would deliver, so he could order something to eat. He'd be here a while. All he needed was William Sidel's social security number. He already had authorization codes and passwords—one of the perks of an important senator's chief of staff.

After a few hours he would have a profile similar to what he had created on Arthur Galloway. Maybe following the money would tell him what the hell William Sidel was up to. And while he was at it maybe he'd check one other profile. Just because it was eating at him and maybe because he needed to find out why it was so easy to murder a member of a senator's staff and keep the news media from pouncing on it.

71

Sabrina hated to see Miss Sadie leave. For the past year she had been Sabrina's only true friend, though she certainly didn't want to keep the old woman from her home. It was probably safer for her back in Tallahassee. By now, anyone looking for Sabrina would have discovered her gone. Yet after only half a day with Eric, Sabrina almost wanted to go back with Miss Sadie. There was something about Eric's new life she didn't trust. She was the one on the run yet Eric was the one who seemed all too prepared and familiar with life on the run.

The instructions he gave the old woman sounded more like a covert operation. It reminded Sabrina of some of the stuff they'd play when they were kids and Eric liked to pretend he was Steve Austin, the Bionic Man.

In a matter-of-fact tone, he had told Miss Sadie what to look for when she got back.

"It may seem like something perfectly ordinary, but doesn't look right," he told the old woman. "Maybe a cement truck at the end of the block, but no road or sidewalk construction. Maybe a cable-TV guy going door to door."

Miss Sadie only nodded, but the information unnerved Sabrina. She wanted to believe Miss Sadie would be safe. She hated herself for having gotten her friend into this mess.

Eric filled the Studebaker's gas tank and stocked a cooler of fresh goodies. He even offered an escort of one of his friends. Instead of the escort, Miss Sadie accepted a cell phone and number.

"You need anything, you call," Eric instructed her. "Anything at all."

After several promises and a somber goodbye, Miss Sadie and Lizzie Borden headed out. Shortly afterward, Eric took the plastic bag with the EchoEnergy glob of waste, saying he knew someone who could help identify the contents. He made Sabrina promise she wouldn't leave his apartment or even answer the door and then he left. And that's when she felt it, the hollow, empty feeling of being alone.

She paced his small apartment out of restlessness more than curiosity. Yet she couldn't help noticing that there was very little here that personalized the place. No photos, no mail, no favorite take-out menus, which she remembered Eric had been famous for when he lived in Chicago. Their mother had kidded him about having more restaurants on his phone's speed dial than women's phone numbers. Eric's quick comeback had always been that the two were his only vices—take-out food and women—noting that he never smoked or did drugs, drank very little alcohol and rarely swore.

Sabrina glanced in a few drawers. Come to think of it, there were no signs of women visitors, either, not even the overnight variety, though Sabrina had always suspected her good-looking, charming brother was more talk than action.

Sabrina had told herself that two years was enough time for a person to change. She wasn't sure she liked the idea. She missed her brother, faults and quirks aside. She peeked inside his closet, hoping for a glimpse of familiarity. Instead, she found Ralph Lauren shirts and khakis and Sperry deck shoes. Everything had a designer label. Since when did Eric care?

Back in the corner was a set of Ping golf clubs and a Head tennis racquet. Outside the apartment door on the second-floor deck Sabrina had noticed a smaller version of what she thought to be a surfboard. Athletics had always come easy to Eric, so this stuff fit, though her very social brother had usually chosen team sports like basketball at the Y and league baseball. Golf was social, she told herself just as she noticed an engraved silver-plated nameplate on the golf bag that read *E. Gallo.* There was more than enough room on the nameplate. Why would he abbreviate his last name? Or was that what Eric was calling himself these days? And if so, why?

72

Eric left the plastic bag down the street at the Santa Rosa Water Treatment Plant with a lab tech who only went by the name Bosco. A few weeks ago she had agreed to do some independent work for Eric in exchange for a chance to do a weekly standup-comedy gig at Howard's place next door, Bobbye's Oyster Bar.

The place was small—a roll-up garage-type door that revealed the bar and enough room on the other side for one bartender, usually Eric, sometimes Howard, to serve from the shelves behind and below. A half-dozen bistro tables and chairs spread out on the board-walk in front were kept full from open to close. Small and intimate, but on Friday and Saturday nights, it could be standing room only.

At the time, Eric knew Howard would be okay with it. He wasn't into making his place a trendy hangout, but he liked the idea of giving someone a shot at her dream. Thankfully for Eric's sake, the fortysomething, nerdy butch lab tech was not just funny, she was hilarious. She had an animated comedic routine that left the patrons in tears and literally holding their stomachs from laughing so hard.

Before Eric went back up to his apartment he decided to drop by the shop. He waved at Howard's crew already cleaning the boat in its slip. He noticed the cowboys' Mercedes already gone from the parking lot. Not a good sign. Howard always invited his deep-sea fishing clients to stay for drinks and a gourmet feast he and Eric would whip up on the short-order flat grill. Instead, he found his boss behind the shop counter, opening the UPS shipments for the day with his cell phone tucked between his ear and his shoulder.

Eric was six foot and lean, probably in the best shape he had been in years. Howard, however, had what Eric would describe as a commanding presence at six foot five, a barrel chest and muscular arms, usually dressed in bright boat shirts—today's an orange and blue marlin pattern—and white linen trousers, sometimes a white captain's cap. Eric guessed Howard to be in his sixties, the thick white hair and mustache the only indicators. He had watched the man handle a five-hundred-pound marlin with little effort and watched him break up a brawl by grabbing unruly patrons by the scruff of their necks. He'd also seen Howard apply fine brushstrokes with a delicate touch to one of his model ships.

Howard gave Eric a nod, a familiar greeting when he was on the phone or with a customer. Something was different this time. Howard grabbed the phone, shoving aside a half-unpacked box and cutting short the conversation with a quick "Let me get back to you."

Eric pretended not to notice his abruptness. Maybe he was being paranoid. And why not, after everything with Sabrina?

"The Texans left already?" Eric asked.

"No catch. And no one had much of an appetite," Howard said, shaking his head, but he didn't sound surprised or disappointed. "The one boy started retching up a storm before we even got settled."

"Mr. Bring-on-the-girls? The guy with the cowboy boots?" Eric smiled. He couldn't help it. He knew it as soon as he saw the guy.

"He's just lucky I ended up feeling sorry for him," Howard said, stroking his mustache out of habit. "We hadn't left the slip and he was being an asshole to Wendi."

Eric knew Howard was protective of his crew though he hired only the best. But Eric also knew Wendi could take care of herself. Without much effort she could probably make Mr. Cowboy Boots cry like a baby.

"Hopefully tomorrow's group will do better."

"Oh, I'm sure they will." Howard sounded confident. "They're from Minnesota. They know a thing or two about fishing up there." He went back to unpacking the boxes.

"I had to close up this morning for a few hours," Eric told him, even though he knew Howard wouldn't mind. And he was right. His boss only nodded, not even looking up for an explanation.

"A friend of mine showed up."

Again he only nodded.

"She's gonna stay with me for several days," Eric added.

This, however, did get Howard's attention. With anyone else Eric might have expected a wink along with some smart-ass comment like "Sure, she's just a friend." But Howard was a gentleman.

"Bring her on down later," Howard invited, meaning the bar to hang out with the others. "I look forward to meeting her."

Eric said he would and caught himself wishing that just once Howard wouldn't be such a nice guy. It'd make what Eric was doing here on Pensacola Beach so much easier.

73

Abda Hassar had spent the day in his hotel room. He put the Do Not Disturb sign on the door as soon as room service delivered his breakfast. Then he connected his laptop to the hotel's wireless network. Qasim and Khaled had checked into the same hotel, only at different times. Each had his own room on different floors. Later they would meet at a coffee shop across the street and pretend to study Qasim's textbooks like university students, not tourists.

Abda had left e-mails at various Web sites. Throughout the day he would pick up the responses and piece together their message. So far they were telling him nothing new. From every indication the plan was still on. Unless something dramatic happened in the next several days, EchoEnergy would grab up contracts that for years had gone to Middle Eastern oil companies. The contracts were small in the scope of business dealings. Their absence would not threaten to bankrupt or even create a ripple of economic harm to any one of these companies. But the contracts were not about money, nor were they about oil, but instead, goodwill and influence.

For years the contracts had been rewards to Abda's countrymen for standing firm with the United States against other Arab states, indifferent to America's fight against terrorism. Taking away these contracts was nothing less than a slap in the face. The current president did not understand this despite its being spoken about over and over in plain diplomatic language, and so perhaps he would understand it in the only language his administration appeared to take notice of.

They had worked hard, or rather Khaled had, for months, creating a plan that would have the greatest impact, but also one that would be undetectable by the hordes of security the president surrounded himself with. At first Khaled thought he had done just that—an explosive device made from purely harmless liquids that separately would draw no attention.

Brilliantly, Khaled contained each liquid in a small plastic bottle that looked no different from an ordinary bottle of water with a pull-top, the type that allowed a drink without twisting off the lid. But Khaled's pull-top included a sharp plastic point, sharp enough to pierce and attach to the bottom of another bottle. It took three bottles, three ordinary bottles of what would appear to be clear water. When the third, the last, pierced the middle bottle, it took but seconds for the liquids to mix, to seep into each other.

The explosion that followed would be massive. It would kill everyone at the reception banquet, including the martyr who stayed behind to combine the bottles.

Khaled had even volunteered to be the martyr. But Abda was the leader. And Abda rejected the idea. He believed an explosion of that magnitude would be dismissed as just another brutal terrorist attack. He believed they needed something as deadly but targeted, so there could be no mistake as to what and for whom their message was meant.

Khaled complied and went back to his test tubes and vials and computer formulas. And again, he delivered a brilliant and deadly solution.

Abda pulled out the innocuous prescription bottle, the capsules inside simple blood pressure medicine. All but one. He knew it from a dimpled marking on the end that he could detect by touch. Instead of medicine, the grains inside were fatal, a concoction Khaled had perfected. More deadly than anthrax, the white, grainy powder had no taste or smell. When applied to food it would not even be noticed. Within seconds the recipient's throat would begin to swell, choking off all breath. There would be no rescue and best of all there would be no indication of what had caused the suffocation.

To Abda, Khaled's potion was brilliant. Its properties were undetectable and fatal, and it allowed them to choose exactly who would die. They would use science to teach this administration a costly lesson. This administration thought they could walk away from promises made only because they thought they had found a scientific freedom with EchoEnergy. And in that sense, Abda believed it was not only a lesson but a sort of poetic justice they were about to serve up.

74

Jason scraped the last of the pad thai noodles from the bottom of the container. He stuffed it all into his mouth without taking his eyes off his computer screen. Everyone had left him behind. The security guard had checked in on him three times. Jason was beginning to wonder if the guy was really worried about him or only wanted to make sure he wasn't stealing congressional secrets of some sort.

Jason went back and forth between William Sidel and Zach Kensor. It was just as easy to run two names through the systems he was intruding on. He hadn't found anything much in Zach's financial profile other than the typical stuff for a guy his age. In some ways it reminded Jason of his own pathetic financial life, decent money but not much to show.

He clicked through another bank statement for EchoEnergy. William Sidel's business accounts, however, resembled a politician's.

It appeared that there wasn't an investment firm or millionaire Sidel wouldn't take money from. By the same token he paid out exorbitant amounts of money to several so-called NFP—not-for-profit—funds. Actually, some of them may have been legit, but Jason recognized a couple as questionable lobbyists. Or at least that's what they pretended to be. As a private, not publicly owned company, EchoEnergy could pick and choose its investors without many limits. It could not, however, use charity fronts to bribe congressional representatives. It would probably be pretty hard for Jason to prove. Still, he printed out the statements and highlighted the questionable NFPs.

He was exhausted. His eyes burned from too many hours in front of the computer screen. He had wasted an entire day. Tomorrow he had to finish up the details for the energy summit reception. There was a load of paperwork he still needed to fill out and hand in. JVC's Emerald Coast Catering had faxed over the menu for approval. And he hadn't even given the Appropriations Committee a second thought. Instead, he was obsessed with finding something, anything, that confirmed his gut instinct about William Sidel. What the hell was it that Sidel could be holding over Senator Allen?

Jason went over and over the phone conversation the senator had had with Sidel that morning. He had never seen the senator back down from anyone and yet that's exactly what he was doing every time with Sidel. It was a gut instinct that had Jason convinced Sidel had given Senator Allen some sort of ultimatum.

In the beginning Jason had thought it was an even exchange. Senator Allen would see to it that the military contract got passed by the Appropriations Committee. For Sidel that meant extra funds as well as respect and credibility. For Senator Allen it boosted his reputation with environmentalists and patriots and would give him a strong made-in-America platform for a possible presidential run. An even exchange, but Jason suspected there was something more. What did Sidel have in his corner that had thrown off the balance and tipped it all in his favor?

Jason had already gone over Sidel's personal accounts, but now he brought up his Visa year-to-date one more time. Again, nothing all that interesting. Sidel collected antiques. He treated himself to expensive haircuts once a month and a pedicure every week. No manicure, though. Sidel spent more money on memberships and fees to exclusive private clubs than Jason made in a year. There was the Champions Golf Club, the Gulf Coast Yacht Club, the South Beach Spa and Resort and the Sandshaker Health Club.

He had made trips to D.C. twice in the last eight months, both times staying at the Washington Grand Hotel. The first time Jason noticed the trips and the hotel, it stopped him cold. He had probably made the reservations for Sidel at Senator Allen's request without even knowing they were for Sidel. But that didn't mean much, either. Of course Sidel would visit D.C. And why shouldn't he stay at one of the city's finest hotels at the recommendation of his friend?

Jason decided to collect all the documents and financial statements he had printed out and go home. He could spread everything out and take another look. If he remembered correctly, he still had a couple of beers in the fridge that might help along the process. He started stuffing copies into his briefcase when he noticed something that made him stop. Maybe he was simply tired and imagining things. He pulled out the only three statements he had printed out from Zach's meager profile.

Jason scanned the credit card charges. He took it line by line, looking for something that had caught his eye earlier. It didn't mean much the first time he had noticed it, but now it seemed too much of a coincidence.

There it was. Five months ago on January 20. A credit card charge at a hotel gift shop. No other charges to indicate the trip except a $29.54 charge at the South Beach Spa and Resort gift shop.

Jason grabbed the pages from Sidel's Visa charges for January. Sure enough, there was a $2,024 charge for January eighteenth through the twentieth. Quite a coincidence that both men would be at the same expensive resort at the same time. Especially since one was living from paycheck to paycheck.

75

Sabrina noticed a tension between her and Eric without Miss Sadie to buffer their two-year separation. She insisted he leave the TV on, so the silence between them wasn't so obvious. She heard laughter and chatter from the oyster bar below. Eric almost had her convinced that it'd be safe to go down in about an hour and get something to eat. By then he told her it would be only the regulars and he reassured her they could be trusted. Sabrina wasn't sure she could believe anything he said. In many ways he was her same old brother, but she kept thinking about the expensive designer stuff in his closet. And she kept wondering why he would call himself Eric Gallo.

Suddenly Eric turned up the TV's volume. Her eyes caught a glimpse of her photo in the corner of the screen.

The news anchor was saying there was a warrant for her arrest while an aerial view of EchoEnergy appeared on the screen.

"The two were coworkers competing for the same position," the anchor explained in a tone that Sabrina thought sounded like enough of a reason or motive for murder. "Earlier this evening, the victim's father announced a hundred-thousand-dollar reward for any information leading to the arrest and conviction of Dr. Sabrina Galloway." Sabrina couldn't help thinking that Anna's father looked nothing like Anna. Instead, he resembled one of the actors on *The Sopranos.*

The anchor went on to the next news story and Eric lowered the volume again. He evidently read her mind because the first thing he said was, "Damn it, Bree. It looks like you're gonna have the entire Florida mafia after you." But then he smiled.

She sat down on the rickety futon. It was soft from wear and smelled like seawater with a hint of Miss Sadie's lemon shampoo rinse. For the moment it was her only safe haven.

"They make it sound so simple."

"Most of the time it is. Greed, envy, lust, hate," Eric said, watching her. "Passions run high and suddenly somebody's dead."

"I didn't kill her. You know that, right?" She couldn't believe she'd need to convince him. But if he had changed, maybe he thought she had, too.

"Hey, you're talking to the guy you beaned with a baseball bat," he joked and fingered the slight indent in the bridge of his nose.

She wasn't in the mood for kidding around, but still she came back with "Only because you were standing too close to home plate."

"You cried at the sight of my bloody nose," he said, laughing.

"I did not," she lied when in fact she remembered bawling uncontrollably. She was only six at the time. She thought she had caused brain damage. Finding out that his nose was only broken hadn't been much consolation.

His eyes were serious now. "You were horrified that you hurt me. I don't think you could hurt anyone."

"You haven't seen me in two years. Maybe I've changed."

"People don't change that much, Bree. They might change careers, religious affiliations, spouses—"

"Or names," she slipped in and watched his face, waiting for his eyes.

"Who told you?"

"What? That you go by Eric Gallo these days?"

"It's not what you think."

"What I think? You disappeared from my life for two years. Your choice. I didn't get a choice." Sabrina wasn't sure where the sudden anger was coming from, but it felt good to get it out. It needed to be said. "I needed you and you just left. Just like that. No forwarding address."

She was hurt and angry and she wanted him to know she wasn't sure she could trust him even now when she didn't have anyone else. "You went to see Dad in Chattahoochee, but you didn't come to see me."

She stopped there and waited out the silence, holding his eyes. She wouldn't look away. She wouldn't let him joke and pretend it wasn't a big deal. And she wouldn't stay here without some explanation...without an apology.

"I left Chicago because I was angry with Dad. Not you."

Sabrina already knew that. She knew Eric blamed their father for their mother's accident.

"There was a lot of crap going on in my life," he continued with little detail. "It was easier to leave and cut off all contact...re-create myself. You were an unfortunate casualty."

Sabrina blinked hard as though the word *casualty* had actually physically stung her. Eric noticed and said, "But I've missed you every single day."

76

Leon tried to block the penlight with his body. It'd been too easy getting into the Galloway woman's condo. Why did people leave spare keys in the most obvious places? He had figured her to be a little smarter than to use a flowerpot on the back porch.

He had noticed a rolled-up newspaper on the front steps. A cheap-ass rental still sat in her garage. He figured the police had already checked flights to Chicago, her obvious escape. A little too obvious, Leon thought, but then maybe he was giving her too much credit. After all, she had left the condo's spare key under a fucking flower-pot.

With the narrow beam of light he did a quick sweep of the furniture, finding only one framed photo. A family photo. He recognized a younger Arthur Galloway. The daughter looked the same, still attractive, maybe a little less intense. The brother had a mix of Hollywood and *Sports Illustrated* good looks with dark hair, brown eyes, a dimpled smile in a square jaw. And he did favor his mother. The lovely Meredith was even prettier than Leon had imagined, a contagious smile, wild but generous eyes. He had trouble taking his eyes away. They were a good-looking family.

He checked the phone, clicking through the caller ID list and the numbers stored on the speed dial. There was nothing on her wall calendar by the fridge. Not a single notation on the scratch pad next to the phone or any indentations in the paper from a message written on the page before it.

Leon did find a leather address book in a desk drawer. This was it, finally. The corners were worn, some entries had lines through them with new information jotted in the margins. There were even dates alongside each entry, probably when she added them. It was obviously well-used and yet there was no recent entry for Eric Galloway. Only a Chicago address and phone number with an *X* over the entire entry. No new information in the margins. Nothing.

Leon was flipping through the address book one last time—maybe she put her brother somewhere else—but he doubted it. He was thinking how organized this Galloway woman was. Suddenly a light clicked on behind him.

He froze, waiting, listening. How could anyone sneak in on him? Sweat trickled down his back and he could feel it on his brow, too, getting ready to slide down his face. He resisted the urge to swipe at it, trying to concentrate on any footsteps coming up behind him, waiting for a voice to say, "Gotcha." Was it possible she had been hiding somewhere? And he was sure she'd never come in on him so boldly without a weapon.

Instead of turning slowly—the expected response—Leon dived behind the sofa. He knocked his elbow against the sofa table and rammed the top of his head into the piano so hard, the vibration set off a musical twang from inside its cabinet.

"Son of a bitch," he mumbled, digging for the gun in his waistband while his eyes darted around and above him from the floor. He was seeing two of everything, but thankfully not a single figure.

That's when he heard a second click. He spun his entire body in the direction of the sound. He held the gun with both hands, arms stretched out and ready to fire. Again, no one there.

He was eye-level with an electrical outlet. And in the outlet was an electronic timer. Leon's eyes followed the cord that was plugged into the timer. Sure enough it led to the lamp that had just turned on.

"Son of a bitch," he said again, pulling himself to his feet.

The woman had timers probably to make it look like someone was here. He shouldn't have been surprised. She looked the type. And sure enough he found timers in the kitchen for the coffee machine and another for a fluorescent light above the sink.

He went through the rest of the condo, leaving the light on in the living room and using it to his advantage. Light or no light, it didn't take long to realize there was nothing here that would tell him where she'd gone or even how she left. Maybe another rental, he thought, and quickly discounted it. The cops would have already thought of that. So how the hell did she leave? By foot?

He looked through each room one last time and took a leak in the upstairs bathroom. He decided he'd watch the place for a few hours from the van he'd left on the street, down a couple houses. Before he left Chattahoochee he had switched license plates, again. He hoped he had another eight-hour shift before the company realized it was missing. And even on a quiet cul-de-sac like this, who'd complain about an air-conditioning service making a late-night call, especially on a bitch of a hot night.

Leon made his way back through the living room, trying to stay away from the front window, though the curtains and blinds were closed. He was at the patio door ready to slide it open when he decided he couldn't leave just yet. He followed the wall back to the framed family photo, grabbed it off the shelf and tucked it under his arm. Then he left the way he came in, replacing the key under the same flowerpot.

Leon had barely climbed into the van when a pair of headlights swung onto the street. He popped open a can of soda from the small cooler beside him and watched the car drive past. It pulled into the driveway next to the Galloway woman's condo. Leon probably wouldn't have paid it much attention except it was a vintage Studebaker, the same Studebaker he'd seen leaving this neighborhood last night.

He watched the garage door slide up and in the bright light from inside the garage he got a glimpse of the driver.

He pulled out a small packet of tissues and dabbed at his forehead and upper lip. He couldn't help thinking it odd that a little old black woman would be out this late at night.

77

Eric talked Sabrina into a truce. They were both hungry. He didn't blame her for being pissed with him. Truth was, he'd been surprised she'd even come looking for him. He told her he wanted to help her. She could decide after this was all over whether or not to forgive him. What he didn't say, what made him nervous as hell, was that if their dad had slipped and told Sabrina where she could find him, he might tell someone else. Someone like the guy trying to kill her.

Now Eric slid his chair so that he sat at the edge of the circle around the small bistro table. He wanted to watch the others while Sabrina told her story. He still wasn't sure he was doing the right thing. And yet, ironically, he knew that if he couldn't trust this group he couldn't trust anyone.

According to Max, they were all lost souls who had found each other. Of course, that was usually after a few glasses of sangria. Eric couldn't really pinpoint when they had all become friends. It was a gradual thing. But it started maybe five months ago, maybe six. They'd end up being the last ones to close down Bobbye's, migrating to one table even if it required pulling up chairs from another table and creating a jagged circle. Eric was notorious for bringing people together. Making friends had always come easy, relationships not so easy.

He knew this group had little in common except for how much they didn't fit in with any other groups that frequented the beach. None of them were tourists or college students, though Russ could certainly pass for either. All of them were from someplace else. None had lived on the beach for very long. The Mayor was the only exception. He had lived in Pensacola most of his life.

Eric always positioned his chair so his back was to the water and he could see anyone coming up the boardwalk or around the building. Tonight he looked for Bosco, hoping she'd show up with the lab results, but he knew that was pushing it. He watched Sabrina, studying her and running through strategies in his head. He hated feeling that his hands were tied, that he couldn't help her all on his own. And he hated that he had to ask for help. At least Sabrina was more relaxed. It was probably the Baileys Irish Cream on ice. He knew she didn't drink, but he was pretty sure she wouldn't mind the sweet, creamy liquor. He had to admit it surprised him when she asked for a second.

The shorter hairstyle made her look younger and it reminded him of when they were kids. She wore it short in the summers so their mother couldn't take up Sabrina's precious summer vacation braiding or curling or perming it. This style looked good on her, but she kept raking her fingers through the bangs, trying to keep them off her forehead.

Max had dressed her in lime green and royal blue. Miss Sadie was right—her eyes were a brilliant blue and they reminded him so much of their dad's. She had been a terrific sport about the makeover, especially during the ear-piercing and the spray-on-tan session. A great sport or perhaps she had been more terrified than he knew.

Over the course of the evening she glanced his way and he tried to read every one of her glances. The first one was definitely "You've got to be kidding." Then slowly the glances were only for reassurance. She had command of the group, not out of shock over her story—Eric didn't think anything could shock them—but rather out of respect. Even Russ, who could be dismissive at times, was listening intently. And hopefully his computer-obsessed mind was grinding out some strategies.

"They have plenty of reason to want to sweep this under the rug pretty quickly," said the Mayor, and he sat back like he had just stated the obvious.

The rest of them waited and watched as the Mayor took a sip of his pink lemonade, always managing to make it look smooth despite the spear of fruit—chunks of pineapple and mango separated by maraschino cherries. Eric and Howard took turns making drinks and were probably the only ones who knew that the concoction—what the Mayor called an exotic pink lady—didn't have an ounce of liquor.

It took the Mayor several sips before he realized they were all waiting for an explanation.

"That $140-million contract they're up for." He waved a hand out like he was literally tossing the information onto the table.

Everyone stared at him, but Eric saw Sabrina sit forward.

"The military contract," she said and the Mayor smiled and nodded.

"It's been in the news," he told the others in a familiar scold. "Don't any of you pay attention to the news?"

It was an old argument, a regular pet peeve of the Mayor's, one that everyone ignored. Fact was, they all knew the old man loved being the one to fill them in on the state of the nation and current events. Eric liked to call him their personal news commentator. Years ago he had been the mayor of Pensacola, but also a U.S. congressman for one of the Panhandle's districts. Eric couldn't remember how many terms the Mayor had served—one or two—but it was enough to have ruffled some D.C. feathers and make some lifelong connections. And though it was years ago, the man talked about the players and the current affairs as though he had left only last year.

"I saw ole Johnny Q last Friday on CNN, right before his tour of the place," the Mayor told them. "Seemed obvious to me he was trying to drum up some last-minute support, which means it might not get approval."

He pushed up his glasses and put his knobby elbows on the table, tenting his arthritic fingers in another familiar gesture that drew the group's attention, because usually it meant "Here's the real scoop." But he surprised them when he looked at Sabrina across the table and instead of providing some juicy tidbit, he asked, "Is it true he up-chucked his lunch on that tour?"

All the attention shifted back to Sabrina and for a moment Eric worried that he had thrown her into this when his sister, by her very nature, wasn't a social being, let alone someone who fed into rumors or innuendo. Here they were supposed to be helping to protect and save her and the Mayor was more concerned with getting the scoop on apparently a former adversary.

"Right over the railing and into the tank of chicken guts," Sabrina told the Mayor, but she was smiling at him.

He rubbed his hands together as if he was relishing the image. "I wish I had seen that."

Eric glanced over at Maxine, who rolled her eyes. Howard and Russ laughed.

That's when Bosco chose to join them. Everyone became silent when she tossed a plastic bag onto the table in front of Eric.

"Was this supposed to be some sort of joke?"

At first Eric wasn't sure if she was being sarcastic. He had seen her do her comedy routine with the same straight face, sometimes feigning anger when she delivered some of her funniest lines.

"What is that?" Howard asked.

"It's a fucking joke, right?" Bosco said again and this time Eric knew she was mad.

"Sabrina pulled this stuff out of a runoff pipe," he said, answering Howard's question. Before he could take the bag off the table, Sabrina picked it up and began fingering the contents as if seeing them for the first time.

"It was supposed to be clear-water runoff. Whatever this is—" and she glanced up at the pissed-off lab tech "—it may have been leaking into the river."

"Oh, that's just perfect," Bosco said, her hands flying up in exasperation. "That's just fucking perfect."

"So what is it?" Eric wanted to know.

"Well, there's your basic poultry DNA with bits of metal, steel mostly or what used to be steel, some plastic by-product and lots and lots of dioxin residue."

"That's what I was afraid of," Sabrina said, and Eric watched her turn the bag over as if she could now see the individual pieces, examining it closely.

"Oh, it gets much better." Bosco glanced at Eric. "I left the L.A. crime lab so I didn't have to put up with crap like this anymore."

"What are you talking about?" Eric was growing impatient with her melodrama.

Now Bosco looked from Eric to Sabrina and back at Eric. "Don't tell me neither of you knew that most of that stuff is human tissue and human blood?"

78

Sabrina didn't want to believe it. But the whole time the woman Eric called Bosco went through the list of contents, Sabrina had been fingering a metal disc through the plastic, trying to get a better look. Before Bosco even mentioned human tissue, Sabrina tried to make out the engraving between the many scratches and grooves on what she guessed might be the back of a watch. It looked like something in Latin above another series of letters. But the only decipherable ones were *DW* followed by scratches and rubbings and then a dissected *L,* more scratches and then *SIK.*

Anna Copello had ended up in a flushing tank. Was it possible that Dwight Lansik had been pushed into a slaughterhouse refuse tank? Before yesterday she would have laughed at such a bizarre idea. Now she realized she might be looking at the only remains of her late boss.

Suddenly she pushed the bag away and bolted from the table, stumbling over chairs.

"Bree," she heard Eric call out, but all she cared about was catching her breath and trying not to give in to her nausea.

She ended up at the edge of the pier, staring out at the black, rolling water and the twinkling lights of homes across the sound. She could hear the water sloshing against the boats in their slips. The sensation of movement was overwhelming. It was enough to make her dizzy. She grabbed on to a piling and maneuvered her way to a sitting position.

She felt Eric's presence, but thankfully he said nothing. No more questions. No more explaining.

She pulled her knees up to her chest, wrapped her arms around them and rested her chin on top, waiting for her stomach to settle and the throbbing in her head to subside.

At some point he sat down next to her and she watched his long legs swing over the edge of the pier. He sat so close his shoulders brushed Sabrina's, but that was their only contact. He was like their dad, Sabrina realized. Not able to find words or gestures to comfort. Only able to offer his presence and his actions. That's where the hot-fudge sundaes usually came in. It used to throw their mother into a dramatic fit, sometimes worse than her original outburst of emotion.

"Sometimes a woman just needs to be hugged," she'd tell their dad and he would quickly accommodate her, almost relieved to be instructed.

Sabrina laid her head against Eric's shoulder and closed her eyes. The urge to retch out her insides subsided little by little. The throbbing in her head eased until it was only the thump of her heartbeat. A cool, gentle breeze came across the water.

"So what do we do?" she asked so softly she wasn't sure if he heard her.

"We find out who the enemy is," he told her calmly and without a hint of anger. "And then we get the son of a bitch before he can get you."

His words surprised her. She jerked her head away from his shoulder so she could look at him. He kept his profile to her as he continued to stare out at the black water. A streak of light appeared on the surface, little by little, as the passing clouds unveiled the moon.

"You think it's William Sidel?" she asked, but she knew the answer. Who else would try to have her killed and when it failed have the power to convince the State Patrol she was the killer instead of the intended victim? Who else would be able to have Dwight Lansik shoved into a tank of chicken guts and announce that the scientist had simply resigned?

"He has access and he definitely has motive. Sounds like he might have some political influence, too."

Sabrina rubbed at her eyes and pushed her fingers up through her hair. She couldn't remember what it felt like not to be exhausted. Her eyelids actually hurt and she knew she was a bit dehydrated. Even her feet seemed to be protesting. She wasn't used to walking in flip-flops. Her internal clock, the one she had spent years disciplining to a daily routine, had been thrown way off track. Once again she was in a place she had never been before, surrounded by people she'd just met—an odd assortment that her brother was insisting she trust. Trust to keep her from being killed by her boss. And why? Because William Sidel was processing Grade 2 garbage without investing the money to do it the right way.

"It doesn't make sense," Sabrina said. "William Sidel has raised millions of dollars from investors. He's garnered millions of dollars in government funds. He's on the verge of locking up a $140-million contract. Why would he risk all that?"

"What is Grade 2 garbage?" Eric asked. He pulled up his legs and shifted to face her.

"Various metals, mostly old appliances. Plastics, PVC, wood, fiberglass. Plastic bottles can yield large amounts of oil. The problem is that with Grade 2 garbage most of the breakdown comes in the second stage and it also takes an extra flushing. The hydrogen in water combines with the chlorine in PVC and some of the other garbage to make it safe. Without doing it properly you get dioxins, which are highly toxic. With Grade 1 garbage, the slaughterhouse waste, the process is more organic. It's full of nitrogen and amino acids, but we're able to separate those off and they're used in liquid fertilizer." Sabrina suddenly realized talking about the process and her work actually calmed her. She checked Eric's eyes to see if he was registering any of it. Sometimes she got carried away with the technobabble.

"So, if Grade 2 garbage takes more steps and is more work, why bother to sneak doing it?"

"That's why I said it doesn't make sense."

"Bottom line, how much does EchoEnergy make for taking slaughterhouse waste?"

"Actually, we pay them twenty-five dollars a ton."

"You're kidding?"

She shook her head. She knew it sounded strange. "We're competing with companies that buy it strictly to make fertilizers."

"Okay. So how much does it cost to haul away Grade 2 garbage?"

"EchoEnergy would be paid to haul away Grade 2 stuff."

"How much?" Eric sat up.

"I'm not sure. We've never done it before so it's never been a part of our calculations."

"But you must have some idea?"

"After the hurricanes there was talk of the federal and state governments paying up to fifty dollars a ton for debris. I remember Dr. Lansik—" Sabrina stopped for a minute. The mention of his name reminded her that they weren't just having a chat about what she did for a living. "Dr. Lansik talked about it last fall, saying it would take EchoEnergy at least two years to add all the necessary equipment and facilities. But the hurricane areas wanted the mountains of debris gone before we could be up and running. He talked about it like it was only a missed opportunity."

"Maybe Sidel didn't want to miss out on it," Eric suggested and she recognized that look, that tone. He thought they had found the motive.

"No," Sabrina told him, shaking her head. "I still can't believe it would be enough to kill two people over."

"How many tons of slaughterhouse waste does EchoEnergy process now?"

"Anywhere from two hundred to three hundred tons a day."

"And they pay five thousand to seventy-five hundred for that. But if they were able to process that much Grade 2 and were paid fifty a ton, that's ten thousand to fifteen thousand dollars a day they'd bring in."

"But murdering people…"

"Bree, do the math—we're talking about three hundred thousand to four hundred fifty thousand dollars a month that EchoEnergy could be taking in without reporting it. That's—" He stopped to do the calculation in his head. "That's almost five million dollars a year. I hate to tell you, Bree, but people have been murdered for a lot less than that."

79

Tallahassee, Florida

Leon sat in the van with the windows rolled down. The hot night air stuck to him. He drank the last piss-warm soda in his cooler, the ice long ago melted. He couldn't risk running the engine and the air-conditioning or he'd draw too much attention to himself. Plus, he was low on gas. What the hell was taking the old lady so long?

He sat patiently while he watched her go through her condo. Her blinds and curtains were pulled tight in every window, but Leon knew where she was by the trail of lights that peeked around the window frames. He figured her condo had to be similar to her neighbor's, the Galloway woman, and he imagined which room she was in as the lights went on and off. If he was correct, she was spending some time in the kitchen. Probably fixing herself a late-night snack. He didn't need a reminder that he was long past dinner. In Leon's book there were two uncontrollable factors in life that could make a man do stupid, impulsive things. Those two factors were hunger and the need to take a leak. He'd hate to whack a little old lady before he got any information out of her just because he wanted a burger something awful.

Finally she was moving upstairs to bed, turning on and shutting off lights as she made her way. But even then her bedroom light stayed on for longer than Leon thought he could endure.

He popped a couple of Tums into his mouth just to have something to chew on. Son of a bitch! What the hell was she doing? It was close to midnight according to his cell phone.

A half hour later the bedroom light went out. Leon waited another grueling fifteen minutes, then he left the sauna of a van and found his way around to the back of the condos. This time his jumpsuit stuck to him in places that made it uncomfortable to even walk. In the silence he thought he could hear the sloshing of his sweat inside his shoes. Served him right for not wearing socks. How could anybody wear socks in this fucking heat?

He didn't remember it being this dark on the patio side. He waited for his eyes to adjust. The moon was almost full. A good thing for seeing, not such a good thing for creating shadows. Finding the key to the Galloway woman's condo had been a piece of cake. Leon doubted he'd find a spare to the little old woman's condo. For one thing, she'd never think to leave a spare because she'd never forget her original.

He was thinking he could pry open a window or dismantle the lock on the sliding glass door. He'd figure something out. It might just take a little more work. He sneaked around the crepe myrtle, keeping close to blend in to the landscape, so close he could feel the branches scratching his back. But when he came to the old woman's patio it was Leon who was startled and actually jumped.

Son of a bitch. He almost pissed his pants. Sitting there in the dark all calm and cool, sipping a glass of something tinkling with ice was the little old black woman, looking right at him.

"What took you so long?" she said.

80

"She could simply disappear," Russ suggested. "Become somebody else."

"I've thought about that," Eric said.

Truth is, he *had* already considered it. He was leaving the idea open as a contingency plan though he didn't think Sabrina would agree. If it did come to that, he knew Russ and Maxine could easily make it a reality.

Russ came off a bit immature. Max had once commented on his dimpled boyish grin being irresistible. Here was a fit, trim, muscular, good-looking young guy who seemed totally unaware of his charisma, a total innocent when it came to women. That was Maxine's take. Eric, on the other hand, knew Russ played the part simply because he could pull it off. He reminded Eric of a younger version of himself. Eric had been doing it for years, figure out who—

not what—people want to see and become that person. That was exactly how he had gone so easily from being Eric Galloway to Eric Gallo.

But he also knew Russ was a gentle sort of intellect who, at first, Eric would never have believed capable of any criminal behavior. Russ told stories about identity theft and online fraud, some of which Eric guessed—though Russ would never admit—were actually tales from his previous life. And Russ never mentioned being incarcerated, not even in jest, but Eric recognized a homemade prison tattoo when he saw one. He suspected Russ Fowler wasn't his real name, either, and he suspected the so-called hobbyist "Dumpster Diver" had not really stopped. He'd only gotten better at not getting caught.

As for Maxine, she came with a story all her own. Eric had actually met her in Washington, D.C., not a great place for starting over when your previous life included senators and congressmen, many of whom Maxine knew from what she liked to joke were "horizontal" relationships. One of those relationships ended up giving her HIV and forcing her into early retirement at the age of twenty-eight. Eric had directed her to a Pensacola physician who was discreet and could care less about politics or gossip. The rest she had done on her own.

She had a nice chunk of money that Eric didn't ask about or want to know the origin of. He only guessed that the source might be a guilty congressman's donation to her health insurance fund. With that donation, Max was able to change her identity and bought the salon on the beach. Seems she was a natural at creating new looks for others, as well. After all, she had already managed a whole transformation for Eric's sister. Sabrina's picture was all over the local and national news, yet a news junkie like the Mayor hadn't recognized her—a true test if ever there was one.

Eric was glad he had talked Sabrina into going up to the apartment and trying to get some sleep. Of course, that was after he convinced her that there was only one way into his second-floor apartment and they were all sitting in front of it. He knew she'd hate this—them batting around her options, trusting strangers to have a hand in her future, her well-being.

"This is serious stuff," Howard was saying. "This company's dumping waste into a major waterway. A company that's getting government funding."

"Not to mention tax incentives," the Mayor added. "Probably some government subsidies, too."

Eric waited for someone to suggest they contact the State Attorney's Office, the EPA, maybe even the Justice Department. Of course, he wasn't surprised when none of them did.

If Sabrina needed to disappear and become someone new, this was the group that could make it happen better than any witness protection program.

81

Tallahassee, Florida

"So what the hell's going on?" Leon tried to remain calm, his head pivoting around, looking for others, maybe the cops. But she was alone.

"You're not going to feed me some line about going door to door checking air conditioners, are you?"

"There's been a lot of outages," he attempted, though he'd already noticed the baseball bat leaning against her chair. How could she possibly have known?

She pointed to a chair across from her and then to an extra glass on the table already filled with ice. A bottle of whiskey sat beside the glass, open and waiting. She had to be kidding. Who the hell did she think he was? Even with a baseball bat she was no match for him. He sat down anyway and pulled the bottle over. He poured a full glass and took a sip. Not the expensive stuff, but not bad. Hell, in this heat he would have drunk gasoline had she served it to him on ice. He chugged the first glass and poured another.

"How did you know?" he finally asked. It was silly to pretend different.

"I noticed your van sitting out there when I drove up. But no one in the neighborhood seemed to be up. No lights. No commotion."

"Coulda been waiting on a part."

"So I called the company," she said as if she hadn't heard his explanation. "Their dispatcher told me they didn't have a van out in this neighborhood."

"Son of a bitch!" He was fucked now.

It was too bad he'd have to wring her neck after all. He thought maybe he could just stumble over something in the condo that would have been enough to find her neighbor. It was a stretch, but he figured he was due some luck. Guess he figured wrong, way wrong.

That was when the cat rubbed up against his legs. A huge white thing that almost glowed in the dark. The purr sounded like a distant engine rumbling. An old woman and her cat, Leon thought. Jesus! He couldn't get a break. He'd have to do the cat, too. Just out of courtesy.

Then he noticed a plastic container on her side of the table. The lid had been removed and left in the middle. In the moonlight he could see the white label with large black lettering that read, PORK CHOPS. His stomach actually growled as if on cue.

"I know who you are," the old woman said.

Leon caught himself licking his lips. Should he eat the pork chops before or after he offed her and the cat? Stupid impulses, he remembered. He probably should eat before.

"I want to hire you," she said and Leon was sure he heard her wrong.

"Hire me? Whadya mean hire me?"

"What's your price to turn the tables?" Her tone was surprisingly professional, not a tinge of fear or apprehension. And she did seem to know exactly who he was.

"Lady, I don't know what you're talking about."

"Whoever hired you to murder Sabrina Galloway," she continued, all matter-of-fact-like. "I want to hire you to make sure that person never, ever hurts her."

"Murder? Old woman, you're talking nonsense."

But Leon started sweating again. Did she know who had hired him? Nah, that was impossible. It didn't matter, anyway. The guy had pretty much told Leon he'd leave it to the State Patrol to take care of Galloway. Leon was on his own to take her out, so technically he was no longer hired. He no longer had a client. There would be no payout. He'd screwed that up royally. Other than the measly ten thousand dollars he got up front for expenses, this was a total fucking waste of a trip.

"I can pay you cash up front," the old woman calmly said like she could read his mind. She lifted a foil-wrapped package from the pork chop container.

He started to tell her to save her breath since it'd probably be her last one. But then she pulled open the foil. Forget about keeping a poker face, Leon felt his jaw drop and his eyes widen.

The old woman was serious and she had a serious wad of cash. She peeled off a chunk about an inch tall, a relatively small chunk considering what was left. Hell, the thing was as tall as a loaf of bread. She slid the small chunk to the middle of the table. On top was a crisp Ben Franklin. If those underneath were also hundred-dollar bills there had to be at least twenty-five to thirty-five thousand in just that one stack.

"It's not only about money, old lady. She saw me. And no matter how plain this mug of mine is, I'm not changing it," Leon told her.

The whole time he tried to keep his eyes off that container. It had made his mouth water when he thought it was pork chops. Now that he knew it was stuffed tight with hundred-dollar bills it made his mouth water even more. "Besides, what makes you think I won't tell you what you wanna hear, slit your throat and take that container full of cash anyway?"

She sat back and nodded like she was considering it. She reached for her glass, rattled the ice to stir it up a bit and took a long sip of the whiskey.

"Now see, I was thinking you were a businessman, not a petty crook." She continued to sip her whiskey. She was pretending it didn't matter to her one way or another whether he took her deal. "Doesn't make sense for a businessman to do something that's not necessary."

"She saw me," he said. It was as simple as that.

"What if I guarantee she won't remember a thing about you? Me, either, for that matter."

Leon laughed. "How the hell can you guarantee a thing like that?"

The old woman sat forward, hesitated, but only for a second. Then wrapping the foil around the huge loaf of cash she slid it over to him.

"Is that enough of a guarantee?" she asked.

Son of a bitch, Leon thought. There had to be over a quarter of a million dollars in that foil.

He looked up at her and this time she caught his eyes and held them. Over the years Leon had seen a lot of things in his clients' eyes: revenge, greed, power, even hate. But he'd never seen anything like this.

Leon opened up the foil. He brought out the solid stack of bills and held it in his hands. It was still cold from its storage in the freezer. It was, indeed, a tight stack of hundred-dollar bills, more than twice the money he'd ever been paid for a hit. He rewrapped it in the foil, including the small chunk from the middle of the table. He stuffed it under his arm and stood up.

"You've got yourself a deal," he said.

Then he left.

82

Natalie Richards despised the media. She hated the way they portrayed her boss and she knew for certain that they didn't always get the facts right. Even before Jayson Blair made up stories for the *New York Times,* quoting people he'd never talked to, let alone met, Natalie had developed a healthy distrust of reporters from her own assorted experiences. Natalie's boss, however, considered the media a necessary evil, so Natalie wasn't surprised to get immediate and full support of her plan.

She had met Gregory McDonald only once, last year when he was an investigative reporter and part-time anchor for ABC News. McDonald was credited with many breaking exposés, including the corruptive handling, or rather mishandling, of FEMA funds after Hurricane Katrina. His work was respected and awarded by his colleagues, but more importantly to Natalie, he had gained the trust of Washington insiders as being tough, accurate and confidential.

Ironically, Natalie hadn't met him while he was working on a story. Instead, they were introduced at a Christmas party thrown by Warren Buffett, of all people. Natalie's invitation had been an accident, at best, especially when her boss had to cancel at the last minute. In the middle of celebrities, politicians and media people, Gregory McDonald had been kind enough to spend time talking to her about teenage boys—he had three of his own—and their expectations for Christmas. At the time he had no clue who Natalie was or who she worked for and that alone had won Natalie over.

Today she was pretty sure no one would recognize her here at the Roosevelt Memorial, either. Nor would they expect to see her dressed in blue jeans and a Smithsonian Museum T-shirt. She wore sunglasses and carried a canvas tote bag over her shoulder imprinted with a colorful panorama of the Washington monuments. With any luck she looked like just another tourist. Maybe she had a bit of Emma Peel in her, after all.

As she waited for McDonald, she couldn't help wondering if this story would be the one to propel him to the evening anchor position he was rumored to be in line for. She shifted the tote bag from one shoulder to the other. It'd be nice to think some good could come out of such a mess.

A man walked up to read one of the monument plaques behind her. He wore running shorts and a T-shirt and lugged an old backpack. She stepped aside and checked her watch. The mall was crowded with June tourists, a few loners and families but mostly field trips of docile senior citizens or screeching high-school students.

The man with the backpack stepped around to stand beside her and she was about to give him her best "shove-off" look when she recognized his smile.

"You sure are skinnier and much shorter than I remember," she told Gregory McDonald.

"Cameras add ten pounds."

"Uh-huh. That's exactly why I stay away from them."

Natalie glanced around. A new group was making its way from room to room in the Memorial. No one seemed interested in the two of them. Satisfied, she nodded toward a bench along the wall.

"Timing's everything in your business," she said to McDonald as she pulled an envelope from her tote bag and handed it to him. He didn't hesitate or ask any questions. He simply took the envelope and slipped it into a side pocket of his backpack.

"I understand the same is true in your business," he said with no threat or urgency, his tone as casual as if they were two friends chatting about the daily grind of their careers. Then as he stood and adjusted his backpack, ready to leave, he added, "You know I wouldn't be doing my job if I didn't ask. So is your boss planning to run next time around?"

She knew without further explanation that he meant "run for president," of course. The speculations were already swirling around, but Natalie's boss had managed to avoid answering while keeping all options open.

Natalie simply smiled. "Let's just say if your timing's right you'll be the first to know."

83

Jason handed off the information he found on Arthur Galloway, but Senator Allen no longer looked interested. Jason knew his boss's mind was, no doubt, preoccupied with more important matters. The Appropriations Committee was set for a vote early tomorrow morning. Jason wouldn't be there. He was scheduled to be in Florida, seeing to the reception details, what he believed would still be a celebration.

Senator Malone's vote would be enough, and yet Senator Allen hadn't stopped pacing his office, the nervous energy jerking the muscles in his jaw all the way down to his shoulders.

"Is there anything else you need?" Jason asked and was surprised to see a grin, no, more of a smirk.

"We've done all we can," he said, without stopping his march, and then adding, like a general preparing for battle, "I won't go down without a fight."

Now back in his office, Jason couldn't concentrate. He had a hell of a lot of work to do before he left for Florida tomorrow morning. He hated being away from the office for three whole days and hated even more the idea of coming back to these piles on his desk.

He had stayed up late, surfing Google and the Net for more connections between Sidel and Zach. The South Beach Resort had been the only one he could find. Maybe it had been a coincidence. To make matters worse, his secretary had brought him a bulging envelope of forms that needed to be filled out and returned ASAP. The label read Contract Renewal. From what Jason could tell, after a quick glance, they looked like standard, mindless stuff—exactly what he needed. He didn't have the attention span for anything more.

Jason pulled out the forms, ready to start filling in the blanks when he noticed EchoEnergy preprinted in the contractor space. He double-checked the envelope and then the description of the contract. This was one he didn't know about and yet it was up for renewal, which meant, in this case, the one-year deadline was coming up.

Jason always prepared the Appropriations Committee contracts that the senator introduced and endorsed. And certainly Jason would have remembered one being awarded to EchoEnergy. He flipped through the pages, but he still didn't recognize any of it. From what he could tell, it had bypassed a subcommittee vote because it had been considered part of the overall disaster package after the onslaught of hurricanes over the last several years. Senator Allen's signature was scrawled across the bottom of the final page with several indecipherable initials in two other approval lines.

Jason grabbed a pen and began filling out the form. So what if he hadn't seen this cross Senator Allen's desk? There had been hundreds of these after the devastation left by the hurricanes. And though it was a bit odd that Senator Allen hadn't mentioned anything, it wasn't unusual. So what if it slipped Senator Allen's mind that EchoEnergy had already been awarded a multi-million-dollar contract with the federal government to dispose of hurricane debris?

Jason sat back and pushed away from the form on his desk. He contemplated throwing a dart, but chose instead to twist and turn it between his fingers.

It wouldn't slip the senator's mind. It would have been another bragging point, a testament of the good and brilliant things EchoEnergy was capable of. In fact, Jason didn't even know EchoEnergy could process hurricane debris. He thought it was only chicken guts. Why wouldn't there have been mention of it on their tour? That did seem odd. Eliminating hurricane debris *and* turning it to oil would be a huge accomplishment Sidel couldn't resist bragging about.

So why wasn't he?

As he leaned back in his office chair, tapping the feathers of the dart against his temple, Jason had a bad feeling in his gut. This wasn't right. Something was going on and he didn't like it. He released the dart and absently looked up at the dartboard.

He'd missed the bull's-eye.

84

Eric took Howard by surprise. At least that's what it looked like. Howard mumbled something into the phone and quickly got off.

Eric wondered if it may have been Howard's old friends who were supposed to be sailing up from Miami. For friends Howard sure seemed to be a bit on edge about their visit, and there didn't seem to be much that put Howard on edge.

Howard didn't talk about his former friends or his previous life. Neither did Eric. None of the group that hung out at Bobbye's did. Eric knew through his own sources that once upon a time Howard Johnson had made millions of dollars trafficking drugs from South America up through Miami. The story was that the feds had made Howard an offer to rat out his suppliers. Instead, Howard decided to thumb his nose at all of them and simply retire before the feds had anything on him and before his suppliers got paranoid. No matter how much of the story was true, Eric was convinced that sort of a life wasn't one somebody just walked away from. He was looking for Howard's friends to be old friends and he wouldn't be surprised if they had a little something for Howard.

"The Minnesotans canceling out?" Eric asked, giving Howard a chance to share his covert phone call.

"No, I haven't heard anything from them." He glanced at his watch. "I expect they'll be here in the next hour." Then he pointed to the TV and the ever-present Fox News channel. "Florida authorities are searching for your friend in Chicago. Media's on it up there, too. They had an interview with some professor at the university where she taught. One of her students, too. Nothing new, just your basic 'I never knew she was capable of such a thing' interview."

"Jesus!" Eric knew it was only a matter of time before the media discovered their dad, maybe even Eric. "Do me a favor. Don't mention it to Bree, okay?"

"Sure, no problem." Howard continued his morning routine, opening the cash register and checking the Visa/MC machine, but then he stopped and turned back to Eric, as if there was something he'd been meaning to tell him. His eyes were serious under bushy white eyebrows.

Here it was, Eric thought. Time for true confessions. Howard was finally ready to give him the dirt on what he was really up to.

"You're a good friend," Howard said, emphasizing *friend*.

It wasn't at all what Eric expected him to say. And now Eric realized he'd mistaken the look in Howard's eyes. Howard wasn't getting ready to confess and come clean. He was encouraging Eric to.

"Look, it's none of my business and you don't have to tell me a damn thing. It's just...Gallo, Galloway..." He shrugged and picked up the inventory clipboard, leaving the conversation there and letting Eric decide to tell him or not.

"It's complicated," Eric said and scratched at his bristled jaw like his answer required some thought. He knew it wouldn't matter all that much if he admitted he'd changed his name.

"Sure, I understand." Again Howard shrugged his huge shoulders, this time the gesture so animated he set in motion the pattern of sailfish on his boat shirt. A gesture that betrayed his words.

It surprised Eric, though not enough not for him to risk an explanation. He'd already gotten too close to Howard, too friendly. It was better that Howard think he was a liar than for him to know the truth, that Eric was only interested in Howard's drug connections.

"I definitely know about stuff being complicated," Howard said just when Eric thought the subject was closed. Maybe he'd luck out, after all, and get Howard to share, not only information, but a piece of the action.

"If something ever happens to me I'd like you to have all my models." He waved his hand up at the shelf that surrounded the shop, a foot from the ceiling and crowded with perfectly crafted and finely detailed boats and ships from various eras.

Again, he surprised Eric. He knew the collection, one that Howard continuously added to, was his prized possession. Never mind that he owned a successful deep-sea fishing service as well as the prime real estate the shop and the parking lot sat on. The model collection was something Howard built with his hands, something uniquely his.

"What are you talking about?" Eric tried to dismiss the tremendous gesture, almost hoping it was some kind of trick. "Nothing's gonna happen to you."

"I'm just saying in case something does."

"What's gonna happen? Nothing's gonna happen."

"What you're doing for Sabrina...not many friends would risk their

ALEX KAVA

necks like that," Howard told him, his eyes still running over his collection, avoiding Eric's. "Not any of mine would. You're a good man."

Eric wasn't prepared for any of this.

85

Sabrina stared at the small, purple notebook. It fell out of the file folder she had taken from Dr. Lansik's desk last Friday. She'd stuffed the folder into her briefcase and forgotten about it. Now there was the notebook on Eric's floor, its worn corners and scratched vinyl cover reminding her of her deceased boss. She recognized it. Lansik usually carried it around with him everywhere. O'Hearn had once jokingly called it Lansik's purple bible.

She started flipping through pages. Not even halfway through, she realized the notes in the margins appeared to have nothing to do with the notes on the pages. Lansik seemed to be writing in code in his own notebook. On the pages everything was in black ink. In the margins the notes were written in blue ink, a few in red. Sabrina couldn't be sure, but she thought some of gobbledygook might be computer code.

There were formulas of some kind, too, but none she recognized. And toward the back of the notebook in a lower corner, printed in red, was what looked like a phone number with the name Colin Jernigan, DOJ above it. The number was important enough that Lansik had scratched a red box around it, outlining it with such pressure the pen had broken through the paper on a second or third pass around one of the corners.

That's when Eric came in the apartment front door. Sabrina slammed the notebook shut as if she'd been caught reading some illicit papers. Okay, so maybe she still didn't trust him.

Eric noticed. Of course he noticed, but all he said was, "Bring that along. Let's get some lunch."

"Out in the open? Just like that? I thought I was supposed to be hiding."

"There's no better place to hide than in plain sight."

They walked to a restaurant called Crabs and got a table on the deck overlooking the crowded beach. It was noisier here than at the marina, with shouts and laughter interspersed with lifeguard whistles. Several of the beachside bars added to the fray with their loudspeakers blaring Bob Marley and Britney Spears. Eric ordered a combination seafood platter. Sabrina ordered the grilled grouper sandwich when she really wanted an egg salad and her old routine back.

She kept the notebook on the bench beside her, not sure she knew what she had found and not sure she wanted to share any of it with Eric. She sat back and watched him. His eyes were everywhere except on her. She glanced over to see what had his attention and saw two uniformed cops at another table. She wondered if Eric was concerned they'd recognize her, or was he worried about himself? Was that the reason he had become Eric Gallo? Eric's roaming eyes reminded her of her dad's, darting off around her. Thinking about her father made her stomach ache. How had this gotten so out of hand?

"We need to see if Dad's okay." She said it out loud before she changed her mind. It brought Eric's eyes to hers. "He might be in danger," she added when she didn't see sufficient concern. Then, as if she had reverted to twelve years old, she heard herself say, "Or don't you care about him anymore?"

She thought she saw a flicker of anger before he looked away. This time he was distracted by his young friend, the one with the shaved head and patient, kind eyes. Eric slid over on the bench and made room for him. He handed Eric an envelope as he plopped down his laptop.

"Bree, you remember Russ." Eric said it so casually that Sabrina stared at him, wondering how he could treat this ordeal like she was on vacation. And yet at the same time she noticed Eric's eyes again, taking in the entire deck, scanning the beach below, watching and looking. Maybe he wasn't so casual.

Russ simply smiled and nodded at Sabrina as he opened his laptop. He reminded her of one of her students, though he was a little older. There was something shy and humble in his demeanor, but she got the impression it might be uncharacteristic and for her benefit. She wasn't totally oblivious to boys or men who had crushes on her.

"I discovered a few things that might be of interest."

He tapped the computer keys with what Sabrina thought was a light touch for such large hands. He moved the laptop to the edge of the table, the screen facing toward them. He tapped a couple more keys then sat back, leaving a bird's-eye view of treetops and buildings.

Sabrina sat forward, elbows on the table, trying to get a closer look. Eric didn't move from his corner of the table, eyes still on duty. But it was Eric who asked, "A satellite picture?"

"Not just any satellite picture," Russ confirmed, smiling now as he reached to move a fingertip over the touchpad and click once. "It's a satellite picture in real time. I saved it from this morning. Made a file on the hard drive and I have a printout." He pointed at the date and time stamp in the corner. It was stamped for Wednesday, June 14th at 6:05 that morning.

The photo zoomed in and Sabrina recognized it immediately. It was EchoEnergy's industrial park.

"How are you able to get real time?" Eric asked and now he huddled up to the table, the computer screen getting his full attention.

"I know a few tricks. Never mind how I did it. Take a look." He clicked again, zooming in even more.

Sabrina could see the maze of pipes and catwalks and rooftops. But most of all she could see down into the trucks with open-top beds. Enclosed tanker trucks brought slaughterhouse waste from poultry processors. These trucks usually came before or after hours. Sabrina had noticed them when she stayed working late. She thought they were part of the ongoing construction. There were constant additions or upgrades to the campus. New construction, however, would mean lumber, bricks, pipes separated out and in new condition. It didn't mean thrown together in what looked like piles of debris in the backs of these trucks.

Her eyes found what she knew was Reactor #5. She followed the maze of pipes that connected the reactor to its outside holding tank. That tank was three stories tall with walled chutes that moved the waste on a conveyor belt from the trucks up into the tank. She believed it was being used as a backup storage facility for oil until Reactor #5 came online. But from this bird's-eye view she could see that wasn't true.

"They're processing hurricane debris," Sabrina said in almost a whisper. How could they have kept this a secret?

86

Eric slid the manila envelope Russ had brought him off the table and onto the bench between them. He had positioned himself so he could keep an eye on what was happening inside and outside the busy restaurant. However, the two Santa Rosa deputies reminded him that no place was safe. Maybe he was simply being cocky and stupid, which wouldn't be the first time. It was fine when he was the only one who could get hurt from his own stupidity. This was different.

He waved at Maxine, who came up the steps to join them. He tried not to look relieved. He was counting on Max to help him convince Sabrina that the contents of Russ's envelope were a necessity. How was he supposed to tell his little sister, whom he hadn't seen for two years, that she needed to disappear? He used to be her best friend—when they were kids, her hero—but he knew he'd abdicated both positions when he left Chicago without even a goodbye.

That was a crazy time for him. How could he explain it to Sabrina when he couldn't explain it to himself? All he remembered was the anger. He was angry at his father for not taking better care of their mother. *How could he let her drive alone in weather like that?* And he was angry with Sabrina for not blaming their dad. Mix all that up with the sense of loss and it felt like he'd been sideswiped by an eighteen-wheeler. Damn, it hurt like hell, but it pissed him off, too.

It sounded childish and immature. Hell, it *was* childish and immature. But all he wanted to do at the time was wrap himself in his anger. It didn't make the hole in his gut go away, but helped keep his mind off it until he could find something else or someone else to channel his anger.

Max looked exhausted, her eyes bloodshot. Eric knew she hadn't had that much to drink last night. He worried it might be the new meds, but she'd made him promise he wouldn't ask. She said she was tired of being asked how she was feeling.

Her eyes met his across the table and he could see the warning, but then there was the slightest of smiles, an acknowledgment, perhaps a subtle thank-you for his concern. Max was the only one who knew Eric's secrets—who he was, what he was really doing on Pensacola Beach. They could trust each other because they knew too much about each other.

Eric's cell phone started ringing and he grabbed it before the deputies three tables away noticed.

"Hello?"

"Is this Eric?"

It took him a second, but he recognized the old woman's voice. "You made it home safely, I hope?"

Sabrina sat up and leaned forward, her entire face instantly registering concern, her eyes holding his eyes, ready to read them.

"Please tell your sister that she doesn't need to worry about her gentleman caller."

"Really? Why is that?"

"Just tell her I took care of things."

"How is that possible?" But the click told him she was already gone. He had told her to keep any calls short and not use specifics.

"Is she okay?" Sabrina wanted to know.

"I guess so. She said you don't have to worry about your gentleman caller."

"She said that?"

"She said she took care of things." He tried to repeat her exact words.

"I don't understand. How could she have taken care of him?"

Eric shrugged. He didn't want Sabrina to worry, but he had no idea how an eighty-one-year-old woman could take care of a hit man.

Besides, right now it looked like they had bigger problems. Eric watched the pair of deputies stand, the older one hiking his pants then heading for the cash register. But the younger one, the one Eric guessed was a thick-necked rookie with an attitude, had glanced in their direction. Something caught his eye after a double take. It seemed impossible that he'd recognize Sabrina. Impossible, but the asshole was coming over to their table.

87

Natalie knew the woman sitting across the table was as different from her as their desserts. Senator Shirley Malone was crème brûlée, upper-class, high maintenance, a little crusty on top, but soft inside. Natalie was strawberry-rhubarb pie, homegrown, unpretentious, straight-forward—what you see is what you get—though maybe a bit tart.

They were also unlikely lunch companions, and seeing them together at a Washington restaurant would certainly raise questions. But here in Senator Malone's suite at the Mayflower no one would know. That fact didn't make Natalie any more comfortable. She was used to having the home-turf advantage, but these were desperate days when adversaries joined as patriots and could be found in the strangest places. This morning was the Roosevelt Memorial, this afternoon the Mayflower Hotel, all a part of what she hoped she could make happen before her forty-eight hours were up.

"They also make a cherry pie that's outstanding," the senator told her before taking a sip of her tea.

Natalie caught herself staring at the woman's long, delicate pinkie extended perfectly from the handle of her teacup. Natalie refrained from rolling her eyes. They both knew this wasn't a social call.

"With all due respect, Senator," Natalie said, sliding her dessert plate to the side. "I know you're a busy woman. I have a full schedule myself. So I hope you don't mind if we dispense with the niceties."

"Tell you what, Ms. Richards, I'll stop with the Betty Crocker niceties if you cut the crap."

Natalie's eyebrows raised before she could stop them, but at least she kept her jaw from dropping.

"For starters," Senator Malone continued, "why are you here instead of your boss?"

Normally, Natalie detested women who had ridden their way to Washington power on the coattails of their husbands, but Malone had won a senatorial term on her own and it hadn't been an easy battle. She had proven herself on the senate floor, too. A mind of her own, not yet jaded by her colleagues or bogged down by favors or paybacks. If she hadn't proven herself, Natalie wouldn't be here right now.

"This one's a bit personal," Natalie confessed.

Senator Malone set down her teacup and sat back, crossing her arms, examining Natalie. For a woman who claimed not to know insider politics she played the game very well. Natalie wondered if perhaps this was a mistake.

"There's a good chance the focus of the energy summit will shift," Natalie told her, choosing her words carefully. "If that happens, there'll be an opportunity and a necessity for someone to step forward and lead."

Malone was silent, but Natalie could see a twitch at the corner of her mouth, an uncomfortable nervous twitch.

"I thought the president controls the focus of this summit?" Malone's question was asked with what sounded like a great deal of uncertainty or perhaps naiveté.

This time Natalie sat back. She let her eyes survey the hotel suite, taking in the senator's attempts to personalize it with framed photographs, stacks of books and a collection of miniature teapots. That Senator Malone would even ask that question confirmed that Natalie had not made a mistake. Instead, she had chosen wisely.

88

Pensacola Beach, Florida

Sabrina saw Eric nudge Russ and the laptop's screen went from the live satellite to a chess game in progress. That was all the warning she got. Suddenly there was a cop in a green uniform standing beside their table.

"Good afternoon," the deputy said, his eyes on Eric and thankfully not her. Otherwise he would have certainly seen a flash of panic.

"Good afternoon, Deputy...Kluger," Eric said, slipping his eyes down to the deputy's badge.

That was Eric, taking time to notice name tags. Usually it was charming. This time Sabrina could feel her teeth clench. Below the table her hands shredded her paper napkin. Eric's hands, however, were on the table, steady and calm, and Sabrina wondered if he was keeping them there for the deputy to see. No funny moves. Isn't that what they always did in the movies?

"You tend bar over at Bobbye's?" the deputy asked Eric.

"Sometimes. Yeah, I do." Eric still looked cool and calm while Sabrina could feel and hear her heart throbbing so hard against her rib cage she thought surely the deputy would also hear the vibration.

"Some of us want to throw a birthday bash for one of the guys. Any chance we could get the place to ourselves?"

Eric stared at the guy. Sabrina glanced at Russ and Max. They were staring at the deputy, too, as if he spoke a foreign language none of them understood. The deputy noticed.

"We wouldn't expect any special discounts," the deputy said. "We just want someplace nice, a little private—you know, off the main beach."

"Oh, sure," Eric told him now, sounding like it was no big deal. "Stop by Howard's shop and we can figure out a day. We'll get it all set up."

"Sounds good. I'll do that."

The deputy left and they all went silent. Russ tapped at the computer keyboard and Max tapped almost in rhythm with a folded newspaper against the table. Sabrina looked from one to the other, uneasy with their calm. Maybe they were used to this sort of stuff. She was not.

Finally Eric smiled at her. "That wasn't exactly what I expected him to want to talk about."

"No kidding," she said and wished she could shrug it off as easily as he seemed to be able to.

"This might actually be a good time to talk to you about this."

He slid a manila envelope onto the table. Sabrina watched his eyes surveying their surroundings again, still cool and calm. He was good. He didn't know what the deputy wanted, but he did know how to act, what to say or more important, what not to say. How did he get so good at this?

He opened the envelope and handed her two plastic cards. One was a driver's license, the other a credit card. She glanced at them and didn't recognize the name. She started to hand them back when suddenly she took a better look at the photo on the driver's license. It was her.

"Where did you get this?"

"Russ put them together," Eric said.

"I found the photo on the university's Web site," Russ explained with a proud grin, mistaking Sabrina's surprise for a compliment. "I copied it, used PhotoShop to change the hair to look like you're wearing it now. I was even able to give you a tan."

When she didn't answer and only stared at the two cards, Russ continued, "The credit card's legit. So is the name. It's okay. Kathryn Fulton's living in London. She's been subletting her place on the beach for over a year." Russ was looking from Sabrina to Eric and then at Max as if trying to get some help in reading Sabrina's reaction.

"She still gets mail here sometimes. You know, like credit card offers. I'm not saying it'll work forever, but it's the best I could do in less than twenty-four hours."

Sabrina didn't know what to say, what to think. It couldn't be that easy, could it? All of this was happening too fast.

"So I just become someone else?"

No one said anything.

"I just change my name and disappear?" Sabrina asked Eric, waiting for him to look at her instead of everywhere else around the damn restaurant. "That's your answer, because it worked so well for you?"

It was a low blow in front of his friends and Sabrina knew it.

"I'm not leaving Dad behind," she told him and she didn't care if his friends had no idea she was his sister. Then the next part surprised her because it wasn't about hurting him or standing up to him, it was about standing up for herself. "And I'm not going to run away and let Sidel continue doing what he's doing."

They sat in silence. Eric's eyes had shifted already, but now she suspected they were avoiding her rather than simply looking out for her. Sabrina wanted to get up and leave, but she wasn't sure where she'd go. If this was Eric's attempt at helping her and she refused it, where did that leave her?

"Actually, I'm glad you said that," Max finally said. She laid the folded newspaper she had brought with her on the table, opening it and pointing to a small article at the bottom of the page. "This was in the *Tallahassee Democrat*. I've been keeping up with the case for a few weeks now." She stopped and glanced at Eric. Sabrina wondered if Max was giving him the chance to shut her up. The look Sabrina saw them exchange told her there was something more between them.

Max slid the newspaper in front of Sabrina. Her first impression of Max was that nothing could surprise or bother her. She envied her street smarts and her "I don't give a damn" attitude. But now Max sounded tentative, her voice a notch lower, her small hands fidgeting without the newspaper. "I have some health challenges that sort of came about from…well, let's just say it's something I didn't expect. This," she said, tapping the article, "is something I don't think any of us can know about and just walk away."

"Toxins found in water." Sabrina read the headline out loud. She remembered reading about this last week before she had any idea that EchoEnergy could have something to do with it. She continued to read the rest of the article in silence, her stomach twisting in knots. The article read:

Jackson Springs, a bottled-water company located outside of Tallahas-see was recently closed down after toxins were discovered in their prod-uct. Several customers had complained of nausea and headaches after drinking the bottled water. One ten-year-old was hospitalized with diox-ins found in her bloodstream. Though the dioxins cannot be traced back specifically to a bottle of Jackson Springs, the company was cited when traces of the deadly toxin showed up in random samples.

Sabrina stopped and looked up at the rest of them. "If it's already contaminated the river, they had to have been dumping the runoff for months."

"And getting away with it," Max added.

89

Jason wanted to go home early to pack. Early, hell, it was almost six. He had an early flight out of Reagan. His boss wasn't scheduled to arrive until just before the evening reception, but Jason needed to make certain all the details were taken care of: caterer, tables and chairs, podiums, microphone. Sidel was supposed to be co-hosting the event, but Senator Allen had asked Jason to take care of setting it up. He'd prepared and ordered and arranged things weeks ago. Hopefully now it would just be a matter of checking and double-checking.

He took the stairs rather than risk running into anyone on the elevators. He didn't need another delay or he'd never leave. His list was still full, despite the load he had tucked under his arm, half of it headed for Senator Allen's secretary and the other half for the senator's desk. He'd made copies of everything that had to go with him. Those copies and everything he hadn't been able to finish waited to be stuffed into his briefcase.

Jason turned the corner and almost ran into Senator Shirley Malone. She had a pile of her own tucked under her arm.

"Looks like we're trying to do the same thing."

"Yeah," he said, but he was wondering why Lindy wasn't toting the pile around and delivering her can't-wait-'til-Monday stuff instead of Senator Malone.

"I thought you'd probably left for Florida," she added. "Lindy took off a couple of hours ago."

Had she read his mind? Jason stopped himself from saying something stupid like, *We're not in a relationship*. He had no idea what, if anything, Lindy had told her boss about their one-night fling. Maybe he was jumping to conclusions that Senator Malone meant for those two statements to be connected.

"I leave first thing in the morning," he told her. "How about you?"

"I leave after the Appropriations Committee vote. Hopefully I'll still be invited to the opening reception."

"Of course you are," he blurted out. He wanted to ask why she thought she might not be. Was she telling him they couldn't count on her vote? No, she was joking. She had to be. "Besides," he continued, trying to tap in to what little charm he had in him, "I'm in charge of invites."

She smiled, and if he wasn't totally mistaken he thought there was even a bit of a blush. Then suddenly her face was serious.

"I've been meaning to tell you how sorry I was about Zach."

"I didn't really know him all that well," Jason said, wondering why she thought he did. What did Lindy tell her? He shifted the pile of envelopes and folders to the other arm.

"Oh," was all she said, but from the look on her face Jason could tell she believed otherwise.

"We played basketball once. Some fund-raiser." He wasn't sure why he felt he needed to explain or deny.

"I knew Zach and Lindy were friends. I guess I thought the three of you..." She shook her head and continued, "I'm sorry. That sounds totally presumptuous."

"I wasn't lying when I told you I hadn't met Lindy before the night of her birthday party." Now he was explaining too much, but he wanted her to know. No matter what Lindy might have told her, suddenly Jason realized he needed Senator Malone to know the truth.

She was distracted, looking over his shoulder at something or someone. Jason turned to find a man he didn't recognize coming up the hallway toward them. His sport jacket was too cheap for him to be a lobbyist and he was too old—at least fifty—to be a staff member.

"Jason Brill?"

If Jason had been alone he probably would have claimed not to know any Jason Brill.

"Yeah, that's me."

The man flapped a badge at him. "Detective Bob Christopher. I just have a few questions if you have a minute."

"Actually, Detective, I don't. I should have had all this delivered an hour ago." Jason indicated the load tucked under his arm.

"It'll only take a minute." The detective was squinting at Senator Malone like he recognized her, but couldn't quite come up with a name.

"I'll leave you two alone," Senator Malone said, and Jason felt her hand brush his shoulder, a sort of good-luck gesture or perhaps in this case a "sorry, you're fucked" gesture.

Detective Christopher watched her all the way until she turned the corner. Not a bad sight, Jason found himself thinking.

"I do need to get this stuff delivered," Jason prompted him. He wondered if Lindy was telling everyone, including the cops, that the three of them were friends.

"There was a picture of you on Zach Kensor's cell phone."

"What?" Jason almost dropped the stack.

"It's time-stamped from the night before he was murdered."

Of course, the party, but Jason didn't think he'd gotten close enough.

Detective Christopher kept his eyes moving back and forth, up and down the hallway, but there was no one else. "And we know you were at the same hotel as Mr. Kensor later that night. I believe until the next morning."

Jason felt his jaw clench. Lindy, he thought, but tried to keep a straight face. It didn't work. He wanted to tell the detective about William Sidel and Zach, that he'd discovered the two of them may have stayed at the South Beach Resort at the same time. But how could he say anything when he'd obtained the information illegally? Without meaning to, he suddenly forgot all about the cool, calm attitude Senator Allen had taught him. Jason found himself, instead, reacting like Uncle Louie.

"Am I a suspect, Detective?" He even felt the snarl of his upper lip, just like his Uncle Louie.

"Of course not, Mr. Brill. If you were I wouldn't be talking to you out here in the middle of the hallway."

"Then this conversation is over," Jason said, and he walked away, forcing his hands to stop shaking, but at the same time keeping his free hand from balling up into a fist. At least until he turned the corner and left the detective's line of vision.

90

Pensacola Beach, Florida

Eric was surprised to come down and find that Howard had closed Bobbye's Oyster Bar to the public. Rope barriers blocked off the boardwalk's entrance. The signs they used—Closed for Private Party—were posted. Howard had the grill fired up, filling the surrounding air with the aroma of garlic, barbecue, pineapple and hickory.

At first Eric thought it was all for the Minnesotans. When Eric asked, Howard laughed, waving the stainless-steel tongs at Eric. "Hell no, they rescheduled."

"But you've got the place cordoned off for a private party?"

"What's the use of having a place of your own if you can't close up once in a while and make dinner for your friends? Russ mentioned we needed to come up with a plan. I figure we'll think better with full stomachs."

Eric simply nodded and got to work restocking the bar. He worried about Sabrina. He hadn't expected this "fight to make it right" attitude. She was looking at this as one of her scientific puzzles, that if only she applied logic and the appropriate formula she'd discover a resolution. Their dad was the same way. Looking at life as if everything were a mathematical equation, a sum of parts that when pieced together would be whole and complete. Life wasn't like that.

Eric emptied oysters from a burlap bag into a plastic bus tub. At the sink he ran cold water over the shells to rinse them before he put them on ice.

He knew it would be easier if Sabrina would accept the new identity, at least temporarily. It'd give him time to come up with something better. He could eventually figure out what to do with their dad, if she insisted. Though he wanted to tell her that in his current mindset their dad was already out of their lives. She obviously hadn't accepted that yet. For scientists with an answer for everything, Sabrina and their dad were pretty good at denial.

Howard brought some shrimp over to be cleaned.

"You mind doing these when you're finished?"

"No problem." Eric drained the bus tub and filled it with ice before he realized Howard was still at his side as if he'd forgotten something.

"Those friends of mine from Miami," he said, waiting for Eric to nod that he remembered. Of course Eric remembered. He'd been looking for their boat since last week.

"They're supposed to be here about midnight," Howard told him, glancing out at the bay. "You mind sticking around and meeting them with me?"

No matter how much he liked Howard, Eric felt like he had plunged his hands elbow deep into the ice. Was that what all this talk about friends was for? To prepare Eric for meeting his Miami friends? What a great time for Howard to trick him, take advantage while Eric was preoccupied with helping Sabrina.

"Sure," Eric told him. He wished Sabrina had taken that new identity and gotten far away from here before Howard's drug-trafficking buddies arrived.

91

A week ago Sabrina remembered whining about being alone. Now suddenly sitting at the beach-bistro table she had a group of strangers plotting her future. She wasn't surprised that Eric had surrounded himself with what, at first appearances, seemed to be misfits. After all, he was the one always bringing home stray dogs and later in college bringing home kids who had nowhere to go for the holidays. "Mr. Charming," as their mom affectionately called Eric, had no problem making friends, getting dates or even getting jobs. It was the keeping part that usually tripped him up.

Between bites of Howard's smorgasbord of shucked oysters, grilled scallops, shrimp, scampi and vegetables, Eric and Sabrina fielded questions and relayed information. The group sat around their favorite table at the edge of the pier, tiki lamps and citronella candles the only light other than the moon. Any other time Sabrina would have enjoyed the sound of the water sloshing up against boats in their slips. The night birds were a bit different here on the gulf than the ones she and Miss Sadie listened to back in Tallahassee. She sighed and once again she hoped Miss Sadie was okay. She missed the old woman, her quiet calm and wise counsel. Sabrina couldn't help wondering what magic the old woman had performed to make Sidel's hired assassin just go away.

"You said a computer software program controlled the process," Russ said, interrupting her thoughts.

"Yes, and Dr. Lansik was the only one with access to change it." It was the second time Sabrina had explained this. Maybe the guy wasn't as much of a computer expert as he pretended to be. He reminded her of male students who wanted her attention though they had no idea what they were talking about.

"The same program would have to be used to process anything that came into the plant then, right?"

Sabrina nodded. "Lansik designed the program alongside another scientist engineer who designed the plant before any of it was built."

"So anything that came through Reactor #5 would have to be done with this computer program," Russ said, pointing a plastic swizzle stick at her as if to emphasize his point, a point Sabrina thought was pointless because they already suspected this might be the reason Lansik had been killed. Russ wasn't finished. "Then there's a file, a record, embedded in the network."

Sabrina stopped with a shrimp halfway to her mouth. Everyone else had stopped, too. Okay, so maybe this guy wasn't just cute and flirting with her.

"Even if they've gone in and erased the files from their particular computer or hard drives," Russ explained, still waving the swizzle stick like it was a wand, "it wouldn't have erased the copy saved on the network's server."

"Wait," Eric said. "Are you saying there may be some sort of record to prove that they've been processing hurricane debris out of Reactor #5?"

"Depends on how detailed the computer program is," Russ said, looking at Sabrina for the answer. "What are you able to see when you access the program to view the various processes?"

"You can't see exactly what's inside the pipes. It tracks the flow, the temperatures, the coking times, what valves are opened or closed." She tried to envision the computer screen and all the data that appeared.

"Would it differentiate between chicken guts and hurricane debris?" Eric looked hopeful.

"Everything would be different," Sabrina said. "The entire formula is different."

"That's it, then." Eric slapped a palm down on the table. "We already have satellite photos of what's being brought in. We just need a copy of the processing file. And Russ here can hack right in and get one, right?"

Sabrina caught Russ's eyes before they dropped. She already knew it couldn't be done before he told them, "I'm afraid it's not possible."

Sabrina could tell Eric wasn't happy with that answer. She could see him sitting on the edge of his chair and even in the dim light she saw his jaw clenched and his eyes narrowed. He'd been on edge since she'd refused his generous offer of a new identity.

"Not possible," Eric said, "or you just don't know how to do it?"

"Easy now." Howard laid a hand on Eric's shoulder.

"You know I'd do it if I could, dude," Russ said, but Sabrina didn't think he sounded defensive as much as hurt.

"But you don't know how. I understand." Eric's tone was one she recognized, a sort of taunt laced with betrayal. He had their mother's talent of using words as weapons.

"He can't do it," Sabrina interrupted, "because he'd have to use a computer at EchoEnergy."

She waited for Eric's eyes to leave Russ and find hers. When they finally did, some of the intensity had softened.

"So we find a way back into EchoEnergy," Maxine volunteered, but Sabrina guessed from her smile that she was simply trying to lighten things up.

"That's not a bad idea," the Mayor joined in, only Sabrina didn't think he was joking. She had counted him at his fifth pink lady.

"Security is pretty tight," she said. "There's only one entrance into the park with a guard hut and gate. Each area can only be accessed by security key cards. I'm sure they voided mine or at the very least attached a security alert to the number," she added, shaking her head.

"What about the grounds?" Eric asked. Sabrina could see him getting hopeful again.

"There's a security fence in the front," she explained. "The forest lines two sides and the river lines the other side." She didn't like where this conversation was headed.

"Is that the Apalachicola River?" Howard asked.

"Yes," Sabrina answered despite the knot beginning to form in the pit of her stomach. She didn't like this one bit and yet, what did she expect when she insisted something had to be done to stop Sidel?

"Is there any security along the river?" Eric asked the next obvious question.

"It doesn't matter if we can get back into the park." Sabrina tried to keep the anxiety out of her voice. "Key card access is required to get into every area, including the administrative building. Even the café and fitness center."

That stopped them. Sabrina looked from one to the next, hoping to see that she had canned the idea of going back to EchoEnergy. There had to be another way.

"This park," the Mayor said, his wrinkled face scrunched up in thought, "it probably has a bunch of vending machines, right?"

Everyone turned to look at him in a way Sabrina thought you looked at someone you respect, but also expect to not make sense, polite but almost dismissive. They were probably thinking the same thing she was— how many pink ladies had he drunk?

"I suppose so," she answered only out of courtesy.

"In pretty much every building?" he asked.

Sabrina glanced at Eric. Was this guy serious? She knew Eric's friends wanted to help, but to what extent was she expected to humor them? Especially an old drunk who only wanted in on the conversation. And yet all of them looked like they were waiting for her answer.

"There's a bank of vending machines in the fitness center," she said, trying to remember. "I suppose there are others around the park. I just don't remember exactly where. I'm a coffee drinker."

"Coke or Pepsi?" The Mayor wouldn't let it go.

She wanted to tell Eric this was ridiculous. "Pepsi," she said with an impatient sigh, hopefully indicating this was the last answer she'd humor him with.

"Excellent," he said, rubbing his crooked arthritic hands together and sitting back, pleased. "I can get you inside," he told Eric. "Piece of cake."

92

Eric sat back and let Sabrina show Russ the notebook she had taken from the dead scientist's office. It was hard to not interrupt, to not be involved even if he didn't understand computer code.

Howard and the Mayor were on their cell phones at opposite ends of the boardwalk, one man arranging for them to get into EchoEnergy's park, the other pulling strings to get them access inside. Eric knew Howard would come through. He wasn't so sure about the Mayor. The old man told great stories. Eric just didn't know how many were true and how many were simply good stories.

"You're doing everything possible." Max's voice startled Eric from his thoughts. "Above and beyond what most brothers would do."

"I don't know about that."

"I'm sorry if I disappointed you," she said and looked out at the water, maybe so he couldn't see her face and her eyes.

"What are you talking about?"

"If I hadn't encouraged her maybe she would have gone off and pretended to be Kathryn Fulton. It would have been safer."

"Sabrina might be quiet and straitlaced when it comes to playing by the rules, but I should have guessed she wouldn't just walk away from something like this."

"I found us a beauty," Howard interrupted, back at the table. For a second, Eric forgot the plan. "Sixteen-foot cabin cruiser with 225 hp."

"I think we found something, too," Russ added as he and Sabrina pulled their chairs back up to the table. Russ held the notebook with gentle reverence, like a preacher with a Bible.

"We think Dr. Lansik already started preparing some evidence," Sabrina declared.

"I recognize a lot of this computer code," Russ said, pointing at the notebook. "I think he saved his files to the network server, only he gave them specific codes so no one would notice or be able to find them easily."

"That's good news, right?" Eric said, hoping this was a turn of luck for them.

"Good news and bad news," Russ answered and Eric didn't like the exchange of glances between Russ and Sabrina, like they had discussed something dangerous, but both had already made the decision what to do.

"The good news is Lansik made it easy enough," Russ said. "I just need someone to get in, get to a computer, open a so-called cyber door for me and leave it open. The bad news..." And he hesitated.

"Lansik says he left a special password in his office." Sabrina took over. "We won't be able to download any of the coded files without it."

"Paranoid bastard, huh?" Eric smiled to disguise his anxiety. This was getting more and more complicated.

"Actually, smart bastard," Russ said. "It has to be someone who knows the lab and his office in order to find the hidden password. Which means..." Russ looked to Sabrina again.

"No," Eric said before she had a chance to answer. "It's too risky to have you go back. We already decided. I'll go in. I can find whatever needs to be found."

"Actually, *you* decided," Sabrina said. "And you'll never find it as quickly as I can."

"It's all set." Another interruption. This time from the Mayor. "Eric, I got you the job. The only problem is they deliver to EchoEnergy tomorrow. You have to report to the Tallahassee distributorship at 7:00 a.m."

"Tomorrow? We can't do this tomorrow," Eric told the old man.

"If not tomorrow they don't deliver again until next week."

"We can't wait until next week," Sabrina said. "They might have already started covering their tracks and deleting evidence."

"And the energy summit begins on Friday morning," the Mayor said. "Opens tomorrow evening with a big reception that Sidel and Johnny Q are probably hoping will be a celebration. They get that contract and all those accolades and recognition at the summit and nobody's going to believe a disgruntled scientist trying to smear them."

Eric glanced around the table. He had brought these people together to help him—his own covert group that had dug into their pasts and now offered to risk their own safe havens. He sighed and nodded reluctantly.

"Okay," he said. "Tomorrow it is."

93

Sabrina knew they were ending the evening early with the hopes of getting some sleep. She, however, simply wanted to end it before Eric changed his mind.

The Mayor gave her a salute as he said good-night. Howard watched Max give her a tentative hug, then took his turn, embracing her in a bear hug, all-encompassing but gentle with the wonderful scent of hickory from the grill and a subtle musk of cologne. Russ, however, stood back, suddenly quiet and shy.

When they got up to Eric's apartment she expected a lecture or perhaps some big-brother words of caution. Instead, he said, "I think he has a crush on you."

"Excuse me?"

"Russ. He's got a little crush on you. Can't you tell?"

"Let's just say it's not at the top of my list right now of things to be concerned about." She plopped down on the squeaky futon. She realized she was still angry with him.

He dragged one of the chairs from the resin bistro set and sat down in front of her. He looked tired. He hadn't shaved. Even his broad shoulders slumped a bit. Here comes the lecture, Sabrina thought. He would still try to boss her around.

"If we're going to do this tomorrow I need one thing from you."

Just one? She kept quiet. He was serious. More serious than she had ever seen him before.

"Okay," she said.

"I need you to forgive me."

Sabrina bit her lip and stared at him. She knew he meant it. He had never intended to hurt her. What was it he'd said yesterday? That she was an unfortunate casualty?

"I forgive you," she said, "but you have to forgive Dad."

In the silence that followed she prepared for a litany of why that couldn't or wouldn't happen. When he met her eyes again he sighed and said, "It's a deal."

He gave her a hug and with the release of tension Sabrina fell asleep while Eric watched the news.

Around midnight Sabrina woke up, almost as if an alarm had gone off, alerting her that she was alone in the apartment. The TV was off, a desk lamp left on. After a quick glance around the apartment, she knew Eric had gone out. She shut off the desk lamp and went to the window. Why in the world would he go at this time of night? And why not at least mention that he needed to go out? Or why not leave a note?

Her eyes searched the empty bistro tables, the boats and the boardwalk down below. Everything was quiet. There was no one around. Then suddenly she saw a flash of light on the beach side of the marina. Four men were walking along the water, two with flashlights, two with long, thin poles. Despite the distance and darkness she recognized her brother's silhouette and his walk. The big guy she guessed was Howard. The other two she knew weren't Russ or the Mayor.

She shook her head. What in the world had Eric gotten himself into this time?

94

"It's called gigging," Eric tried to explain to the one Howard introduced only as Manny, a thick-chested Cuban with a thin mustache
that made him look like he was constantly smiling.

At least Manny pretended to be interested. The other guy who
Howard called Porter—tall, thin with a marine-style crew cut and
tattoo to match—nodded and agreed to carrying a flashlight, but
kept saying things like, "I'd rather get my flounder hot off the grill."

Eric had no clue why Howard had even suggested they go
gigging for flounder. Maybe it was his way to loosen them up for
the real business of the evening. Eric had to admit he was surprised.
He expected some hard liquor, maybe a sample line of product.
He had tried to prepare himself as best he could, especially hoping
it wouldn't influence his effectiveness the next day. Invading
EchoEnergy would be tricky enough without a hangover and no

sleep. He didn't, however, prepare himself for a night of gigging for flounder.

"I thought this was something you did in the fall." Eric didn't want Howard to believe he was as easy as his two Miami buddies.

"They're around at other times. October through December's usually when they're headed in masses out into the gulf."

"Why at night?" Manny wanted to know. "We gettin' them while they sleep? That doesn't seem fair."

"No, no." Howard laughed. "You get them while they're hiding just under the sand waiting to prey on other fish."

"Always showing off what you know." Porter laughed and slapped Howard on the back. Eric thought he saw Howard wince. "We know you're this big, successful fisherman now. You don't have to prove it."

Eric found himself wanting to defend Howard. Hell, yes, he was a successful fisherman, a charter-boat captain with one of the most reputable deep-sea-fishing businesses on the gulf. He avoided glancing at Howard, afraid if he saw one more wince he'd blow this whole meeting.

"We can't stay," Porter said, not wasting time. He lit a cigarette and in the blue flame of the butane lighter, Eric thought his skin looked yellow. "We're headed to Texas as soon as we're finished here."

"Sure," Howard said and Eric thought he heard relief. "Why don't you let Eric show you some gigging, and I'll get what you need."

They watched Howard head back to the shop. Eric tried his best. Manny still showed interest. Porter sucked on his cigarette and stared out at the water as if he couldn't wait to get back on it.

In minutes Howard returned with a leather satchel he handed to Porter in exchange for a two-grip handshake from Porter, the only emotion, the only thank-you the man had shown.

Inside an hour they were gone, back on the water. Eric didn't ask for any explanation. He and Howard walked to the shop in silence. Eric brought in the gigs, the prongs never meeting a flounder that night. Howard stowed the flashlights.

The shop was dark except for a small fluorescent light behind the counter. Eric might not have noticed the three model ships from Howard's collection down on the counter with cracked hulls. His first guess was that they had fallen and needed repair. That is, until Howard picked up one of the pieces and started shoving a wad of rolled-up bills held together by a rubber band back into the hollow center of the broken ship.

He didn't look away. Howard wanted him to see. Without glancing up at Eric, Howard said, "Porter saved my ass, pulled me from a burning helicopter just outside of Da Nang."

"So what business is he in now?" Eric didn't expect Howard to tell him even if it was cocaine or heroin.

"Business?" Howard laughed. "Hell, he has cancer. One of the bad ones. He just wants to live out what days he has left on the water. Maybe stop along the way and see some of his old friends. I'm glad I can help out. What's the use of having any of this if you can't help out your friends?" He waved his hand and at first Eric thought he meant the success of the shop and business. But then Eric realized that wasn't it at all.

Eric's eyes followed along the shelves and what had to be over a hundred model ships, the collection Howard had just the other day told Eric he wanted him to have if something happened to him. And in his own way Howard was telling him, showing him, that the rumors were true. All the drug money the feds never found was stashed inside Howard's collection of model ships, and it was here only to help out his friends.

95

Jason hadn't gotten any sleep. He'd showered and shaved, but that was about all. No breakfast. No newspapers. Earlier he had caught a reflection of himself. His swollen eyes and disheveled hair, along with the untucked shirt, faded blue jeans and worn Nikes gave him an uncharacteristic grunge look. It also gave him an unintentional disguise. After his run-in with Detective Christopher last night, he found himself looking over his shoulder as he walked through the airport, keeping his head down when he met up with anyone close enough to recognize him.

He had shut his cell phone off before he boarded his flight. Normally he was one of those guys still getting in one last call as the plane taxied to the runway and the flight attendant asked for any electronic devices to be turned off. Today he was in no mood to fix any last-minute problems or answer "urgent" questions.

Luckily it was too early for any problems at the office. And every-thing had already been arranged for the energy summit's reception. He'd check all the details himself when he got to Florida. In the meantime, his secretary and the senator knew he couldn't be reached while he boarded and was in flight.

That no one could bother him for almost three hours ended up being a wonderful escape. He had a Bloody Mary, even eating the celery stick since he hadn't had breakfast. He decided to stay off his laptop and started listening to the latest Jack Reacher novel on his iPod. By the time the plane landed in Tallahassee, he knew he'd be more relaxed than he had been in weeks.

He had arranged for early check-in at the hotel. Maybe he'd order brunch up to his room. He'd have all afternoon to check e-mail and see to the reception details. Senator Allen's private jet would arrive at Tyndall Air Force Base late afternoon. Jason had a limo scheduled to pick him up. For himself, Jason had reserved a BMW Z4, a red convertible. Not a bad way to eliminate a bit of stress. He planned on a drive along Highway 98, which he understood included some amazing views of the gulf.

Jason nodded when the flight attendant asked if he'd like another Bloody Mary. He glanced at his watch. Not quite seven o'clock, but he figured he had reason to kick back. He deserved it. Later this morning the Appropriations Committee would award EchoEnergy the $140-million military contract. And Senator Allen would be the darling of the energy summit. He didn't even care if the senator had to share the limelight with William Sidel.

In fact, Jason decided he wouldn't stress out over the connection Sidel may have had with Zach Kensor. After this summit it wouldn't matter—both Sidel and Senator Allen will have gotten what they wanted.

And Jason decided he wouldn't worry about what Lindy may have told Senator Malone or Detective Christopher. By the time he got back to Washington that whole mess with Zach could be old news. He needed to sit back and enjoy the results of his hard work.

96

The Apalachicola River

Sabrina hated boats. Now, however, was probably not a good time to tell them.

She had gotten deathly ill on a whale-watching cruise six hours off Boston harbor. Her one-time venture from an academic conference had left her weak-kneed and drained after several hours of retching and vomiting and then dry retching over the railing when she could no longer wait in line for the boat's bathrooms, already filled with other nauseated patrons.

She had caught only a glimpse of the whales that day, but actually met a handsome gentleman who brought her cool napkins for her forehead and a Coke to wash away the foul taste in her mouth. At the end of the cruise they had exchanged phone numbers and e-mail addresses, but it was difficult to maintain a long-distance relationship when the only thing they had in common was Sabrina's marathon retching, something she'd rather forget. She should have remembered that about long-distance relationships, and if she ever made it back to her condo she'd deliver Daniel's ring back to him. Easy to make promises when confronted with hit men and seasickness.

This boat was much smaller than the whale-cruiser. Yet Sabrina felt dizzy just looking at it. And all the while Howard pointed out the postage-sized amenities like they were luxurious showstoppers.

"Twin aft seats and twin helm seats." He waved toward the two back corner seats and the cockpit seats like a game-show host showing them what they had won.

And all Sabrina could think about was how much room this big man would take up. He'd have to sit in one of those twin helm stools to fit in the wheelhouse. No way could he stand. Each time he disappeared down into the cabin to stow their equipment it reminded Sabrina of a magic trick, a round peg fitting into a square hole two sizes too small.

She kept telling herself the river would be much different from the Atlantic Ocean. This should be a piece of cake. But as soon as she boarded the small fishing boat she felt the rocking and immediately she had to fight back the nausea. She refused to let any of them know.

Eric had already relayed very clearly his belief that she was a liability when it came to matters that involved physical stealth and a degree of cunning. Attributes that came naturally to Eric and his odd group of friends.

Okay, so unlike them she'd never had to elude the IRS, the FBI or any other law enforcement agency…at least not until now. She was a late bloomer. Didn't mean she couldn't be a quick study.

"It's best you and Russ sit portside," Howard instructed. "I'll balance our weights."

Russ immediately took the other seat in the wheelhouse and started setting up his laptop and several electronic contraptions Sabrina didn't recognize.

It made sense to Sabrina that Russ would be in the front under the protection of the wheelhouse roof and surrounded by the glass. She'd stay dry seated in the back corner where mere inches of railing were supposed to keep her from bouncing out of the boat. The rocking of the stationary boat made her nauseated, but that had been nothing compared to the Tilt-A-Whirl of the motorized boat.

The one good thing, Sabrina decided, was that by the time they reached their destination she'd want off the boat so badly she wouldn't care if she faced security guards, guns or even tanks filled with chicken guts.

97

Outside Tallahassee, Florida

Eric heaved another case of Pepsi products onto the hand truck. It was only their first delivery of the day and his formerly crisp uniform shirt stuck to his skin. His cap no longer held back the tiny rivulets racing down his face. He discarded the gloves almost immediately because his hands felt on fire. And according to his partner, he owed his employer for five bottles of Aquafina. He hadn't thought to bring his own kegger-sized water jug like his experienced partner, a young guy named Bubba who had an amazing talent of keeping his pants up despite them being fastened clear down under his bulging waistline. He did, however, manage to keep his shirttail tucked and could probably outhoist anyone.

Eric had never known anyone who asked, no insisted, he be called Bubba even after Eric asked his real name.

"My daddy started calling me Bubba when I was two and a half. I can't see changing it now," he told Eric.

At first Bubba didn't talk much. Immediately he slipped in a cassette of the Rolling Stones. He blasted the volume, joining in on certain words like *"can't get no,"* but leaving *"satisfaction"* to Mick.

Eric quickly realized he didn't need to worry about his young partner being suspicious of the sudden substitution. He seemed to like showing new guys the ropes, especially since his showing included letting them do the lion's share of the work while he explained things. But he wasn't a slacker, which he'd shown every once in a while by hoisting two crates at a time. After the first delivery Bubba asked Eric, "So did you work for that bottled-water company that went out of business?"

"No, but that was something else, wasn't it?"

"I heard it was some crazy bastard at their bottling plant playing Russian roulette by putting stuff in only a few bottles."

"Really?" Eric was always amazed at the stories people came up with, as if the truth wasn't bad enough.

"A shame we couldn't have something like that happen with Coke, huh?" Bubba let off a squawk of a laugh.

"Hey, they have their own problems," Eric said. "It's called Coca-Cola BlaK. What were they thinking with that? Soda drinkers drink soda 'cause they hate coffee."

When Bubba didn't respond, Eric glanced over, afraid he'd broken some industry code that didn't allow slamming the other's innovations.

Bubba was nodding and when he finally said something it was with genuine appreciation. "You're absolutely right, dude."

And this time when he went to punch in the Rolling Stones cassette he stopped. "You like the Stones? 'Cause I've got the Doobie Brothers and the Boss, too."

"Stones are good for me," Eric said, and for the first time he thought they might actually pull this off, if they didn't get shot or arrested.

98

The Apalachicola River

Although she could barely see through the thick undergrowth, from the river EchoEnergy's industrial park reminded Sabrina of a deserted city, something out of the *The Twilight Zone* where only machines existed. With the sun just coming up through the trees, she could hear the first tankers arriving, their air brakes hissing, along with the grinding of gears and rumbling conveyor belts.

Sabrina knew there wasn't a single person on the grounds. The few who were here at this time of day were where they needed to be, not venturing back out into the sultry morning.

Last year when Sabrina arrived at EchoEnergy, she learned quickly that all but the plant's shift workers arrived before nine. Some stayed late, but no one came earlier than they had to. So they had an hour, tops, to get in and get out.

Howard maneuvered the boat expertly around logs and debris in the river and under branches overhanging the water. She watched his monster hands on the wheel and clutch, gentle, smooth touches that steered the boat to the right and then to the left with very little motion, which Sabrina was grateful for. Her stomach had settled a bit, but her nerves had taken over. Earlier on the road trip to Tallahassee, the men had eaten breakfast burritos and hash browns while she had forced down a cup of coffee. Now she could feel the acid churning in the empty pit of her stomach, sour and unforgiving.

Without having navigated the river before, Howard seemed to know how close they'd be able to get to the bank. The propellers scraped once, then she caught him wince when it happened a second time. Even Russ stopped plucking at the computer keys. She saw Howard shift something and the engine started to idle while he came to the back of the boat. Sabrina didn't look to see what he was doing. She seemed to be fine as long as she didn't look down at the water.

Howard was but a few minutes then she felt his hand on her shoulder.

"I'm going to get you as close as possible," he said, and she offered him a weak smile.

As close as possible was still two or three feet from the bank. Howard helped her into Russ's hip-high rubber waders that on Sabrina came up to her chest. At the same time Russ attached what looked like a miniature hearing aid over her right ear, gently, almost apprehensively moving her hair aside. She could feel the short microphone stem brush her cheek.

While Howard tightened the straps on the waders, Russ turned back to the laptop and electronic equipment he had set up in the small space next to the cockpit. A dozen lights flashed. He picked up one of the miniature hearing aids and put it on his ear, adjusting the short microphone stem. Then he turned his back to them and spoke softly. "Test, test one, test two, test three."

Sabrina could hear him clearly in her ear and told him so.

"You try," he said and Sabrina repeated the test.

He gave her a thumbs-up.

"Try not to get it wet, okay?"

She nodded, but felt a tingle of panic. Why did he think it might be possible that it would get wet? They had told her she'd be able to walk to the riverbank and not have to swim. She was an okay swimmer, but she had been in Florida long enough to know you didn't swim in rivers unless you could see there were no water moccasins anywhere on the surface.

"Keep these on," Howard told her as if he could read her panic. "At least until you get out of the tall grass. Snakes can't bite through this rubber."

"Great," she said. "And here I was only worried about security guards with guns."

She meant it as a joke. Howard didn't laugh. Neither did Russ. Instead, Russ pointed to a map he had of EchoEnergy's park.

"You get in trouble, any trouble at all, you tell us exactly where you are and we'll come get you."

She knew he meant it, so she didn't bother to remind him they wouldn't be able to get in without key card access.

They helped her down into the dark water. The sun had risen only enough to seep through the trees and create shadows. The water sloshed almost to the top of the waders. She had to keep her arms high, taking small steps, each one sinking just a little deeper.

"Careful," she heard Russ whisper in her ear.

"To your right," Howard instructed, his voice calm and reassuring. "Keep to the right, Sabrina."

At the moment all she could think about was how ungodly hot the rubber waders were. She wiped sweat off her forehead and pushed her hair back behind the earpiece remembering not to get it wet. Strands of her bangs stuck to her face.

"More to the right," Howard insisted.

Sabrina reached the bank and found several dead tree stumps and large roots. They were sturdy enough to help her secure her balance. She lifted herself up, the rubber waders like lead weights, sucking and pulling against her steps. She made it up onto the bank and let out a sigh of relief. That's when she heard something drop into the water. It was to her left where she had just been. Although daylight hadn't set in, Sabrina could see well enough to make out the snake riding the surface of the water. It crossed exactly where she had walked just seconds before, under a low, overhanging tree branch. Her stomach took a roller-coaster plunge and sent a chill down her back despite the saunalike waders.

"You did good," Howard called to her with that same calm that had guided her away from a snake hanging a foot or two above her.

Suddenly she wished she was back on the boat.

99

EchoEnergy

Eric hoped Sabrina wasn't waiting for him. He had spent a good hour of their road trip from Pensacola to Tallahassee with a penlight and a map of EchoEnergy's park, trying to commit it all to memory. He was dead tired, getting only a few hours' sleep after his gigging with Howard's buddies. He wasn't sure how much had stuck in his memory. Now as Bubba drove up to the guard hut, Eric stared out at the expanse of buildings and trucks where his sister used to work. This place was a hell of a lot bigger than he imagined.

The security guard checked Bubba's ID, then asked for Eric's. Russ had done an excellent job with the fake employee badge, whipping it together from a file the Mayor's friend had e-mailed. The same friend who managed to get Eric the last-minute substitute job. No clue what pull the Mayor or his friend had. Eric sure hoped he wouldn't be sorry he'd trusted the old man.

The ID had passed Bubba's inspection, which hadn't been more than a dismissive glance. The guard, however, fingered the ID and turned it around. Was there something on the back Russ had missed? Eric figured he could play stupid and say he didn't know it was fake.

Damn! The guard slid his window shut and was picking up the phone. Maybe they were on a special alert because of the murder. And Eric had no way of letting Sabrina know. Russ had tried to talk him into wearing a wire. He had compromised by agreeing to a GPS tracking device instead. Okay, so at least Russ could notify Sabrina when they took him away from the park to a jail cell back in Tallahassee.

"They do this crap all the time," Bubba finally said. "You'd think they housed the Holy Grail here or something."

Bubba pulled out a package of gum and popped a couple of pieces, then offered the package to Eric. He'd scored big on the Coke BlaK comment. He thanked Bubba and helped himself to a couple of pieces. He wondered whose side Bubba would be on if the guard announced the badge a fake.

The guard slid the window open and handed Bubba Eric's badge, waving them through without a word while he kept the phone tucked between his shoulder and ear.

Paranoid, Eric thought. He was way too paranoid.

They drove around the corrugated-steel building that Eric knew was the processing plant. From the parking lot he could see a slice of the river between the trees and brush. He couldn't see the boat. He couldn't see Sabrina. That was a good thing.

"So what do they make here?" Eric pretended he didn't have a clue or interest.

"Supposedly they take chicken guts and compress them or something and then they get oil." Bubba didn't really sound interested, either.

"No shit?"

"No shit. Just the guts." And this time Bubba squawked out another laugh at his own joke. Eric joined him. For the next hour Bubba was his best friend.

They parked in a loading zone between the plant and one of the administrative buildings. Eric tried to visualize the map he'd left in his head.

"It's a hell of a big place," he told Bubba. "Every building have machines?"

"At least one. They're on the main floors. No stairs or elevators, at least, to slow us down." He shoved a clipboard at Eric and got out of the truck.

Eric followed, pretending to study the order form. From a glance he knew he'd be here a while. But he still wasn't sure how he was going to persuade Bubba to let them stock the EchoLab building first. Then he'd need to lose him long enough to find Sabrina and let her in.

He looked around as they got their hand trucks out. There wasn't anyone else in sight except the tanker trucks and drivers. Not much of a chance to load up his crate and wait by the right door for someone to come along and play Good Samaritan. He'd be stuck following Bubba.

Eric checked off options in his head. He needed to get Sabrina in early or she'd risk getting caught. He was deep in thought when Bubba tapped him on the shoulder.

"You'll need this to get in."

Eric stared at the security key card Bubba was handing him. He barely heard the rest of what his partner said.

"I'll take the plant, fitness center and café. You take the rest. You think you can handle that?"

"No problem," Eric said, restraining a smile and a sigh of relief.

100

Sabrina struggled out of the rubber waders, finally sitting on the ground, safe ground, no snakes. She yanked and rolled the rubber hip waders over her sneakers to free her feet. She kept watch on the tree branches above her. Her T-shirt was soaked with perspiration and clinging to her so that she felt like she had been swimming.

"Eric just left the gate." She jumped from the sudden voice in her ear.

"He's early," she whispered, her head swiveling around to make sure no one was within listening range. She wasn't sure Russ could hear her over the rumble of engines, though the trees muffled the sounds and hum of gears. "Can you hear me okay?" she asked just a bit louder.

"I can hear you fine. How you holding up?"

"Hot and sweaty."

"Just the way I like my women."

The comment surprised her and she smiled. Both Russ and Howard were trying their best to keep her calm and steady.

"And dressed in sexy rubber waders, right?" she joked.

"You betcha."

She rolled rather than folded the waders, hoping she had made it difficult for anything to crawl inside while she was away. Then she tucked them into the crook of a tree, the whole time her eyes darting around, above and below. She'd need to stay out of sight until Eric was able to get into the building that housed EchoLab.

From where she stood she could see only a piece of the boat through the trees. On the other side of the brush was the parking lot. Somewhere close by was where the clogged water pipe had been. That seemed like ages ago, instead of days. How did she ever get to this place? Two people were dead, dozens, maybe thousands, sick, and all because one man decided to take advantage of making a few extra million dollars. It seemed inconceivable to Sabrina.

The idea, the mission behind EchoEnergy, had inspired her move from academia to the corporate sector. When she'd decided to be closer to her father she had contemplated a position at Florida State in the same department where her father had been. But Dr. Lansik wooed her with promises of scientific breakthroughs. Break-throughs he claimed would change not only the environmental landscape, but the political landscape, as well. But William Sidel had taken it all—promises and breakthroughs—and exploited it all for his own greed.

"He's almost in place." Russ's voice startled her again.

"That was quick. Do we have any idea if he's alone?"

"Can't tell. Remember, he didn't wear a communication system. Don't worry. He won't open the door unless it's safe."

Or he has a security guard with a gun at his back. She couldn't stop thinking about the guard during the thunderstorm outage who'd acted like a manic Robocop.

"I'm on my way," she said. Then slowly, hesitantly, she ventured away from the safety of her temporary hiding place.

101

Abda Hassar could see the security perimeter dotted by men in flak jackets and helmets and carrying automatic weapons. On this side of the estate where the energy summit was getting under way the soldiers' presence would be needed more than their tactics. Abda had counted five limousines, two flanked by a half-dozen black SUVs. All were stopped at the gated entrance by more men. These talked into their cuffs and wore sunglasses with black suits, despite the Florida heat.

Abda expected nothing less than this show of security force. He knew the badges he, Khaled and Qasim had acquired, the badges with the magic strip of bars at the bottom, would allow them entrance. But he also knew there would still be metal detectors they would need to pass through. Perhaps even body searches. It made no difference. None of them would be carrying any weapons. There would be no explosives, not even liquid explosives.

ALEX KAVA

He glanced at the time. Soon he would report for work at the catering company. He planned to arrive five minutes before his shift was to begin. He believed five minutes would be early enough to satisfy his temporary employer, but not so early that he looked too eager.

Khaled would report several hours before. As a part of the pre-reception group he would be setting up tables and chairs, arranging table linens, flatware and centerpieces. Khaled had accepted the assignment with no protest when Abda insisted, even though Khaled understood the concoction, its properties and dosage better than any of them. As its creator it would make sense that Khaled would want to be the one who personally saw it to fruition. And yet, he had accepted and recognized that as their leader Abda would be the one. It would be Abda's responsibility to administer the fatal concoction.

It would be Abda who presented the deadly meal to the President of the United States.

102

Jason stopped to get a mocha latte as soon as he got off the plane. The two Bloody Marys had gone straight to his head. Of course they did this early in the morning and without anything else in his stomach. He had to admit it was nice to sit back and chill, but he'd forgotten that he'd need to be able to drive. He had plenty of time. He'd sip his coffee, go down and get his bag. Give his head some time to clear, then get the rental car.

He was thinking about the BMW Z4 and smiled. He'd never owned or driven anything like it.

He passed by one of the airport terminal gates and caught a glimpse of the overhead TV screen. What he saw stopped him dead in his tracks. No one noticed. People simply went around him. Passengers were lined up, ready to board. Very few paid attention to the TV screen. No one paid attention to Jason. While everyone else left their seats to claim their place in line, Jason, without taking his eyes off CNN's crawl, found a seat directly under the TV and dropped into it.

At first he thought it might be an announcement about the Appropriations Committee vote. Then he saw the handcuffs.

On the screen a handcuffed Senator Allen was being escorted down the Capitol steps. The noise around Jason drowned out the sound, so he had to read the crawl at the bottom of the screen:

Senator Allen calls the charges bogus. Gregory McDonald broke the story early this morning. The ABC news exclusive claims McDonald has seen irrefutable evidence that implicates the senator in the murder of Zach Kensor. Kensor, a congressional staff member to Senator Max Holden, was found murdered early Sunday at the Washington Grand Hotel.

103

EchoEnergy

It took Eric three tries before he remembered and found the building that housed the lab. He quickly stocked a couple of soda machines to get rid of his load. Then he left the empty hand truck in a corner. If Bubba or anyone else caught him he'd say he was trying to find a bathroom. Not such a stretch of the truth. The maze of hallways took him one way and then another. At this rate he'd never find a bathroom, let alone the EchoLab.

He pulled the miniature GPS handheld device out of a holster attached to his belt. The holster looked like a cell phone carrier, but the tracking system fit perfectly with a slight bulge. Eric stopped for a minute to view the tiny screen and get his bearings. Russ had programmed in all the locations. He was sure the door he needed was to his right, but when he pushed the door open there was no Sabrina. The steam of the morning hit him in the face with a smell he couldn't quite place. He was just about to close the door when he heard a rustle in the crepe myrtle against the building.

"Bree?"

Somehow she looked more vulnerable in the T-shirt and running shorts. She didn't say a word until the door closed gently behind her.

"I'm in," she said, but Eric realized it was for Russ and Howard's benefit, not out of relief.

"He gave me a key card," Eric told her, holding it up like the prize it was.

"Really?"

He could see her mind going somewhere they hadn't planned, exactly like his had been ever since Bubba handed the thing to him.

"I'm just saying it made it easier," he explained, now wishing he hadn't opened his mouth.

"He has a key card," she said in the tiny microphone. And then to Eric she said, "Just please don't run off playing Steve Austin with it."

He gave her his best hurt look and readjusted his uniform cap on his sweat-soaked head. "Gotta go. I have a lot of soda machines to fill."

They stood there staring at each other for a moment. Despite his earlier assessment of her looking vulnerable he saw only determination in her eyes. She was in familiar territory and on a mission. He hoped that would be enough to drive her. Covert missions were more his style.

"You gonna be okay?" he asked anyway.

"Yeah," she said, nodding, but her eyes shifted away and back like it was a decision she still had to make.

"Be careful, okay?"

"I will. You be careful, too. Don't get cocky with that key card."

"Me? Cocky?" He smiled and turned, starting down the hallway. When he glanced back over his shoulder, Sabrina was already disappearing through the stairwell door.

He checked his watch and pulled out the GPS device again. He needed to backtrack, get his hand truck and return to the vehicle to get another load. Then he thought he might just wander by William Sidel's office.

104

Sabrina knew the best thing Eric could do for her now was let her do what she came to do. Still, it was hard watching him go in the opposite direction. He needed to move on to the next building, stocking soda machines. Anything out of the ordinary would draw too much attention.

She took the stairs, stopping on each landing to listen. Other than Pasha and O'Hearn, she didn't think anyone would recognize her with the new haircut and in running shorts and a T-shirt. She checked her arms to see if the spray-on tan had streaked in the flood of humidity.

She leaned her ear against the stairwell door.

"Are you there yet?"

Russ's voice made her jump again.

"Jesus!" she whispered. "You have to stop doing that."

"I'm just checking on you."

"You're scaring the crap out of me."

"Sorry," he said. "I never thought I'd hear you say crap."

"Yeah, well, I never thought I'd be sneaking back into this place."

"Okay, so I won't scare the crap out of you. Just remember to update us, okay?"

"Okay."

On the other side of the door she listened again before she started down the hallway. It was still quiet. No computers or copiers were humming yet. Not even the fluorescent lights were on. The sun streamed in through the small milky-glass window set in the laboratory doors.

She tried the entrance closest to Dr Lansik's office. Sometimes it was locked. Today she lucked out. Silence here, too. Lab coats hung from the antique stand. Freshly washed test tubes dried on a paper towel by the sink. Bottles containing various degrees of brown liquid lined the samples shelf. Sabrina was struck by how normal everything looked, as if she'd never left. *What did she expect?* Life goes on. Even without her and Anna Copello the lab ran smoothly. Maybe she, at the very least, expected to see a mess. Weren't she and Anna always cleaning up after the guys?

Her father had told her once that he didn't believe in teams of scientists. One ego would always bruise more easily than another. And brilliant minds weren't necessarily generous ones, especially when it came to sharing credit. But Sabrina thought it was absurd that anyone would believe she'd murder Anna Copello over a promotion.

Dwight Lansik's office remained the same. No one had even moved out the old blue sofa. They had, however, removed his framed credentials. Bright white squares revealed their existence where the walls had stained around them.

First things first. She sat down at Lansik's computer and turned it on. Everything booted up normally, which meant the computer was still connected to the network server.

She clicked on Control Panel and found the program file under Network that Russ had instructed her he'd need. Then she accessed her own e-mail simply by typing in her password. No one had thought to cancel her account. She typed in Russ's e-mail address, attached the program file and hit Send. He had told her he needed her to open a door for him and leave it open. Sending him the e-mail opened that door. The attached program file would allow access to anything and everything stored on the network server. It was similar to how hackers managed to download viruses. Sabrina didn't completely understand it. But she understood enough to know that if the processing plant's files of hurricane debris were still on the server, Russ would be able to find them now.

"I just sent the e-mail," she said into her mic. "Let me know if you've received it."

She waited. Damn! What if it wasn't as easy as Russ had made it sound? Seconds ticked by. It felt like an eternity of silence.

"Got it!" he finally came back.

Sabrina closed her e-mail, but left the computer on. Now she needed Lansik's password for Russ to be able to download all those coded files that were stored on the network server. In his notebook he said he'd left it back in his office "in plain sight for any true scientist to discover." Russ insisted it would be at least six to eight characters. What if it was part of the degrees and certificates that had been removed? It was possible. All of them were scientific degrees of some sort.

The small bulletin board behind Lansik's desk contained the usual stuff that most people put on their office cubicles or bulletin boards, with the exception that Lansik's had a scientific flavor. There were several *NewYorker* cartoons, a newspaper article on EchoEnergy that included quotes from Lansik, and a small strip of paper that looked like it had come from a fortune cookie: "You will be rich and famous one day." At the bottom was a series of lucky numbers. It couldn't be that easy.

"Are you ready to try one?" she asked.

"Ready," came his quick reply.

"Okay. 43590."

"That's only five numbers."

"I know," she told him. "It probably isn't it, but you said it might be something overly simple."

Silence.

While she waited she kept examining the room. There wasn't much here. Lansik kept decorating to a minimum. On one wall was a small periodic table, one of those ancient eleven-by-seven laminated posters like the ones found in high-school science classrooms. On the opposite wall was a small clock.

"Nada," Russ said. "I tried it backward and forward."

She glanced at her watch. She was taking too much time. In plain sight, she repeated to herself, for a true scientist. She stared at the periodic table. Could it be some combination? Some joke like oil and water?

Something made her look back at the bulletin board.

There were two quotes from Albert Einstein. The first:

One must divide one's time between politics and equations. But our equations are much more important to me.

The other was one she hadn't seen or heard before:

If A is success in life, then A equals x plus y plus z. Work is x; y is play; and z is keeping your mouth shut.

She stared at both for what seemed much too long then finally she said, "Russ, try this, AAxyzxyz."

She waited again, but not long.

"That's it! I'm in. Come on back."

Sabrina smiled and let out a sigh of relief. In a matter of minutes they would have copies of every process the hurricane debris had gone through, including dates and times that they could connect to the satellite photos Russ had copied.

"You have a lot of balls coming back here."

It took Sabrina a second to realize the voice wasn't Russ in her ear. It came from behind her. She spun to find O'Hearn standing in the doorway.

"It's all been a mistake," Sabrina said. Certainly he'd understand as soon as she told him that she was right about Reactor #5 and about the hurricane debris.

"That's right. A huge mistake. You were the one who should be dead."

That's when she saw the gun in his hand.

105

Jason sat in front of another TV at the airport. Everything appeared in a haze. Sounds were jumbled together. His reflexes felt delayed. Maybe it was still the effects of the Bloody Marys. Several times he bumped into people, not even noticing them.

He had moved three times to different passenger waiting areas so he wouldn't draw attention to himself. He'd lost track of how many flights he'd watched board, how many he had seen arrive. He'd lost all track of time. He toted his carry-on and briefcase from one end of the terminal to the next.

He turned on his cell phone long enough to panic at the full queue of missed calls and voice messages. It started ringing, startling him so much he almost dropped it. He didn't recognize the number on the caller ID. He shut the phone off and slipped it into his pocket.

CNN's crawl added new information in bits and pieces. Jason had

seen most of it often enough that he had it memorized, so he immediately noticed anything new that came across the bottom of the
screen. He thought he'd seen the worst of it. He was wrong.

The newest information read,

*The senator's chief of staff, Jason Brill, is wanted for questioning. Brill
is believed to have left Washington, D.C. Anyone with information as to
his whereabouts has been asked to call 1-800-555-0700.*

Jason sat up at the edge of the chair. *This was crazy.* Of course he'd left
D.C., for the energy summit. It had nothing to do with Zach's murder.
How could they believe he had anything to do with Zach's murder?

He glanced around. There were more lines waiting to board
flights. Regular airport personnel picked up trash and drove trams
with handicapped passengers. Once or twice a security guard passed
through the area. No one seemed to notice him. No one looked like
they were watching him.

That's when it occurred to Jason that there might be someone
waiting down in baggage claim or at the rental-car counter. Jesus!
They had to know he had taken the morning flight here and that he
had arrived. They'd be able to check that out. He couldn't just take
another flight somewhere else. They might be watching for that, too.

He hadn't picked up his checked garment bag. In his mind he
flipped through its contents trying to decide if he could do without
it. Almost everything except his suits he had stuffed in his carry-on
or his briefcase.

He slouched down in the vinyl seat, suddenly very aware of how
alone he was. He pulled out his cell phone. He had it turned on and
started to dial before he snapped it off. They could track a cell phone,
couldn't they?

He scoped out the crowds again, then grabbed his carry-on and briefcase. He found a bank of pay phones with no one standing around. It'd been so long since he'd used one he had to read the instructions before he dialed. If he got a voice-messaging service he'd just hang up and no one would recognize the recorded phone number.

"Hello," she said after the third ring.

"Lindy, it's Jason."

"Where are you?" She changed to a whisper, a panicked whisper. No, not panicked—conspiratorial.

"Never mind that. What the hell's going on?"

"Hold on a minute," she said and his stomach clenched. Was she going to give him up? But then he heard her tell someone she'd catch up, that she had to take this call. If he remembered correctly she was already down here in Florida. Isn't that what Senator Malone told him last night? She was probably at the estate. "Your boss is in a whole lot of trouble," she finally said. "Word is his fingerprints were in Zach's hotel room."

"Jesus! I can't believe this."

"Jason, he says he was covering for you."

"What?"

"He claims you called him and he came to help you."

"What are you talking about?"

"I thought you said you didn't know Zach?"

"I didn't know him."

"He says you and Zach have been meeting there at the hotel for months. You reserved the same room. You made the reservations from your office. There are phone records."

Jason gripped the phone, needing to hang on to something. Jesus! He had reserved the same room at the Washington Grand several times over the last few months—for Senator Allen.

"Jason?"

"You don't believe any of this. I was with you."

Now there was a pause.

"You left early, before I woke up," she finally said.

"Lindy, it was four o'clock." He shoved his fingers through his hair and glanced around him, wondering if anyone could smell his panic.

"I don't have any idea what time you left."

"Lindy, you know I didn't do this."

There was silence, again. He couldn't believe this.

"Is that what you told the police?" he asked, bracing himself against the wall. His knees were threatening to wobble.

"I haven't told them…look, they haven't asked…yet."

"Lindy, why would I…" He glanced around and lowered his voice. "Why would I sleep with you if I was gay?"

"How do I know why you guys do anything?" He heard a bit of anger in her voice. "It certainly didn't stop Zach from sleeping with me the first time we met."

Silence. Again.

Jason closed his eyes and leaned his head against the wall of the pay phone. So that was it. She didn't believe him.

"Jason, maybe you should just go to them and tell them what happened."

The panic caught in his throat and he swallowed hard. How could she believe he was capable of murder? She would be worthless as an alibi. If the woman he fucked and left too early thought he was capable of going to another room in the same hotel and passionately killing a male lover, then what would the cops believe? Evidently the story Senator Allen had provided was convincing.

"Jason?"

He placed the phone gently back in its cradle.

He wasn't sure how much time had gone by while he stood there. The noises around him couldn't puncture the throbbing in his head. His feet guarded the only belongings he now owned. The scent of cinnamon reminded his empty stomach to gather in knots.

He had no place to go and the one person he thought he could count on, the one person he had pledged his loyalty to, had just thrown him in front of a moving train.

106

EchoEnergy

"What's going on?" Sabrina heard Russ whisper in her ear.

"What are you doing with a gun, Dr. O'Hearn?"

She didn't move. Was he serious? He couldn't possibly be worried that she had come back to knock off the rest of her colleagues.

"A gun? Who's O'Hearn?" She ignored Russ, slightly turning the earpiece away so that O'Hearn couldn't spot it as easily. O'Hearn's black eyes were as wild and unsettled as his mop of hair.

"Why in the world would you come back?" he asked, then looked around the office. He noticed the computer screen though Sabrina had closed out her e-mail so nothing was left except the screen saver. "What could be so important that you'd risk coming back?"

"I didn't kill Anna," she said, trying to explain. She figured O'Hearn was defending himself from her. As soon as she explained he'd understand. Then it occurred to her. How did he know she had been the real target?

"What did you mean I should be the one dead?"

"He left you something, didn't he?" O'Hearn seemed focused on the computer, his eyes darted back and forth. "That son of a bitch left you something on his computer."

She'd never seen O'Hearn angry. Usually he had been the voice of reason, the calm within the storm. Now his silver goatee caught spittle, his bushy eyebrows met in an angry *V*. With his shirtsleeves rolled and pushed up, she could see the veins bulging in his arms, especially the one holding the gun.

"I have no idea what or who you're talking about."

"What is it? What did he leave for you?" He jabbed the gun at her.

"Honestly, you're not making sense." She caught herself backing away from him and didn't notice until she was up against the old blue sofa.

"You almost ruined everything. You and Lansik. Too bad neither of you could be like good ole Ernie Walker, satisfied with retiring to Cancún with a nice little bank account."

"You're in on it," Sabrina said in almost a whisper. She couldn't believe it. But of course, Sidel would have needed someone to change the computer program, someone who would know how to set the correct temperature and coking times.

"What do you mean 'in on it'?" O'Hearn looked insulted. "Lansik may have come up with the formula for thermal conversion of chicken guts. He certainly took all the credit." O'Hearn emphasized his points with the gun. Sabrina couldn't take her eyes off it. "I was the one who kept saying we needed to do Grade 2 garbage in order to be efficient and make a profit."

"But the upgrades to the equipment were never made," Sabrina reminded him. "As a scientist, how could you do it incorrectly?"

"Are you kidding? Do you have any idea how much the government is paying to haul away that goddamn hurricane crap? Getting
paid to haul away the garbage is the only way this process will ever
be able to compete. We'd never be able to put out enough oil with
chicken guts to be taken seriously. What's the use of doing any of
this if we're not taken seriously?"

"But Dr. Lansik didn't agree." Sabrina wanted to keep him talking.
It was almost as if he forgot about the gun when he talked except
that he swung it around recklessly.

Out of the corner of her eyes she scanned the small office for
weapons. Would Russ or Howard come to her rescue? No, of course
not. They couldn't get into the building. And Eric was off somewhere
stocking soda machines. They couldn't even contact him.

"Dwight was very narrow-minded," O'Hearn continued. He
didn't sound angry so much as vindicated.

"Why didn't Sidel just fire him?"

"Sidel?" O'Hearn laughed. "You think that dimwit clown could
comprehend any of this? He might know how to charm investors,
but he doesn't have a clue about thermal conversion. You ever
heard his explanation? It's magic." O'Hearn laughed again and
Sabrina noticed the gun hand dropped to his side. O'Hearn had a
killer ego, not a killer instinct. If she could talk him out of this
small office and into the lab, she might have a chance at making a
run for it.

"The oil's not the same," she said. O'Hearn quit laughing and
stared at her. "Oil from Grade 2 garbage has too many impurities."

"You don't know what you're talking about."

She knew it wasn't true, but she continued, "I've seen samples with
so many impurities they sink to the bottom."

"Not this stuff."

It worked. He waved her out of the office and gave her a shove toward the sample bottles lined up on the shelf across the lab.

This could work. She just needed to be patient. She'd humor him and get him to forget about the gun. It was small, practically looked like a toy. She could put a counter between them and make a run for the door. She had to believe O'Hearn wasn't much of a shot.

Just when she felt hopeful, the lab door opened and filled with a stocky, square-shouldered man with slick-backed hair, a widow's peak, deep-set eyes. She thought she recognized him.

"Well, look who's here. It's about time you showed up," O'Hearn told the man. "You can finally take care of your mistake." And he pointed at Sabrina.

That's when Sabrina realized who the man was. He looked bigger close up, not like when he was on the catwalk over the tank. And unlike O'Hearn, Sabrina knew this man would kill.

107

Eric brought a partially loaded hand truck with him to the fourth floor. Down in the lobby he had met up with his first security guard who gave him a curt, dismissive nod, like he didn't waste time even greeting lowly vendors. That's when Eric realized the uniform and hand truck didn't just give him credible admittance, they made him invisible.

The fourth floor opened to a reception lobby. There were no hallways and only three doors off the lobby. The main door had a simple gold-plated and engraved plaque, not a nameplate, but a plaque: William Sidel.

Eric had expected to find the CEO's secretary here. Weren't CEO's secretaries in early to organize their day before their bosses arrived? Eric had even come up with several charming excuses on the elevator for why he had ended up on the wrong floor.

Sidel's huge office door with the name plaque opened easily. And why not, Eric thought. If the man didn't have anything to hide he shouldn't need to lock his office door at night, especially when a security key card was required to get in the building and then required again to gain access in the elevator to the fourth floor.

Sidel's office was a huge triangle with two of the walls floor-to-ceiling glass. Eric had theorized that if a security tape existed of Anna Copello's murder—and Sabrina was confident that every reactor had cameras—then William Sidel would have wanted the tape in his safe-keeping. He obviously had not given it to the police. But as Eric began searching the office, he found few hiding places. Finally he found a false bottom in one of the CEO's drawers. There was no video, no CD. However, there were a half-dozen interesting Polaroid photos.

Eric slipped the photos into his shirt pocket. Before he left, he looked out over the campus, wondering if Sidel spent a great deal of time in this exact spot, admiring the kingdom he had created. It was quite an accomplishment and it could have been an amazing business if only the bastard hadn't gotten so cocky and greedy.

Then Eric realized he could say the same thing about himself. He had gotten cocky and greedy with the key card. Of course Sidel didn't need to lock his office. There were probably hidden security cameras. Somewhere a guard could be watching his every move and by now be sending up guards to remove him.

Eric turned slowly, his eyes examining every shelf, frame and fixture in the room. In the meantime he listened for the elevator. Experience and training reassured him there were no hidden cameras. He did, however, need to get the hell out of there and get to their agreed-upon pick-up place or he would, literally, miss the boat.

108

Leon sure hated loose ends. This woman, this Dr. Sabrina Galloway, represented the biggest fuckup of his career. He figured it was even bigger than Casino Rudy. Well, at least she had the decency to look scared shitless.

"You even know how to use one of those things, Doc?" He pointed to the .22-caliber revolver, a nice little brain rattler, but the way Michael O'Hearn tossed it around it wouldn't do much damage.

"I wouldn't have to do this if you'd finished what you got paid to do."

"Actually, Doc, I haven't been paid yet. And if I remember correctly, you told me to leave it to the cops. So…" Leon glanced at his watch. "The cops must be on their way, right?"

"Don't be a smart-ass. Just take care of her."

"You were the one who hired him?" The Galloway woman looked

at O'Hearn. Leon shook his head. She was still seeing her colleague instead of the mad little scientist.

"Yeah, it's amazing," Leon said to Sabrina, "what people, even scientists, are willing to do out of greed."

"This wasn't about greed."

Now Leon had made the man angry.

"Not for me it wasn't."

"Really?" Leon cocked his head to the side and grinned enough to ignite O'Hearn.

"This is about being taken seriously and being seen as a true competitor. Something that would never happen under Lansik and definitely not as long as we were using only chicken guts."

"How could we ever be taken seriously?" Galloway said, surprising them both. "How could we gain any credibility by making people sick?"

"What? Oh yeah, that stupid little bottled-water company?" O'Hearn laughed and Leon thought he sounded a little like a foghorn—not a pretty sound.

Leon didn't know anything about people getting sick from the water. Hell, every time he was out here he couldn't believe people didn't get sick from the smell. He glanced at his watch again. He really just wanted to get this over and done with.

"Let's get on with this," he said. He crossed the room and put out his hand. To his surprise, O'Hearn relinquished the revolver without a protest.

"Get it right this time," he told Leon, reminding him of an old teacher he had in high school, one that Leon didn't particularly like.

"You can come along. Make sure it's done right."

"No, that's quite all right."

Leon thought he saw the cocky scientist get a bit squeamish.

"Actually, I'm gonna have to insist. It's my policy when something like this happens." He took the Galloway woman's wrist, his fingers easily wrapping and overlapping. She didn't flinch...much. "Oh, and Doc, I'll need that video from the security camera."

"Video? I'm not sure I know what you're talking about."

Leon almost let another grin loose. This guy might be a brilliant scientist but he was a god-awful liar.

"The video of me bashing that poor woman into the tank. I know you have security cameras in every one of those reactor buildings. Me and Dr. Galloway will wait here while you get it."

He could see O'Hearn's mind churning around the alternatives. Finally, without a word he went to a row of footlockers and twisted open the combination padlock on one of them. He pulled out a CD case and tossed it to Leon.

Leon couldn't help thinking the brilliant mad scientist threw like a girl. He wouldn't be much help at all, but then he also wouldn't be much trouble, either.

109

This is what had happened to Dwight Lansik, Sabrina told herself as she looked over the railing down into the swirling tank of chicken guts. All that was left of him was a piece of his watch and a glob of tissue. She might not even be that lucky. And yet all she could think about was her dad. He had lost so much. For his daughter to literally become a part of a scientific formula seemed a particularly cruel injustice.

O'Hearn had ended up being the one dragging and prodding her. Her wrist hurt. So did her jaw. She had tried to twist away from him and he slapped her hard. His hit man followed, wiping sweat from his forehead, using tissues from a small packet. He seemed indifferent, almost reluctant, not exactly cold and calculating like she imagined a hit man would be. O'Hearn, on the other hand, acted like a man on speed, pumped full of energy, jerky and anxious and strong.

Leon pocketed her wireless earbud as soon as he noticed it. Oddly he didn't mention it to O'Hearn. He had plucked it off as they left the lab and slipped it into his trouser pocket without a word or a look. So there was no longer a way for her to even get a message to Russ and Howard. It didn't matter. They wouldn't be able to hear her.

The steel-grated catwalk swayed and vibrated from the steady rumble of pulleys, engines and conveyor belts down below. A few tanker trucks started to load and unload. Up here, three stories above the noise, no one would notice a wave for help or a scream or even a gunshot.

Leon pulled out O'Hearn's gun now. He flipped open the chamber and looked at O'Hearn.

"Loaded," he said. "I'm impressed. I didn't think you had it in you." Then suddenly he surprised both of them by shoving the gun's muzzle up against O'Hearn's temple.

"What the hell is this?"

Sabrina could hear the panic in O'Hearn's voice despite the roar of trucks below and the whine of conveyor belts.

"Oh, I forgot to tell you," Leon said. "I have a new client. Sorry to drag you up here, ma'am, but I'd never get him all the way out here without you." He managed a casual glance at Sabrina. The gun didn't budge from O'Hearn's head. "You're free to go."

"Excuse me?"

O'Hearn still had a grip on her arm, and now his fingernails were digging deep into her skin. Maybe this was part of some sick joke between the two of them. But Leon gave the muzzle another shove, this one enough to tilt O'Hearn's head to the side.

"Let her go before I start breaking your fingers one by one."

"This is ridiculous." But O'Hearn let go, giving her a hard shove.

Sabrina slammed against the railing. It hit her in the small of her back, the force enough to throw her off balance. She grabbed on to the railing, trying to steady herself. A slightly harder shove would have sent her over. She didn't know if she could trust him. After all, she had seen him bash Anna when Anna wasn't looking. Would he do the same to her as soon as she turned her back?

Her eyes met Leon's and in what looked like an afterthought he said, "Tell your neighbor I don't plan on coming back down to Florida for a while."

Miss Sadie, of course. She really had made some kind of deal with this man. How was that possible?

Sabrina didn't hesitate this time. She gripped the railing and hand over hand found her way to the end of the catwalk. She didn't look back. She crawled down the steel ladder, missing the last step and stumbling to the ground. Somewhere in the distance she thought she could hear a security alarm going off. It had to be her imagination, triggered by the memory of the last time she had fled this place.

Anyone who saw her—and employees' vehicles had started to come onto the grounds—might think she was getting in a morning run before work. Except she didn't stick to the sidewalks, or the roads. She took the shortest route, over landscaped berms, through the middle of parking lots and around tanker trucks. And she didn't stop until she hit the tall grass.

She found the rubber waders where she had left them and struggled to pull them up over her running shoes and sweaty legs. All the while she watched where she had just come from, her heart pounding, her breathing coming in machine-gun gasps. She expected to find someone racing to stop her, especially now that she could hear the alarm. It was not her imagination.

Sabrina stumbled through the trees, her feet suddenly awkward and heavy. She skidded to a halt at the riverbank and thought she'd faint from the wonderful sight of the boat and Howard waving frantically at her. She was so relieved that when she felt the hand on her shoulder she simply froze. She closed her eyes, not wanting to look, too exhausted to fight or care.

"I had to do something." She heard Russ's voice and she opened her eyes to see him, beside her now. He was dripping wet, his shaved head glistening, but he was smiling. He put his arm around her shoulder and she leaned against him to get her balance back. He smelled of river water and perspiration.

"You pulled an alarm somewhere," she said.

"Yeah, so we better get the hell out of here."

Soon her concern switched to snakes again. By the time she flopped onto the boat she was pretty sure she wouldn't be getting seasick on the trip back.

110

Natalie Richards stepped the short distance from the airport doors into the waiting limousine and yet she could swear she felt her hair already frizzle in the hot, humid air. Colin Jernigan was waiting for her inside the car. He smiled at her patting her hair.

"This might help." He handed her a glass of something frosty and lime green with a spear of fruit balanced against the rim.

"You do know how to pick up a girl in style."

She slid in, taking the seat opposite him. She carefully set down a long, narrow, gift-wrapped box beside her before she accepted the drink from him. She took a sip, smooth and tangy. If all went well she hoped to treat herself with a day or two of these on a beach.

"You really didn't have to bring me a gift."

"This?" She held up the package carefully, almost reverently, with her free hand. "This is the only reason I am here."

"That's some special delivery."

"I told you we like to do things the old-fashioned way. My boss wants to make sure the president receives this gift before the reception tonight."

"Must be something special indeed."

"You don't know the half of it," Natalie said, waving her hand at him like she usually did when emphasizing a point. "You have any idea how difficult it is to find a solid-red silk necktie on short notice?" Actually, finding a solid-red necktie had been quite easy, but joking about it helped her stop thinking about it and treating the necktie like it was a ticking bomb.

She took another sip of the glorious creation. The last-minute trip preparations had been the least of her unraveling. Things were moving fast, locking into place. Yes, both of them were being a bit flippant, a tactic to relieve tension and stress. Like soldiers in a war zone or cops at a grisly crime scene. She and Colin were the only ones who truly knew how close to out of control this situation had gotten.

Now in a matter of hours they would know whether or not they had succeeded in foiling a terrorist plot or had succeeded in instigating one.

111

EchoEnergy

Leon couldn't believe how bad this guy smelled. He almost smelled worse than the chicken guts down below. And he was pathetic, too. A grown man pissing his pants.

"Not so brilliant now, huh, Doc?"

"Who paid you?" O'Hearn wanted to know. "It was Sidel, wasn't it?"

Leon simply shook his head, not as an answer so much as out of disgust. He never understood why anyone wasted his dying breath wanting to know who had done him in.

He had the mad scientist backed against the railing, sweating and crying and pissing his pants. His forehead was raw where Leon had pressed and jabbed the barrel of the gun. If the idiot would hold still instead of jerking around, this part wouldn't have to hurt.

"Please don't kill me." It was a whimper. Finally, maybe the asshole would settle down. Leon liked the idea of making him squirm a little. Maybe just because this whole goddamn job had been such a bitch.

Christ! It was hot up here now that the sun had broken out of the trees. All this fucking steel and concrete. And that stink! Leon would be glad to finish this up and finally get back home.

Somewhere down below he heard an alarm. He cocked his head, trying to listen over the groans of hydraulics and the roar of motors. Or was it a siren? That Galloway woman wouldn't have been so stupid to sic the security guards on him, would she?

It distracted Leon. Sent his eyes off O'Hearn long enough for the scientist to notice. Long enough for O'Hearn to believe he had one desperate chance left. He grabbed for the gun. Son of a bitch! Leon pushed back, but the guy was already attached. Why the hell did they always grab for the gun?

The mad little scientist was strong. He arm wrestled Leon so that both of them were pressed against the railing. Leon tried to keep his footing solid while O'Hearn dug long fingernails into his skin. He tried to keep his own finger on the trigger, but O'Hearn had managed to shove their arms down, against each other's bellies. And now Leon knew his best option was to shift the balance. Use his bulk to shove the madman over the railing.

He had O'Hearn where he wanted him. He just needed to brace himself against the railing and kick one of O'Hearn's legs. The man's grimace tilted up right into Leon's face. It wasn't a pretty sight: gritted yellowed teeth, silver goatee glistening with spittle, eyes wide, forehead veins bulging. And there was a growl. Even with all the surrounding noise Leon could hear the madman growling like some rabid dog.

Leon had control. He had the advantage of a solid balance. He was ready to fling the little bastard over the railing. There were two gunshots. Leon wasn't sure he would have even recognized them as gunshots, both muffled and small, but their force jabbed both men.

Leon watched O'Hearn's grimace slide into shock—raised eyebrows, eyes still wide. The struggle stopped. O'Hearn slipped away, falling sideways, his torso simply tipping over the railing. There was no grasping, no straining, no scream. And Leon stood still, staring as another scientist plunged into the churning feedstock.

It wasn't until Leon swung his legs over the catwalk to connect with the steel ladder down that he realized it wasn't all O'Hearn's blood on the front of his shirt. He could feel the pain in his side with every step.

The sirens were louder on the ground. He'd never make it to the back parking lot where he'd left his latest ride. And he couldn't just walk out of here with all this blood. What an absolute fucking way to end. That fortune-teller was probably smiling somewhere about now.

Leon thought for sure he was fucked until he saw the Pepsi truck. The driver was closing up the back, getting ready to move out. Leon made a dash for the truck, running between whining conveyor belts and making it to the passenger door without anyone noticing. Or at least he hoped. He opened the door and pulled himself up into the seat just as the driver opened his door on the other side. Leon showed him the gun, keeping it down on the seat.

"Get in."

The guy obeyed, climbing up behind the wheel, staring at the bloody mess that covered the front of Leon's shirt.

"I won't hurt you," Leon said, trying not to concentrate on the fire starting to sear his insides. "I just need a ride out of this goddamn place."

The guy continued to stare for a minute or two. Leon wondered if maybe he should shove him out and attempt to drive the truck himself. They didn't stop employees or vendors on the way out of the park. Finally the guy pulled on his seat belt and started the engine. But he stopped before he put it into gear and glanced over at Leon.

"Do you like the Boss, Rolling Stones or the Doobie Brothers?"

112

Jason kept going through all his options and came up blank each time. All he had was a couple of changes of clothes and his computer. That's when he realized he had something else—a briefcase stuffed with documents and a hard drive filled with files. He'd already found a connection between William Sidel and Zach Kensor. What else could he find if he dared to check Senator Allen's records? Sure, the police would be checking that stuff, too, but maybe Jason could see something they wouldn't notice or recognize.

He pulled out his laptop. The airport had wireless Internet service and in a matter of minutes Jason had access to Senator Allen's bank statements and credit card accounts. Using all his tricks, it only took an additional five minutes to access the senator's e-mails—both business and personal. When he found the senator's deleted cache of e-mails he knew he had hit a bull's-eye.

Jason downloaded copies of everything to a separate jump drive. The trick—and yes, trick was the appropriate term—was to get the information into the right hands. The cops would laugh if he presented it, but there had to be someone…

He packed up his laptop and stopped at a gift shop. He bought a Florida State baseball cap and a nine-by-twelve mailing envelope with URGENT printed in tall red letters. From his messenger days he knew that word garnered attention no matter what the package was. He stuffed some copies inside, sealed it and scratched out the recipient's name on the outside.

Down in baggage claim he saw his garment bag off to the side abandoned with a group of others. A couple of flights had just come in and the area was crowded. Jason gave a college kid ten bucks to rescue the garment bag. Another ten bucks if he held a cab for him. All the while, Jason watched from the middle of a crowd at the turnstile to see if anyone followed the kid. No one did.

He asked the cabdriver to drop him off at the corner of the hotel he wanted, and instructed him to drive around the block before he dropped off Jason's bags in the lobby. That gave Jason enough time to slap on his baseball cap and walk in with only the URGENT envelope. He handed it to the concierge with the practiced indifference and impatience of a messenger.

"This has to get into the client's hands ASAP," he told the concierge who barely glanced up at him, instead focusing on the name on the envelope.

By the time Jason stepped away from the desk the guy was already on the phone. Jason left the lobby just as his cabdriver dropped his bags on the sidewalk.

"Thanks, man." Jason handed him an extra twenty. He stowed the baseball cap in the side pocket of his garment bag, slung straps and bags over his shoulder and entered the lobby again. He headed for a bank of pay phones and then he waited and watched.

It didn't take long. A small, well-dressed black man Jason didn't recognize picked up the URGENT envelope from the concierge. Jason followed him onto the elevator. He played the weary traveler, offering only a weak smile and nod when the man glanced his way. He poked at the already lit fourteen as if he hadn't noticed his floor had already been selected.

At the fourteenth floor he let the small man out while he pre-tended to readjust his bags and determine which way his own room was. The man march-stepped to the end of the hall, knocked on a door and delivered the envelope with only a brief exchange.

Jason turned a corner and waited until he knew the man was back on the elevator. Then he went to the room at the end of the hall. He took a deep breath and knocked.

When she opened the door, she was the one who looked relieved.

"I wondered what happened to you," Senator Shirley Malone said.

113

Eric didn't like the idea of them meeting in a suite at the airport Marriott, but the Mayor hadn't let them down yet. Howard had to return the cabin cruiser. Eric had hoped Sabrina would go with him, but she insisted on coming along to the Marriott. There wasn't much of an argument. It was her neck that was still at risk.

Russ carried a leather briefcase that included his laptop and copies of all the processing files. The satellite images and Polaroids Eric had found at EchoEnergy in Sidel's desk drawer were also in the case.

"You think we have enough?" Russ asked the Mayor as the four of them stepped off the elevator.

"This guy's a straight shooter. He'll tell us if it's enough. I'm hoping the combination of stuff will be the proverbial last nail in the coffin."

"As long as he doesn't nail us for how we got the information," Russ said.

Eric didn't blame him. He felt a bit uneasy about this deal, too.

The Mayor found the suite and knocked while the others stayed back a few paces.

When the door opened, Eric couldn't believe he didn't see this coming. He knew the man though they would both pretend otherwise. So when the Mayor introduced Colin Jernigan, Eric greeted him as if it were their first introduction.

They spent less than twenty minutes presenting their information. Jernigan nodded a lot and when they finished he rewarded them with, "This is quite a collection."

"But can you use it?" the Mayor wanted to know.

"I'm sure we'll figure something out."

"They'll have to stop processing the hurricane debris, right?" the Mayor asked.

"I would think so." But Eric didn't think Jernigan sounded convincing.

"What's the punishment these days for contaminating Florida's waterways?" Russ asked.

"Punishment? Probably a fine. I'm not sure."

"A fine?" Sabrina sat on the edge of her seat. Eric could feel her frustration. "Are you telling me they hired someone to kill me, then they framed me for murder and all to avoid a fine?"

"There is no proof here that they tried to kill you," Jernigan said. "I'll talk to the State Patrol," he added as if that were her only concern. "I can probably get the charges dropped for your cooperation in this investigation. But I have to be honest with you—" and he waved a hand over the documents and computer files on the coffee table "—none of what you have here will probably add up to a felony charge."

"What about the Polaroids?" Eric wanted to know.

"Those will definitely finish off Senator Allen's career."

"And Sidel?" Sabrina asked.

"Unless any of those young men are under eighteen, there's no crime for him to have pornography in his private office."

The Mayor and Russ sat quietly. Eric glanced at Sabrina and saw her studying Jernigan. She wasn't impressed or satisfied. Neither was Eric. But he wasn't sure what else they could do.

"I don't mean to sound so negative," Jernigan told them. "Altogether the information is compelling—"

"I just remembered where I've seen your name," Sabrina interrupted.

Everyone looked at Jernigan. Eric thought she had to be mistaken. The Colin Jernigan he knew didn't have his name up and out in public much. In fact, it was usually one of those names whispered around Washington. Eric had never been sure who Jernigan exactly worked for in the Justice Department. Nobody seemed to know except that it was someone high in the administration and anything he was involved with was top secret.

Sabrina pulled out the small purple notebook that Eric knew belonged to Dr. Lansik and she flipped through the pages. She found what she wanted and slid the notebook across the coffee table to Jernigan.

"Dr. Lansik had your name and phone number written down," she said, tapping the notebook. "You've known about this."

Eric stared at Jernigan and he could see the truth, though Jernigan was good. He didn't shift or jerk in the least. Only his eyes moved, looking up at Sabrina the way someone looks up over reading glasses to be able to see in the distance more clearly.

"Dr. Lansik had been in touch with me, yes."

"So you knew what was happening?"

Eric could hear her anger just on the fringes. She was talking to Jernigan like he'd heard her talk to an errant student.

"We didn't know exactly what was happening. Dr. Lansik backed out. He never showed up." Jernigan sighed and sat back as if it was something he had no control over. Eric knew better. He knew there probably wasn't anything Jernigan didn't have some control over.

"And you never thought to follow up," Sabrina said, her voice bordering on sarcasm. "You didn't bother to see why he didn't show up."

Jernigan glanced at his watch, exaggerating the gesture. He was finished here and wanted them to know he was finished. "No. Some people simply change their minds."

Sabrina stood and walked over to Russ's briefcase. She unzipped a side pocket and took something out. "Dr. Lansik had his mind changed for him," she said as she placed the plastic bag down on the coffee table in front of Jernigan. "This is all that's left of him." Then she headed for the door.

Russ grabbed his briefcase and followed her out. The Mayor stood waiting for Jernigan to do the same. The old man shook his hand and, without a word, he left, too.

That left Eric alone with Colin Jernigan. He fingered the plastic bag, then left it on the table.

"She's quite a spitfire," he told Eric.

"What'd you expect? She's my sister."

"I didn't realize you were working on this EchoEnergy thing."

"I wasn't," Eric said. "I'm with Sabrina. I didn't know there was an EchoEnergy thing. I just stumbled into this because of her. So what will happen to Sidel?"

"I'm not sure." Jernigan looked at his watch again. "Unfortunately, he'll still be hosting the opening bash for the energy summit this evening. There's no one to confront him. All the attention for scandal and smear is on Senator Allen right now."

Eric shook his head. He couldn't help thinking Sidel had tried to have Sabrina killed and yet he still got to celebrate with the president. It wasn't right.

"So, who'd you end up with?" Jernigan asked Eric.

"Excuse me?"

"Who did you decide to work with?"

"DEA."

Jernigan nodded his approval. "So you're here in Tallahassee?"

"Pensacola Beach."

"Drug runners?"

"Ex-dealer," Eric said. "We've never been able to connect him to anything that would stick. The money was never found." And that's what Eric's report would say. Howard had gone straight. He deserved to be left alone.

"Well, I have a reception I need to prepare for."

There was a knock on the door. Jernigan glanced at Eric and Eric only shrugged.

It was Sabrina. A cooler, calmer Sabrina.

"I'm sorry I left like that," she said, but she was looking at Eric, not Jernigan. "There has to be something more we can do."

Jernigan looked to Eric as if waiting for an answer.

"Maybe there is," Eric said, getting an idea. "But first there's something I've got to tell you, Bree."

114

Energy Summit
The Reid Estate

William Sidel straightened his bow tie in the mirrored glass between him and the limo driver. The tuxedo was a little tighter since the last time he'd worn it, but he still looked good. And he felt good, better than ever. Actually, he felt as though he'd dodged a bullet. He figured it was only a matter of time before John's lifestyle caught up with him, but Christ! Why the hell did it have to be this week?

Now the Appropriations Committee would put off voting on the military contract until next week. Or, at least, that's what he heard. He suspected something else was up and he feared the opposing factions may have already gotten their way. Without John he wouldn't be privy to the deals that were made in the bars and cafés and even hotel rooms instead of on the floor of Congress.

He decided tonight he wouldn't worry about it. He owned tonight, had bought it fair and square. And no one could mess that up.

115

Abda couldn't believe how smoothly the preparations had gone. His polite manner and meticulous eye for detail had earned him a head-table assignment just as he had hoped and anticipated.

He had seen Khaled shortly after he arrived. His friend looked exhausted, but there was something else in his eyes. Impatience? Anticipation? Abda knew Khaled looked forward to being in this banquet room. He was anxious to witness the exact moment when the President of the United States brought his hands to his throat, gasping for air and ripping at his own flesh in the hopes of relieving the suffocating feeling.

Unlike Khaled, Abda felt no eagerness. But there was, also, no hesitation, no regret in Abda that it had come down to this. He was prepared to do what was necessary though he looked for every sign that compromise may have been reached. He had heard that a decision had been made, though publicly it appeared to be a quagmire. He understood and accepted that whatever the decision was, it may require death to preserve his country's interests and reinforce their nation's status and influence in the global economy. They could not be taken for granted year after year by president after president only to be swept aside for some temporary political maneuver.

Some might call their tactics extreme and dare to compare them to other radical factions. Others might say it's only about greed and oil. All of them would be wrong to be so shortsighted.

Abda stood over the tray with appetizer plates waiting for him to serve as soon as the guests were seated and ready. The powder he was to add would blend in with the Parmesan cheese and never be noticed. He watched with disinterest as the rich man who owned the estate introduced the head table.

The president had not arrived yet. He would make a grand entrance, no doubt. And when he did, Abda would be ready.

116

Natalie Richards nodded and gave a slight wave to Senator Shirley Malone as she entered the room. The woman did look like a class act, tall and stately in black silk with silver sequins. Didn't hurt to have that handsome young man on her arm though she wasn't sure she agreed with the Indiana senator's timing.

Actually, Natalie was relieved to see that the fallout, the crashing and burning of Senator Allen, wouldn't include any of his staff. That he would even try blaming Jason Brill was something she had not anticipated, but she couldn't say she was surprised. It was called survival in Washington. Or collateral damage, as her boss had called Zach Kensor. She wasn't anxious to see another casualty. Didn't matter if she did think Brill was a major pain in the ass.

She continued to watch the door after a glance at her watch. Where in the world was Colin Jernigan? The president was due to arrive any minute, and here Natalie sat surrounded by three empty chairs.

117

Jason Brill proudly held the chair out for Senator Shirley Malone at her place next to the podium, the place that would have been Senator John Quincy Allen's. She would be replacing him tonight in more ways than simply on the program.

She had told Jason no one would dare to question his being here, especially if he arrived as her escort. And she was right. No one did, though he felt their eyes like darts in his back. Even Lindy couldn't stop her jaw from dropping. He wanted to tell her that although she didn't believe in him, someone else did.

Earlier in Senator Malone's hotel room he had come clean, confessed everything he knew and, more importantly, everything he did not know. He had been convinced that Senator John Quincy Allen was powerful enough to make him take the blame for Zach Kensor's murder. Almost every visible connection Senator Allen had with

Zach, Jason had either arranged, made payment for or scheduled. And perception was everything in Washington. Jason really did believe he was screwed.

But Senator Malone simply told him, "The truth can be a powerful weapon."

Now, as Jason watched William Sidel take the podium, he wasn't so sure that was true. Sidel was still here, untouched, unscathed and stronger than ever, surrounded by those who had invested, lobbied, promoted and trusted him. There was something wrong with that, Jason thought, as he took his place.

118

Abda paid close attention. Mr. Reid had introduced William Sidel, the head of EchoEnergy. He would be the one introducing the President of the United States.

Abda's fingers found the small prescription bottle in his jacket pocket. He had practiced over and over again, so that no one could possibly notice. He rolled the lid off with little trouble. He found the capsule easily and gently pinched it between his fingertips.

He caught Khaled watching him from the corner where he also waited with a tray.

"Ladies and gentlemen," Mr. Sidel was saying, "I have the privilege to introduce with great pride our President of the United States of America."

The banquet hall resounded with applause. Chairs skidded out as guests rose to their feet. No one was even looking Abda's way and he used the distraction to take out the capsule. It was difficult to see the man they were applauding. Abda had little time. He craned his neck and twisted his body to get a glimpse between the applauding bodies.

He brought out the capsule, pleased that his hands were dry and his fingers steady, though he could feel the vibration of excitement pumping in his chest. This was the moment they had planned for. All their hard work, their secret meetings, their sleepless nights had brought them to this one moment.

Abda was ready. His fingertips squeezed the capsule. He was about to break it over the appetizer. The fatal powder would become a part of the sprinkles of Parmesan. And then it would be too late. It would be over, a lesson that would teach them all.

That's when Abda noticed the red necktie. The President of the United States was wearing a solid-red necktie.

They had won. His nation had won. He and Khaled and Qasim had won. Abda should have felt relieved. No one would die today. But as he dropped the unbroken capsule back into his pocket he felt it would only be a matter of time.

119

William Sidel could barely contain himself. Here he was seated next to the president and surrounded by a roomful of Fortune 500 CEOs, senators, foreign diplomats and celebrities. He was supposed to make a short speech. John had told him to keep it light and charming. Like John could instruct him on being charming. Who was he kidding? Sidel was in his element. He'd tell a few jokes, roast a couple of easy targets, work the room.

He didn't even wait for all the salads to be served. Sidel couldn't wait. He was back up on his feet and at the podium, anxious and ready. He noticed a trio arrive late, but paid little attention to them. And neither did anyone else. Instead, they were awaiting his words.

Eric expected to feel relief when Sabrina so easily accepted his confession that he worked as an undercover agent. Any relief was short-lived, however, and replaced by more clandestine planning. Maybe he was even a little worried that she was so anxious to join in his suggested covert operations.

It had happened quickly and rather smoothly. Within an hour of their decision, Colin Jernigan appeared with a gown and tuxedo, invitations and dinner seating down in front of the podium. They were only a few minutes late and even that Colin had orchestrated so that they walked in just as Sidel made his way to the podium. So what if they missed the appetizers; Sabrina looked ready to deliver the main course.

Sabrina tapped her foot impatiently under the table. The shoes Jernigan had gotten for her were a size too big and too tall. She'd stuffed tissues in the toes, but they still slipped off her heel. Even as she tapped her foot she could feel the shoe swinging and just when she needed every ounce of confidence.

Sidel started in with his lame frat-boy jokes. Actually, she'd be doing everyone a favor by shutting him up. And yet, her stomach continued to twist into knots. Her throat was dry despite having gulped her entire goblet of water. Jernigan even slid his glass over to her. Was it that obvious?

The attractive black woman across the table watched her out of the corner of her eye. She had nodded when Jernigan brought them in, even offered Sabrina a slight smile as she gestured for them to sit down.

Sabrina glanced at Eric. He had told her she could back out if she wanted and they'd simply enjoy the meal. In the last week she had survived her car being shoved off the road and exploding. She'd witnessed the death of her coworker. She'd had her reputation smeared and her life threatened. She'd come much too close to a water moccasin and face-to-face with a hired killer. And the man in front of her, standing at the podium, had been responsible for all of it. She stood up.

"Mr. Sidel," she called out. Silverware clinked and stopped. "Is it true your processing plant is responsible for the contamination of Jackson Springs Bottled Water?"

Complete silence.

Sidel still had a smile left over from the joke he had just told. It took him a few seconds before the attack registered. "Excuse me?"

"Dozens of people have gotten sick. A ten-year-old girl was hospitalized with dioxins found in her bloodstream. Dioxins that your processing plant released into the Apalachicola River."

She could see two Secret Service agents starting toward her, but Jernigan waved them off.

"I'm quite certain you don't know what you're talking about, ma'am."

There were whispers now and shuffling of chairs as guests tried to get a better view.

"Oh, but I do." And just as she saw the recognition start to register on his face she said, "I used to be one of your scientists."

Abda had finished serving the head table just as the woman began to jeer Mr. Sidel. He had felt a disappointment, a physical draining of energy. The trays weighed him down. Every plate, every serving became an effort. He had not realized how difficult it would be to go from assassin to ordinary waiter. He should have felt relief. He should feel joy, for their mission had obtained their goal. They would, indeed, be awarded a portion of the military oil contract and their nation's influence and standing would remain strong and steady. But instead of accomplishment, Abda lacked focus.

He listened to this woman and he heard the passion in her voice. Perhaps that's what he worried he had lost somewhere between the appetizers and the salads, his passion. No, he had replaced passion for resolve. That was not a bad thing. Passion could be dangerous. And that's when Abda saw Khaled approaching the head table. He balanced a tray on one hand above his head. All eyes were on the woman. No one noticed him. He was just another waiter. But Abda saw what was on the tray, three small, plastic bottles with pull-top caps.

Abda froze and watched as Khaled set the tray down next to the head table. He picked up two of the bottles. No one paid him any attention. He shoved the top of one bottle into the bottom of the other. He picked up the third bottle.

"He has a bomb," Abda yelled.

Eric grabbed Sabrina and shoved her down onto the floor. Jernigan already had his gun out. Secret Service agents were scrambling toward the president. And the Middle Eastern man in a waiter's uniform held his hands up for everyone to see he was serious. Two bottles already attached in one hand. Another bottle in his other hand. Liquid explosives, Eric thought. The man would need only to shove the last bottle into the others. As soon as the three liquids mixed they would explode.

Jesus! All this security and a waiter could stand two feet from the President of the United States and blow up an entire banquet hall.

Eric's eyes raked the room.

"Take it easy," Jernigan said to the man as he approached him, walking slowly, his gun held down by his side. "Whatever it is you want, we can get for you."

The man wouldn't answer, his eyes darted back and forth from the bottles in his hands to Jernigan to the frantic guests at the head table.

"You don't want to do this," Jernigan continued in a tone Eric recognized. In training, Eric used to joke and call it the lullaby tone. "Tell me what you'd like me to get for you."

The man looked at Jernigan now. And Eric thought perhaps the lullaby tone really did work. But then the man smiled and his hands moved together. Before they connected, his head exploded with a blast from above. Eric didn't even see the sniper.

120

Natalie Richards sank into the leather seat and stretched her legs out in front of her, pushing off her right shoe then her left. Having this solo limo ride to the resort was something new for her, a definite treat. No business to be conducted. No egos to stroke. No deadlines or special deliveries. No phone calls. No madmen with bombs.

Everything had worked out perfectly. Well, *perfectly* wasn't the word she'd use out loud. They had come damn close this time. Too many risks, and she was glad none of them were her decision. If it were up to Natalie, she wouldn't give these assholes the time of day, but then she wasn't the diplomat her boss was. To Natalie they all looked like the enemy and sometimes she couldn't see the greater picture. Sometimes she had moments of doubt. Not that she would ever admit it.

In her line of work, at this level of security, you accepted that there might be casualties, though she wasn't used to almost being one of them. But Natalie could sleep well knowing that blood had not been shed on her shift…*this time.* That there would be another and another could be unsettling if she gave it much thought.

This past week when she was missing her boys she had brief thoughts of packing them up and moving to the Midwest, maybe Chicago, maybe even Omaha. She had friends in both places who kept tempting her to come live "a normal life." Natalie smiled at that. She supposed what she had just been through didn't really count as normal. Maybe it was time to start thinking about a change.

She looked over the driver's shoulders out the front windshield and saw a sign that read Destin, sixty miles. She had forty-five minutes to go before their arrival at the private resort. She'd have plenty of time to think and make decisions.

Her cell phone interrupted her thoughts. Why hadn't she turned the damn thing off? She picked it up, intending to do just that, when she recognized the caller's number.

"This is Natalie Richards."

"Are you there yet?"

"Sixty more miles," Natalie said, smiling at the obvious excitement in her boss's voice. "And thank you again."

"You deserve every bit of this. It's not just me saying thank-you, it's the entire country. Sometimes it's not easy keeping the president focused and in line."

"Well, we make a good team."

"Exactly. And that's why I'm calling. I want you to think about something while you're out there basking in the sun on those sugar-white beaches. I've decided to run for president, and Natalie, I want you to be my campaign manager."

Natalie was speechless. All the continued risks and secrets, all the hopes for a normal life were suddenly overshadowed by her sense of pride and duty.

"With all due respect, sir, you came damn close to becoming the president last night," Natalie said. "Despite all that, I'd be honored to be your campaign manager, Mr. Vice President."

121

Chattahoochee, Florida

Sabrina set the foil-wrapped corn bread on the tray in front of her father. It was still warm, fresh out of Miss Sadie's oven. He looked good today though his fingers were tapping the recliner's arms. His eyes lingered in one place for longer periods of time. They almost seemed focused on her. She thought she saw him smile when he noticed Eric standing behind her.

"Hey, Dad," Eric said, but he stayed where he was.

"We're talking to your doctor about taking you on an outing for the weekend," Sabrina told him. "How would you like to take a drive and go to the beach? Maybe go deep-sea fishing."

"As long as I don't miss my friend Mick," Arthur Galloway said, his eyes flashing back and forth from Sabrina to Eric. "He came to visit again last night. Brought me a Snickers."

"Mick?" She didn't remember anyone in her dad's life named Mick. She glanced back at Eric and he shrugged.

"How would you like to spend a couple of days on Pensacola Beach?" Eric asked. "You can meet some of my friends."

His fingers frantically tapped. "Howard Johnson?"

Sabrina smiled. He did remember. But just when she was feeling confident he added, "My friend Mick had to go to the vet to get stitched up. He showed me the sutures."

She wanted to correct him. How could he get confused with vets and doctors?

"Your friend Mick's not a dog, is he?" she joked.

"No, no." Then he leaned forward and in a whisper he said, "You see, doctors have to report certain...wounds. Vets don't."

It made no sense to Sabrina and she could see Eric was beginning to get frustrated, too. She wanted them to have two days of enjoying the sun and water and each other. She hoped she wasn't being naive in thinking that was possible. After all they had been through they deserved some normalcy.

"Can we stop and get cheeseburgers on the way?" he asked suddenly. "With pickles and onion?"

She felt Eric's hand on her shoulder and she was nodding and smiling even before their dad added, "Maybe some fries and a chocolate shake?"